PENGUIN BOOKS

Beyond the Ultimate Trivia Quiz Game Book

Beyond the Ultimate Trivia Quiz Game Book

Edited by Maureen Hiron, Alan Hiron and David Elias

Penguin Books

PENGUIN BOOKS

Published by the Penguin Group
Penguin Books Ltd, 27 Wrights Lane, London W8 5TZ, England
Penguin Books USA Inc., 375 Hudson Street, New York, New York 10014, USA
Penguin Books Australia Ltd, Ringwood, Victoria, Australia
Penguin Books Canada Ltd, 10 Alcorn Avenue, Toronto, Ontario, Canada M4V 3B2
Penguin Books (NZ) Ltd, 182–190 Wairau Road, Auckland 10, New Zealand

Penguin Books Ltd, Registered Offices: Harmondsworth, Middlesex, England

First published 1985
10 9 8 7 6

Printed in England by Clays Ltd, St Ives plc
Typeset in Century

Contents

Introduction

How to Play the Book vii

Onwards, Ever Onwards viii

Quizwrangle ix

Tic Tac Trivia xii

Count-up xiv

Travel Trivia xiv

Get Out of That xv

BEYOND THE ULTIMATE TRIVIA QUIZ 1–468

Introduction

We were astonished and delighted by the reception accorded to *The Ultimate Trivia Quiz Game Book* when it was published in late November 1984. So, when Puffin Books asked us for a version for younger players, we readily agreed to write it. However, when Penguin suggested a follow-up to *The Ultimate*, our first thoughts were, 'How do you go beyond the ultimate?' So, here it is – *Beyond the Ultimate Trivia Quiz Game Book*, with over 6,300 more questions, by popular request.

One of the questions *we* are often asked is, 'How do you collect the material to all the quizzes?' – and the answer is, 'Slowly – very slowly!' Undoubtedly we have to include some 'pot-boilers' but we like to think that the bulk of the questions have a touch of originality.

One of the things that your authors find awkward is to be asked trivia questions themselves. Meeting a random trivia enthusiast we were asked, 'In which year did *two* red-haired, slow, left-arm bowlers take exactly 99 wickets for their county?' We made a lucky guess – that it was a joke question – and (as far as we know) there is no genuine answer.

What is even more unsporting is for the *publishers* to ask us a question. Just as we were going to press they came up with, 'Which stations on the London Underground and the Paris Métro share the same name?' Bluffing valiantly we suggested *Le Tooting Broadway* – the wide boulevard where Parisian motorists hoot more than usual – but scored no points. The real answer? *Temple*. Well, it is in the book, and if you get asked this particular question, you have a head start.

How to Play the Book

All answers are on the following left-hand page, overleaf, so that there is no need to grub around the back of the book. Nor is there any need to turn back, unless your questionee has forgotten the question. Keep going through the book in numerical order. Even if only one question is answered from each quiz, ask the next contestant a question from the following quiz. This eliminates cheating. Only when you have reached Quiz 234 do you return to the beginning of the book, to start again with the middle section (235–468), and again for Quizzes 469–702. In the fullness of time, you may be lucky enough to be asked a question that you or someone else has had before – and you might even remember the answer!

All the Trivia Quizzes contain nine questions. They are roughly grouped into the following categories, which remain the same throughout the book:

1. Ragbag
2. Mainly historical
3. Mainly geographical
4. Literature, mythology and the Bible
5. Sport
6. Entertainment
7. Leisure, people and art
8. Music, in all its manifestations
9. Loosely, science and natural history

So, if you choose or are given question 5, be prepared for sport.

Following are some of the games that you can play competitively, between individuals or teams. Game charts are provided.

Some hints on equipment

If you haven't got any dice or, for Quizwrangle, the rather special ten-sided dice which are not readily available in the shops, then you can easily find an alternative way of selecting question numbers. For Quizwrangle, take a pack of cards and remove the Kings, Queens and Jacks. Shuffle the remaining forty cards and simply turn up the top three for the first player (10 counts as zero in Quizwrangle). Any rejects are put in a discard pile and new cards taken from the top of the pack (this is the equivalent of rerolling dice). Only when the stockpile is finished are the cards reshuffled and used again.

Similarly, if you are playing a game such as 'Onwards, Ever Onwards' that needs only six categories, you can sort out the appropriate twenty-four cards and use them in the same way. Use two packs if you like; not everyone has dice in the house, but a pack of cards is usually within range.

Onwards ever Onwards

Equipment needed This book; 1 standard six-sided die; a distinguishing marker for each player.

All players place their marker on the *Start* square. Decide the order of play. Then each player throws the die and moves his or her marker the number of squares shown on the die, following the direction of the arrows. If you land on a zero your turn is over, and the die passes to the next contestant. Land on any other number, and an opponent asks you the question appropriate to that number from the next quiz. If you answer correctly you retain the die and throw again, and continue to do so until you answer incorrectly or land on a zero, when your turn ends.

To win You *must* answer a question that takes you on to or past the *Finish* square. You *cannot* win just by throwing the dice and galloping past the post.

Note In theory, you could win without your opponents ever getting their paws on the die; but it won't happen – well, it hasn't yet.

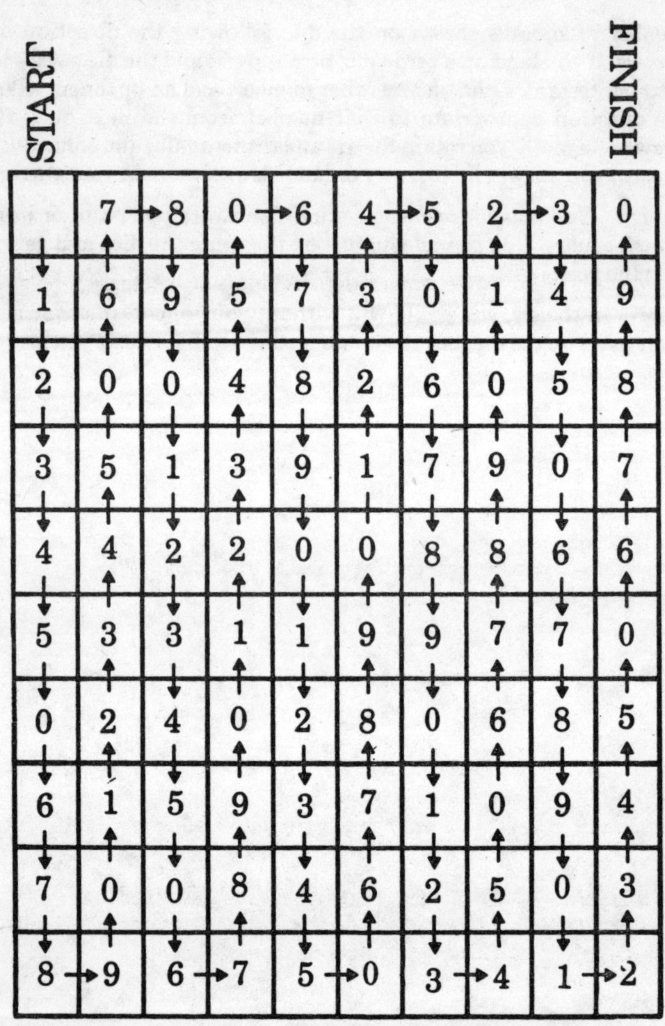

ONWARDS, EVER ONWARDS

Quizwrangle

Quizwrangle was Britain's first Trivia game, devised by the authors of this tome. It has become quite a cult, and the constant requests for even more questions from Quizwrangle *aficionados* provided the inspiration for this book, which can also be used in conjunction with Quizwrangle.

Equipment needed This book; 3 decahedral (ten-sided) dice; 9 counters.

Quizwrangle is played between two individuals or two teams of players. Place the board so that the dark squares at each end face the players. Place one counter on each of the central numbered spaces. Teams take turns to roll the three dice: either the original numbers may be accepted, or the player can reroll one, two or all three dice – but only one reroll is allowed. (Have you ever played poker dice? It's the same idea.)

You automatically move your counter one square towards you in the lanes indicated by the numbers on the dice. If you throw a zero, though – you miss a question!

Now your opponents will ask you questions from the appropriate numbers. If you answer correctly, move an extra square towards you in that lane; if you answer incorrectly, stay where you are.

If your dice include the same number two or three times, you only get to answer the question once – but if you answer correctly, you move *two* extra squares in the appropriate lane, rather than the usual one, if *two* dice show the same number, and *three* extra squares if all *three* dice show the same number.

Continue on to the next quiz after each player or team has had a turn.

In order to nullify the advantage of having a first roll, the team or player which starts rolls only two dice and is not permitted a reroll. After this, all three dice are used throughout by both sides.

To win The game is won by the first player or team to get three (or four – decided *before* play begins) counters into the dark squares nearest to them. It's rather like nine simultaneous tugs-of-war.

QUIZWRANGLE BOARD

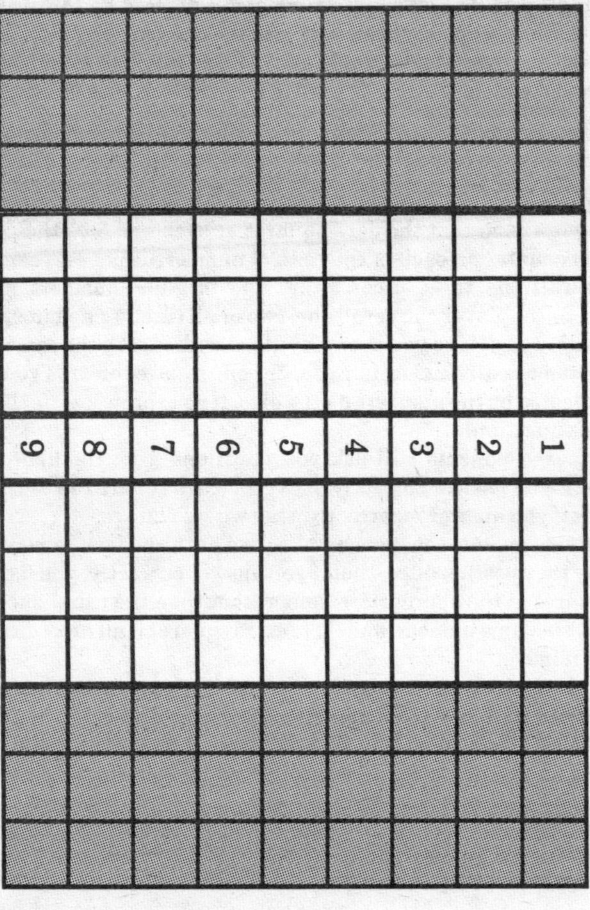

Tic Tac Trivia

For two or more players or teams.

How to win Get your initials, or other distinguishing feature, in a consecutive row of three, horizontally, vertically or diagonally.

How to play Choose any section. Another player asks the question, and if you answer correctly, place your mark in any space along the line of that section only. One question per turn, and play passes in rotation. There is no penalty for a wrong answer.

Note It can pay to defend as well as attack!

TIC TAC TRIVIA CHART

T I C T A C T R I V I A

1									
2									
3									
4									
5									
6									
7									
8									
9									

Count-up

For any number of players

Equipment needed A pack of cards with Kings, Queens, Jacks and 10s removed; scorepad.

First decide the order to play. Then shuffle the cards and place them face down. Each player turns up the top card and is asked the question relating to the number on that card from the next quiz. Score 1 point for each correct answer. The first player to reach 10 points wins (or any other number of points that you agree upon *before* play starts).

Travel Trivia

You can play a very simple game to while away the time spent in travelling by car, train, coach or plane.

In turn, each player has the option of selecting a category of his choice – for which he scores *1* point if he gets the answer right – or allowing the opposition (the player on his left, if there are more than two contestants) to choose the category. If the player gets this one right, he scores *2* points. The winner is the first player to collect 15 points (or any other tally that you choose).

Get Out of That

Equipment needed This book; a small distinguishing marker for each player.

For any number of players.

All players place their markers in the centre circle. Each player is asked question 1 in turn – not question 1 from the same quiz: plough on through the book. (There is an advantage to being quizzed early, so we suggest that you cut a pack of cards to determine the order of play.)

If you answer correctly, move your marker one space outwards on the circle to any number, even if there is already someone else's marker on it. If you answer incorrectly, stay put, and have another go at category 1 when it is your turn again.

The procedure for the next round is as follows. If you have moved, you must now correctly answer a question from the category whose number you are occupying, so that you can continue your journey outwards. You may choose which of the two adjoining numbers to move on to, but once you've moved, you cannot change your mind. That is the category on which you will next be quizzed in the next round. If you answer incorrectly, you remain where you are until your next turn, when you will be asked another question from the same category.

The first player to reach the *Winner's Enclosure* is the winner.

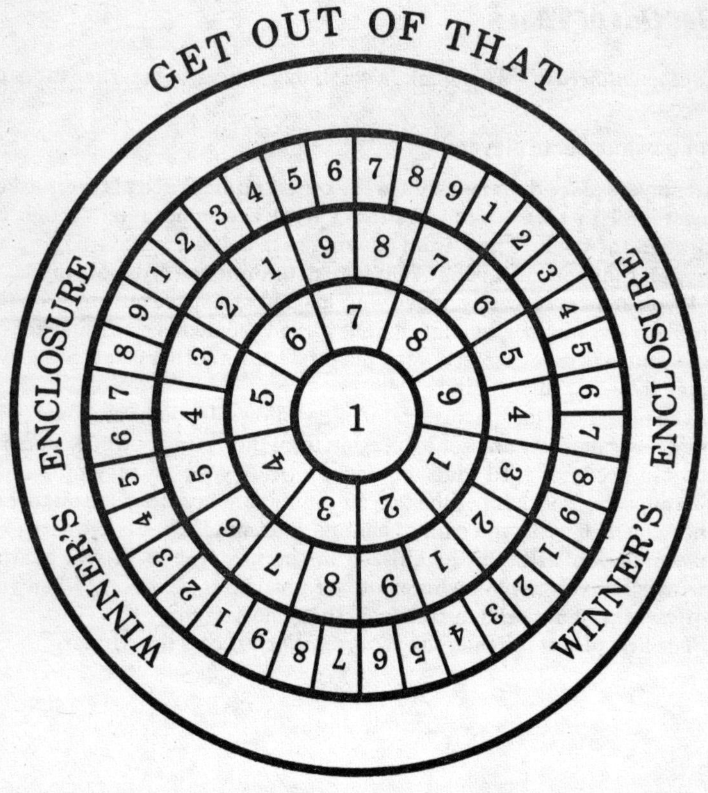
GET OUT OF THAT
WINNER'S ENCLOSURE
WINNER'S ENCLOSURE

Q

1

1. What does the wail of a banshee reputedly foreshadow?
2. During World War II what was Iva Toguri d'Aquino's nickname?
3. Between which two cities did the old Orient Express run?
4. What did the crocodile remove from Captain Hook?
5. What height is the net in squash?
6. What type of shark was *Jaws*?
7. Which comedian uses the catch-phrase 'Katanga'?
8. Who is *Top of the Pops*' longest-serving DJ?
9. Which part of the body is affected by astigmatism?

235

1. Proverbially, what is it impossible to find in a haystack?
2. What was Brummell, the Regency leader of fashion, known as?
3. Sweden, Finland and the USSR all border on which country?
4. In which language was the Old Testament originally written?
5. Whom did Muhammad Ali nickname 'The Turtle'?
6. What do Americans usually call films?
7. What colour scarf does Rupert Bear wear?
8. How many movements does a symphony normally have?
9. What is the minimum number of metals needed to form an alloy?

469

1. How many nickels make a quarter?
2. Who was described by Lloyd George as 'A good Mayor of Birmingham in an off year'?
3. To what did Idlewild Airport change its name?
4. Who wrote the story *The Ant and the Grasshopper*?
5. What are table-tennis balls made of?
6. Who played the part of Polly in the TV series *Fawlty Towers*?
7. What do photographers call developer?
8. Who was John Lennon's second wife?
9. What is the modern name for brimstone?

A

1

1. Approaching death.
2. Tokyo Rose.
3. Paris and Istanbul.
4. His hand.
5. There is no net in squash.
6. A Great White Shark.
7. Lenny Henry.
8. Jimmy Savile.
9. The eyes.

235

1. A needle.
2. Beau.
3. Norway.
4. Ancient Hebrew.
5. Joe Frazier.
6. Movies.
7. Yellow, with a black check.
8. Four.
9. Two.

469

1. Five.
2. Neville Chamberlain.
3. John F. Kennedy Airport.
4. Somerset Maugham.
5. Celluloid.
6. Connie Booth.
7. 'Soup'.
8. Yoko Ono.
9. Sulphur.

2

1. In 1967, Pat McGuigan, father of boxer Barry McGuigan, was Ireland's representative – in what capacity?
2. Which battle of 1942 did Churchill call 'the end of the beginning'?
3. Duffel coats are named after a town in which country?
4. What nationality is Patrick White, winner of the 1973 Nobel Prize for Literature?
5. Which boxer is nicknamed 'The Cyclone'?
6. Which film ends with 'Rosebud' burning?
7. Which comedian used to reminisce about 'the day war broke out'?
8. Which complete-sounding group recorded the soundtrack for *Dune*?
9. What is the common name for 'Scrivener's Palsy'?

236

1. Why was a 'wideawake' hat so called?
2. Who was the USA's second President, and father of the sixth?
3. On a map, what does an isobath show?
4. Which villainous creatures did Terry Nation invent in 1963?
5. Who are 'The Potters', in football?
6. In films, who met Captain Kidd, the Mummy, the Invisible Man and the Keystone Kops?
7. Which actor lists among his hobbies, 'Plotting to overthrow Willy Rushton'?
8. *The Slave of Duty* is the subtitle of which Gilbert and Sullivan opera?
9. Windmills and tulips are mostly associated with which country?

470

1. Midas was king of which country?
2. Which island did the Romans call Vectis?
3. What is the most southerly city ever to hold the Olympic Games?
4. Which poem ends, 'Fled is that music – do I wake or sleep?'?
5. Who, in 1976, was the only person allowed into Montreal's Olympic Village without an identity card?
6. Which film begins with the words 'Most of what follows is true' and ends in Bolivia?
7. Which comedian once had as his catchphrase, 'I've arrived, and to prove it, I'm here!'?
8. Which punk group brought out an LP, *The Raven*, which had a 3-D cover?
9. Which bird, in days of old, was known as the laverock?

2

1. He performed in the Eurovision Song Contest.
2. El Alamein.
3. Duffel, in Belgium.
4. Australian.
5. Barry McGuigan.
6. *Citizen Kane.*
7. Rob Wilton.
8. *Toto.*
9. Writer's cramp.

236

1. It was made from felt with no 'nap'.
2. John Adams.
3. The depth of water.
4. The Daleks, in *Doctor Who.*
5. Stoke City FC.
6. Abbott and Costello.
7. John Junkin.
8. *The Pirates of Penzance.*
9. Holland.

470

1. Phrygia.
2. The Isle of Wight.
3. Melbourne, which held them in 1956.
4. *Ode to a Nightingale*, by Keats.
5. Queen Elizabeth II.
6. *Butch Cassidy and the Sundance Kid.*
7. Max Bygraves.
8. *The Stranglers*, in 1979.
9. The lark.

3

1. In the 17th century, what job was done by 'Charlies'?
2. Why did Disraeli not want Queen Victoria to visit him as he was dying?
3. What is the most northerly city ever to hold the Olympic Games?
4. What do Obadiah, Philemon and Jude have in common in the Bible?
5. Which city should have held the cancelled 1944 Olympics?
6. Who played 'Gloria' in *It Ain't Half Hot Mum*?
7. The 1985 musical *Who's A Lucky Boy*? was based on which sequence of engravings?
8. Which *Boney M* hit had the oldest lyric ever to top the charts?
9. Which part of your body does the tragus protect?

237

1. Which Conservative Cabinet Minister was called 'Smuggins' at school?
2. Which king was married to Anne Hyde, though she died before he became king?
3. How many official languages has Singapore?
4. Who said, 'I will never desert Mr Micawber' in Dickens' *David Copperfield*?
5. How many minutes does the winner take to complete the Grand National?
6. In which 1971 film did Tom Courtenay spend 24 hours in a Siberian prison camp?
7. What did singer Ernest Evans, a fan of Fats Domino, call himself?
8. Brian Francis Connerly was lead vocalist for which 1970s star group?
9. Which element has the lowest boiling point?

471

1. What were Bow Street Runners nicknamed, because of their coloured waistcoats?
2. Against which king did Hereward the Wake rebel?
3. In which country are Akureyri and Kopavogur the second and third largest towns?
4. Which poet's cocker spaniel was kidnapped and ransomed three times?
5. Child care expert Dr Benjamin Spock once represented the USA in the Olympics – at what?
6. Why did Buddy Ebsen give up his role as the Tin Man in *The Wizard of Oz* in 1939?
7. Which US politician is nicknamed 'Fritz'?
8. Which solo pop singer belonged to the *Streetband*, then the *Q-Tips*?
9. Which mammal is also called an urchin?

3

1. They were night-watchmen.
2. He thought she might want him to take a message to Prince Albert!
3. Helsinki, which held them in 1952.
4. They are all books of only one chapter.
5. London.
6. Melvyn Hayes.
7. Hogarth's *The Rake's Progress.*
8. *Rivers of Babylon*, which was a hit in 1978.
9. The inner ear – it is the flap at the entrance to the ear.

237

1. Nigel Lawson.
2. James II.
3. Four.
4. Mrs Micawber.
5. Between nine and ten.
6. *One Day in the Life of Ivan Denisovitch.*
7. Chubby Checker.
8. *Sweet.*
9. Helium.

471

1. Robin Redbreasts.
2. William I.
3. In Iceland.
4. Elizabeth Barrett Browning's dog, Flush.
5. At rowing, in 1924.
6. The metal paint made him ill.
7. Walter Frederick Mondale.
8. Paul Young.
9. The hedgehog.

4

1. What does the inhabitant of the crow's nest on a ship keep?
2. Khartoum, on the orders of Kitchener, was built to represent which flag?
3. Which country has compulsory military service for women?
4. Who was Zeus's wife?
5. Which former world heavyweight boxing champion, the day before his birthday, was killed in a plane crash?
6. In which country is TV's *The Children of Fire Mountain* set?
7. Approximately how many people worldwide have the surname of Chang?
8. Who composed the music to *Lullaby of Broadway*?
9. Which planet is called both the 'morning star' and 'evening star'?

238

1. Which is Britain's most dangerous occupation – having a 1 to 5 injury-to-employee ratio?
2. For how long was Oliver Cromwell's head displayed on the roof of the Houses of Parliament?
3. From which language does the prefix 'tele' come?
4. Graham Greene's *The Confidential Agent* was set during which war?
5. How many laps are run in a 10,000 m track race?
6. Which comedians starred in *A Chump at Oxford*?
7. *The Fosdyke Saga* cartoon strip was created by whom?
8. Whose second symphony was known as the 'Little Russian'?
9. What sort of triangle has just two sides of equal length?

472

1. Women of which religion wear the 'burqa'?
2. For how long were the American Embassy staff in Tehran held captive?
3. Where in London is Hangman's Corner?
4. Who was 'the voice of one crying in the wilderness'?
5. Where is the Irish Sweeps Derby run?
6. In the 1972 film *The Poseidon Adventure*, how many passengers escaped from the overturned ship?
7. Who led the Labour Party, prior to Harold Wilson?
8. Which instrument did George Gershwin play professionally from a young age?
9. What is Britain's largest bird?

4

1. Look-out, or watch.
2. The Union Jack, or Union Flag.
3. Israel.
4. Hera.
5. Rocky Marciano.
6. In New Zealand.
7. 70–80 million.
8. Harry Warren.
9. Venus.

238

1. Coal-mining.
2. About 25 years.
3. From Greek. (It means 'far off'.)
4. The Spanish Civil War.
5. Twenty-five.
6. Laurel and Hardy.
7. Bill Tidy.
8. Tchaikovsky's.
9. Isosceles.

472

1. Islam.
2. For 444 days. (Nov. 1979 – Jan. 1981.)
3. At Marble Arch.
4. John the Baptist.
5. At the Curragh.
6. Six.
7. Hugh Gaitskell.
8. The piano.
9. The Sea Eagle. (Recently re-introduced, its wingspan is about one foot broader than that of the Golden Eagle.)

5

1. What is the first of the seven canonical hours in religion?
2. Which monarch lost the battle of Actium?
3. In which country is Cape Wrath?
4. Who said she had believed 'as many as six impossible things before breakfast'?
5. On which 38-mile course are Kate's Cottage and Ginger Hall?
6. Michael Curtiz won an Oscar for his contribution to the film *Casablanca*. What was it?
7. Which writer called himself 'Public Anemone No. 1'?
8. Which composer, who died in 1971, said 'My music is best understood by children and animals'?
9. What unusual food do South Pacific robber crabs eat?

239

1. In 1973, where did the Summerland fire disaster happen?
2. Which war was described as 'The war to end all wars'?
3. For every widower in Britain, how many widows are there?
4. Who lived in a gamekeeper's cottage in Dorset called Clouds Hill?
5. On which day of the week do the Russians reckon most great chess-players were born?
6. What is Diana Moran's nickname on Breakfast TV?
7. Which politician is sometimes called 'Dr Death'?
8. Which great composer is buried at Bayreuth?
9. For how many months each year does a woodchuck sleep?

473

1. Which tree is sometimes called the 'Hampshire weed'?
2. Who were called 'the shrieking sisterhood' by their critics?
3. Near which town with a famous public school is Savernake Forest?
4. About which town did Sam Weller say the waters tasted 'like warm flat-irons'?
5. For what is the Lugano Trophy awarded?
6. In 1985, which beauty queen joined Frank Bough to present *Breakfast Time?*
7. Who was nicknamed 'The Nabob of Sob' and 'The Prince of Wails'?
8. Who turned the cartoon strip *Andy Capp* into a stage musical?
9. Which creatures are named after the Baghdad suburb of Attab?

5

1. Matins.
2. Cleopatra.
3. In Scotland.
4. The White Queen, in *Through the Looking Glass.*
5. The Isle of Man TT course.
6. He won the award for Best Director.
7. Beverley Nichols.
8. Igor Stravinsky.
9. Coconuts – they have *very* powerful pincers.

239

1. At Douglas, Isle of Man.
2. World War I. It wasn't.
3. Four, approximately.
4. T.E. Lawrence.
5. On Thursday.
6. The Green Goddess – she does exercises.
7. Dr David Owen.
8. Wagner.
9. For eight months.

473

1. The yew.
2. The suffragettes.
3. Marlborough.
4. Bath.
5. Team race-walking.
6. Debbie Greenwood.
7. Johnny Ray, the crying singer.
8. Alan Price.
9. Tabby cats. They made Attabiya, a striped fabric, there.

6

1. What is 'snuff-dipping'?
2. Who said of Viscount Montgomery, 'In defeat unbeatable, in victory unbearable'?
3. Approximately how deep is the Grand Canyon?
4. Who wrote *A Portrait of the Artist as a Young Dog*?
5. Who, on 1 May 1985, collected his 110th International soccer cap – a record for the home countries?
6. Which married couple star in *A Fine Romance*?
7. Whose ghost is said to haunt Hastings Castle?
8. Which singer married Claude Wolff?
9. Which fruit is a cross between a peach and a plum?

240

1. Which two words were substituted for swear words on the Watergate tapes?
2. When were England and Scotland joined under one ruler?
3. What is the principal language of Iceland?
4. Which Poet Laureate wrote detective stories under the name Nicholas Blake?
5. What is a backward handspring called?
6. Barbra Streisand portrayed which daughter of Charles and Rose Borach?
7. Which rank did Idi Amin hold in the British Army?
8. What was Mischa Elman's instrument?
9. What does pasteurization do to the enzymes in milk?

474

1. At the 1981 census, how many males were there in Britain?
2. Which P.M. presided over the founding of the Open University?
3. Where is the Forbidden City?
4. Who wrote, 'Money is like muck – not good except it be spread'?
5. For prowess in which sport is the Podoloff Trophy awarded in the USA?
6. Who said, after finishing a BBC TV series on Peter the Great, 'I made some money so I can now afford to work for the BBC'?
7. What was I.K. Brunel's nickname?
8. The tiktiri is mostly played by whom?
9. What is the mole's preferred sustenance?

6

1. The new name for holding tobacco, possibly in a miniature tea-bag, between the cheek and the gum.
2. Winston Churchill.
3. One mile deep.
4. Dylan Thomas.
5. Pat Jennings. (N. Ireland.)
6. Judi Dench and Michael Williams.
7. Thomas à Becket's.
8. Petula Clark.
9. A nectarine.

240

1. Expletive deleted.
2. In 1707.
3. Icelandic.
4. Cecil Day-Lewis.
5. A flic-flac.
6. Fanny Brice.
7. Sergeant-major.
8. The violin.
9. It destroys them.

474

1. 26,286,000.
2. Harold Wilson.
3. In Peking, China.
4. Francis Bacon.
5. Basketball.
6. Omar Sharif.
7. The Little Giant.
8. Snake charmers.
9. The worm.

7

1. What does 'cave canem' mean?
2. Which General founded the Scots Greys and reputedly haunts Blackness Castle?
3. On which river were the Queen Mary, Queen Elizabeth and QE2 built?
4. In the Bible, whom does Ruth marry?
5. For which country did Bob Wilson keep goal?
6. To which Mr Universe was Jayne Mansfield once married?
7. Which questionmaster was elected *Pipeman of the Year* in 1978?
8. For what do the letters W.S. stand in W.S. Gilbert's name?
9. The original wheels, in prehistoric times, were made from what?

241

1. In 1984, 70-year-old Peggy Barlow attempted to hold up a Kensington bank with what?
2. What particular use did the US Army make of Navajo Indians in World War II?
3. Which is the most populated city in Northern Ireland?
4. Who wrote *A Spaniard in the Works*?
5. Since the age of 16, Herb Elliott was never beaten over two distances in any race. Name one.
6. Who was nicknamed 'The It Girl'?
7. At what card game was Iain Macleod a top-class player?
8. Which musician was elected *Pipeman of the Year* in 1981?
9. Pulex Irritans is better known as what?

475

1. What were Quakers originally called?
2. Which French king did Joan of Arc assist to defeat the British?
3. In which desert do the nomadic Tuaregs live?
4. How did Aaron's serpent deal with the Egyptian serpents?
5. Which French skier took three Gold Medals at the 1968 Winter Olympics?
6. On which island are the Bible and Shakespeare permanent fixtures?
7. What was wrong with the blue plaque put up in Covent Garden to commemorate Thomas de Quincey?
8. In 1981, who had a hit with *Let's Get Physical*?
9. In nuclear reactors, which metal acts as a shield?

7

1. 'Beware of the dog'.
2. General Dalyell.
3. The Clyde.
4. Boaz.
5. For Scotland.
6. Mickey Hargitay.
7. Magnus Magnusson.
8. William Schwenk.
9. Solid slices of tree trunk.

241

1. A perfume spray.
2. They used them to communicate with each other on radio and walkie-talkies – in their native tongue – which the enemy couldn't understand.
3. Belfast.
4. John Lennon.
5. The mile and the 1500 m.
6. Clara Bow.
7. Bridge.
8. James Galway.
9. The human flea.

475

1. Seekers.
2. Charles VII.
3. In the Sahara.
4. It ate them.
5. Jean-Claude Killy.
6. On Roy Plomley's Desert Island.
7. His surname was mis-spelt!
8. Olivia Newton-John.
9. Lead.

8

1. Who holds the catalogue of the 1851 Great Exhibition on his Memorial?
2. In which castle was King Edward the Martyr murdered in AD 978?
3. Which peninsula did Hardy call 'the Gibraltar of Wessex'?
4. Zeal-of-the-land Busy and Bartholomew Cokes are characters created by which dramatist?
5. In which event did Nurmi win an Olympic gold medal for Germany?
6. *The Celestial Toyroom* and *Zerinza* are magazines for fans of which TV series?
7. Which famous painting shows the sea wall at Budleigh Salterton, Devon?
8. Which rock star has the nickname 'Phyllis'?
9. From which country do King Charles spaniels originally come?

242

1. In 1985, how much did the average couple spend on their wedding and honeymoon?
2. After which prince was Dartmoor's Princetown named?
3. On which Roman road is Ilchester?
4. Who wrote *Giles Goat-Boy* and *The Sot-Weed Factor*?
5. How far apart are the goal-posts in polo?
6. Which TV programme features Bungle, Zippy, George and Geoffrey?
7. In the Sistine Chapel, how many square metres a day did Michelangelo paint?
8. Which disc jockey is often called 'Fluff'?
9. What is the appropriate name of the largest type of frog?

476

1. What are Klondike, Canfield and Scorpion?
2. Which English monarch owned a pleasure boat called 'The Rat of Wight'?
3. London's Little Venice is a basin of which canal?
4. Which bird in *The Arabian Nights* could lift elephants in its claws?
5. What sort of sports competition is called a 'powder puff'?
6. The film *The Choirboys* was about which body of men?
7. For what was Dr Livingstone searching when he was found by Stanley?
8. Who was the first singer to get five Top Ten hits from one album?
9. How is a husky's tail different from a wolf's?

8

1. Prince Albert, on the Albert Memorial.
2. In Corfe Castle, Dorset.
3. The Portland peninsula.
4. Ben Jonson. They appear in *Bartholomew Fair*.
5. The three-day event in 1936. He was the winning *horse*!
6. *Doctor Who*.
7. *The Boyhood of Raleigh* by Millais.
8. Rod Stewart.
9. From Japan.

242

1. £2,576 – between £2000 and £3000 will do!
2. The Prince of Wales, who became George IV.
3. On Fosse Way.
4. John Barth.
5. Eight yards – the same as in soccer!
6. *Rainbow*.
7. Six, on average.
8. Alan Freeman.
9. The Goliath frog of West Africa.

476

1. Games of Patience, or Solitaire.
2. Queen Elizabeth I. It was built at Cowes.
3. The Grand Union Canal.
4. The roc.
5. An event for women in a programme otherwise all-male.
6. It was about policemen in Los Angeles.
7. The source of the Nile.
8. Michael Jackson. *Thriller* was the name of the album.
9. The husky's curls up on his back, the wolf's hangs down.

9

1. How can Queen Elizabeth II tell which milk bottles are hers?
2. How many murders did Burke and Hare commit, in order to supply corpses for medical schools?
3. Approximately what proportion of Singapore's inhabitants are Chinese?
4. T.S. Eliot's *Jellical Cats* are which two colours?
5. Which team won the 1985 Milk Cup Final?
6. Who is American TV's equivalent of Alf Garnett?
7. Pope John Paul II was the first Pope from which country?
8. According to Egyptian mythology, which God conquered the world with music?
9. Lack of which vitamin causes scurvy?

243

1. The harvest moon appears in which month?
2. Why were bells originally rung at funerals?
3. Which ocean is nicknamed the 'herring-pond'?
4. Who refused Oliver Twist more gruel?
5. Which part of the judo costume indicates the grade achieved?
6. In the film *Bedknobs and Broomsticks*, what made the bed fly?
7. Which is the most popular flavour for ice-cream?
8. Which group contained Agnetha, Annifrid, Benny and Bjorn?
9. Which bird picks the teeth of a crocodile clean?

477

1. Worldwide, approximately how many people die per minute?
2. Which was the last year to read the same upside down as the right way up?
3. The soup 'artsoppa' comes from where?
4. Who created Noddy?
5. Which so-called 'sport' was termed the 'Royal Diversion'?
6. Whom did Snowy White assist?
7. In weaving, what is the name of the thread carried by the shuttle?
8. What was Stravinsky's first name?
9. Which vegetables are nicknamed 'black diamonds'?

9

1. Hers have the Royal Crest on them.
2. Sixteen.
3. 75 per cent.
4. Black and white.
5. Norwich City.
6. Archie Bunker.
7. Poland.
8. Osiris.
9. Vitamin C.

243

1. In September.
2. To keep evil spirits at bay.
3. The Atlantic.
4. Mr Bumble.
5. The belt.
6. Turning one of the bedknobs.
7. Vanilla.
8. *ABBA*.
9. The plover.

477

1. Sixty-eight.
2. 1961.
3. Sweden.
4. Enid Blyton.
5. Cock-fighting.
6. Dick Barton.
7. The weft.
8. Igor.
9. Truffles.

10

1. Which English firm once made a 'Bullnose' car?
2. Where did King Aggabodhi and King Parakrama Bahu rule?
3. Where are Cape Everard and Cape Otway?
4. In which capital city is Oscar Wilde buried?
5. What was the rhyming nickname of Wilton Chamberlain, the great basketball player?
6. What is the only film to come after *Zulu* in Halliwell's *Film Guide*?
7. Which film producer said, 'The public is always right'?
8. Which famous composer wrote love letters to Antonie von Brentano?
9. What are male and female moles called?

244

1. Which weapon takes its name from the French for 'pomegranate'?
2. How many states formed the Confederacy in the American Civil War?
3. Which country in South America was called Banda Oriental before independence?
4. Who wrote the *Sword of Honour* trilogy?
5. In horse-racing, a photo-finish is called for if the winning distance is less than *what*?
6. In which film does Laurence Olivier torture Dustin Hoffman by drilling into his teeth?
7. British pilot John Pendry in 1985 became world champion at what?
8. *The Israelites* by Desmond Dekker was the first record of this sort of music to reach number one. Which?
9. What sort of creature mates only when the female has its mouth full?

478

1. We may say 'It's a cinch!' for something easy, but what *is* a cinch?
2. In 1832, Prince Otto of Bavaria became the first king of which country?
3. Where in Britain is the National Horseracing Museum?
4. Which hero marries Arabella Donn, then Sue Bridehead?
5. On which racetrack is *Stirling's Bend* encountered?
6. Who played the title role in TV's *Winston Churchill – The Wilderness Years?*
7. The largest British park containing *what* is at Margam in South Wales?
8. Who was the 'fastest milkman in the West'?
9. Which tree has the largest seeds?

10

1. Morris.
2. Ceylon, or Sri Lanka.
3. In south-east Australia.
4. In Paris – in the Père Lachaise cemetery.
5. 'Wilt the Stilt'.
6. *Zulu Dawn*, made in 1979.
7. Cecil B. De Mille.
8. Beethoven.
9. Boars and sows.

244

1. The grenade.
2. Eleven.
3. Uruguay.
4. Evelyn Waugh.
5. Half a length.
6. *Marathon Man.*
7. Hang-gliding.
8. Reggae. (It was a hit in 1969.)
9. A spider called *Pisaura listeri.*

478

1. The saddle-girth, or belt for a horse.
2. Greece. They expelled him in 1862.
3. At Newmarket.
4. Jude Fawley, in *Jude the Obscure.*
5. Brands Hatch.
6. Robert Hardy.
7. Sculpture.
8. 'Ernie', according to Benny Hill.
9. The double coconut, or coco de mer.

Q

11

1. Which German word for 'lightning war' was used for 'air-raid' in Britain?
2. Which British king's coronation was postponed because he had appendicitis?
3. From 1980 to 1985, which was the world's most expensive city to live in?
4. Whose autobiography was called *Courting Triumph*?
5. In soccer, what became compulsory in 1875, replacing the use of a tape?
6. Which Great Dane puppy is the cartoon friend of Heathcliff the cat?
7. In which English city is the National Lifeboat Museum?
8. Which composer used to shoot at neighbours' cats with a bow and arrow?
9. Which element does a Venus's Fly-Trap most need from flies?

245

1. The name of which animal originally meant 'little thief' in Latin?
2. Which language did Napoleon first speak?
3. Which red-bonneted female symbolizes the French republic?
4. Which soccer-player called his life story *It's All About A Ball*?
5. With which sport do you associate Cottesmore, Fernie and Pytchley?
6. *Emmerdale Farm* is set around which fictional village?
7. What did Dr Johnson say was 'the liquor for boys'?
8. Who wrote the coronation anthem *Zadok the Priest* in 1727?
9. A sika is a small *what*?

479

1. What, in South African slang, is a 'warm patat'?
2. The Prince of Saxe-Coburg-Gotha married which English Queen?
3. Where do Orcadians live?
4. Which poet was the son of Charlotte Champe Stearns?
5. In which sport was Admiral Rous famous in the 19th century?
6. With which TV programme do you associate Michael Sundin and Janet Ellis?
7. St David, according to tradition, was the uncle of which king?
8. Which American musical star was called 'The Golden Foghorn'?
9. A springbok can defend itself by 'pronking'. What does it do?

11

1. Blitzkrieg, or Blitz.
2. Edward VII's, in 1902.
3. Lagos, Nigeria.
4. Virginia Wade's.
5. The use of crossbars above goalposts.
6. Marmaduke.
7. In Bristol.
8. Brahms.
9. Nitrogen.

245

1. The ferret.
2. Italian.
3. Marianne.
4. Alan Ball, of course!
5. Fox-hunting.
6. Beckindale.
7. Claret.
8. Handel.
9. Deer.

479

1. A good-looking girl – a 'hot potato'.
2. Queen Victoria.
3. In Orkney.
4. Thomas Stearns Eliot.
5. Horse-racing – he devised the weight-for-age handicap.
6. *Blue Peter*.
7. King Arthur.
8. Ethel Merman.
9. It bounces up and down, very high.

12

1. What is the usual first indication of the presence of a ghost, so it is reported?
2. What was the laneuage of ancient India?
3. Right up to the beginning of this century, how did the Chinese mark criminals for life?
4. In Greek mythology, who killed Ladon, the dragon of a hundred heads?
5. Which club won the Rugby League Cup Final in 1985?
6. Name Dr Zhivago's mistress.
7. Which 4 chess pieces start on the 4 corners?
8. At what time of dhe day should aubades be played?
9. What is the other name for quicksilver?

246

1. Of what is haphephobia the fear?
2. Which Queen reputedly haunts Windsor Castle's library?
3. Which British islands are serviced by a scheduled helicopter service?
4. Which is the second novel in the *Dune* series?
5. The centre player in the front row of a rugby scrum is called *what*?
6. In April 1985, against which BBC TV programme was some £1¼ million pounds awarded in damages in a libel action?
7. Which politician is nicknamed both 'Goldilocks' and 'Tarzan'?
8. In *The Pirates of Penzance*, whom does Frederic love?
9. Bone marrow manufactures *what*?

480

1. Who or what is the biggest landowner in Britain?
2. Why was 17 June of special significance to King John III of Poland?
3. What does the name Addis Ababa mean?
4. Whom did Aphrodite love?
5. What game did the Haringey Racers and Wembley Lions play?
6. Lord Harewood succeeded the late Lord Harlech as what?
7. What does SEX score in the game SEDUXION?
8. In which musical did Billy Bigelow feature?
9. By the end of April 1985, how many heart transplants had been carried out at Papworth Hospital?

12

1. The room suddenly goes cold.
2. Sanskrit.
3. By branding them with hot irons.
4. Hercules.
5. Wigan.
6. Lara.
7. Rooks, or castles.
8. In the morning.
9. Mercury.

246

1. Physical contact.
2. Queen Elizabeth I.
3. The Scilly Isles.
4. *Dune Messiah.*
5. The hooker.
6. *That's Life.*
7. Michael Heseltine.
8. Mabel.
9. Blood cells.

480

1. The Crown.
2. Because he was born, crowned, married and died on that date. (Not on the same day, though!)
3. New flower.
4. Adonis.
5. Ice hockey.
6. President of the British Board of Film Censors.
7. Thirty.
8. *Carousel.*
9. One hundred.

13

1. What does the 'T' stand for in FIAT, the Italian car company?
2. Who founded the British Union of Fascists?
3. Where do the Ashanti people live?
4. In the Bible, what was a publican's job?
5. What do horse-racing people call 'the nanny'?
6. Which was Britain's first sound film studio?
7. Which famous person has blue plaques on six London houses he lived in?
8. What was Morecambe and Wise's signature tune?
9. Which medical complaint is nitroglycerin used to treat?

247

1. As what did the Princess of Wales replace Tom Baker in 1981?
2. In the sixteenth century, John Knox preached against which religion?
3. In which forest is the Rufus Stone?
4. Which veteran actor called his life story *Early Stages*?
5. With which sport do you associate Guzzi and Gilera?
6. Which radio series made Arthur Askey's name, in 1938?
7. What percentage of Englishmen sleep in the nude?
8. What does the title of the opera *La Traviata* mean?
9. What colour light will a magnesium lamp give out?

481

1. Where is the Mound of Mars Positive?
2. What was Bob Ford's reward for killing Jesse James in 1882?
3. Which sacred volcano last erupted in 1707?
4. Which European country's people borrow most books each from public libraries?
5. How long is the standard Olympic rowing course?
6. Who plays Jenna in *Dallas*?
7. In American jewellery, how are karats different from carats?
8. Which hymn did the Rev. Augustus Montague Toplady write after a rainstorm forced him to shelter?
9. Which creature could be lappet-faced or griffon?

13

1. Torino, or Turin, where the cars were first made.
2. Sir Oswald Mosley.
3. In Ghana.
4. He collected taxes, he did *not* serve drinks!
5. The Tote, or 'nanny-goat'.
6. Ealing.
7. Charles Dickens.
8. *Bring Me Sunshine.*
9. Heart trouble, or *angina pectoris.*

247

1. The favourite character in Madame Tussaud's waxworks.
2. Roman Catholicism.
3. The New Forest.
4. Sir John Gielgud.
5. Motor-cycling – they are makes of Italian bike.
6. *Bandwagon.*
7. 41% – between 35 and 45 will do.
8. 'The Wayward One'.
9. Green.

481

1. On your palm, between the thumb and fore-finger.
2. 10,000 dollars.
3. Mount Fuji, in Japan.
4. Denmark's.
5. 2000 metres.
6. Priscilla Presley.
7. Karats measure gold, carats measure gems.
8. *Rock of Ages.*
9. The vulture.

14

1. Britons say 'anticlockwise'. What do Americans say?
2. The Edict of Nantes gave religious freedom to whom?
3. Which members of the Royal Family live at Thatched House Lodge, Richmond Park?
4. Who wrote the poem beginning, 'Half a league half a league'?
5. What are kept in a quiver?
6. What was the film sequel to *The Exorcist* called?
7. Who is Karel Wojtyla?
8. Where did the Beatles last all play together?
9. In which part of the body is the largest muscle, the gluteus maximus?

248

1. *Resolution* and *Renown*. Which is the missing nuclear submarine?
2. How did the stagecoach get its name?
3. Mount Kilimanjaro, Africa's highest mountain, is in which country?
4. How long did it take Solomon to have his palace built?
5. Which boxer first beat Muhammad Ali in a professional fight?
6. What was the sequel to *Bedtime for Bonzo*, in which Ronald Reagan co-starred with Bonzo the Chimp?
7. By what title was Mickey Hargitay known?
8. What did the old lady swallow that killed her?
9. Name the first part of the small intestine.

482

1. What is the minimum age at which one can legally purchase fireworks?
2. How did Somerset Maugham serve his country in World War I?
3. Where do financial 'gnomes' congregate?
4. Who is Byron's *Bride of Abydos*?
5. Dr Frank Stableford devised a scoring system for which game?
6. Name the annual trophy awarded in the USA for the best porn film.
7. Who preceded Giscard d'Estaing as President of France?
8. Who 'packed her trunk and said goodbye to the circus'?
9. Where would you find places called 'Little Rushing In' and 'Insect Ditch'?

14

1. Counterclockwise.
2. The Huguenots.
3. Princess Alexandra and the Hon. Angus Ogilvy.
4. Alfred, Lord Tennyson.
5. Arrows.
6. *Exorcist II: The Heretic.*
7. Pope John Paul II.
8. On top of the *Apple* building, in Savile Row, London.
9. The buttocks

248

1. *Repulse.*
2. It had to have fresh horses at stages on its journey.
3. Tanzania.
4. Thirteen years.
5. Joe Frazier.
6. *Bonzo Goes to College* – but Ronald Reagan did *not* appear in it.
7. Mr Universe.
8. A horse.
9. The duodenum.

482

1. Sixteen.
2. He was a spy.
3. In Zurich.
4. Zuleika.
5. Golf.
6. The Erotica Award.
7. Georges Pompidou.
8. Nellie the Elephant.
9. On your body! They are names of acupuncture points.

15

1. What do the French call 'earth apples'?
2. Who ordered Lady Jane Grey to be executed?
3. What is called 'The Sorrow of China'?
4. What is this book's colophon?
5. Whom did Hippomenes defeat in a race, in mythology?
6. In which TV show did Molly Weir play Hazel the McWitch?
7. In which game might you play a 'stepping stone squeeze'?
8. Which long-necked musical instrument has eighteen strings?
9. Around what would you find Himalia, Ananke and Europa?

249

1. Before 1969, you were legally an infant in the UK until you reached what age?
2. Which ruler used to prefer his armies to attack on the seventh of the month?
3. Its inhabitants call it Kerkira – what do Britons call it?
4. In Indian myth, the earth is supported by eight *what*?
5. In which sport might you worry about a borrow?
6. In which horror musical film did Tim Curry play Frank N. Furter?
7. Who was the last peer to be Prime Minister of Britain?
8. Who sang with Michael Jackson on *The Girl is Mine* and *Say Say Say*?
9. Which acid was called 'aqua fortis' or 'strong water'?

483

1. What do scuba diving, lasers and Pakistan have in common?
2. 'AuH_2O in 1964' was whose slogan?
3. Which country is called Chosen by its inhabitants?
4. What do Coleridge's, George Eliot's, Karl Marx's, and Charles Dickens's parents have in common?
5. Which six-a-side game was invented in 1895 by William G. Morgan?
6. In which TV series does Max take care of Jennifer and Jonathan?
7. Which mixed drink takes its name from the Hindi word for five?
8. Americans call it a sixteenth-note. What is the British term?
9. What do you measure with a venturi meter?

15

1. Potatoes (*pommes de terre*).
2. Mary Tudor, Queen Mary I, in 1554.
3. The Hwang-ho, or Yellow River, because it often floods.
4. The picture of a penguin on the cover.
5. Atalanta.
6. *Rentaghost.*
7. Bridge.
8. The sitar.
9. Jupiter. They are satellites.

249

1. Twenty-one.
2. Adolf Hitler.
3. Corfu.
4. White elephants.
5. Golf.
6. *The Rocky Horror Picture Show.*
7. Lord Salisbury.
8. Paul McCartney.
9. Nitric acid.

483

1. They are all acronyms, or words made up of initials.
2. Barry Goldwater's, when he was standing for President of the USA.
3. Korea.
4. They are all buried in London's Highgate Cemetery.
5. Volleyball.
6. *Hart to Hart.*
7. Punch, from 'panch'. (It has five ingredients.)
8. A semiquaver.
9. How fast a liquid or gas is flowing.

16

1. How many old pennies are there in a guinea?
2. Who first suggested the possibility of man-made satellites?
3. In which city is the Little Mermaid statue sited?
4. Who is called the 'weeping prophet'?
5. Which was the first-ever race run in the Modern Olympics (1896)?
6. Wrapped in *what* was actor Bela Lugosi buried, in 1956?
7. Which Hurricane has been a snooker world champion?
8. Which great contralto won the *Daily Mail Kathleen Ferrier Award*, in 1956?
9. Whose third Law of Motion states that to every action there is an equal and opposite reaction?

250

1. How does a fountain pen behave in a plane?
2. On which king's birthday was the Battle of Hastings fought?
3. What is the birth rate in the Vatican City?
4. Who wrote *Crime and Punishment*?
5. How many divisions has the Scottish Football League?
6. Which actor often signed hotel registers as Lord Greystoke?
7. What is the surname of the brothers Robert and Charles, who founded a watch-manufacturing company in 1887?
8. Who sent a musical *Message in a Bottle* in 1979?
9. The lack of which vitamin causes beriberi?

484

1. Who can be charged with infanticide?
2. Did Henry Stanley, who found Dr Livingstone in Africa, serve with the Confederate or Union army during the American Civil War?
3. Which is the largest island of the Inner Hebrides?
4. Which was the first book ever printed outside China?
5. Where is the H.Q. of the Jockey Club?
6. Which actor has played Worzel Gummidge and Dr Who?
7. How did Buhram, a member of the Indian Thuggee sect, kill more than 900 people?
8. How many reeds are used to play an oboe?
9. Who or what is Agent Orange?

16

1. 252.
2. Sir Isaac Newton.
3. In Copenhagen.
4. Jeremiah.
5. The 100 m sprint for men.
6. The cape that he had so often worn playing Count Dracula.
7. Alex Higgins, nicknamed Hurricane Higgins.
8. Dame Janet Baker.
9. Sir Isaac Newton's.

250

1. The ink overflows because of the altitude.
2. King Harold's.
3. Zero.
4. Dostoyevsky.
5. Three.
6. Marlon Brando.
7. Ingersoll.
8. The pop group *Police*.
9. Vitamin B.

484

1. Only the mother of the infant.
2. Both.
3. Mull.
4. The (Gutenberg) Bible.
5. At Newmarket.
6. Jon Pertwee.
7. He strangled them all.
8. Two.
9. The chemical used to spray and kill vegetation in Vietnam.

17

1. What, in army slang, are 'green goddesses'?
2. Which peer was a British aviation pioneer?
3. Across which African river is the Owen Falls dam?
4. Who wrote *79 Park Avenue*?
5. Which sport was controlled by the Broughton Rules from 1743 to 1867?
6. Which establishment did Nicola Freeman take over in 1985?
7. Who was commemorated on a special British postage stamp in August 1980?
8. Who made 1964's top-selling record *I Love You Because*?
9. What does a somatologist study?

251

1. What, in Ireland, is a gravy ring?
2. In which cathedral was the first Prince of Wales proclaimed in 1301?
3. In which city is Krasnaya Ploshchad?
4. Who wrote *The Black Tulip?*
5. Tennis player Manuela Maleeva comes from which country?
6. Which TV actor usually wears about £200,000-worth of jewellery on screen?
7. About which game did Herbert Spencer say that to play it well was a sign of a mis-spent youth?
8. Where do the Three Little Maids from School sing together?
9. What is rubber called as it flows out of tapped trees?

485

1. What do Americans understand by 'a muffler'?
2. Rehoboam was the last king of *where*?
3. In which country are the Reichenbach Falls?
4. To which poet did Maud Gonne say, 'The world will thank me for not marrying you'?
5. Which sport is governed by FOCA and FISA?
6. Which politician was short-listed for the lead role in *National Velvet*?
7. Which great furniture designer died in 1786?
8. Anthony Dowell is a virtuoso at which activity?
9. In the West Indies, what is a pinguin?

17

1. Fire engines.
2. Lord Brabazon of Tara.
3. The Nile.
4. Harold Robbins.
5. Boxing.
6. The Crossroads Motel.
7. The Queen Mother, on her 80th birthday.
8. Jim Reeves.
9. The human body.

251

1. A ring doughnut.
2. Lincoln Cathedral.
3. In Moscow. It is better known as Red Square.
4. Alexandre Dumas.
5. Bulgaria.
6. Mr T., in *The A-Team.*
7. Billiards.
8. In *The Mikado.*
9. Latex.

485

1. A car silencer.
2. Israel.
3. Switzerland.
4. W.B. Yeats.
5. Motor racing.
6. Shirley Williams. Elizabeth Taylor won.
7. George Hepplewhite.
8. Ballet dancing.
9. A pineapple.

18

1. How many days did people think they had 'lost' in the 1752 calendar changes?
2. Wed. 2 Sept. was followed by Thurs. 14 Sept. in which year?
3. Which country did Cetewayo once rule?
4. Which high British honour did George Bernard Shaw turn down?
5. At which sport did Douglas Bader excel, before losing his legs?
6. What was the Third Man's name?
7. Which British political party contained the Gang of Four?
8. In ballet, what does 'sauter' mean?
9. What is loess, in geology?

252

1. How long did Paul Dowdeswell take to swallow 144 prunes, in 1985?
2. What is the meaning of the name Kwame Nkrumah's people usually called him?
3. Which country's cars carry the letters SK?
4. What did Aaron Ward produce in 1874 that was 8 pages long?
5. What nickname was used for Henry Cooper's left hook?
6. Who won her second Oscar for the film *Coming Home*, in 1978?
7. Who originally starred in *The Nerd* on stage?
8. Which instrument did band-leader Harry James play?
9. To regulate which disease is insulin used?

486

1. Where did Mrs Margaret Thatcher have her nose cut off in May 1985?
2. Where in Britain did the Romans mine gold?
3. Which Italian city is called 'La Superba'?
4. Which playwright was sentenced to have his nose cut off for making fun of Scotsmen?
5. Which peer used a teddy bear as the symbol for his Grand Prix motor-racing team?
6. Which actor was born Larushka Skikne?
7. What did ancient Greek prostitutes have carved on the soles of their shoes?
8. American DJ Alan Freed was said to have coined which phrase?
9. What, in fact, are flying foxes?

18

1. Eleven.
2. 1752.
3. Zululand.
4. The Order of Merit.
5. Rugby.
6. Harry Lime.
7. The SDP.
8. Jump.
9. Yellow dust.

252

1. 34 seconds. Perhaps he suffered gross indigestion?
2. The Redeemer.
3. Sarawak's.
4. The first mail-order catalogue.
5. 'Enery's 'ammer.
6. Jane Fonda.
7. Rowan Atkinson.
8. The trumpet.
9. Diabetes.

486

1. Dublin's waxwork museum.
2. North Wales.
3. Genoa. It means 'the proud'.
4. Ben Jonson, in 1605, but he was reprieved.
5. Lord Hesketh.
6. Laurence Harvey.
7. 'Follow Me'.
8. 'Rock 'n' Roll'.
9. Bats.

19

1. Vox populi means *what*?
2. Which PM was nicknamed 'Pam'?
3. Of which hills is Will's Neck the final summit?
4. Which British author turned down $250,000 from Steven Spielberg to write the book of *E.T.*?
5. Who presented the 1985 F.A. Cup to Manchester United?
6. Whose enemy is Texas Pete?
7. How many men does the average American woman kiss (passionately) before she marries?
8. What did Reginald Dixon play?
9. Through where will a camel not pass – so goes the saying?

253

1. When is a solider given an oak leaf cluster?
2. Who reputedly started the newspaper called *Acta Diurna*?
3. Where, today, can you travel on the *Lusitania*?
4. Whom did Jane Austen's Emma marry?
5. Where do Anderlecht football club come from?
6. In 1977, Harry Evans was the first winner of which TV quiz?
7. Which famous cricket commentator was once a police detective?
8. Which pop singer made his stage debut in 1985 as Sloane in *Entertaining Mr Sloane*?
9. What is the great maple tree called in Britain?

487

1. Which letters stand for 505 in Roman numerals?
2. How many days were there in a week in ancient Greece?
3. What is the highest African capital city?
4. By which of his 151 pseudonyms do we best know Vladimir Ilyich Ulyanov?
5. Which former England cricketer has become Bishop of Liverpool?
6. Which famous film star had the middle name 'Spencer'?
7. Who was nicknamed 'Concrete Bob'?
8. Who wrote the music for *Les Sylphides*?
9. What did Kellogg and Rice invent in 1927?

19

1. Voice of the people.
2. Lord Palmerston.
3. The Quantocks.
4. Jeffrey Archer.
5. The Duke of Kent.
6. Superted's.
7. Seventy-nine.
8. The organ – mainly at Blackpool Tower.
9. The eye of a needle.

253

1. When mentioned in despatches.
2. Julius Caesar.
3. Between Madrid and Lisbon. It is an express train.
4. George Knightley.
5. Brussels.
6. *The Krypton Factor*.
7. John Arlott.
8. Adam Ant.
9. The sycamore.

487

1. DV.
2. Eight.
3. Addis Ababa.
4. Lenin.
5. David Sheppard.
6. Charlie Chaplin.
7. Robert McAlpine.
8. Chopin.
9. The moving-coil loudspeaker.

20

1. What is an albacore?
2. What was the Irish politician Daniel O'Connell's nickname?
3. In Britain, which city is reached by dialling 061 on a telephone?
4. Into what animal was Actaeon turned for watching Artemis bathing?
5. Which game used Winston Churchill to be especially fond of playing as a young man?
6. Who played the parson in the 1963 British comedy *Heavens Above*?
7. Who designed the Spitfire?
8. Who had a big hit in 1969 with *Sugar, Sugar*?
9. Jargonelle is an early variety of which fruit?

254

1. Whose statue stands on the traffic island outside Buckingham Palace?
2. What type of planes did the RAF use for the first bombing raid on Germany in World War II?
3. In which English county is Boothferry?
4. Sydney Carton dies at the end of which book?
5. What colour jacket does a greyhound from Trap 3 wear?
6. *The Philadelphia Story* became which film musical?
7. Who married his secretary, Frances Stephenson?
8. In which town was Gustav Holst born?
9. What do sericulturists breed, apart from more sericulturists?

488

1. What colour ribbon does the Victoria Cross have?
2. Against which king was a plot hatched by Father Wilson and Lord Cobham?
3. In which city is there a cathedral nicknamed 'Paddy's Wigwam'?
4. Whose sister was Morgan Le Fay?
5. What is the minimum distance of a National Hunt race?
6. In the film of Graham Greene's *Travels With My Aunt*, who played Alec McCowen's aunt?
7. In Japan, which colour of car may only the Royal Family drive?
8. Where did Ska originate?
9. Which bird is called a mavis?

20

1. A kind of fish.
2. The Liberator.
3. Manchester.
4. A stag.
5. Polo.
6. Peter Sellers.
7. R.J. Mitchell.
8. *The Archies.*
9. The pear.

254

1. Queen Victoria's.
2. Blenheims.
3. In Humberside.
4. *A Tale of Two Cities.*
5. White.
6. *High Society.*
7. David Lloyd George.
8. In Cheltenham.
9. Silkworms.

488

1. Purple.
2. James I, in 1603.
3. In Liverpool.
4. King Arthur's.
5. Two miles.
6. Maggie Smith.
7. Maroon.
8. In Jamaica.
9. The thrush.

21

1. Which chicken dish is named after a Ukrainian city?
2. To which French leader did President Bokassa give diamonds?
3. For what is Dijon, in France, famous?
4. In *Ring of Bright Water*, what is Mijbil?
5. To what number does a wrestling referee count to determine whether a fall is good?
6. Which film was the inspiration for an American snack food called *Screaming Yellow Zonkers*?
7. Degas was especially famed for painting which two subjects?
8. Which clarinet is the biggest and has the deepest sound?
9. Where does the halibut have its two eyes?

255

1. What is the smallest quantity of draught beer that may legally be sold in Britain?
2. Which monarch is featured on the 'Penny Black'?
3. The original Church of the Nativity is where?
4. Which book was the sequel to *Little Women*?
5. Kenny Dalglish transferred to Liverpool from which club?
6. Whom does Jack Coleman portray in *Dynasty*?
7. Of which country was Salvador Allende president?
8. Who had a big hit with *See ya Later, Alligator*?
9. Is the *Sagnac Effect* to do with medicine, geology, relativity or American football?

489

1. Of what is gymnophobia the fear?
2. Who were expelled from England in 1291?
3. Which US state borders four of the five Great Lakes?
4. For which profession is the *Lancet* written?
5. What does Zola Budd prefer to wear on her feet when racing?
6. Which TV show gave *The Flying Fickle Finger of Fate Award*?
7. In the early nineteenth century what did billiards players begin to use to improve the accuracy of their play?
8. Which instrument does the Hardangerfele closely resemble?
9. What is the maximum cc for a moped?

21

1. Chicken Kiev.
2. Valéry Giscard d'Estaing.
3. Mustard.
4. An otter.
5. Three.
6. *Yellow Submarine.*
7. Ballet dancers and horses.
8. The contrabass clarinet.
9. Both are on the right side of the head.

255

1. $\frac{1}{3}$ pint.
2. Queen Victoria.
3. In Bethlehem.
4. *Good Wives.*
5. Glasgow Celtic.
6. Steven Carrington.
7. Chile.
8. *Bill Haley and the Comets.*
9. Relativity.

489

1. Nakedness.
2. The Jews.
3. Michigan.
4. The medical profession.
5. Nothing.
6. *Rowan and Martin's Laugh-In.*
7. Chalk on the top of the cue.
8. The violin.
9. 49cc.

22

1. How many firkins are there in a hogshead?
2. Between World War I and World War II, what was the school-leaving age?
3. Which British museum attracts the most visitors?
4. Who wrote of a doctor's rise to Harley Street in *The Citadel?*
5. Rodnina and Zaitsev were World Champions at what form of skating?
6. Name the film sequel to *King Kong*, also released in 1933.
7. What was snooker first called?
8. *Away We Go* was the original working title of which musical film?
9. What is the name given to the flower truss of the willow tree?

256

1. Which massive wheeled vehicle takes its name from that of a Hindu god?
2. What did a colour TV licence first cost, in 1968?
3. What do Argentinians call the Falklands?
4. Who was Ebenezer Scrooge's original partner?
5. In 1947 and 1967 the Grand National was won by 100-1 outsiders. Name either.
6. Who plays Robby Box on TV?
7. Highwayman Robert Ferguson was known by what nickname?
8. Which musical was originally due to be entitled *Welcome To Berlin*?
9. What name is given to the world's largest emerald?

490

1. Which common coin has the Prince of Wales feathers on one side?
2. Name Queen Isabella I's husband, co-financier of Columbus.
3. Which Scottish town shares a name with a candle component?
4. How many syllables are there in an iambic pentameter?
5. Who was the first runner to break 3 min. 50 sec. for the mile?
6. Which is the scruffy one in *Last of the Summer Wine*?
7. Who kept a World Championship title from 1927 to 1946?
8. Name the march William Walton composed for King George VI's coronation.
9. What is the main difference between a black leopard and a panther?

22

1. Six.
2. Fourteen.
3. The British Museum.
4. A. J. Cronin.
5. Pairs skating.
6. *Son of Kong*.
7. Snooker pool.
8. *Oklahoma*.
9. Catkin.

256

1. The juggernaut.
2. £10.
3. Las Malvinas.
4. Jacob Marley.
5. *Caughoo* – 1947. *Foinavon* – 1967.
6. Ray Brooks.
7. Galloping Dick.
8. *Cabaret*.
9. The Star of Delhi.

490

1. The 2p piece.
2. Ferdinand.
3. Wick.
4. Ten.
5. John Walker, in New Zealand 1975.
6. Compo.
7. Joe Davis, the snooker champion.
8. *Crown Imperial*.
9. None – they are one and the same.

Q

23

1. Why do Americans use hickory wood to make axe handles?
2. Bessarabia was taken over by which country, in 1947?
3. The Kikuyu live in which country?
4. Which British news magazine closed down suddenly in April 1981?
5. Which rugby player was nicknamed 'Desperate Dan'?
6. What is the name of the Minister played by Paul Eddington in *Yes Minister*?
7. With whom did Charlotte Vernay get lost in 1982?
8. Who sang the title song in *Friendly Persuasion* in 1956?
9. In geology, what is a moraine?

257

1. What is a cabochon-cut gemstone?
2. Which Midlands city had Britain's first telephone kiosk?
3. What is the largest medieval cathedral in Britain?
4. Who wrote *Magnolia Street*?
5. Which cricketer wrote *Put to the Test* and *Opening Up*?
6. Who played the title role in the 1972 film *Young Winston*?
7. What do Scots celebrate on 25 January?
8. Who made the best-selling record of 1971, *My Sweet Lord*?
9. To which Army corps do doctors belong?

491

1. What would you do with a cullen skink, if given it by a friend?
2. In heraldry, what is the shape of a lozenge?
3. Which city has been called 'The Mistress of the Adriatic'?
4. The mother of which Dickens hero marries Mr Murdstone?
5. Andy Mapple and Mike Hazelwood have both been British champion *what*?
6. What was the name of the character played by Tony Perkins in *Psycho*?
7. Which painter's last words were 'The Sun is God'?
8. Who had his first hit for 17 years in 1975?
9. If an animal is a tetradactyl, what does it have?

23

1. Because it is very springy.
2. The USSR.
3. In Kenya.
4. *Now!*, which became 'Then . . .!'
5. Fran Cotton.
6. Jim Hacker.
7. Mark Thatcher, in the Sahara.
8. Pat Boone.
9. The deposit left in the wake of a glacier.

257

1. It is a stone without facets.
2. Nottingham, in 1908.
3. York Minster.
4. Louis Golding.
5. Geoff Boycott.
6. Simon Ward.
7. Burns Night.
8. George Harrison.
9. RAMC.

491

1. Eat it – it is a Scottish fish soup.
2. It is diamond-shaped.
3. Venice.
4. David Copperfield.
5. Water-skiers.
6. Norman Bates.
7. J.M.W. Turner's.
8. Johnny Mathis.
9. Four fingers or toes.

24

1. What would you do to serve a wine *chambré*?
2. Which PM referred to the colonies as 'A millstone around our necks'?
3. Barcelona is which country's second city?
4. Which word was coined to describe nude runners at public events?
5. What do relay runners pass to each other?
6. In *Brideshead Revisited*, at which university did Sebastian and Charles meet?
7. Whose mummified body, dressed in its own clothes, is preserved on display in a glass showcase at University College, London?
8. At which instrument is Julian Bream a virtuoso?
9. What is the fruit of the Citrus Paradisi tree?

258

1. What is the heraldic word for 'black'?
2. Which Chancellor of the Exchequer introduced Old Age Pensions?
3. In which country might you shop at ISUM?
4. Who wrote 'We call him tortoise because he taught us'?
5. Name the 3 divisions of the Scottish Football League.
6. What word is used to describe an amateur radio operator?
7. At the beginning of a chess game, which two pieces flank the queen?
8. How many piano sonatas did J.S. Bach write?
9. What makes a stink bomb stink?

492

1. If you were born on Christmas day, what would be your Zodiac sign?
2. Francis Drake was knighted on which ship?
3. Where is Gander airport?
4. ______ ______, *a Romance of Exmoor*. What is missing?
5. To April 1985, how many people have successfully reached the summit of Everest?
6. Who starred in the film *The Blob*, apart from the blob?
7. Of which public school was Sir Thomas Arnold headmaster?
8. How was a dustman related to the singer?
9. What has been named 'The Farmer's Nightmare'?

24

1. Bring it to room temperature.
2. Disraeli.
3. Spain's.
4. Streakers.
5. A baton.
6. Oxford.
7. Jeremy Bentham's.
8. The guitar.
9. The grapefruit.

258

1. Sable.
2. David Lloyd George.
3. In Russia.
4. Lewis Carroll.
5. The Premier, the First, and the Second.
6. Ham.
7. The king and a bishop.
8. None, as the piano had not yet been invented.
9. Hydrogen sulphide.

492

1. Capricorn.
2. *The Golden Hind.*
3. In Newfoundland.
4. *Lorna Doone.*
5. 169.
6. Steve McQueen.
7. Rugby.
8. He was 'My old man'.
9. A mixture of seeds of wild flowers to be sprinkled on verges and unused ground.

25

1. What is the English equivalent of the Italian name Giovanni?
2. Which is the world's remotest inhabited island?
3. On which river does Leicester stand?
4. Who won the Booker Prize in 1980 with *Rites of Passage*?
5. Kitty O'Neil, a Hollywood stunt star and racing driver, set over 20 records in various types of racing. Which sense did she lack from birth?
6. What is the TV character, Arthur Daley's favourite tipple?
7. Who is the Duke of Normandy?
8. Whom does Tamino seek to rescue in Mozart's *The Magic Flute*?
9. Who commanded the first space shuttle flight?

259

1. Of what is pantophobia the fear?
2. Richard Neville, Earl of Warwick, was known by what nickname?
3. What is the centre of attraction on the Acropolis in Athens?
4. What was Erich Segal's sequel to his novel *Love Story*?
5. Who once rode *St Paddy* to victory in the Derby?
6. Who is 'faster than a speeding bullet'?
7. Sir James Goldsmith had dual nationality: British and *what*?
8. Which musical film was adapted from Lynn Rigg's book *Green Grow the Lilacs*?
9. Normal human body temperature is 98.4°F. What is the highest temperature attained by a human – who lived?

493

1. For what does TGIF – the teachers' prayer – stand?
2. When did Concorde first become commercially operative?
3. How many lighthouses are there on Lundy?
4. What date is now generally recognised to be Jesus's birthday?
5. Over how many days is the Tour de France bicycle race held?
6. Who plays the drunken aristocrat in *Sir Henry at Rawlinson End*?
7. For what type of design was John Gilroy best known?
8. Louis Armstrong once spent six months in jail. What was unusual about his incarceration?
9. Relating to radio, what do the letters FM represent?

25

1. John.
2. Tristan da Cunha.
3. The River Soar.
4. William Golding.
5. Hearing.
6. VAT – Vodka and Tonic.
7. The Queen!
8. Pamina.
9. John Young.

259

1. Everything.
2. The 'Kingmaker'.
3. The Parthenon.
4. *Oliver's Story.*
5. Lester Piggott.
6. Superman.
7. French.
8. *Oklahoma.*
9. 112°F.

493

1. 'Thank God It's Friday'.
2. In 1976.
3. Two.
4. 3 April.
5. Twenty-three.
6. Trevor Howard.
7. Poster design.
8. He was allowed out nightly to play with his band.
9. Frequency Modulator.

26

1. In the 19th century, what happened if you had 'January chickens'?
2. What is India's main political party called?
3. In which city is the last Shah of Iran buried?
4. In the phrase 'Hobson's Choice', Hobson's customers were looking for what?
5. In which sport is the Wrigley Trophy awarded for an indoor competition?
6. On which TV quiz does Geoffrey Wheeler ask the questions?
7. Who was nicknamed 'Sir Cumference' when knighted in 1981 for services to show business?
8. Who composed *Sinfonia Antarctica* in 1953?
9. A rock-hopper is a kind of *what*?

260

1. In the USA, what is meant by an RV?
2. Who died in Medina in AD 632?
3. Which seaside resort used to be called Meols?
4. In P.D.James's book, what was *An Unsuitable Job for a Woman*?
5. What was Mrs E. Cawley's maiden name?
6. Who played the husband in the TV comedy series *My Wife Next Door*?
7. Which unhygienic puppet does Bob Carolgees 'control'?
8. Kate St John belongs to which pop group?
9. A dew-hopper is another name for which animal?

494

1. 'Husch' or 'Husha' is an old word for what?
2. Where was Emily Davison killed by Anmer?
3. When is the monsoon season in India?
4. What is the colour of Kipling's bear, Baloo?
5. Which car manufacturer made the British 'Nimrod' that competed at Le Mans?
6. Name Mervyn Johns' actress daughter.
7. Which ventriloquist's doll was Archie Andrews?
8. Whose first two hit albums were *No Parlez* and *The Secret of Association*?
9. Where on your body could you suffer from a whitlow?

26

1. You had children late in life.
2. The Congress Party.
3. In Cairo.
4. A horse to hire.
5. Cricket – six-a-side.
6. *Winner Takes All.*
7. Harry Secombe.
8. Vaughan Williams.
9. Penguin.

260

1. A recreational vehicle, or motor-caravan.
2. The Prophet Muhammad.
3. Southport.
4. The job of private detective.
5. Evonne Goolagong.
6. John Alderton.
7. Spit the Dog.
8. *Dream Academy.*
9. The hare.

494

1. 'Atishoo'.
2. Tattenham Corner, in the 1913 Derby. She ran in front of Anmer, the king's horse.
3. It lasts from June to September.
4. Brown.
5. Aston Martin.
6. Glynis Johns.
7. Peter Brough's.
8. Paul Young's.
9. On your finger.

Q

27

1. How many sen make a yen?
2. During the 1960s, where were winkle-pickers to be seen?
3. Formerly in East Anglia, where is the town of Dunwich now sited?
4. Which playwright classed his plays as 'pleasant' and 'unpleasant'?
5. Who captained Brazil to their third World Cup win?
6. In which TV show do Stadler and Waldorf heckle from the balcony?
7. What does double-top score at darts?
8. With whom does Michael Jackson sing on the single *State of Shock*?
9. The presence of which vitamin is necessary for blood to clot?

261

1. Which company manufactures the Civic car?
2. Charles Edward Stuart was also called *what*?
3. Who are the Contras?
4. During which events in Massachusetts is Arthur Miller's play *The Crucible* set?
5. In basketball, how many points is a non-penalty goal worth?
6. To whom were David McCallum and Charles Bronson both married?
7. Which game is played with four balls coloured blue, black, yellow and red?
8. What is Paul McCartney's middle name?
9. What part of the body is the trachea?

495

1. Who has the key to the front door of 10 Downing Street?
2. How long *after* his death was Tsar Peter II of Russia crowned?
3. 'See ______ and die.' Which city?
4. Which poet wrote the novel *Zastrozzi*?
5. On which day of the week did 1924 Olympic Gold Medallist Eric Liddell refuse to run?
6. In the 1954 film *The Creature from the Black Lagoon*, the creature was a cross between a man and *what*?
7. As what was the yo-yo originally used?
8. Who wrote the opera *Elektra*?
9. How often does a deciduous tree shed its leaves?

27

1. One hundred.
2. On the feet – they were long, pointed shoes.
3. At the bottom of the sea – it fell off the cliff.
4. G.B.Shaw.
5. Pelé.
6. *The Muppet Show.*
7. Forty points.
8. Mick Jagger.
9. Vitamin K.

261

1. Honda.
2. Bonnie Prince Charlie, or 'The Young Pretender'.
3. The rebel forces in Nicaragua.
4. The Salem Witch Trials.
5. Two points.
6. Jill Ireland.
7. Croquet.
8. Paul – his first name is James.
9. The windpipe.

495

1. No-one, as the door can only be opened from inside.
2. 35 years – his coffin was opened for the ceremony.
3. Naples.
4. Shelley.
5. Sunday.
6. A frog.
7. A weapon.
8. Richard Strauss.
9. Once a year.

28

1. In which month of the year does the feast of the Epiphany fall?
2. The Royal Family of which country are called Bernadotte?
3. In which field are *Viking* and *Silja* keen rivals?
4. Who wrote *Household Management*, which originally came out in parts?
5. At what club did Sir Stanley Matthews both begin and end his soccer playing career?
6. In which studio did the 007 sound stage burn down in 1984?
7. 'Even _____ sometimes nods'. Who?
8. Who told us in a song 'I feel like Buddy Holly'?
9. Aerolite and siderite are the two types of what?

262

1. What is the central colour of a Gucci belt?
2. Rakesh Sharma was the first Indian to do what?
3. In which English city is the Martyrs' Memorial?
4. What did the 'M' stand for in Louisa M. Alcott's name?
5. Which tennis player was nicknamed 'The Rocket'?
6. Which actor played rock singer Nigel Cochran in *Roll Over Beethoven* on TV?
7. What are non-star ballet dancers called as a group?
8. Which black singer was shot dead by his father in April 1984?
9. What would you look like if you were prognathous?

496

1. Which year uses all the Roman numerals in order, MDCLXVI?
2. Who was the assassinated sixteenth President of the USA?
3. Where is there a smaller version of the Statue of Liberty?
4. Who wrote *The Tenth Man*, rediscovered and published in 1985?
5. Which sport is played at The Belfry?
6. In 1985, who left Sherwood Forest for Denver?
7. What is the Junior TV Times called?
8. Which musical has singers on rollerskates pretending to be trains?
9. The three secondary colours are orange, purple and . . .?

28

1. In January.
2. Sweden.
3. The field of Baltic ferry shipping. They are, respectively, Finnish and Swedish companies.
4. Mrs Beeton.
5. Stoke City.
6. Pinewood.
7. Homer.
8. Alvin Stardust, but he didn't look like him.
9. Meteorite.

262

1. Red.
2. Go into space, in 1984 in a Soyuz T11.
3. In Oxford.
4. May.
5. Rod Laver.
6. Nigel Planer.
7. Corps de ballet.
8. Marvin Gaye.
9. Your jaw would stick out.

496

1. 1666.
2. Abraham Lincoln.
3. Paris.
4. Graham Greene.
5. Golf.
6. Michael Praed, ex-Robin Hood, who joined *Dynasty*.
7. *Look-In*.
8. *Starlight Express*.
9. Green.

29

1. How many times did the Duchess of Windsor marry?
2. What did the German monk Berthold Schwartz invent in the 14th century?
3. What is the official language of Fiji?
4. Who was the 'Beloved Physician'?
5. What sort of football is played on an oval field 200 yards long?
6. Where could you see Henry Wilks in *The Woolpack*?
7. What was the Duchess of Windsor's maiden name?
8. When Michael Jackson sang *PYT*, what did the initials mean?
9. What is an animal's pancreas called, when used as food?

263

1. For whom was the Tower of London's largest suit of armour made?
2. Who succeeded Lord Carrington as British Foreign Secretary?
3. In which country is Fiordland the largest national park?
4. What is the next line after 'A wandering minstrel I'?
5. What is golfer Craig Stadler's nickname?
6. Which actor did his own stunts when playing the lead in the film *Condorman*?
7. Who is the cartoon strip 'minx'?
8. How many strings has a ukulele?
9. What orbits between Mars and Jupiter in our solar system?

497

1. What does an uxoriphobe hate?
2. Which European capital suffered a severe earthquake in 1755?
3. To which country does Kharg Island belong?
4. What is the name of the river which features in *Three Men in a Boat*?
5. In which sport do the Peterborough Panthers compete?
6. Who is the TV proprietor of the Stratford Inn, in Vermont?
7. Which member of the Royal Family took part in *The Archers* in 1984?
8. Which group did John Moss join after leaving *The Clash*?
9. Which South American bird looks like an ostrich?

29

1. Three times.
2. The cannon.
3. English.
4. St Luke.
5. Football played according to Australian rules.
6. In *Emmerdale Farm.*
7. Warfield.
8. Pretty Young Thing.
9. Sweetbread.

263

1. An Indian elephant.
2. Francis Pym.
3. In New Zealand.
4. 'A thing of shreds and patches'.
5. The Walrus.
6. Michael Crawford.
7. Minnie.
8. Four strings.
9. The asteroid belt.

497

1. His wife.
2. Lisbon.
3. To Iran. It lies in the Persian Gulf.
4. The Thames.
5. Speedway racing.
6. Bob Newhart, in *Newhart.*
7. Princess Margaret.
8. *Culture Club.*
9. The rhea.

30

1. What traditional dress do Indian women wear?
2. Who was the first protestant Archbishop of Canterbury?
3. Hamelin is on which river?
4. In *Hamlet*, who drowns herself?
5. Which game is played at Cowdray Park?
6. Which film star became involved with Eva Perón and had to flee Argentina?
7. To whom was Xanthippe married, before her husband killed himself?
8. The film *Death In Venice* uses music by which great composer?
9. How many moons has the planet Mercury?

264

1. On what do local authorities currently spend the greatest part of their revenue?
2. Which earl, executed in 1322, reputedly haunts Dunstanburgh Castle?
3. Where were the secret police known as the Tonton Macoute?
4. Who wrote *Arms and the Man*?
5. In which country was cricketer Tony Greig born?
6. Which Beatles film title contains a colour?
7. What position does Robin Leigh-Pemberton hold?
8. Who composed the hymn *Nearer My God to Thee*?
9. What is the technical name for the flap of a dog's ear?

498

1. The people of which two countries buy the most Rolls-Royces?
2. Zeno founded which school of philosophy in Athens?
3. The Samurai were warriors of which country?
4. Who infatuates Humbert Humbert?
5. Which soccer team plays home matches at Ewood Park?
6. Which Anne was featured in the film *Anne of the Thousand Days*?
7. What career did Claude Duval and John Clavell pursue?
8. Which pianist and composer gave his last public concert at the Guildhall in 1848 – in aid of Polish refugees?
9. Which is the first animal in a dictionary?

30

1. The sari.
2. Thomas Cranmer.
3. The Weser.
4. Ophelia.
5. Polo.
6. Errol Flynn.
7. Socrates.
8. Mahler.
9. None.

264

1. Education.
2. The Earl of Lancaster.
3. In Haiti.
4. G.B.Shaw.
5. In South Africa.
6. *Yellow Submarine.*
7. He is Governor of the Bank of England.
8. Lowell Mason.
9. The leather.

498

1. People from the UK and the USA.
2. Stoicism.
3. Japan.
4. Lolita.
5. Blackburn Rovers.
6. Anne Boleyn.
7. They were highwaymen.
8. Chopin.
9. The aardvark.

31

1. If you worked as a pedagogue, what would you be?
2. When was the Channel Tunnel first proposed?
3. Which country produces the wine Tokai?
4. Who wrote the book *One Hundred and One Dalmatians*?
5. What are the pupil grades in Judo called?
6. Name Peter Seller's last film.
7. Which comedy actor said, 'A man is only as old as the woman he feels'?
8. From which operetta comes 'When constabulary duty's to be done/A policeman's lot is not a happy one'?
9. The additives cyclamates were withdrawn from use, as they were said to cause *what*?

265

1. Who 'had so many children she didn't know what to do'?
2. The son of which former Soviet Premier allegedly shot his father's successor in 1983?
3. After which British Queen is Africa's largest lake named?
4. According to John, what were the last words of Jesus?
5. Which great inventor invented water-skiing, although he never attempted it himself?
6. Who was the third Dr Who?
7. What was Malcolm X's surname?
8. The song *Que Sera Sera* originated in which film?
9. From which fish are rollmops made?

499

1. Of what is blennophobia the fear?
2. Who was in charge of the *Pinta*, the *Nina* and the *Santa Maria*?
3. Pluckley, in Kent, has what peculiar distinction?
4. In mythology, how many heads had the Spanish king Geryoneus?
5. In 1829, which two-team race first took place?
6. Sean Connery and Audrey Hepburn starred together in which Nottingham-based film?
7. If the Union Jack is flying over Buckingham Palace, who is at home?
8. How far is it to Tipperary?
9. What colour are deadly nightshade berries?

31

1. A teacher.
2. In 1802.
3. Hungary.
4. Dodie Smith.
5. Kyu.
6. *Being There.*
7. Groucho Marx.
8. *The Pirates of Penzance.*
9. Cancer.

265

1. The old woman who lived in a shoe.
2. Leonid Brezhnev – his son is Yuri.
3. Victoria.
4. 'It is finished.'
5. Benjamin Franklin.
6. Jon Pertwee.
7. Little.
8. *The Man Who Knew Too Much.*
9. From herrings.

499

1. Slime.
2. Christopher Columbus.
3. It is said to have more ghosts than anywhere else in England.
4. Three.
5. The Oxford v Cambridge Boat Race.
6. *Robin and Marian.*
7. Queen Elizabeth II.
8. A long way.
9. Red.

32

1. In Italy, what was the 'Settebello' or 'Seven of Diamonds'?
2. How many sons did King George V have?
3. In which county is Redcar, the seaside resort?
4. What title did Kit Williams give to his sequel to *Masquerade*?
5. Which county tied three successive Sunday League cricket matches in 1983?
6. At which film festival are Golden Bears awarded?
7. Which artist did a series of etchings called *The Disasters of War*?
8. What is Toyah's surname?
9. In measuring, 200 milligrams equal one *what*?

266

1. From July 1984, how much did an MOT test for cars cost?
2. In which city was the atom first split in 1932?
3. In which country are the Golan Heights?
4. Whose autobiography was called *Let's Get Through Wednesday*?
5. Aptly located, which soccer team is nicknamed the 'Gulls'?
6. The grand-daughter of which author played the lead in *Star 80*?
7. What was the name of the rabbit the *Daily Mail* flew back from the British Embassy in Libya?
8. Who had hits with *Let's Go Crazy* and *1999*?
9. A Bonne Louise is a kind of *what*?

500

1. Who carries a leather case called a sabretache?
2. Which famous siege occurred in 1884?
3. On which island is Akrotiri RAF base?
4. Tom Stoppard's play *Squaring the Circle* is about which trade union leader?
5. What is the equivalent of a fullback in American football?
6. Which TV pop show of the 1960s was repeated in 1985?
7. Who became the Mayor of New York in 1978?
8. Ringo, Frog, J.T., Charley and Sniffer make up which group?
9. What is measured in Lamberts?

32

1. An express train, withdrawn in 1984.
2. Five, and one daughter.
3. In Cleveland.
4. No title – the competition was to find it out.
5. Worcestershire. Statistically, it happens once in 58,000 years.
6. The Berlin festival.
7. Goya.
8. Wilcox.
9. Carat.

266

1. £10.70.
2. In Cambridge, England.
3. In Syria.
4. Reggie Bosanquet's.
5. Torquay United.
6. Ernest Hemingway's grand-daughter, was the star of the film.
7. Honeybun.
8. Prince.
9. Pear.

500

1. A cavalry officer.
2. The siege of Khartoum.
3. Cyprus.
4. Lech Walesa.
5. The safety.
6. *Ready, Steady, Go!*
7. Ed Koch.
8. *Duran Duran.*
9. Light.

33

1. Which make of car bore the very first number plate – A1?
2. During which century did Popocatepétl last erupt?
3. What is the capital of the US state of Nevada?
4. Who divorced Vashti to marry Esther?
5. How are showjumpers Liz Edgar and David Broome related?
6. In the 1958 film *The Fly*, what happened to make Vincent Price unrecognisable?
7. What percentage of Eskimos have even *seen* an igloo, let alone lived in one?
8. For what type of songs was Orlando Gibbons noted?
9. Which part of the body suffers from gastroenteritis?

267

1. What transforms Yorkshire pudding into toad-in-the-hole?
2. In China, which dynasty began in 1368?
3. The Azores are in which ocean?
4. Who was made from Adam's rib?
5. Which vehicles does Randy Mamola race?
6. Barbra Streisand starred with Ryan O'Neal in which 1979 film?
7. Bobby Leech, the stuntsman who fell over the Niagara Falls in 1911, breaking many of his bones, miraculously lived. How did he die?
8. Who had a hit record with *Happiness*?
9. In which country is the condor sacred?

501

1. 12 March '45. 23 April '56. What is unique about these dates?
2. What type of traders were once called 'flesh-floggers'?
3. Which two countries does the Simplon Railway Tunnel link?
4. Who wrote *Jude the Obscure*?
5. In Venezuela there is a 'sport' called *Toros Coleados*. What does this involve?
6. Why is 27 May an auspicious day for would-be horror film stars to be born?
7. What type of plane does Snoopy imagine he is flying?
8. Who wrote the 1971 bestseller *Grapefruit*?
9. How often do deer grow new antlers?

33

1. A Napier.
2. The eighteenth century. (1702.)
3. Carson City. (not Las Vegas.)
4. Ahasueras.
5. They are brother and sister.
6. His head became that of a fly.
7. About two per cent.
8. Madrigals.
9. The stomach.

267

1. The addition of sausages.
2. The Ming dynasty.
3. The Atlantic.
4. Eve.
5. Motorcycles.
6. *The Main Event.*
7. As a result of tripping over a banana skin some years later.
8. Ken Dodd.
9. In Peru.

501

1. They are the only dates in which the days, month and last two digits of the year form five consecutive numbers.
2. Butchers.
3. Switzerland and Italy.
4. Thomas Hardy.
5. Pulling the tails of bulls.
6. Peter Cushing, Christopher Lee and Vincent Price, three of the greats, were all born on that date.
7. A Sopwith Camel.
8. Yoko Ono.
9. Annually.

34

1. Why is a plane's flight recorder also known as the 'black box'?
2. Which British king was nicknamed 'Farmer George'?
3. Name two of the three flags erected on the summit of Everest in 1953 by Hillary and Tenzing.
4. According to the Bible, how many proverbs did Solomon know?
5. For what were 'plus-fours' worn?
6. The *Hot Shoe Show* dance company was led by whom?
7. Which Pope was Michelangelo's patron?
8. Which two colours is lavender, in the song?
9. Molten animal fat used for candles and soap is called what?

268

1. What is the only word in regular use in English containing three consecutive sets of double letters?
2. Whose best troops were known as the Young and Old Guard?
3. Nadi Airport is where?
4. Where in Turkey was St Paul born?
5. On which horse did Bob Champion win the 1981 Grand National?
6. Which game do Death and the Knight play in *The Seventh Seal*?
7. Who was Sir Winston Churchill's only son?
8. What is Paul McCartney's first name?
9. Which mineral plays a major part in maintaining the health and strength of teeth and bones?

502

1. Describe a pawnbroker's sign.
2. Whom did Mehmet Ali Agca attempt to assassinate in 1981?
3. In which country are the Cantabrian mountains?
4. What relation was Lot to Abraham?
5. Which liquid is at the centre of a golf ball?
6. To whom was Alfred Hitchcock referring when he said, 'If he doesn't like an actor, he just tears him up'?
7. Fred Dibnah is famed at which profession?
8. How many rows of keys has the Janko piano?
9. In healthy humans, how long does blood normally take to congeal?

34

1. Because Dr Black invented it.
2. George III.
3. The flags were those of the UK, India, and Nepal.
4. Three thousand.
5. Golf.
6. Wayne Sleep.
7. Pope Julius II.
8. Blue and green. 'Lavender's blue, dilly dilly, Lavender's green.'
9. Tallow.

268

1. Book-keeping.
2. Napoleon's.
3. In the Fiji Islands.
4. In Tarsus.
5. *Aldaniti.*
6. Chess.
7. Randolph Churchill.
8. James.
9. Calcium.

502

1. It consists of three hanging brass balls.
2. Pope John Paul II.
3. In Spain.
4. His nephew.
5. Castor oil.
6. Walt Disney.
7. He is a famous steeplejack.
8. Six.
9. 4–6 minutes.

Q

35

1. In the British Army, what is a Ferret?
2. What do we use today instead of the old-fashioned 'pouncepot'?
3. The Grande Place is the main square of which capital city?
4. In Shakespeare, who murders his wife Emilia?
5. What is the nickname of rugby international P.J. Winterbottom?
6. In the film, who or what was *The Mighty Joe Young*?
7. Which national museum is in Greenwich?
8. Which group sang *Lonely This Christmas* in 1974?
9. What is the surname of Liverpool sextuplets Hannah, Lucy, Ruth, Sarah, Kate and Jennifer?

269

1. Which American President has given his name to the world's largest aircraft carrier?
2. In which city did the Holy Roman Emperor live in the 17th and 18th centuries?
3. Which Republic was once called the Kingdom of a Million Elephants?
4. What nickname did John Dawkins use, in a book by Dickens?
5. What is the difference between rowing and sculling?
6. Which serial was originally called *Little Twittington*?
7. How old must you be to take out a Citizens' Band radio licence?
8. Who wrote the *Raindrop Prelude*?
9. What is colostrum?

503

1. What is kept in an amphora?
2. What did John Burns describe as 'liquid history'?
3. The Cabora Bassa dam lies on which river?
4. What is Lady Chatterley's first name in D.H. Lawrence's novel?
5. How many perfect marks of 6 did Torvill and Dean score in the 1984 Olympics free dance programme?
6. Whose life story was told in the film *PT109*?
7. What was Nelson's rank when he was killed at Trafalgar?
8. Who made 1975's best-selling record *Bye Bye Baby*?
9. Which name of a garment is used for aconite, or wolf's-bane?

35

1. An armoured car.
2. Blotting paper.
3. Brussels.
4. Iago, in *Othello*.
5. 'The Strawman'.
6. A giant gorilla.
7. The National Maritime Museum.
8. *Mud*.
9. Walton.

269

1. Eisenhower.
2. In Vienna.
3. Laos.
4. The Artful Dodger, in *Oliver Twist*.
5. A sculler uses two oars, a rower one.
6. *The Archers*.
7. Fourteen.
8. Chopin.
9. The first milk secreted by a mammal.

503

1. Wine, usually.
2. The River Thames.
3. The Zambesi.
4. Constance.
5. 12, out of 18.
6. John F. Kennedy's.
7. Vice-Admiral.
8. *The Bay City Rollers*.
9. Monk's hood.

36

1. What is Ogham?
2. Which Prime Minister's mother was one-eighth Iroquois Indian?
3. Which capital city contains a Temple of Peace and Health, and Cathays Park?
4. Who is Adrian Mole's girl-friend?
5. In which two athletics jumping events do women not compete?
6. In the cartoons, which cat chased Speedy Gonzales?
7. Who did not like the way Rodrigo Moynihan painted her eyes in 1984?
8. Who made the hit record *Like a Virgin*?
9. How many sides has a rhombus?

270

1. Which animal carries a palanquin?
2. What were Bright and Cobden opposed to?
3. In which English city is the Byker Wall?
4. In the sequel to *Tom Brown's Schooldays*, which university did the hero attend?
5. What are the relative starting positions for pursuit cyclists?
6. What was the first regular TV programme in colour?
7. Who was more famous for faking Samuel Palmer's work than for his own painting?
8. In which US state was Elvis Presley born?
9. For what property is the limpet best known?

504

1. What used to be called Bradburies?
2. In which year was the minimum voting age reduced to 18 in the UK?
3. In which country is the volcano Cotopaxi situated?
4. A wyvern has the tail of a serpent and the head of *what*?
5. Which sporting equipment do Purdy's make?
6. Which actor in *The A-Team* took his surname from an item on a restaurant menu?
7. Handsome Dan the bulldog was the original mascot of which university?
8. Which group sang *Robert de Niro's Waiting*?
9. What is treen?

36

1. Ancient Celtic writing.
2. Winston Churchill's.
3. Cardiff.
4. Pandora.
5. The triple jump and the pole vault.
6. Sylvester.
7. Mrs Thatcher.
8. Madonna.
9. Four.

270

1. The human being.
2. The Corn Laws.
3. In Newcastle-upon-Tyne.
4. Oxford.
5. Opposite sides of the track.
6. *Late Night Line-Up*, BBC2.
7. Tom Keating.
8. Mississippi, in 1935.
9. Its ability to cling.

504

1. Treasury notes.
2. In 1969.
3. In Ecuador.
4. A dragon.
5. Shot-guns.
6. Dirk Benedict, formerly Niewoehner, from 'Eggs Benedict'.
7. Yale.
8. *Bananarama.*
9. A small antique object made of wood.

37

1. Where would you find Rouge Dragon Pursuivant and Garter King of Arms working?
2. How many cohorts make a Roman legion?
3. Name one of the joint capitals of Libya.
4. Who was the very first *Time* magazine *Man of the Year*, in 1927?
5. In which sport is the Strathcona Cup competed for?
6. Whose first husband was Jim Dougherty?
7. Which style of card dealing has the same name as a stew?
8. Neil Diamond obtained a degree in biology at New York University. For what did he achieve a scholarship to gain his place?
9. Which bone connects the pelvis to the knee?

271

1. What is the colour of bottles containing Moselle wine?
2. Name the German pocket battleship scuttled in 1939 off Montevideo harbour.
3. Which is Scotland's most-visited building?
4. Who wrote the play *The Caretaker*?
5. Who once broke Muhammad Ali's jaw?
6. Whose autobiography is entitled *Somebody Laughed*?
7. Which British art gallery attracts the most visitors?
8. In *The Twelve Days of Christmas*, how many birds are given in total?
9. A leporine is what type of animal?

505

1. What is the difference between English and American pyjamas?
2. In which year was Singapore founded?
3. Which is Wales' second most populated city?
4. Who said, 'The only thing to do with good advice is pass it over'?
5. Which British player was European Footballer of the Year in 1978 and 1979?
6. To whom was Henry Fonda married when he died?
7. Which Greek philosopher looked all his life for an honest man?
8. Who, in 1959, had a hit with *Oh Carol*?
9. To which bird family does the jackdaw belong?

37

1. In the College of Arms. They are Heralds.
2. Ten.
3. Benghazi or Tripoli.
4. Charles Lindbergh.
5. Curling.
6. Marilyn Monroe's.
7. Goulash.
8. Fencing.
9. The femur, or thigh bone.

271

1. Green.
2. The *Graf Spee*.
3. Edinburgh Castle.
4. Harold Pinter.
5. Ken Norton.
6. Des O'Connor's.
7. The National Gallery.
8. 184.
9. A hare.

505

1. Americans spell it 'pajamas'.
2. In 1819.
3. Swansea.
4. Oscar Wilde.
5. Kevin Keegan.
6. Shirlee Adams.
7. Diogenes.
8. Neil Sedaka.
9. The crow family.

38

1. What is the name of the electric tricycle launched in 1984 by Sir Clive Sinclair?
2. The Romans used a liquid called sepia for writing. From what did this come?
3. Which is Africa's largest country?
4. Name Postman Pat's cat.
5. Which soccer team plays home matches at Maine Road?
6. How tall was King Kong in the 1933 film?
7. Who was Polly Nichols?
8. Which Benjamin Britten opera features a fishing village?
9. What usually cause tidal waves?

272

1. What is the earliest date that Easter can be?
2. In 1431, which English king was crowned as King of Paris?
3. Manama is the capital of where?
4. Who wrote the stories *Winter Cruise* and *Gigolo and Gigolette*?
5. Which sport did Major Killander invent?
6. 'The Golden Turkey Awards' were given for what?
7. Who discovered the colours of the spectrum?
8. In *Das Rheingold*, who steals the Rhine gold from the Rhine maidens?
9. The milk from which animal is most used in making cheese?

506

1. What do the Chinese words 'Kung Fu' actually mean?
2. In the American Civil War, which Confederate General was accidentally killed by one of his own soldiers?
3. Where in Devon can Drake's Drum be seen?
4. Genius is said to be 1% inspiration and 99% ______?
5. In which year was the first London Marathon held?
6. Which of the two Ronnies stars in TV's *Sorry!*?
7. In which city did Eva Perón's body turn up, three years after her death?
8. Which of Puccini's operas led to a law suit?
9. What does a whale use for breathing?

38

1. The C5.
2. Cuttle fish.
3. The Sudan.
4. Jess.
5. Manchester City.
6. Six inches – he was a hand puppet!
7. Jack the Ripper's first victim.
8. *Peter Grimes.*
9. Earthquakes under the seabed.

272

1. 22 March.
2. Henry VI.
3. Bahrain.
4. Somerset Maugham.
5. Orienteering.
6. The worst films made in the USA.
7. Sir Isaac Newton.
8. Alberich, the Nibelung Dwarf.
9. The cow.

506

1. 'Leisure time'.
2. 'Stonewall' Jackson.
3. At Buckland Abbey.
4. Perspiration. (The authors agree!)
5. In 1981.
6. Ronnie Corbett.
7. In Milan.
8. *La Bohème.*
9. Lungs.

39

1. How much were GCHQ employees offered to give up Union membership?
2. Which Emperor married Messalina?
3. In which country is Mount Logan?
4. Michael Hastings' play *Tom and Viv* is about which famous poet?
5. How long is a golfer allowed to search for a lost ball?
6. In the 1984 film *1984*, who played Big Brother?
7. Which political party leader was named 'Head of the Year' in 1984?
8. *Frankie Goes To Hollywood* took the title of their LP *Welcome to the Pleasure Dome* from which poem?
9. From what is amber made?

273

1. What used to be called Belishas?
2. Who was 'El Caudillo'?
3. Of what has Venice been called the 'mistress'?
4. In Hindu myth, what sort of animal is Kurma, the beast that Vishnu turns into?
5. What was tennis player Little Mo's surname?
6. In 1983, the National Theatre staged its first pantomime – which one?
7. What did the Gobelins workshop in Paris make?
8. Who called music 'the brandy of the damned'?
9. What does a rheostat control?

507

1. The *Western Mail* is the only daily morning newspaper published in which country?
2. What happened to George Mallory and Andrew Irvine in 1924?
3. In which city is the Palace of the Nations?
4. On which voyage did Gulliver visit Brobdingnag?
5. Which sport featured in the film *Gregory's Girl*?
6. Whose catchphrase was 'Didn't he do well?'?
7. Who was the famous husband of Roxana?
8. Mick Talbot and Paul Weller are from which pop group?
9. Which part of the body is afflicted by gingivitis?

39

1. £1,000 each, in February 1984.
2. Claudius.
3. In Canada.
4. T.S. Eliot.
5. Five minutes.
6. Nobody – the character didn't appear.
7. David Steel.
8. *Kubla Khan*, by Coleridge.
9. Tree resin.

273

1. Pedestrian crossings.
2. General Franco.
3. The Adriatic.
4. A tortoise.
5. Connolly.
6. *Cinderella.*
7. Tapestries.
8. G.B. Shaw.
9. Voltage: it is a variable resistance.

507

1. Wales.
2. They were lost on the final slopes of Mount Everest.
3. Geneva.
4. His second.
5. Soccer.
6. Bruce Forsyth's.
7. Alexander the Great.
8. *The Style Council.*
9. The gums.

40

1. How much soda is there in a gallon of soda water?
2. When did the Great Train Robbery take place?
3. How many official languages has Switzerland?
4. Name Gepetto's cat in *Pinocchio.*
5. At what long odds did *Snow Knight* win the English Derby in 1974?
6. When Fidel Castro appeared on the American TV show *Person to Person*, what was he wearing?
7. For what do the letters A. A. stand, in A. A. Milne's name?
8. Which bridge is burning down?
9. Who founded the science of electromagnetism?

274

1. What percentage of the total British population regularly attends places of worship?
2. Who reputedly haunts Hermitage Castle?
3. Which is the most populous city in the Republic of Ireland?
4. By what name is writer Mrs McCorquodale better known?
5. At what odds did Lester Piggott bring home *Never Say Die* to win first place in the 1954 Derby?
6. Who played Jennie Cavalleri in *Love Story*?
7. Who was elected *Pipeman of the Decade* in 1976?
8. On the sale of *what* was the Top 20 originally based?
9. Who discovered the conditioned reflex through experiments on dogs and rats?

508

1. For what does the acronym AWOL stand?
2. Shih Huang Ti was responsible for building which massive structure?
3. What was the former name of Wellington, New Zealand?
4. Who wrote the patriotic poem *Drake's Drum*?
5. Mildred Didrikson won two Gold Medals at the 1932 Olympics, then became a professional golfer. What was her nickname?
6. What was Marji Wallace's claim to fame in 1973?
7. Who was Socrates' most famous student?
8. *One o'Clock Jump* is particularly associated with whose big band?
9. How many moons has the planet Venus?

40

1. None.
2. In 1963.
3. Four.
4. Figaro.
5. 50–1.
6. His pyjamas.
7. Alan Alexander.
8. London.
9. Michael Faraday.

274

1. About 10 per cent.
2. Mary, Queen of Scots.
3. Dublin.
4. Barbara Cartland.
5. 33–1.
6. Ali McGraw.
7. Sir Harold Wilson.
8. Sheet music.
9. Ivan Pavlov.

508

1. Absent without leave.
2. The Great Wall of China.
3. Britannia.
4. Sir Henry Newbolt.
5. 'Babe'.
6. She became Miss World.
7. Plato.
8. Count Basie's.
9. None.

41

1. *Widseth*, dating from the 6th century, is the earliest known *what*?
2. Which king's death was caused by 'a little gentleman in black velvet'?
3. Where do the Dyaks live?
4. In *A Midsummer Night's Dream*, what is Starveling's job?
5. How many Grand Slam tournaments are there in tennis?
6. Who is the Incredible Hulk when he is not angry?
7. What was the *Morning Star* newspaper formerly called?
8. What did a barber called Buddy Bolden reputedly start in 1900?
9. According to a *Sunday Express* survey, which zoo animals do children like most?

275

1. What colour is pistachio-flavoured ice cream?
2. Who, reputedly dubbed a joint of beef 'Sir Loin'?
3. In which county is the town of Wellington, from which the Duke took his title?
4. Which poet was MP for Hull for 20 years, and wrote *To His Coy Mistress*?
5. 'Berm' and 'bunny hop' are terms used in which sport?
6. Which children's TV quiz is based on the game of Battleships?
7. Which newspaper was edited in 1985 by Peter Preston?
8. Who had a number one hit with *The Finger of Suspicion* in 1954?
9. What is a Cinnamon Norwich?

509

1. Who is the patron saint of tax collectors?
2. Which king had the first passenger lift, called the 'Flying Chair', in his private apartments?
3. Which country is ruled by the Kuomintang?
4. Which poet died running for a tram, in Liverpool, in 1888?
5. Which stadium was built for the 1908 Olympic Games in London?
6. What is the name of ITV's teletext service?
7. In which country was Shaker furniture made?
8. Whose 1985 hit album was called *No Jacket Required*?
9. What does a gravimeter measure?

41

1. English poem.
2. William III's: his horse stumbled over a molehill.
3. In Borneo.
4. He is a tailor.
5. Four.
6. David Banner.
7. The *Daily Worker*.
8. Jazz, in New Orleans.
9. Monkeys.

275

1. Green.
2. Henry VIII.
3. Somerset.
4. Andrew Marvell.
5. BMX biking.
6. *Finders Keepers*.
7. The *Guardian*.
8. Dickie Valentine.
9. A breed of canary.

509

1. St Matthew.
2. Louis XV of France.
3. Taiwan.
4. Matthew Arnold.
5. The White City Stadium.
6. Oracle.
7. In the USA.
8. Phil Collins's.
9. Specific gravity.

42

1. 'Dabs' is police slang for *what*?
2. Which country did Rhodri Mawr once rule?
3. What landed unexpectedly on the Australian town of Rawlinna in 1979?
4. What was the French novelist Zola's first name?
5. Before 1985, who was the last Australian man to win the Wimbledon Singles title?
6. Eddie Calvert once had a golden *what?*
7. What is Princess Diana's second name?
8. What makes an opera a Grand Opera?
9. What is deuterium oxide usually called?

276

1. At what age must British Field-Marshals retire?
2. Which French politician was called 'The Tiger'?
3. Which country's name means 'Resplendent Isle'?
4. Which famous American writer's works were all out of print when he died?
5. In which city is Meadowbank Athletics Stadium?
6. Which TV puppet's make-up tip is 'Never use yellow lipstick'?
7. What is the Soviet Union's highest decoration?
8. Who wrote *Where Have All The Flowers Gone?*?
9. What is nacre?

510

1. Which trade got its name because it used a lot of lead?
2. Which London railway station's name commemorates Queen Eleanor, who died in 1290?
3. Which US state capital has the same name as the state, plus 'City'?
4. Which day of the week is called, by the French, after the god Mercury?
5. Whose nickname was 'Smokin' Joe'?
6. What is the motto on the loop of film round the MGM lion's head?
7. Which black-bearded captain is Tintin's friend in the comic strip?
8. Which singer has been called 'the Divine Miss M'?
9. In which of the sciences does Margaret Thatcher have a degree?

42

1. Fingerprints.
2. Wales.
3. Pieces of Skylab.
4. Emile, not Budd . . .
5. John Newcombe, in 1971.
6. Trumpet.
7. Frances.
8. Nothing is spoken – everything is sung.
9. Heavy water.

276

1. They never retire.
2. Georges Clemenceau.
3. Sri Lanka.
4. F. Scott Fitzgerald's.
5. Edinburgh.
6. Miss Piggy's.
7. The Order of Lenin.
8. Pete Seeger.
9. Mother-of-pearl.

510

1. Plumbing, from the Latin 'plumbum', meaning lead.
2. Charing Cross. (Wherever her body rested on its journey to Westminster a cross was erected.)
3. Oklahoma City.
4. Wednesday – Mercredi.
5. Boxer Joe Frazier's.
6. 'Ars Gratia Artis'.
7. Captain Haddock.
8. Bette Midler.
9. In chemistry.

43

1. How often, worldwide, is a person murdered?
2. Giving birth to whom did Jane Seymour die?
3. In which city is the smart Ginza district?
4. Which angel told Mary that she was to bear God's son?
5. Whom did Arthur Ashe beat in the 1975 Wimbledon Final?
6. In which country is *Casablanca* set?
7. Who was Israel's first Prime Minister?
8. Who sang with Chesney Allen in *Underneath the Arches*?
9. What did it rain on 12 July 1961 in Shreveport, Louisiana?

277

1. What is tarragon?
2. What was special about Torgou in World War II?
3. In which county is the Caractacus Stone – under which legend says treasure is buried?
4. Where did Jesus spend his childhood?
5. Competitive Judo developed from *what*?
6. Who played Quentin Crisp in *The Naked Civil Servant*?
7. Who was the subject of Sir Joshua Reynolds' painting *The Tragic Muse*?
8. What sort of instrument was the Kit?
9. What colour are the stripes on the side of a perch?

511

1. Which is the sixth most common form of accidental death?
2. The proposal to reduce whose wages initiated the General Strike in 1926?
3. By law, what is the maximum age of a Singapore taxi?
4. Who wrote *Starship Troopers*?
5. Which tennis player is nicknamed 'Nasty'?
6. Who played Percy Brand in the comedy film *Law and Disorder*?
7. Sir Stanley Spencer set many of his paintings around which Berkshire village?
8. How many separate horns has the weird-looking altohorn?
9. Which necessary element in our diets is provided by kelp?

43

1. Every 20 seconds – but not the same person.
2. Edward, later Edward VI.
3. In Tokyo.
4. Gabriel.
5. Jimmy Connors.
6. In Morocco.
7. David Ben-Gurion.
8. Bud Flanagan.
9. Green peaches!

277

1. A herb used for seasoning.
2. It was where the Allied troops met the Russians.
3. In Somerset.
4. In Nazareth.
5. Ju Jitsu.
6. John Hurt.
7. Sarah Siddons.
8. A very small violin that could be carried in the pocket.
9. Black.

511

1. Choking.
2. Those of the miners.
3. Seven years.
4. Robert Heinlein.
5. Ilie Nastase.
6. Michael Redgrave.
7. Cookham.
8. Seven.
9. Iodine.

44

1. Who rules an Emirate?
2. Right up to 1819, what was the maximum penalty for illegal tree-felling in Britain?
3. What has killed the greatest number of Americans?
4. Who is Shakespeare's King of the Fairies?
5. Ilie Nastase comes from which country?
6. Whom did Frank Sinatra marry in 1966 at a casino in Las Vegas?
7. Contract Nullos is a form of which card game?
8. Kiki and Dave share which surname?
9. What is the more colloquial name for 'pernio'?

278

1. In which country would you be most likely to eat *bigos?*
2. How many of his eight wives did Bluebeard murder?
3. In Japan, which is the unluckiest number, equating to our number 13?
4. Who wrote *Daniel Deronda*?
5. Why, in the last century, was Frank Lentini particularly adept at playing football?
6. Harry Hamlin was the hero of which 1981 film?
7. In which event in April 1985 was the very last black highly significant?
8. A policeman's lot was not *what*, according to Gilbert and Sullivan?
9. The National Grid distributes which form of power?

512

1. What is the chief ingredient of the cocktail 'Margarita'?
2. Why did surgeons in ancient Egypt take particularly good care of their patients?
3. Where do Novocastrians live?
4. Who said to whom on their first meeting, 'I perceive you have been in Afghanistan'?
5. How many 20-minute periods make up an ice-hockey game?
6. Which actress was nicknamed 'The Statue of Libido'?
7. Wands, cups, swords and pentacles appear on what cards?
8. Johnny Cash only performs dressed in one colour. Which?
9. In which province were the first Artesian wells sunk?

44

1. An Emir.
2. Hanging.
3. Car accidents.
4. Oberon.
5. Romania.
6. Mia Farrow.
7. Bridge.
8. Dee.
9. Chilblains.

278

1. In Poland.
2. Seven.
3. Four.
4. George Eliot.
5. He had three legs.
6. *Clash of the Titans*.
7. The final of the World Professional Snooker Championship.
8. 'A happy one'.
9. Electricity.

512

1. Tequila.
2. Because their hands were cut off if their patients died.
3. In Newcastle.
4. Sherlock Holmes to Dr Watson.
5. Three.
6. Mae West.
7. Tarot.
8. Black.
9. In Artois.

45

1. Jimmy Olsen is a reporter friend of which comic book hero?
2. Louis Montcalm was killed in 1759, defending which city?
3. In which Scots city is the Wallace monument?
4. Who wrote *Love Story*?
5. Which sport has world records for the 100 km Triangle, and Goal and Return?
6. Which film star was called 'the Sweater Girl'?
7. Who led the 'Hole in the Wall' gang?
8. What is Stephen Duffy's nickname?
9. What was the first turbojet-powered airliner?

279

1. *Sois Prêt* is the French version of whose motto?
2. Which war lasted from 1337 to 1453?
3. In which county is the Duke of Portland's Welbeck Abbey?
4. By what name is the heroine Diana Prince better known?
5. Which sporting gift from the French insulted King Henry V?
6. Which doctor is Dr Kildare's mentor in the old TV series?
7. In which English city is the renowned 'Hole in the Wall' restaurant?
8. Paul, Nasher, Pedro and Mark are members of which group?
9. What is a Rhodesian Ridgeback?

513

1. Miss Betty Trask left £400,000 to provide an annual prize for *what*?
2. Which country was once ruled by Boleslaw the Generous?
3. Which animal is shown on the California State flag?
4. In the Bible, who is the father of Ishmael?
5. What, in horse racing, is a 'Bumpers' race?
6. Which actor starred in the stage musical *Barnum*?
7. Which American film star appeared on the London stage in 1985 in *The Caine Mutiny*?
8. Which group sang *Michael Caine*?
9. How many pips make up the Greenwich time signal?

45

1. Superman.
2. Quebec.
3. Stirling.
4. Erich Segal.
5. Gliding.
6. Lana Turner.
7. Butch Cassidy.
8. 'Tin Tin'.
9. The Comet.

279

1. The motto of the Boy Scouts – 'Be Prepared'.
2. The Hundred Years' War – really about 116.
3. In Nottinghamshire.
4. Wonderwoman.
5. Tennis balls.
6. Dr Gillespie.
7. In Bath.
8. *Frankie Goes To Hollywood.*
9. A breed of dog.

513

1. Romantic fiction.
2. Poland.
3. The bear.
4. Abraham.
5. One for amateur riders only.
6. Michael Crawford.
7. Charlton Heston.
8. *Madness.*
9. Six.

46

1. What should be used for eating asparagus?
2. What is the modern name of the town called Dubris by the Romans?
3. Which city does Haneda International Airport serve?
4. To whom did Tennyson dedicate *In Memoriam*?
5. What are the balls used in bowls called?
6. Who starred in the 1971 film *Kotch*?
7. For what was Anne Baites tried and convicted in 1673?
8. Who wrote the *Hammerklavier Sonata*?
9. Which bird's name means to flinch, or cower away?

280

1. What do Americans call a 'Chipwich'?
2. What was known as the 'Whiskey on the Rocks' episode?
3. Which country has the world's most crowded railway system?
4. Name Sebastian's twin sister in *Twelfth Night*.
5. When pole vaulting, which part of the body crosses the bar first?
6. In the 1965 film *A Study in Terror*, who is being hunted by Holmes and Watson?
7. What do pot-holers explore?
8. What does Roger Taylor play, in the group *Queen*?
9. Lambs' Tails is one of the colloquial names for what?

514

1. Which is the next year that will read the same upside-down and the right way up?
2. On which side did Spain and Sweden fight during World War II?
3. On which continent is Ethiopia?
4. What is the eccentric family's surname in *Arsenic and Old Lace*?
5. In a regular relay race, how often is the baton passed?
6. Name Brody's wife, in *Jaws*.
7. What is the occupation of BBC TV's 1985 *Mastermind* winner?
8. How old was Mozart when he died?
9. In which part of the body is the bone called the trapezium?

46

1. One's fingers.
2. Dover.
3. Tokyo.
4. Arthur Henry Hallam.
5. Woods.
6. Walter Matthau.
7. Witchcraft.
8. Beethoven.
9. That of the quail.

280

1. A sandwich of icecream between two biscuits.
2. The Whiskey-class Soviet submarine running aground near Karlskrona (Sweden) in 1981.
3. Japan.
4. Viola.
5. The feet.
6. Jack the Ripper.
7. Caves.
8. The drums.
9. Catkins.

514

1. 6009.
2. Neither – they were neutral.
3. Africa.
4. Brewster.
5. Three times.
6. Ellen.
7. A hospital driver.
8. He was 35.
9. In the wrist.

Q

47

1. What did Tom Smith invent in the 1840s that his company still makes?
2. Before the seventeenth century, what did 'pencil' mean?
3. Which city is called 'Mile High City' in the USA?
4. Which Asiatic master criminal was nicknamed 'the Yellow Peril'?
5. How many Gold Medals did Carl Lewis win in the first World Championships for athletics?
6. How many crew are on *Star Trek*'s *USS Enterprise*?
7. Which Russian world chess champion has a name which means 'Saviour'?
8. Who was backed by the *Blue Flames*?
9. Which university controls the Jodrell Bank radio telescope?

281

1. In 1985, which country's army had its phones cut off for not paying its bills?
2. Which ruler, son of a shoemaker, was intended by his mother to be an Orthodox priest?
3. Which city is traditionally famous for 'jute, jam and journalism'?
4. Whose first novel was *Hatter's Castle*?
5. Which cricketer was nicknamed 'The Big Cat'?
6. Which character did Noele Gordon play in *Crossroads*?
7. What was the original first name of TUC leader Len Murray?
8. Who had a hit with *You Spin Me Round* in 1985?
9. Where is your sartorius muscle?

515

1. Which vegetable do the French call 'flageolets'?
2. Who was nicknamed 'Stuffy', and ran Fighter Command in the Battle of Britain?
3. The Dutch call it Vlaams – what do we call it?
4. Which magazine was intended to be called the *Bladder*?
5. From which country do the football clubs Penarol and Nacional come?
6. Which odd couple live in Stackton Tressel?
7. What can you buy with a mortgage called 'bottomry'?
8. Which pop singer's real surname is Panayiotou?
9. Which animal is called 'Simba' in Swahili?

47

1. Christmas crackers.
2. A brush,
3. Denver.
4. Fu Manchu.
5. Four.
6. 430.
7. Spassky.
8. Georgie Fame.
9. Manchester.

281

1. Israel's.
2. Josef Stalin.
3. Dundee.
4. A.J. Cronin's.
5. Clive Lloyd.
6. Meg Richardson.
7. Lionel.
8. *Dead or Alive.*
9. In the thigh.

515

1. Green beans.
2. Sir Hugh Dowding.
3. The Flemish language.
4. *Private Eye.*
5. Uruguay.
6. Dr Evadne Hinge and Dame Hilda Bracket.
7. A boat or a ship.
8. George Michael, of *Wham!*
9. The lion.

48

1. What does MOP stand for in a British Police report?
2. What do members of the House of Commons call the House of Lords?
3. Which country's inhabitants have the longest life expectancy?
4. How was the martyr St Stephen killed?
5. Women compete for the Marcel Corbillon Trophy at which game?
6. Which actor, who provides the voice of Paddington Bear, was knighted in 1983?
7. Which member of the Royal Family was attacked in the Ideal Home Exhibition by a man dressed as a wolf?
8. Who composed 33 variations of a Waltz by Diabelli after being paid to write just one?
9. What sort of vehicle is called an LEM by astronauts?

282

1. Which Embassy owed Camden Council £517,000 in unpaid rates in 1983?
2. Aldo Moro was once Prime Minister of where?
3. Which city, originally called 'Pile O'Bones', is now capital of Saskatchewan?
4. Which comic-book hero's name is Lamont Cranston?
5. Which sport uses the terms 'rover peel' and 'cross-wire'?
6. In which TV series does the Sunshine Cab Company feature?
7. Why is Princess Michael of Kent referred to as 'Our Val' inside the Royal Family?
8. Which record by *Dexy's Midnight Runners* was the best-selling single of 1982?
9. John Young has made most trips into space – how many?

516

1. What significance does 'S4C' have in Wales?
2. Which English king suffered a nervous breakdown in July 1453?
3. Which US city is called 'Gateway to the West'?
4. In which play by Marlowe is Barabas the central character?
5. Who partnered Martina Navratilova to win her first Wimbledon Doubles title?
6. Which actress gave up the licence of the *Rover's Return* in *Coronation Street*?
7. What is the organisation STOPP opposed to?
8. In which Puccini opera do Ping, Pang and Pong appear?
9. When Concorde goes supersonic, does it get shorter, longer, or stay the same?

48

1. Member of the Public.
2. 'Another place'.
3. Japan's.
4. He was stoned to death.
5. Table-tennis.
6. Sir Michael Hordern.
7. Princess Michael of Kent.
8. Beethoven.
9. A Lunar Excursion Module – a car to be used on the moon.

282

1. The Soviet Embassy.
2. Italy.
3. Regina.
4. The Shadow.
5. Croquet.
6. *Taxi.*
7. It is short for 'Our Valkyrie'.
8. *Come On Eileen.*
9. Five.

516

1. It means Sianel Pedwar Cymru – the Welsh Channel 4 on TV.
2. Henry VI.
3. St Louis.
4. *The Jew of Malta.*
5. Chris Evert, in 1976.
6. Doris Speed.
7. The caning of children in schools.
8. *Turandot.*
9. It gets 9 inches longer, because of the effects of heat.

49

1. What is the English equivalent of the Spanish name Juan?
2. Which Italian family produced a Pope and a poisoner?
3. In which US state is Amarillo situated?
4. Who wrote *The Human Zoo*?
5. Whom did Floyd Patterson beat to become World Heavyweight Boxing Champion?
6. What was the sequel to *2001: A Space Odyssey*?
7. Which American became famous for his paintings of subjects such as Campbell Soup tins?
8. *Springtime for Hitler* is the musical featured in which film?
9. Which vehicle is known as a 'chopper'?

283

1. A supplement to a will is called what?
2. The first assassination attempt on an American President in 1835 went wrong, from the assassin's point of view. What happened?
3. Baghdad stands on which river?
4. In the Bible, at what age did Sarah, Abraham's wife, die?
5. In which country does the soccer club CSKA Sofia play?
6. At what club do Arthur and Terry in *Minder* do most of their drinking?
7. Who won the 1985 Embassy World Snooker Championship?
8. Whose first No. 1 hit was *Release Me*?
9. The enlargement of which gland is called a goitre?

517

1. Which dish derives its name from the Latin 'lasanum'?
2. Whose official residence was St James's Palace between 1698 and 1837?
3. Name the fault that extends from San Francisco to Los Angeles, along which earthquakes occur'
4. Maundy Thursday commemorates *what*?
5. Who, in 1983, rode *Teenoso* to victory in the Derby?
6. Name the motel in *Crossroads*.
7. For which author is 48 Doughty Street in London 'blue-plaqued'?
8. Which instrument does the German dudelsack most closely resemble?
9. What is the maximum speed of a human heart?

49

1. John.
2. The Borgia family.
3. In Texas.
4. Desmond Morris.
5. Archie Moore.
6. *2010: Odyssey Two*.
7. Andy Warhol.
8. *The Producers*.
9. A helicopter.

283

1. A codicil.
2. Both his guns misfired.
3. The Tigris.
4. 127.
5. Bulgaria.
6. The Winchester Club.
7. Dennis Taylor.
8. Engelbert Humperdinck's.
9. The thyroid gland.

517

1. Lasagne.
2. Britain's reigning sovereign's.
3. The San Andreas Fault.
4. The Last Supper.
5. Lester Piggott.
6. *The Crossroads Motel*.
7. Charles Dickens.
8. The bagpipes.
9. 220 beats per minute.

50

1. Which current British coin weighs exactly five grams?
2. Which country was ruled by the New Jewel Movement, until it was invaded by the USA?
3. In which English city is King Alfred's statue?
4. Which writer was called 'the performing flea of English literature' by Sean O'Casey?
5. How old must a horse be to run in a 'nursery'?
6. Which TV quiz show host was once a shipyard worker in Glasgow?
7. What pseudonym did Prince Andrew and Koo Stark use when they flew to the West Indies in 1982?
8. *The Witch's Curse* is the subtitle of which Gilbert and Sullivan operetta?
9. What would an ombrometer or a Dines tilting syphon measure?

284

1. Which cartoon character frequently exclaims 'Leapin' Lizards!'?
2. Who set up shop at the Sign of the Red Pale, by Westminster Abbey, in 1476?
3. Which country's anti-terrorist commandos are called 'Leatherheads'?
4. Which priest writes 'the words of a sermon that no-one will hear' in a Beatles song?
5. Which organisation protested about Martina Navratilova's clothes at Wimbledon in 1983?
6. In what sort of circus would 'pulex irritans' perform?
7. Who was Elizabeth Taylor's second husband, her first being Nick Hilton?
8. Who had hits with *Tonight* and *This is not America*?
9. What other name is used for the linden tree?

518

1. What did Presbyterians call 'the Devil's picture-book'?
2. Where did Michael Fagin break in, leading to the 1982 Dellow Report on security?
3. Which English county used to be known as Wigorn?
4. Which humorist wrote about dogs called Muggs, Barge, and a peke named Darien?
5. On which televised sport does Kent Walton commentate?
6. By what name is former bodyguard, Lawrence Tureand, better known?
7. Who changed the name of Clarty Hole to 'Abbotsford' when he went to live there?
8. Which musical instrument's name means 'large trumpet' in Italian?
9. Cambridge Rival, Redgauntlet and Grandee are varieties of *what*?

50

1. The twenty pence piece.
2. Grenada, before 1983.
3. In Winchester.
4. P.G.Wodehouse.
5. Two years old.
6. Nicholas Parsons.
7. Mr and Mrs Cambridge.
8. *Ruddigore.*
9. Rain – they are rain-gauges.

284

1. Little Orphan Annie.
2. William Caxton.
3. Italy's.
4. Father Mackenzie, in *Eleanor Rigby*.
5. ASH, or Action on Smoking and Health, as she wore a badge advertising a tobacco company.
6. In a flea circus.
7. Michael Wilding.
8. David Bowie.
9. The lime.

518

1. A pack of playing cards.
2. Buckingham Palace.
3. Worcester.
4. James Thurber.
5. Wrestling.
6. Mr T, in *The A-Team*, who changed his name in 1970.
7. Sir Walter Scott.
8. The trombone.
9. Strawberry.

51

1. With what type of sweetmeat is Montelimar associated?
2. For what purpose was Eau de Cologne originally manufactured?
3. The Madeira Islands belong to which country?
4. In which language was the New Testament originally written?
5. Who was the first player capped for England at all *five* levels in soccer?
6. In which film was 'flubber' invented?
7. Which gangster was called 'Lucky'?
8. Musical directions are mainly written in which language?
9. Who invented the Bessemer process for making steel?

285

1. How long is a decade?
2. Which town in Glamorgan is renowned for its castle and its cheese?
3. What are Macgillycuddy's Reeks?
4. In the nursery rhyme, what did Jack break?
5. Which soccer club has the nickname 'The Cottagers'?
6. Who said, 'I'm feeling a little tired today. One of these fellows'll have to go home'?
7. Which gangster was called 'Machine Gun'?
8. By what name was *Sex Pistol* John Lydon known?
9. Which branch of chemistry deals with the compounds of carbons?

519

1. The addition of what turns a Welsh rarebit into a Buck rarebit?
2. What were the secret state police of Nazi Germany called?
3. Where are the headquarters of Interpol?
4. 'More haste, less ______'?
5. What colour caps do English cricket internationals wear?
6. The climax of which Spielberg film takes place at Devil's Tower?
7. Which are the weakest pieces in chess?
8. Tom-toms and bongos are types of *what*?
9. Which creatures have the most legs?

51

1. A kind of nougat.
2. As a protection against the plague.
3. Portugal.
4. Greek.
5. Terry Venables.
6. In *The Absent Minded Professor*.
7. Charles Luciano.
8. Italian.
9. Bessemer.

285

1. Ten years.
2. Caerphilly.
3. Mountains in Ireland.
4. His crown.
5. Fulham.
6. Mae West.
7. George Kelly.
8. Johnny Rotten.
9. Organic.

519

1. A poached egg.
2. The Gestapo.
3. In Paris.
4. Speed.
5. Blue.
6. *Close Encounters of the Third Kind.*
7. The pawns.
8. Drums.
9. Millipedes.

52

1. How many Pope Urbans have there been to date?
2. What did the *SS Carpathia*, the *SS Virginian*, the *SS Parisian* and the *SS Olympic* do in common?
3. Name one of the two cities which win the *Britain in Bloom* award most frequently.
4. What colour stockings did Shakespeare's Malvolio sport?
5. At which boxing weight was Terry Downes World Champion?
6. Why did Stewart Granger change his name?
7. Who succeeded William Temple as Archbishop of Canterbury?
8. How many played in *The Dave Clark Five*?
9. For what does the acronym AIDS stand?

286

1. Who claim to 'put a tiger in your tank'?
2. What was the great female fashion craze of 1971?
3. Where is the administrative centre of the Open University?
4. Approximately what percentage of items in London Transport's Lost Property Office is claimed by the owners?
5. Which game is played at Muirfield, Carnoustie and Troon?
6. Which football team does Arthur Mullard support?
7. What profession did Colin Campbell and Sir John Vanbrugh both follow?
8. As high as which animal's eye was the corn, in *Oklahoma*?
9. Which snake has the largest fangs?

520

1. What is a doch-an-doris?
2. Who led the party which may possibly have reached the summit of Everest in 1924, but, since all were killed, no-one was left to tell the tale?
3. How many hours ahead of GMT is Egyptian time?
4. Who wrote *Eugene Onegin*?
5. At which weight was Walter McGowan world boxing champion?
6. What is Sir John Gielgud's first name?
7. Who first employed the phrase 'Lunatic fringe'?
8. Which instrument has been termed the 'clown of the orchestra'?
9. What, in 1906, did Ralph Wedgewood invent?

52

1. Eight.
2. They all rushed to the rescue of the Titanic.
3. Aberdeen or Bath.
4. Yellow.
5. Middleweight.
6. His real name was James Stewart, already the name of a well-known actor.
7. Geoffrey Fisher.
8. Five.
9. Acquired Immunity Deficiency Syndrome.

286

1. Esso.
2. Hot pants.
3. Milton Keynes.
4. 33 per cent.
5. Golf.
6. Arsenal.
7. Architecture.
8. An elephant.
9. The gaboon viper.

520

1. One last drink before going home.
2. George Leigh Mallory.
3. Two hours.
4. Pushkin.
5. Flyweight.
6. Arthur.
7. Theodore Roosevelt.
8. The bassoon.
9. Carbon paper.

53

1. What are Barlinnie and Long Lartin?
2. In which century did evangelist John Wesley live?
3. Of which English bridge is Sydney Harbour Bridge a copy?
4. Who rode a winged horse called Al Borak?
5. How often is tennis's Davis cup contested?
6. Which Baron is Dangermouse's enemy in the TV cartoon?
7. Which English county has a tradition of clog dancing?
8. What name does New York's 28th Street have in common with London's Denmark Street?
9. Which wood is most often used to make pencils?

287

1. What sort of creature is a Welsh Black?
2. What job did William Rees-Mogg do from 1967 to 1981?
3. If a pilot flew directly west from Paris, which country would he come to first?
4. In which book is Heaven called 'the Celestial City'?
5. Which sport does Peanut Louie play?
6. The TV serial *By The Sword Divided* was about which war?
7. In which month of 1982 was Prince William born?
8. John Gorman, Roger McGough and Mike McGear sang in which group?
9. In Scotland, what's a 'bubblyjock'?

521

1. What is a posset?
2. What was a 'berlin' in the 18th century?
3. In which town is the Great Orme's Head?
4. Who is Hamlet's murderous uncle?
5. How did Geraldine Rees enter the record books of her sport?
6. In which TV series could you see Doozers?
7. What do you need to play 'Cat's Cradle'?
8. To which heavy metal group do Ozzy Osbourne and Geezer Butler belong?
9. What colour is anil dye?

53

1. British prisons.
2. The eighteenth century.
3. The bridge at Newcastle-upon-Tyne.
4. Muhammad.
5. Annually.
6. Greenback.
7. Lancashire.
8. Tin Pan Alley.
9. Cedar.

287

1. A cow.
2. He edited *The Times*.
3. Canada.
4. *The Pilgrim's Progress*.
5. Lawn tennis.
6. The English Civil War.
7. In June.
8. *Scaffold*.
9. A turkey.

521

1. A drink of milk and ale.
2. A kind of carriage.
3. Llandudno.
4. Claudius.
5. She was the first woman to complete the Grand National.
6. *Fraggle Rock*.
7. String, and your fingers.
8. *Black Sabbath*.
9. Indigo, or purple.

54

1. Which tax, soon after it was introduced, became irreverently known as 'Vear and Tear'?
2. How was it that Bluebeard's last wife was not murdered?
3. What is the capital of the Shetland Isles?
4. Whom did the wolf impersonate in *Little Red Riding Hood*?
5. After how many points do players change service at table-tennis?
6. Who was the first PM to broadcast on radio?
7. k2; sl1; psso; k2; p2. What are you doing?
8. Who starred in the film *Brimstone and Treacle*?
9. How many moons has Uranus?

288

1. Which shoe heel and thin dagger share a name?
2. What was the pig called that was run for President in the USA in 1968?
3. Which is the third largest ocean?
4. Ian Fleming used De Beers' slogan for one of his novels. Which?
5. In 1976, who became the first woman golfer to earn over $100,000?
6. Who starred with Judy Garland in *A Star is Born*?
7. Whose ghost reputedly haunts Marwell Hall in Hampshire?
8. Name the *Soft Machine* drummer who unfortunately became paralysed.
9. The Glaistig, a Scottish monster, was half woman, half *what*?

522

1. We know that grapes are used for making wine, but what is used as the basis of tequila?
2. What did a TV licence cost in Britain in 1946?
3. What was Sir Winston Churchill's Kent home called?
4. What are the two top-selling (not given away with a newspaper) weekly magazines?
5. At which weight was John H. Stracey world boxing champion?
6. Which character did David Carradine play in *Kung Fu*?
7. Which game features blots, points and gammons?
8. What is the stage name of Stephen Judkins Saginaw?
9. What is the more colloquial name for the antirrhinum?

54

1. VAT – Value Added Tax.
2. She found the bodies of the other seven, and so got the message.
3. Lerwick.
4. Little Red Riding Hood's grandmother.
5. Five.
6. Stanley Baldwin.
7. Knitting.
8. Sting.
9. Five.

288

1. The stiletto.
2. Pigasus.
3. The Indian Ocean.
4. *Diamonds are Forever*.
5. Judy Rankin.
6. James Mason.
7. Jane Seymour's.
8. Robert Wyatt.
9. Serpent.

522

1. Cactus.
2. £2.
3. Chartwell.
4. *Radio Times* and *T V Times*.
5. Welterweight.
6. Kwai Chang Caine.
7. Backgammon.
8. Stevie Wonder.
9. The snapdragon.

55

1. Which egg dish takes its name from the French 'alemelle'?
2. In 1867, which four animals came to provide company for Nelson in Trafalgar Square, London?
3. Which international airport is identified by the letters JFK?
4. Who wrote *Thomas the Tank Engine*?
5. Who assists Jimmy Hill in introducing BBC TV's *Match of the Day*?
6. Which character does John Thaw play in TV's *Home To Roost*?
7. Which fashion designer is married to Alexander Plunket Greene?
8. How tall are most double-basses?
9. Where in the body is the retina?

289

1. What relation was the founder of the Girl Guides to the founder of the Boy Scouts?
2. From which French beach were over one third of a million soldiers evacuated in World War II?
3. Where was cambric linen originally made?
4. Which writer created Bilbo Baggins and Frodo?
5. What was soccer's Milk Cup formerly called?
6. In *Star Wars*, what species is *Chewbacca*?
7. Whom did Baroness Marie-Christine Von Reibnitz marry?
8. Who had a great hit with *Stranger on the Shore*?
9. What colour blood has a lobster?

523

1. Gin and 'It' – what's 'It'?
2. In about AD 543, how many people a day died from bubonic plague, worldwide?
3. Since April 1985, why are servants in the Mississippi basin happier?
4. Who wrote the play *Volpone*?
5. In which game would you use a caman?
6. Which football team does Bernie Winters support?
7. By trade, what was Shakespeare's father?
8. How many movements does a concerto usually have?
9. After which creature are false tears named?

55

1. The omelette.
2. Four lions.
3. New York City (John F. Kennedy).
4. Reverend W. Awdry.
5. Bob Wilson.
6. Henry Willows.
7. Mary Quant.
8. Just over six feet.
9. In the eye.

289

1. She was his sister.
2. Dunkirk.
3. Cambrai.
4. J.R.R. Tolkein.
5. The Football League Cup.
6. A wookie.
7. Prince Michael of Kent.
8. Acker Bilk.
9. Blue.

523

1. Italian Vermouth.
2. 10,000.
3. It is now no longer legal for their employees to beat them to death.
4. Ben Jonson.
5. Shinty.
6. Arsenal.
7. A butcher.
8. Three.
9. The crocodile.

56

1. Which huge bird can be found at Grosvenor Square's west end?
2. From what did Australian outlaw Ned Kelly make his armour?
3. In which English city have two cathedrals been built in the twentieth century?
4. Who made a Biblical riddle out of bees nesting in a dead lion?
5. Which cricket club's home is Fenners?
6. In which fictional town is *Coronation Street* set?
7. Who blessed married couples on York racecourse in 1982?
8. What does Roger Nelson of Minneapolis call himself when he sings?
9. Which metal is the base for plating Sheffield Plate?

290

1. What are a carrick bend and a Turk's head?
2. What was unusual about the Roman consul Incitatus?
3. In which US state is Cajun Country?
4. Whose first novel was *The Loving Spirit*?
5. George Herman Ruth; by what name is he better known?
6. From which country did actress Beatrice Lillie come?
7. Which left-handed darts player, nicknamed 'The Ton Machine' usually wears black?
8. Which bizarrely-dressed pop duo are made up of Jill Bryson and Rose McDowall?
9. What does the disease phylloxera affect?

524

1. Which current British coin shows a portcullis?
2. Which historian became Lord Dacre?
3. Biafra is part of which country?
4. As what was John Evelyn best known?
5. Which Scottish soccer league club are 'Academicals'?
6. Which is probably TV's most famous farm?
7. Periwinkle is a shade of what colour?
8. Who had a big hit called *Goody Two Shoes*?
9. What sort of creature is a sewin?

56

1. An eagle, above the US Embassy.
2. Old plough-shares.
3. In Liverpool.
4. Samson.
5. Cambridge University's.
6. Weatherfield.
7. The Pope.
8. Prince.
9. Copper.

290

1. Types of knot.
2. He was Caligula's horse.
3. Louisiana.
4. Daphne du Maurier's.
5. Babe Ruth.
6. Canada.
7. Alan Glazier.
8. *Strawberry Switchblade*.
9. Vines.

524

1. The one-penny piece.
2. Hugh Trevor-Roper.
3. Nigeria.
4. As a diarist.
5. Hamilton.
6. Emmerdale.
7. Blue.
8. Adam Ant.
9. It is a fish – a sea trout.

57

1. Who wear 'Something old, something new, something borrowed, something blue'?
2. When was the Atlantic first crossed by steamship?
3. Where do Monégasques live?
4. Who wrote *The Abbess of Crewe*?
5. What gesture does a cricket umpire use to indicate a no-ball?
6. Who starred in the film *Tootsie*?
7. Who was often referred to as 'The First Lady President'?
8. What nationality is violinist Yehudi Menuhin?
9. How many horses pull a troika?

291

1. How long before leaving harbour would you hoist the Blue Peter?
2. Who were the original 'Tories'?
3. According to German folklore, the Lorelei threw herself into which river?
4. According to the rhyme, how many whacks did Lizzie Borden give her father?
5. Which horse won the Derby, St Leger and 2,000 Guineas in 1970?
6. Who plays Edward the Lionheart, the ham Shakespearian actor, in the 1973 film *Theatre of Blood*?
7. Ten-pin bowling pins are ideally made of which wood?
8. Who wrote the song *Camptown Races*?
9. What is an otoscope used to examine?

525

1. Which drink is nicknamed 'Nelson's Blood'?
2. Alexandra Palace was destroyed by fire in 1873. It happened again more recently. When?
3. Which English town gives its name to an invalid chair?
4. Yahoos are imaginary animals in which book?
5. Which game is played in the Britvic League?
6. Translate MGM's motto 'Ars Gratia Artis'.
7. Where would you find Alexander, Caesar, Charles and David together?
8. The ancient Turkish qanum is the forerunner of which instrument?
9. The Rh factor derives its name from which animal?

57

1. Brides.
2. In 1826.
3. In Monaco.
4. Muriel Spark.
5. He raises one arm horizontally.
6. Dustin Hoffman.
7. Edith Wilson, the wife of Woodrow Wilson, who conducted his affairs after his stroke.
8. He is American.
9. Three.

291

1. 24 hours.
2. Irish bandits.
3. The Rhine.
4. 41.
5. Nijinsky.
6. Vincent Price.
7. Maple.
8. Stephen Foster.
9. The inside of the ear.

525

1. Rum.
2. In 1980.
3. Bath.
4. *Gulliver's Travels.*
5. Volleyball.
6. 'Art for Art's sake.'
7. In a pack of cards – they are the four kings.
8. The zither.
9. The rhesus monkey.

58

1. According to legend, if it rains on St Swithin's day, for how many days afterwards will it rain?
2. How many times was Davy Crockett elected to Congress?
3. In which country would you spend satangs and bahts?
4. Which is the shortest book in the Old Testament?
5. How wide is a competition basketball court?
6. In *2001: A Space Odyssey*, name the spaceship bound for Jupiter.
7. Which occupation had Bartholomew Roberts and Mary Read in common?
8. Whose autobiography was entitled *My Own Trumpet*?
9. How many eyes has a caterpillar?

292

1. How many cents make a nickel?
2. For what purpose was Parliament's ceremonial mace formerly used?
3. Which British colony is served by North Front Airport?
4. With which county is the poet A.E. Housman chiefly associated?
5. At what long odds did *Psidium* win the 1961 English Derby?
6. What name for light entertainment came from the French 'Chanson du vau de Vire'?
7. How many cards are used in pinochle?
8. Which crooner enjoys playing with his vast collection of toy trains?
9. To which bird family does the jay belong?

526

1. What is the chief ingredient of junket?
2. Members of which army were the Desert Rats of World War II?
3. Shantung silk comes from which country?
4. Remember 'The Dam Busters'? What was the title of the original book?
5. Who scored the most goals for West Germany in the 1970 and 1974 World Cups?
6. Who is radio's 'Diddy David'?
7. By what name is painter Anna Mary Robertson better known?
8. *The Marseillaise* features in which Tchaikovsky overture?
9. What type of creature is a sand mason?

58

1. Forty.
2. Three.
3. In Thailand.
4. The book of Obadiah.
5. 50 feet.
6. *Discovery*.
7. They were pirates.
8. Sir Adrian Boult's.
9. Twelve.

292

1. Five.
2. Hitting nuisances.
3. Gibraltar.
4. Shropshire.
5. 66–1.
6. Vaudeville.
7. 48.
8. Frank Sinatra.
9. The crow family.

526

1. Milk.
2. The 8th Army.
3. China.
4. *Enemy Coast Ahead*.
5. Gerd Muller (14).
6. David Hamilton.
7. Grandma Moses.
8. The 1812.
9. A worm.

59

1. What would you do with an Abernethy?
2. Which famous mutiny occurred in the 1850s?
3. In which country is Pusan?
4. Who wrote about Pigling Bland?
5. Who beat Anderlecht on penalties to win the 1984 UEFA Cup?
6. Who plays Gladys Pugh in *Hi-De-Hi*?
7. In which county was the poet Tennyson born?
8. Which street in New Orleans is famous as the cradle of jazz?
9. Spirits of Salt is another name for which acid?

293

1. What do we call the sweetmeat that Turks call Rahat?
2. At whom were the 1913 'Cat and Mouse' Acts aimed?
3. What is the main language of Ethiopia?
4. In which seaside resort is *The French Lieutenant's Woman* set?
5. Errol Tobias was the first black to play rugby for which country?
6. Which comedian once presented *It's A Square World* on TV?
7. What job does a bencher do?
8. To which group did Nick Heyward belong before going solo?
9. What is a Lent Lily usually called?

527

1. 'Zero Hour' is CB jargon for what time?
2. Who lost the battle of Borodino, 1812?
3. What is the USA's most southerly state?
4. Who created Gollum and Gandalf?
5. In which sport could you see a flying camel?
6. The film *The Italian Job* is about a robbery in which city?
7. Who is Harlequin's girl friend?
8. What does the name of the opera house 'La Scala' mean?
9. How many Laws of Thermodynamics are there?

59

1. Eat it, as it's a kind of biscuit.
2. The Indian Mutiny.
3. South Korea.
4. Beatrix Potter.
5. Tottenham Hotspur.
6. Ruth Madoc.
7. In Lincolnshire.
8. Basin Street.
9. Hydrochloric.

293

1. Turkish Delight.
2. The Suffragettes.
3. Amharic.
4. In Lyme Regis.
5. South Africa.
6. Michael Bentine.
7. He or she is a lawyer.
8. *Haircut 100.*
9. A daffodil.

527

1. Midnight.
2. Russia.
3. Hawaii.
4. J.R.R.Tolkien.
5. In ice-skating.
6. In Turin.
7. Columbine.
8. 'The Staircase'.
9. Three.

60

1. What is the main ingredient of risotto?
2. The Spanish Inquisition was formed chiefly to wipe out *what*?
3. Diplomats of which country collected most traffic tickets in London in 1984?
4. In which book does Injun Joe die when trapped in a cave?
5. In golf, which number iron is called a 'mashie'?
6. Who is Dee Dee McCall's detective partner?
7. How is the ex-ambassador Peter Jay related to James Callaghan?
8. In which century was the piano invented?
9. How old is a colt?

294

1. What is Prince Andrew's last Christian name?
2. Where was London's Zoo before 1834?
3. Which landmark do the Nepalese call Sagarmartha?
4. What kind of animal was Tuppenny in Beatrix Potter's *The Tale of Tuppenny*?
5. Gay Meadow is the home of which football team?
6. What was the name of the character called 'The Bionic Woman'?
7. Which French singer's nickname was 'Little Sparrow'?
8. To which conductor was Evelyn Rothwell married?
9. Which year (in the 1980s) was World Communications Year?

528

1. In which year did the Profumo scandal and the Great Train Robbery happen?
2. Who nailed 95 Theses to Wittenburg church door in 1517?
3. Under which European mountain range are the world's deepest caves?
4. Who wrote the novel *Fame is the Spur*?
5. Which Olympic event did Bruce Jenner win in 1976?
6. In which TV drama series did Bernard Hill play Yosser Hughes?
7. What was the Yorkshire Ripper's surname?
8. Which planet did Gustav Holst call 'The Mystic'?
9. Is heat kinetic, radiant or conserved energy?

60

1. Rice.
2. Heresy.
3. Egypt.
4. *Tom Sawyer*.
5. Five.
6. Rick Hunter.
7. He is his son-in-law.
8. In the eighteenth century.
9. Between one and four years old.

294

1. Edward.
2. In the Tower of London.
3. Mount Everest.
4. A balding guinea-pig.
5. Shrewsbury.
6. Jaime Summers.
7. Edith Piaf's.
8. Sir John Barbirolli.
9. 1983.

528

1. In 1963.
2. Martin Luther.
3. The Pyrenees.
4. Howard Spring.
5. The Decathlon.
6. *The Boys from the Black Stuff*.
7. Sutcliffe.
8. Neptune.
9. Kinetic.

61

1. Relating to cruise ships, what do the letters P & O stand for?
2. What was curious about the teeth of Louis XIV of France?
3. In April 1985, which unlikely place acquired a barbed wire fence?
4. Who wrote the play *The Trojan Women*?
5. In basketball, a successful free shot scores how many points?
6. When Vivien Leigh died in 1967, how did all London's West End theatres mark this?
7. What name did the painter Paolo Di Dono use?
8. Who is the world's most successful composer of popular music?
9. A tercel is what sort of bird?

295

1. How many pounds of grapes are needed to make one bottle of champagne?
2. Which Queen was called 'Gloriana'?
3. Which country annexed Transylvania in 1920?
4. Which of D.H. Lawrence's novels is set in Australia?
5. A competition bowling alley is how many feet long?
6. What do we call the one the Japanese call Miki Kuchi?
7. The Parthenon in Athens was built in which architectural style?
8. Who conducted the very first performance of Holst's *The Planets* in 1918?
9. Which hormone stimulates the development of male characteristics?

529

1. What is the minimum age at which one can legally purchase a pet?
2. From 1937–1975, who was Spain's dictator?
3. Which is the largest of the three Great Pyramids of Egypt?
4. Name Moses' father-in-law.
5. Which great miler was made Chairman of the Sports Council in 1972?
6. Who plays Haskins in *The Sweeney*?
7. Which American painter became famous for his illustrations of bird books? (A society for the preservation of wildlife was named after him.)
8. Who made the LP *Can't Fight Lightnin'*?
9. Of what is entomophobia the fear?

61

1. Peninsular & Oriental.
2. He was born with a full set.
3. Stonehenge – to prevent damage from Druids and pop-fans.
4. Euripides.
5. One.
6. By turning out all outside lights.
7. Uccello.
8. Paul McCartney – judging by monetary rewards.
9. A falcon (male).

295

1. Three – minimum.
2. Elizabeth I.
3. Romania.
4. *Kangaroo.*
5. Sixty feet.
6. Mickey Mouse.
7. Doric.
8. Sir Adrian Boult.
9. Testosterone.

529

1. Twelve.
2. Francisco Franco.
3. Cheops.
4. Jethro.
5. Sir Roger Bannister.
6. Garfield Morgan.
7. John James Audubon.
8. Ringo Starr.
9. Insects.

62

1. At the 1981 census, how many people admitted to being in Britain?
2. Which battle won Scotland's freedom in the Wars of Independence?
3. In which South American country would you spend guarani?
4. 'They also serve who only stand and wait.' Who wrote it?
5. By what name is the game minnonette now known?
6. Which brewers supply the *Rover's Return* in *Coronation Street*?
7. Highwayman John Cottington was known by what nickname?
8. Who wrote 'Abide With Me'?
9. Approximately how many teeth has the whale shark?

296

1. For what do the letters W.H. stand in W.H.Smith?
2. On the banks of which river did William III defeat James II in 1690?
3. Stirling is sited on which river?
4. Who was the Greek god of mockery?
5. Where is Britain's highest golf course?
6. Whose autobiography is entitled *Goodness Had Nothing To Do With It*?
7. What was Pilin Leon's title in 1981?
8. The beautiful aria *One Fine Day* is from which opera?
9. To which bird family does the blackbird belong?

530

1. Which wedding anniversary is crystal?
2. Who was Portugal's dictator from 1932–1968?
3. Between which two rivers does the Wirral lie?
4. Which prophet denounced Ahab and Jezebel?
5. Whom did Muhammad Ali nickname 'The Bear'?
6. Which actor's previous jobs included professional boxer and dance hall bouncer?
7. By what name was pirate Captain John Rackham better known?
8. Christopher Isherwood's novel *Goodbye to Berlin* gave rise to which musical?
9. In the main, what does a camel's hump contain?

62

1. 54,129,000.
2. Bannockburn, in 1314.
3. In Paraguay.
4. Milton.
5. Volleyball.
6. Newton and Ridley.
7. 'Mulled Sack'.
8. Henry Lyte.
9. None.

296

1. William Henry.
2. The River Boyne.
3. The Forth.
4. Momus.
5. Leadhills, in Scotland.
6. Mae West's.
7. Miss World.
8. *Madame Butterfly*.
9. The thrush family.

530

1. The fifteenth.
2. Salazar.
3. The Dee and the Mersey.
4. Elijah.
5. Sonny Liston.
6. Arthur Mullard's.
7. 'Calico Jack'.
8. *Cabaret*.
9. Fat.

63

1. What would you do with a 'Winston Churchill'?
2. How many Russian diplomats were expelled from Britain on spying charges in April 1985?
3. What colour are New York cabs?
4. To where did Orpheus travel in an attempt to recover his wife?
5. How many wrestlers compete in a tag match?
6. What followed *Beyond Our Ken*?
7. After whom was Rhodesia named?
8. Who sat among the cinders?
9. Which animal appears on the coat of arms of the city of Madrid?

297

1. At the 1981 census, how many females were there in Britain?
2. In 1873, which most prolific British murderess was hanged?
3. Approximately how many islands comprise Indonesia?
4. Who wrote 'Dying is the very last thing I wish to do', then did?
5. In which city did the 1924 Olympics, the subject of *Chariots of Fire*, take place?
6. What was the film sequel to *Funny Girl*?
7. Who was the first President of the State of Israel?
8. 'See ya later, Alligator.' What is the next line?
9. What blood was used in the early blood transfusions?

531

1. What is special about Akha Teej day in India?
2. Stone balls atop posts on London's bridges replaced what?
3. In the USA, what name was given to the national medical plan, introduced in 1966?
4. Relating to the Arthurian legends, what was the land of heroes called?
5. *In the Fast Lane* is whose autobiography?
6. The title of which porn film was used as an alias for an unidentified Watergate informer?
7. What is the English equivalent of trèfles, carreaux, coeurs and piques?
8. *The Impossible Dream* came from which musical?
9. The Clumber spaniel takes its name from a park in which county?

63

1. Smoke it – it is a cigar.
2. Five. (Thirty-one more went in September 1985.)
3. Yellow.
4. The Underworld (Hades).
5. Four usually.
6. *Round the Horne*.
7. Cecil Rhodes.
8. Little Polly Flinders.
9. A bear.

297

1. 27,842,000.
2. Mary Ann Cotton (she had 14 or 15 murders to her credit).
3. 13,000.
4. Samuel Pepys.
5. In Paris.
6. *Funny Lady*.
7. Chaim Weizmann.
8. 'In a while, Crocodile.'
9. Animal blood – with little success.

531

1. It is the most auspicious day for marriages.
2. Decapitated heads of criminals.
3. Medicare.
4. Avalon.
5. Geoffrey Boycott's.
6. *Deep Throat*.
7. Clubs, diamonds, hearts and spades.
8. *Man of La Mancha*.
9. In Nottinghamshire.

64

1. Who dubbed Miss Piggy's singing voice in *The Muppet Movie?*
2. Which Queen lost her head in 1587?
3. Which state of the USA today contains the Liberty Bell and Gettysburg?
4. Who wrote *Rachel Rosing*?
5. Which forest animal provides the nickname of Mansfield Town?
6. Who used to ask the questions in *The Sky's The Limit*?
7. Ronnie and Reggie were the first names of which notorious twins?
8. In which city is the Metropolitan Opera House?
9. Which continent has fresh-water electric eels?

298

1. Jerez de Rodrigo was the first European to do *what*, when taught by American Indians?
2. Which nursery rhyme is generally thought to be about the symptoms of the plague of 1665?
3. In which Indian city is the Red Fort of the Mughals?
4. Who wrote 'We are the hollow men'?
5. What is the largest number of letters and spaces allowed in a British racehorse's name?
6. Which chilly Alistair Maclean film did millionaire Howard Hughes watch over 150 times?
7. What was the first name of both Burke and Hare, the corpse-stealers?
8. Edward Elgar, as well as composing, was a professional player of which instrument?
9. Synthetic *what* was called 'buna' by the Germans in World War II?

532

1. Which general was nicknamed 'the Kansas cyclone' at West Point?
2. Nine days after Westminster Abbey was consecrated, which king was buried there?
3. From which country does Emmenthal cheese come?
4. Which Poet Laureate lived from 1770 to 1850?
5. What nationality was Jaroslav Drobny when he won Wimbledon in 1954?
6. Who was cloned 94 times in *The Boys From Brazil*?
7. What was James J. Corbett's nickname?
8. What was the real first name of both Bix Beiderbecke and Chuck Berry?
9. In the olden days, what was a 'curtal horse'?

64

1. Johnny Mathis.
2. Mary, Queen of Scots.
3. Pennsylvania.
4. Howard Spring.
5. Stag – 'The Stags'.
6. Hughie Green.
7. The Kray brothers.
8. In New York.
9. South America.

298

1. Smoke tobacco.
2. Ring-a-ring-o'-roses.
3. In Delhi.
4. T.S. Eliot.
5. Eighteen.
6. *Ice Station Zebra.*
7. William.
8. The violin.
9. Rubber.

532

1. Dwight D. Eisenhower, when playing football.
2. Edward the Confessor, in 1066.
3. From Switzerland.
4. William Wordsworth.
5. He was Egyptian.
6. Adolf Hitler.
7. 'Gentleman Jim'.
8. Leon.
9. One with its tail docked, or cut short.

65

1. For which speedy father and daughter has a teddy called Mr Whoppit served as a mascot?
2. Who 'Nothing common did or mean, upon that memorable scene'?
3. On which border are 42,000 people a month arrested?
4. In which Shakespeare play is Falstaff's death described?
5. What is the song-title motto above the gates of Liverpool football club?
6. Which TV puppet family had a charwoman called Mrs Scrubbit and a huge spotty dog?
7. Whose catchphrase was 'You lucky people!'?
8. What instrument did Evelyn Rothwell play?
9. What sort of creatures were Aunt Pettitoes, Aunt Dorcas and Aunt Porcas in Beatrix Potter's books?

299

1. What is a Shaded Cameo?
2. Why did Boadicea commit suicide?
3. According to the saying, where do all roads lead to?
4. Geneva, Wicked and Breeches are three names for versions of *what*?
5. Where was Kevin Moran when he heard the FA would let him have a cup-winner's medal?
6. Which famous singer played Jack Warner's daughter on radio in *Meet the Huggetts*?
7. In which game did Paul Masson captain the Scots team?
8. What distinction does Al Martino's *Here In My Heart* have in pop music?
9. Which apple tree parasite is much in demand for festivities?

533

1. What is a South African doing if he puts money in a 'tickey-box'?
2. What sort of food was once called 'marchpane'?
3. Which Asian capital city has a name which means 'Town of Victory'?
4. In which 1945 novel does Lord Marchmain appear?
5. Which firm makes the sports shoes with three stripes?
6. In the radio series *The Archers* which character wears a buckskin shirt?
7. Who has a little sister called Skipper and a boy-friend called Ken?
8. How many players were there in the *Temperance Seven*, the Sixties band?
9. Durmast and common are the two British species of *what*?

65

1. Donald and Gina Campbell.
2. Charles I at his execution, according to Andrew Marvell.
3. The border between Mexico and the USA.
4. In *Henry V*.
5. *You'll Never Walk Alone*.
6. *The Woodentops*.
7. Tommy Trinder's.
8. The oboe.
9. Pigs – or, rather, sows.

299

1. A breed of cat.
2. To avoid capture by the Romans.
3. Rome.
4. Translations of the Bible.
5. In an aeroplane flying to the West Indies with his Manchester United team-mates.
6. Petula Clark.
7. Darts.
8. It was the first-ever Number One in the first pop chart, in 1952.
9. Mistletoe.

533

1. Making a telephone call from a pay-phone – a 'tickey' was a threepenny bit.
2. Marzipan.
3. Djakarta, in Indonesia.
4. *Brideshead Revisited* by Evelyn Waugh.
5. Adidas.
6. Eddie Grundy.
7. Barbie, the doll.
8. Nine – they were always 'one over the eight'.
9. Oak tree.

66

1. What sort of drink is a 'St Clement's'?
2. Who died in 1814, leaving a box of prophecies to be opened by bishops?
3. Where are Sabra, Chatilah and Bourj-al-Barajneh which made the news in 1985?
4. Which famous lovers were the subject of Dryden's play *All For Love*?
5. Kayles, or 'quilles' in France, is an early form of which game?
6. Which 1969 film did Richard Burton make because he wanted his children to be able to see a film he had made?
7. In the *Daily Mirror* cartoon, who is Andy Capp's wife?
8. Which British rock band has backed Bob Dylan on several albums?
9. What do American newspaper horoscopes call people born under the astrological sign we know as 'Cancer'?

300

1. Why was convict Jimmy Simmonds recaptured within 30 minutes of escaping from High Point prison in Suffolk in 1985?
2. Who was the last English king to have a queen called Catherine?
3. Which American city has a name which is the Indian for 'the Place of the Skunk Cabbage'?
4. Which novelist edited the 1985 *Oxford Companion to English Literature*?
5. In which sport is the star's personal servant called the 'mozo de estoques'?
6. After making which film did Bert Lahr complain, 'I was typecast as a lion'?
7. Which actor is the brother of Sheila Mercier (Annie Sugden in *Emmerdale Farm*)?
8. Which musical selection was made first by Vic Oliver and last by Sheila Steafel?
9. Which gas did Joseph Priestley discover and call 'dephlogisticated air'?

534

1. What does the surname 'Kaufmann' mean?
2. What was the name of William Shakespeare's only son?
3. Which Asian capital city has a name which means 'muddy river mouth'?
4. Who wrote *The Great Hoggarty Diamond* and *The Fitzboodle Papers*?
5. The Knighthood Tournament, held at Southampton, is the world's oldest competition in which sport?
6. Which film about a mental hospital won all five major Oscars in 1975?
7. Flower Garden, Spite and Malice, and Napoleon at St Helena are all *what*?
8. Why might Creedence Clearwater Revival's only number one hit remind you of a werewolf?
9. Which technique of decorative metal-work comes originally from Syria's capital?

66

1. Mixed orange juice and bitter lemon.
2. Joanna Southcott.
3. In Lebanon; they were three Palestinian camps in Beirut.
4. Antony and Cleopatra.
5. Skittles.
6. *Where Eagles Dare.*
7. Florrie.
8. *Dire Straits.*
9. Moon Children.

300

1. He hitched a lift from a police car!
2. Charles II.
3. Chicago.
4. Margaret Drabble.
5. In bull-fighting: he looks after the swords.
6. *The Wizard of Oz.*
7. Brian Rix.
8. *Desert Island Discs*, with Roy Plomley.
9. Oxygen.

534

1. Merchant.
2. Hamnet – *not* Hamlet!
3. Kuala Lumpur, Malaysia.
4. W.M.Thackeray.
5. Bowls.
6. *One Flew Over The Cuckoo's Nest.*
7. Games of patience.
8. It was called *Bad Moon Rising*, and was a hit in 1969.
9. Damascening, from Damascus.

67

1. What colour are the Royal Air Services Research and Rescue helicopters?
2. Who was the second husband of Mary, Queen of Scots?
3. Which particular pilgrimage has a Haji made?
4. Who wrote *Man and Superman*?
5. Which British cricketer has walloped the most runs in his first-class career?
6. What was John Inman's job, prior to acting?
7. What occupation had Ann Bonney and Captain Gow in common?
8. Which group had a hit with *Good Vibrations*?
9. What colour is a sorrel horse?

301

1. Which are Britain's two most widely used credit cards?
2. Which king of England was termed 'Harefoot'?
3. Which river meets the Mediterranean at the Gulf of Lions?
4. Who wrote the play *John Bull's Other Island*?
5. What colour shirts do Norwich City wear by choice?
6. Which actor's previous occupations included cement mixer and coffin polisher?
7. What is James Callaghan's first name?
8. Which pop singer starred in the film *The Man Who Fell To Earth*?
9. Which ghastly medicine did Dr John Hughes Bennet introduce?

535

1. What is a trigamist?
2. Who preceded Creon as King of Thebes?
3. Where is the Potala Palace?
4. Who wrote *The Quare Fellow*?
5. What was Cindy Nicholas the first woman swimmer to do?
6. Which former contestant sets the questions for TV's *Krypton Factor*?
7. Which Home Secretary was described by the *Daily Mirror* as Mrs Thatcher's 'house-trained poodle'?
8. Which Gilbert and Sullivan opera is subtitled *The Merryman and His Maid*?
9. By what more familiar name is an aircraft's flight recorder known?

67

1. Yellow.
2. Lord Darnley.
3. To Mecca.
4. G.B.Shaw.
5. Jack Hobbs – 61, 237 runs between 1905 and 1935.
6. He was a window dresser.
7. Piracy.
8. *The Beach Boys*.
9. Light brown.

301

1. Barclaycard and Access.
2. Harold.
3. The Rhône.
4. G.B.Shaw.
5. Yellow.
6. Sean Connery's.
7. Leonard.
8. David Bowie.
9. Cod liver oil.

535

1. Someone with three spouses.
2. Oedipus.
3. In Lhasa, Tibet.
4. Brendan Behan.
5. To swim the English Channel in both directions.
6. David Elias.
7. Leon Brittan.
8. *The Yeomen of the Guard*.
9. The black box.

68

1. How many 'S's are there in 'scissors'?
2. Which famous dog was found in a foxhole during World War I?
3. In April 1985, where did Mrs Thatcher think she was when she wasn't?
4. How does Robert Browning's *Home Thoughts From Abroad* begin?
5. Which soccer manager is nicknamed 'The Doc'?
6. Who starred in the 1954 film *You Lucky People*?
7. Who was the first Roman Catholic President of the USA?
8. Why, for nearly 200 years, was the music of Mozart banned in the Vatican?
9. What is the common name for the tree Salix Babylonica?

302

1. Of what is lalaphobia the fear?
2. The people of which group of islands murdered the explorer Magellan?
3. Over 2,000 people died in 1984 from deadly fumes. In which Indian city?
4. Which part of Black Beauty wasn't black?
5. In the USA, which racehorse is sometimes called the 'chalk horse'?
6. Who wrote the scripts for *Till Death Us Do Part*?
7. Who taught Prince Philip to sail?
8. According to the song, who was 'King of the Wild Frontier'?
9. Systolic and diastolic are the upper and lower rates of what?

536

1. Potted hock is made from which joint of beef?
2. In which year was VAT introduced in Britain?
3. Which English city has unbroken city walls?
4. How long did it take Solomon to build the Temple?
5. Who was the first man to break 3 min 30 secs in the 1,500 metres race?
6. Who produced *The Producers*?
7. Sylvia Plath was the wife of which Poet Laureate?
8. Who, in 1985, was presented with the Burma Star – 40 years after earning it?
9. It always used to be the first cuckoo that was reported in *The Times* letters. What has taken its place?

68

1. Four.
2. Rin Tin Tin.
3. She momentarily confused Malaysia with Indonesia on her Far East tour.
4. 'Oh to be in England, now that April's there'.
5. Tommy Docherty.
6. Tommy Trinder.
7. John F. Kennedy.
8. Although a Roman Catholic, he became a Freemason just before his death.
9. Weeping willow.

302

1. Speaking in public.
2. The Philippines.
3. Bhopal.
4. The white star on his forehead.
5. The favourite.
6. Johnny Speight.
7. Uffa Fox.
8. Davy Crockett.
9. Blood pressure.

536

1. The shinbone.
2. In 1973.
3. Chester.
4. Seven years.
5. Steve Cram.
6. Mel Brooks.
7. Ted Hughes.
8. Dame Vera Lynn.
9. The first sighting of a cormorant fishing in the Thames.

69

1. What is made of canvas coated with oxidised linseed oil?
2. Of which country was Vittorio Emanuele the king before he became King of united Italy in 1861?
3. In which English town do bananas grow in Queen Mary's garden?
4. Whose autobiography is called *As It Happens*?
5. What do touring South African rugby sides give to the first team to beat them?
6. What is the name of the alligator in *Miami Vice*?
7. Who writes the bridge column in *The Times*?
8. What is 'Opera buffa'?
9. Which noisy bird do Australians call 'the bushman's clock'?

303

1. Who got into the Kremlin in 1985 using a GLC bus pass for OAPs?
2. Which king did Robin Hood support?
3. What do inhabitants of Los Angeles call themselves?
4. Whose eyes make up the peacock's tail in myth?
5. In which sport would you find the Poppies, Angels, Chicks and Dollies?
6. The first House of Lords debate to be televised discussed *what*?
7. Who was Lady Constance de Coverlet in radio's *I'm Sorry, I'll Read That Again*?
8. About whom did 'Mad Jocks and Englishman' make a record called *Just Like Kenny*?
9. Ninety-five percent of the atmosphere of Mars consists of which gas?

537

1. Where is the Ocean of Storms?
2. Who was given the Cullinan Diamond for his 66th birthday?
3. Which Mediterranean island has just one railway line, 71 miles long?
4. In myth, for what was Stentor famous?
5. In which sport is 'Canine Catch and Fetch' a class?
6. Who played Lord Emsworth in TV's *The World of Wodehouse*?
7. As what has Stan Flashman become famous in London?
8. Who has written operas about Einstein, Gandhi and an Egyptian Pharaoh?
9. The Focke Wulf 61 was the world's first successful *what*?

69

1. Lino, or linoleum.
2. Sardinia.
3. In Falmouth.
4. Jimmy Savile's.
5. A stuffed and mounted springbok head.
6. Elvis.
7. Jeremy Flint.
8. Comic opera.
9. The kookaburra, or laughing jackass.

303

1. Denis Healey.
2. Richard I.
3. Angelenos.
4. Argus's.
5. Football – they are nicknames of non-league clubs.
6. The economy.
7. Tim Brooke-Taylor.
8. Footballer Kenny Dalglish.
9. Carbon dioxide.

537

1. On the moon.
2. King Edward VII, in 1907.
3. Cyprus.
4. His extremely loud voice.
5. Frisbee throwing.
6. Ralph Richardson.
7. As a 'scalper', or tout, who sells hard-to-get tickets.
8. Philip Glass.
9. Helicopter. It took to the air in 1937.

Q

70

1. For which month is topaz the birthstone?
2. Name the whopping white diamond that Richard Burton bought for Elizabeth Taylor in 1969.
3. Which is the largest lake in Ethiopia?
4. Which of Chaucer's pilgrims told the first Canterbury Tale?
5. What is the full name of the chief Rugby League knockout cup?
6. Whom did Jean Alexander play in *Coronation Street*?
7. In 1923, who founded a car rental company originally called *The Drive-Ur-Self System*?
8. Who had a hit with *For Once in my Life*?
9. From what is penicillin made?

304

1. Who or what is the second biggest landowner in Britain?
2. In pagan times, why did girls tie holly onto their beds before retiring?
3. Mahón is the capital of which island?
4. Which king ordered John the Baptist to be beheaded?
5. Which bone do jockeys break most often?
6. Which of Charlie's Angels did Kate Jackson play?
7. What was Lawrence of Arabia's military title?
8. YMO are the initial letters of which orchestra?
9. Approximately how many sightings of the Loch Ness monster are there each year?

538

1. What is the motto of the Institute of Builders?
2. When were driving tests introduced in Britain?
3. Which country's flag is green with a central red circle?
4. How many years of happiness does the devil promise Dr Faustus in Marlowe's play?
5. Which club did Kevin Keegan leave to go to Newcastle?
6. *Son of the Sheik* was which great screen lover's last film?
7. Which American President's statue is in Grosvenor Square, London?
8. Which pop band have a deadly sense of humour?
9. After which creatures were the Canary Islands named?

70

1. November.
2. The Cartier-Burton Diamond.
3. Lake Tana.
4. The Knight.
5. The Silk Cut Rugby League Challenge Cup.
6. Hilda Ogden.
7. John Hertz.
8. Stevie Wonder.
9. Fungus or mould.

304

1. The Church of England.
2. To stop themselves turning into witches.
3. Minorca.
4. Herod.
5. The collar-bone, or clavicle.
6. Sabrina.
7. Aircraftsman.
8. *Yellow Magic Orchestra*.
9. Twenty.

538

1. 'Diligently and Faithfully'.
2. In 1933.
3. Bangladesh's.
4. 24 years.
5. Southampton.
6. Rudolph Valentino's.
7. F.D.Roosevelt's.
8. *Killing Joke*.
9. Dogs!

71

1. What is the speed limit on Japanese motorways?
2. What connection did Copenhagen have with the Battle of Waterloo?
3. Which capital city is surrounded by a 68-mile outer ring road?
4. Who wrote 'How do I love thee? Let me count the ways'?
5. What was the official car of the 1984 Winter Olympics?
6. Who played Adam Adamant on TV?
7. Who was the official hair stylist for the 1984 Olympic Games?
8. Which group did the *Mugwumps* and the *Lovin' Spoonful* become?
9. What does a badger eat, mainly?

305

1. In 1980, how many gunmen were in the Iranian Embassy when the SAS stormed in?
2. Each month, Napoleon bathed in about 13 gallons of *what*?
3. The world's largest *what* is at Cholula di Rivadabia in Mexico?
4. What pseudonym does Betty Kenward use for her social diary in *Harper's and Queen*?
5. From which West Indies island does fast bowler Malcolm Marshall come?
6. Which chat show host is nicknamed 'Sooty'?
7. With which other chessman does the castle castle?
8. What nationality is singer Helen Reddy?
9. What is the only land mammal with more than forty-four teeth?

539

1. What did Thomas Austin take to Australia in 1859, for hunting?
2. Who did not become King of Britain until he was nearly 65, then ruled for seven years?
3. In which European country do the highest percentage of people have a telephone?
4. Which book by Harold Robbins was modelled on arms-dealer Adnan Khashoggi?
5. Which boxer said, 'I was black once – when I was poor'?
6. Who is the housewife megastar from Moonce Ponds?
7. Who holds British passport Number One?
8. Which sweet-sounding group were called 'first of the heavy bands' in 1967?
9. In what do arboreal animals live?

71

1. 49 mph, or 79 kph.
2. He was the Duke of Wellington's famous horse.
3. Moscow.
4. Elizabeth Barrett Browning.
5. The Chevrolet.
6. Gerald Harper.
7. Vidal Sassoon.
8. *The Mamas and The Papas.*
9. Earthworms – they comprise about 60 per cent of its diet.

305

1. Six. Five were killed.
2. Eau de Cologne.
3. Pyramid.
4. Jennifer.
5. From Barbados.
6. Russell Harty.
7. The king.
8. She is Australian, born in Melbourne.
9. The opossum.

539

1. Twelve pairs of rabbits, from which all Australia's rabbits came.
2. William IV.
3. In Monaco – 84 per cent.
4. *The Pirate.*
5. Larry Holmes. World Heavyweight Champion.
6. Dame Edna Everage.
7. Prince Philip.
8. *Vanilla Fudge.*
9. Trees.

72

1. Which is Britain's third most common surname?
2. How old was Harold Macmillan when he became Prime Minister?
3. With which country is the drink Tokai chiefly associated?
4. Who said to customs officers, 'I have nothing to declare but my genius'?
5. Who plays home matches at the Filbert Street ground?
6. Whose autobiography is called *Jacob's Ladder*?
7. What are the three primary colours of light?
8. Which pop singer starred in the film *The Hunger*?
9. What are the approximate odds against your being struck by lightning this year?

306

1. Which of these famous London stores still trade; Derry and Thoms; Swan and Edgar; Bourne and Hollingsworth; Whiteleys?
2. Who receives the most from the Civil Lists?
3. On which continent do the wandering Hottentots roam?
4. Who, in Genesis, dreamt of seven fat and seven lean kine?
5. Who was the first 'Footballer of the Year'?
6. *Puss Gets the Boot* was the first cartoon to feature which pair?
7. Which is the world's most popular collecting hobby?
8. At what instrument is John Lill a virtuoso?
9. What is the other name for the all but extinct snow leopard?

540

1. What was founded by John Elias, which flourishes on Sundays?
2. What preceded the Royal Air Force?
3. Which country produces the most timber?
4. Name Captain Marryat's midshipman.
5. To the nearest 100,000, how many Mars Bars placed end to end are needed to cover the distance run in the London Marathon?
6. Which actor's previous jobs included butcher's boy and rag and bone merchant?
7. Which Prime Minister immediately preceded Margaret Thatcher?
8. Which line precedes 'Mother of the free'?
9. Which gardens in Britain attract the most visitors?

72

1. Williams.
2. 62 years old.
3. Hungary.
4. Oscar Wilde.
5. Leicester City FC.
6. David Jacobs'.
7. Red, blue and green.
8. David Bowie.
9. 2,000,000–1.

306

1. None of them.
2. Queen Elizabeth II.
3. Africa.
4. Pharaoh.
5. Stanley Matthews, in 1948.
6. Tom and Jerry.
7. Stamp collecting.
8. The piano.
9. The ounce.

540

1. Sunday School.
2. The Royal Flying Corps.
3. The USSR.
4. Easy.
5. 400,000 (413,305 to be exact).
6. Arthur Mullard's.
7. James Callaghan.
8. 'Land of Hope and Glory'.
9. The Royal Botanical Gardens at Kew.

Q

73

1. Should a clock strike 13, what does this supposedly foretell?
2. Cesarewitch was the name used for which relative of the Tzar?
3. Why cannot you enter Leningrad's harbour between December and April?
4. To which writer was Catherine Hogarth married?
5. Name Hull's two Rugby League teams.
6. Who played Olive Oyl in the 1980 film *Popeye*?
7. Who painted the portraits of hanged men that adorn the walls of the Chief Magistrate's Palace in Florence?
8. John Lydon formed which group – post-*Sex Pistols*?
9. What percentage water is the human brain?

307

1. What is contained in the despatch box on the Government side of the table in the House of Commons?
2. Who succeeded Richard the Lionheart as King of England?
3. Which river marks the border between England and Scotland?
4. Who wrote *Mysterious Island*?
5. What colour is the caution flag in motor racing?
6. Who was supposed to have lived at 23 Railway Cuttings, East Cheam?
7. Who shouted 'Sic Semper Tyrannis!' in dramatic circumstances?
8. Which country's National Anthem set the fashion for National Anthems all over the world?
9. Which vitamin aids healthy vision?

541

1. Who or what is the the third biggest landowner in Britain?
2. In the 14th century, a pig was once publicly hanged for doing *what*?
3. Edinburgh's Royal Mile leads from the Castle to *where*?
4. In *Oliver Twist*, what famous quote did Mr Bumble make about the law?
5. Who was the original 'Brylcream Boy'?
6. Who did James Cagney portray in *Man of a Thousand Faces*?
7. Pelham Grenville were the forenames of which writer?
8. Who wrote the operas *Almira* and *Rodrigo*?
9. The blowfly is more frequently called *what*?

73

1. An imminent death.
2. His eldest son.
3. Because it is iced up.
4. Charles Dickens.
5. Hull and Hull Kingston Rovers.
6. Shelley Duvall.
7. Botticelli.
8. *Public Image Limited.*
9. About 80 per cent.

307

1. The Old and New Testaments and the Oath.
2. His brother, King John.
3. The Tweed.
4. Jules Verne.
5. Yellow.
6. Tony Hancock.
7. John Wilkes Booth, after assassinating President Lincoln and leaping on to the stage.
8. Britain's.
9. Vitamin A.

541

1. The National Trust.
2. Killing a child.
3. Holyrood House.
4. '... the law is a ass – a idiot.'
5. Denis Compton, the cricketer.
6. Lon Chaney, Senior.
7. Wodehouse.
8. Handel.
9. The bluebottle.

74

1. What are the Wedge, the Scrunch and the Chop?
2. Who did not find out he was King of England for nearly three days after the previous monarch died?
3. In which city is the Jorvik Viking Centre?
4. Who writes the 'Father's Day' column in *Punch*?
5. Which French racing driver did John Watson call 'a pain in the backside'?
6. Mick Jagger first appeared on TV doing *what*?
7. What was the business in which Emil Savundra conned people?
8. Who received an Oscar for his music to the film *Oliver*?
9. In maths, the first 'perfect number' is six. What is the second?

308

1. 'Noisettes' usually refers to cuts of which meat?
2. Who is the only person represented by two of London's 68 statues?
3. On which island is Peel Castle?
4. Which Somerset Maugham novel features Sadie Thompson?
5. What was the real first name of champion jockey 'Scobie' Breasley?
6. Which character did Penelope Keith play in *To The Manor Born*?
7. Whose first stage appearance, at the age of 15, was as Katharina in *The Taming of the Shrew* in 1922?
8. Which Christian rock band had hits with *New Year's Day* and *Pride*?
9. The moon has an albedo of 7%. What does albedo mean?

542

1. Which hobby uses the terms 'serpentine roulette' and 'dominical labels'?
2. Which huge building project began in the third century BC?
3. By what name is the Thames known as it flows through Oxford?
4. Who wrote *Ode to the West Wind* in a wood near Florence?
5. From which country do the martial arts Bando and Krabi-Krabong come?
6. Which character did Penelope Keith play in *The Good Life*?
7. Which actress who starred in *Camelot* was once the Max Factor girl?
8. Which planet entered the charts five times for Dickie Valentine?
9. What do you call the process of metal extraction by heating ores?

74

1. 1980s hair-styles for women.
2. James I. It took a messenger 62 hours to reach Edinburgh.
3. In York.
4. Hunter Davies.
5. René Arnoux.
6. Demonstrating rock-climbing, as a schoolboy.
7. Insurance.
8. Johnny Green, for his adaptation of Lionel Bart's work.
9. Twenty-eight.

308

1. Lamb.
2. The Duke of Wellington.
3. The Isle of Man.
4. *Rain*.
5. Arthur.
6. Audrey fforbes-Hamilton.
7. Lord Olivier's.
8. *U2*, from Ireland.
9. Ability to reflect light.

542

1. Stamp collecting.
2. The Great Wall of China.
3. The Isis.
4. Shelley, in 1819.
5. Burma.
6. Margot Leadbetter.
7. Fiona Fullerton.
8. *Venus*, in 1959.
9. Smelting.

75

1. What does 'kamikaze' actually mean?
2. When did Concorde first fly?
3. What great edifice stands on Ile de la Cité in Paris?
4. Who, in 1921, wrote *Etiquette*, which set the standard for acceptable social behaviour?
5. Whom did Muhammad Ali nickname *The Rabbit*?
6. Name one of John Derek's three actress wives – all of whom posed for *Playboy* magazine?
7. For what do the letters P. C. stand, in P. C. Wren's name?
8. Who was invited to 'Come into the garden'?
9. Which is the smallest of the dairy cattle breeds?

309

1. What did Seth Wheeler register for a US patent in 1871?
2. For what is the Purple Heart awarded in the USA?
3. The Tuscany district of Italy is famed for producing which Italian wine?
4. Who were King Solomon's parents?
5. What were *Shergar*'s winnings in 1981?
6. Whom did Peter Ustinov portray in the film *Quo Vadis*?
7. Name the McWhirter brother who was killed.
8. Which is the smallest instrument in a string quartet?
9. The launch of which American space shuttle was aborted four seconds before lift-off?

543

1. How many new pence would the old florin have been worth?
2. When did a hovercraft first cross the Channel?
3. Which is Scotland's most populated city?
4. The magazine *Over 21* rose from the ashes of which previous magazine?
5. Arthur Wellard of Somerset once hit Frank Woolley of Kent for how many successive sixes?
6. Which horror actor said, 'I never drink – wine'?
7. 'As no man is born an artist, so no man is born an angler.' Who said it?
8. How many strings has an oboe?
9. For how long does a C-60 cassette tape play?

75

1. 'Divine wind'.
2. In 1969.
3. Notre Dame Cathedral.
4. Emily Post.
5. Floyd Patterson.
6. Ursula Andress, Linda Evans, and Bo Derek.
7. Percival Christopher.
8. Maud.
9. The Jersey breed.

309

1. Gift-wrapping paper.
2. Wounds received on active military service.
3. Chianti.
4. David and Bathsheba.
5. £394,646.
6. Nero.
7. Ross.
8. The violin.
9. *Discovery*.

543

1. Ten.
2. In 1959.
3. Glasgow.
4. *Vanity Fair*.
5. Five.
6. Bela Lugosi.
7. Izaak Walton.
8. None.
9. One hour.

76

1. When is there never jam?
2. In English universities, 'Regius' professorships were set up by which king?
3. Where was the HQ of the National Union of Mineworkers relocated in 1984?
4. Which Nobel Prize-winning novelist, whose middle name was Ernst, died in 1968?
5. What was jockey Harry Wragg nicknamed because of his patient tactics?
6. In which city are the Pebble Mill studios?
7. Which fashion designer has a busy bee as his motif?
8. What is the only number one hit, so far, to begin with an X?
9. What did Cornelius van Drebbel show King James I?

310

1. The nine ranks of *what* are distinguished by the buttons on their caps?
2. Pubs called 'White Hart' are named after which king's badge?
3. Mount Kebnekaise is the highest point in which country?
4. Of whom did Ben Jonson say, 'He was not of an age, but for all time'?
5. In which athletics event is it illegal to carry weights?
6. Who starred in a series called 'Yus, my dear'?
7. Who was Jerry Hall's boy-friend before Mick Jagger?
8. Which university did Bob Dylan attend?
9. Which metal comes from cinnabar?

544

1. In 1985, David Trippier was appointed Minister for *what*?
2. Which large embroidery depicts D-Day?
3. In which US state is the port of Mobile?
4. Who left her last novel, *Wives and Daughters*, unfinished?
5. What does 'Dormy 3' mean in golf?
6. Which 1985 film is about mercenaries trying to snatch Hess from Spandau?
7. Which overcoats did Lord Kagan make?
8. Who wrote the lyrics for Julie Covington's 1971 album *The Beautiful Changes*?
9. In 1985, what did the National Vegetable Research Station say you should do to seedlings to help them grow?

76

1. Today. 'Jam tomorrow and jam yesterday, but never today.'
2. Henry VIII.
3. Sheffield.
4. John Steinbeck.
5. 'The Head Waiter'.
6. In Birmingham.
7. Bill Gibb.
8. *Xanadu*, in 1980.
9. A primitive submarine.

310

1. Mandarins.
2. Richard II's.
3. Sweden.
4. Shakespeare.
5. The long jump.
6. Arthur Mullard.
7. Bryan Ferry.
8. Minnesota University – but he didn't graduate.
9. Mercury.

544

1. Waste, in the Board of Trade.
2. The Overlord Embroidery, in Portsmouth.
3. Alabama.
4. Mrs Gaskell.
5. At match play, three holes ahead, with three left to play.
6. *Wild Geese II*.
7. Gannex raincoats.
8. Clive James, the critic.
9. Stroke them, or brush them.

77

1. What is the main ingredient of Foo Yung in Chinese cooking?
2. What was the patriotic name of Nelson's flagship before the battle of Copenhagen?
3. Which country calls itself Al-Mamlaka al-Maghribiya?
4. Which British humorous writer's father became a judge in Hong Kong?
5. Why was Scotland's Willy Johnston sent home from the 1978 World Cup Finals?
6. In which film did Sarah Douglas (of *Falcon Crest*) play Queen Taramis?
7. Which entrepreneur did Jean Rook call 'the winged chubby cherub'?
8. Which group, known as AWB for short, had their first break as support to Eric Clapton?
9. What is the name of the National Trust campaign to protect Britain's coastline?

311

1. Which famous London street of Piccadilly was once called Portugal Street?
2. Which Caribbean island was invaded by the USA in October 1983?
3. Which US state is north of Wyoming?
4. In which novel does Mr Knightley live at Donwell Abbey?
5. At which sport does Jackie Stewart excel, besides motor racing?
6. In which film about a three-day-event did Tatum O'Neal ride Arizona Pie?
7. Who won the 1983 Nobel Peace Prize?
8. Which pop singer nearly picked 'Terry Tinsel' as his stage name?
9. The flowers of which shrub are used for flavouring tea and perfume?

545

1. What size is a Crown sheet of paper?
2. Where did German Field-Marshal Friedrich Paulus surrender to the Russians in 1943?
3. Which place lies near Inaccessible Island and the Three Nightingale Islands?
4. What did the slithy toves do in the wabe?
5. Which England cricket captain was nicknamed 'the Goose'?
6. Which 1985 film is about an all-day Saturday detention at an American high school?
7. Who became Chairman of the National Coal Board in 1971?
8. At what age did Anatole Fistoulari first conduct at a concert?
9. Edible, fat and squirrel-tailed are kinds of *what*?

77

1. Eggs.
2. *St George.*
3. Morocco.
4. P.G. Wodehouse's.
5. He failed a drugs test.
6. *Conan The Destroyer.*
7. Sir Freddie Laker.
8. *Average White Band.*
9. Enterprise Neptune.

311

1. Old Bond Street.
2. Grenada.
3. Montana.
4. *Emma.*
5. Clay pigeon shooting.
6. *International Velvet.*
7. Lech Walesa.
8. Gary Glitter.
9. Jasmine.

545

1. 20 inches by 15 inches.
2. At Stalingrad.
3. Tristan da Cunha.
4. 'Gyre and gimble' (in Lewis Carroll's *Jabberwocky*).
5. Bob Willis.
6. *The Breakfast Club.*
7. Sir Derek Ezra.
8. Seven.
9. Dormouse.

Q

78

1. What is the basis of the superstition 'See a pin and pick it up, All the day you'll have good luck'?
2. Which part of his anatomy did Nelson lose at Santa Cruz?
3. On which day of the week should you not eat snakes in Iraq?
4. The creature Barguest gave Conan Doyle the idea for a story. Which one?
5. Which major sporting event does Britannia Assurance sponsor?
6. Name the 'Thing' that beat Godzilla in *Godzilla vs The Thing.*
7. Sir Max Aitken, who had been a leading newspaper publisher, died in 1985. Who was his father?
8. Who sang *The Ugly Duckling* in the film *Hans Christian Andersen*?
9. Which fish is known as the River Wolf?

312

1. What is the minimum distance from the shore that a burial at sea may take place?
2. After whom was the Tate Gallery named?
3. In which country are Pulitzer Prizes awarded?
4. Who won a Booker Prize with *Staying On*?
5. The Bol d'Or race is for which machines?
6. Which town was invaded in the film *Gremlins*?
7. How are the Earl of Carrick and the Duke of Rothesay related?
8. Who wrote the harpsichord piece known as *The Harmonious Blacksmith*?
9. How many poles are there in a chain?

546

1. Proverbially, what does a watched kettle never do?
2. With how many men did Cortez take Mexico from the Aztecs?
3. From which country do Bretons come?
4. Who wrote *Anna and the King of Siam*?
5. Spencer Gore was the first to win what, in 1877?
6. Who was the star of the Mercury Theatre Company?
7. How many draughts pieces are on one row at the beginning of a game?
8. The theme of BBC TV's *Face the Music* comes from which Walton work?
9. What is the approximate length of each of the giraffe's seven neckbones?

78

1. If you didn't, a witch might find it and use it for a bad luck spell. Well – it's a theory.
2. His arm.
3. On Sunday.
4. *The Hound of the Baskervilles.*
5. The County Cricket Championship.
6. Mothra – a giant moth.
7. Lord Beaverbrook.
8. Danny Kaye.
9. The pike.

312

1. Three miles.
2. Henry Tate (later Sir Henry), of Tate and Lyle, the Liverpool sugar merchants and refiners.
3. In the USA.
4. Paul Scott.
5. Motor-cycles.
6. Kingston Falls.
7. They are the same person, namely Prince Charles.
8. Handel.
9. Four.

546

1. Boil.
2. 500 men.
3. France – Brittany, more precisely.
4. Margaret Landon.
5. The Wimbledon Men's Singles title.
6. Orson Welles.
7. Four.
8. *Façade.*
9. One foot.

79

1. Of what is erotophobia the fear?
2. Which American President made the Louisiana Purchase?
3. Cetinje is the capital of *where*?
4. Who plays Pyramus in *A Midsummer Night's Dream*?
5. Which two teams were playing in 1971 at Ibrox, Glasgow, when 66 spectators died?
6. Who plays Clayton Farlow in *Dallas*?
7. Who was made a peer for his poetry?
8. Which pop group is featured in the film *Take It or Leave It*?
9. What was Halley's first name – of comet fame?

313

1. Name the Greenpeace trawler which was sunk in July 1985.
2. Which king of Egypt abdicated in 1952?
3. From which country does teak mainly come?
4. From which mountain did Moses view all of the Promised Land?
5. Seven books about which cat made the New York Times best-sellers list simultaneously?
6. Which actress's autobiography was entitled *By Myself*?
7. What is Enoch Powell's first name?
8. Who wrote the cycle of operas called *The Ring*?
9. C_2H_5OH is the chemical formula for what?

547

1. Whose wife would eat no lean?
2. The treaty of 1922 in Rapallo restored diplomatic relations between Russia and which other country?
3. In Scotland, which title is given to the Chief Herald?
4. Name Moses' wife.
5. Which soccer player was nicknamed the 'Black Pearl'?
6. Which 1973 film starred Sean Connery and Charlotte Rampling, and was set in the Wicklow Mountains?
7. What is the surname of Sherpa Tenzing, conqueror of Everest in 1953?
8. What would you hear at Ronnie Scott's?
9. What colour is a panther?

79

1. Sexual intimacy.
2. Thomas Jefferson.
3. Montenegro.
4. Bottom.
5. Rangers and Celtic.
6. Howard Keel.
7. Alfred, Lord Tennyson.
8. *Madness*.
9. Edmund.

313

1. *Rainbow Warrior*.
2. King Farouk I (forcibly, following a military coup).
3. Burma.
4. Mount Nebo.
5. Garfield.
6. Lauren Bacall.
7. John.
8. Wagner.
9. Alcohol.

547

1. Jack Spratt's.
2. Germany.
3. Lord Lion King of Arms.
4. Zipporah.
5. Pelé.
6. *Zardoz*.
7. Norkay.
8. Superb jazz.
9. Black.

80

1. In medieval times, what was a psaltery?
2. What job did the Ninja do in ancient Japan?
3. Where is the British National Lifeboat Museum?
4. In *Troilus and Cressida*, who was Cressida's uncle, and acted as go-between?
5. Crane, dragon, leopard, tiger and snake are styles of *what*?
6. When the Beirut hostages were released in June 1985, one American TV company accused another of 'pigging'. What is that?
7. Sir Billy Butlin was raised in Canada, but where was he born?
8. Who composed the *Manfred Symphony*, in 1885?
9. A swelling or knot on a nerve or tendon is called *what*?

314

1. What is a burgee used for on a yacht?
2. What did Henry IV of France say was 'well worth a Mass'?
3. Why did 25 trade unions organize a massive demonstration in Singapore in 1985?
4. Who was Sir Galahad's father?
5. Which silver emblem appears on New Zealand rugby jerseys?
6. Which musical is a fantasy about a dead man returning after 15 years to help his family?
7. In which resort did the first Butlin holiday camp open in 1936?
8. What does singer Clementina Campbell call herself?
9. Which is the most corrosion-resistant metal known?

548

1. In Turkey, what was an odalisque?
2. What sort of work did a cordwainer do?
3. In which Canadian province is Gander airport?
4. Who wrote the novel *Our Mutual Friend*?
5. Which firm sponsored the 1985 London Marathon?
6. Which pop singer played Miranda in a film of *The Tempest*, in 1979?
7. What distinction has Shigechiyo Izumi?
8. Which dance did Ponchielli write for Act 3 of *La Gioconda*?
9. What is studied in histology?

80

1. A stringed musical instrument.
2. They were assassins and spies.
3. In Bristol.
4. Pandarus.
5. Kung-fu.
6. Holding on to a scarce telephone line to prevent a rival getting through.
7. In South Africa.
8. Tchaikovsky.
9. A ganglion.

314

1. Not a lot – it is a small flag or pennant.
2. Paris, so he became a Catholic.
3. Because of an offered pay rise – they said it was too *high*!
4. Sir Lancelot.
5. A fern leaf.
6. *Carousel.*
7. Skegness.
8. Cleo Laine.
9. Iridium.

548

1. A female slave.
2. He made shoes and worked in leather.
3. Newfoundland.
4. Charles Dickens.
5. The makers of Mars bars.
6. Toyah.
7. He is the oldest man in the world who can prove his age.
8. *Dance of the Hours.*
9. Tissues, or layers of cells.

81

1. How were Franklin and Eleanor Roosevelt related to each other, apart from being married?
2. Which was the first of the great Livery Companies of the City of London?
3. Which weather forecast area comes between Fisher and Tyne?
4. Who said, 'The Irish are a fair people – they never speak well of one another'?
5. Who won the 1985 London Marathon?
6. Two of which three actress sisters has actor George Sanders married?
7. Who painted The *Fighting Téméraire*?
8. Name Georgie Fame's backing group.
9. Approximately how long is the lifespan of a robin?

315

1. In which religion does a guru give spiritual guidance?
2. Who reputedly haunts Hever Castle?
3. New Orleans stands at the mouth of which river?
4. What subject did Mr Chips teach?
5. Who was the first jockey to win $6,000,000 in one season?
6. In *Winner Takes All*, what are the top odds?
7. Which is the lowest card used in bezique?
8. Britain's first win in the Eurovision Song Contest was with which song?
9. What is the technical term for the study of children's diseases?

549

1. What would you say to someone who sternutates, if you are polite?
2. Martin Luther nailed how many Propositions to a church door, in Wittenburg, Germany?
3. Where was the Rosetta stone found?
4. In Genesis, who was Joseph's younger brother?
5. In which country was cricketer Basil D'Oliveira born?
6. In *Clochemerle*, the building of *what* caused ructions?
7. Who is known as Evans the Arrow?
8. How many necks had a theorbo, an old style of lute?
9. Approximately how many hairs does a healthy human scalp possess, per square inch?

81

1. They were cousins.
2. The Mercers.
3. Dogger.
4. Samuel Johnson.
5. Steve Jones.
6. The Gabor sisters.
7. Turner.
8. *The Blue Flames.*
9. Just over one year – it is about the shortest-lived British bird.

315

1. Hinduism.
2. Anne Boleyn.
3. The Mississippi.
4. Latin.
5. Steve Cauthen.
6. 10–1.
7. Seven.
8. *Puppet on a String.*
9. Paediatrics.

549

1. 'Bless you' – they have just sneezed.
2. 95.
3. Rosetta, in Egypt.
4. Benjamin.
5. In South Africa.
6. A urinal.
7. Darts player Alan Evans.
8. Two.
9. 1,000.

82

1. Between which two British airports is there a scheduled helicopter service?
2. Name England's last Anglo-Saxon king.
3. Ian Smith was the PM of which country?
4. Who was the Roman god of sleep?
5. Who was the only Briton to be boxing's World Heavyweight Champion?
6. Which actor starred in *Operation Petticoat*?
7. Who was the defeated finalist in the 1985 Embassy World Snooker Championship?
8. Who wrote the operetta *The Grand Duke*?
9. When are mumps contagious?

316

1. What is special about the ship *Godspeed*?
2. In ancient times, why were Chinese corpses often buried with pieces of jade?
3. Hokkaido is the northernmost island of which country?
4. What is the VAT rate for books?
5. Where is the Oaks run?
6. In which city is the series *Van der Valk* set?
7. In which London square is there a statue of Simon Bolivar?
8. Off which bridge did Billie Joe McAllister jump?
9. To which dog, who would not leave his master's grave, is there a statue in Edinburgh?

550

1. At least how far below ground should foundations be sited for buildings?
2. The inhabitants of which country were once called 'Scottis'?
3. La Guardia airport is named after a mayor of which city?
4. In what type of construction did the Minotaur live?
5. On which race track was Jim Clark killed, in 1967?
6. Who was nicknamed 'The Blue Angel'?
7. How many squares forward can a rook move in chess?
8. At what time of the day should serenades properly be played?
9. At one time, fried mice were considered to be a cure for which disease?

82

1. Gatwick and Heathrow.
2. Harold, who was killed in 1066.
3. Rhodesia.
4. Somnus.
5. Bob Fitzsimmons (1897–9).
6. Cary Grant.
7. Steve Davis.
8. Gilbert and Sullivan.
9. Whilst the swelling is in evidence.

316

1. She is a replica of one of the ships that sailed for America in 1606 – and is repeating the trip.
2. Because they thought this prevented the body from decaying.
3. Japan.
4. Zero.
5. At Epsom.
6. Amsterdam.
7. In Belgrave Square.
8. The Tallahatchie Bridge.
9. Greyfriars Bobby.

550

1. One metre.
2. Ireland.
3. New York.
4. A maze.
5. Hockenheim.
6. Marlene Dietrich.
7. Seven.
8. In the evening. (And always properly!)
9. Smallpox.

83

1. In Greece, what is a fustanella, worn by men?
2. Which town was the capital of Saxon England?
3. Walachia and Moldavia united to form what?
4. Which epic novel about the Roman Empire did Lewis Wallace write?
5. Who received an honorary degree in law at Sussex University in July 1985, aged 39?
6. The play *Trafford Tanzi* was about women playing which sport?
7. What was Linda McCartney's maiden name?
8. Which group, formerly called *Hotlegs*, had their first number one hit with *Rubber Bullets*?
9. What is a fer-de-lance?

317

1. What could you buy second-hand that could be 'foxed'?
2. Which English king was killed with a red-hot poker?
3. Which city is called Firenze by its inhabitants?
4. In Dorothy L. Sayers' book, what were *The Nine Tailors*?
5. In which sport do players compete for the Middleton Cup at Mortlake?
6. Who was the first coloured performer to appear in the *Black and White Minstrel Show*?
7. Which painting by Andrea Mantegna fetched £8.1 million at Christie's in 1985?
8. Which dance did Salome do before Herod?
9. What would a mycologist study?

551

1. 'Ensate' describes the shape of which weapon?
2. How did Miss Madeleine Smith become well-known in Glasgow in 1857?
3. What is the native language of Liechtenstein?
4. Who created *Rogue Herries*?
5. Which South African-turned-American knocked John McEnroe out of the 1985 Wimbledon singles?
6. Which musical was based on Shaw's *Arms and the Man*?
7. Who created Old Mother Riley?
8. Name Borodin's operatic Prince.
9. What is the purpose of an analgesic?

83

1. A stiff white petticoat.
2. Winchester.
3. Romania, in 1859.
4. *Ben Hur*.
5. Virginia Wade.
6. Wrestling.
7. Eastman.
8. *10 cc.*, in 1973.
9. A poisonous snake.

317

1. A book, slightly discoloured by age.
2. Edward II.
3. Florence.
4. Church bells.
5. Bowls.
6. Lenny Henry.
7. The Adoration of the Magi.
8. The Dance of the Seven Veils.
9. Muscles in the body.

551

1. The sword.
2. She was accused and acquitted in a famous poisoning case.
3. German.
4. Hugh Walpole.
5. Kevin Curran.
6. *The Chocolate Soldier*.
7. Arthur Lucan.
8. Igor.
9. It is a drug to counteract pain.

84

1. In which city does the Equal Opportunities Commission have its HQ?
2. Which tribe did Geronimo lead?
3. Which city did Wordsworth call 'the safeguard of the West'?
4. For works in which field of literature is William Cowper known?
5. Which song is associated with Llanelli rugby club?
6. Woody Allen made a film called 'The Purple Rose of...' *where*?
7. Which pseudonym did Harry Longbaugh use when working?
8. The musical *Man of La Mancha* is based on the story of which hero?
9. Which letter symbolizes potassium?

318

1. What is 'prosciutto'?
2. Who was nicknamed 'Jack Amendall'?
3. Which sea is between Korea and Shanghai?
4. Who created the schoolmaster Ichabod Crane?
5. In the name of a rugby club, such as Heriot's FP, what does FP stand for?
6. *The Gold Rush* is often considered to be which actor's best comedy?
7. What did Elizabeth Taylor's ex-husband John Warner do?
8. In the opera *Parsifal*, the magician Klingsor has a sacred *what*?
9. What sort of creature is a cayman?

552

1. How many years make a chiliad?
2. Who was considered to have been the central figure of the Reformation?
3. Where is Graham Land, or the Palmer Peninsula?
4. Which of the James Bond novels is set almost entirely in Japan?
5. Which England batsman was nicknamed 'Arkle'?
6. What colour is Kryptonite in *Superman*?
7. Celeste is a shade of which colour?
8. Janáček's opera *The Makropoulos Affair* is about a magic formula for *what*?
9. Where do littoral creatures live?

84

1. In Manchester.
2. The Apache.
3. Venice.
4. Poetry.
5. *Sospan Fach*, or 'little saucepan'.
6. Cairo.
7. The Sundance Kid.
8. Don Quixote.
9. The letter K.

318

1. Italian ham.
2. Jack Cade, who led a rebellion in 1450.
3. The Yellow Sea.
4. Washington Irving.
5. Former Pupils.
6. Charlie Chaplin's.
7. He was a US Senator.
8. Spear.
9. It is a reptile like a crocodile.

552

1. A thousand.
2. Martin Luther.
3. In Antarctica.
4. *You Only Live Twice.*
5. Derek Randall, also nicknamed 'Spider'.
6. Green.
7. Blue, like the sky.
8. Immortality, or prolonging life.
9. On the seashore.

85

1. How much money passed over London's licensed gaming tables in 1984?
2. What was Napoleon wearing when he died?
3. What is particularly curious about the cake we call 'Swiss Roll'?
4. To which wind did Shelley write an ode?
5. If you went to Wookey Hole and Swildon's Hole, in which sport would you be participating?
6. Which sport featured in the 1969 film *Winning*?
7. What was the first name of author H. Rider Haggard?
8. Which musical instrument has a name which means 'leaping flea'?
9. Which flowering plant was so named for its supposed wolfishness?

319

1. Rose Noble, George Noble and Angel Noble were all what?
2. Where was Jean Marat when Charlotte Corday killed him in 1793?
3. Why is Caldron Snout famous?
4. Who wrote the historical romance *Hypatia*?
5. Ice dancers Jayne Torvill and Christopher Dean were given the freedom of which city?
6. In which film did Groucho Marx say, 'Look at me, I worked my way up from nothing to a state of extreme poverty'?
7. Who are the 'Primate of England' and the 'Primate of All England'?
8. Four pupils from which public school formed the rock group *Genesis*?
9. Which stone is the granular form of gypsum?

553

1. How many miles of publicly maintained roads are there in Britain?
2. To which party did Oswald Mosley belong, before he founded the British Fascists?
3. On which river is Caldron Snout, on the Durham-Cumbria border?
4. Who wrote *The Gulag Archipelago*?
5. Which British soccer club won nine successive League Championships between 1966 and 1974?
6. For which film did Julie Andrews win her only Oscar?
7. In which city did the composer Johannes Brahms die?
8. Who composed *Eine Alpensymphonie*?
9. A hamadryad could be a snake, or what other creature?

85

1. One billion pounds. (Give or take a million.)
2. The uniform of a Field Marshal, with boots and spurs – in spite of having been six weeks in bed with a fatal illness.
3. By all accounts, it is unobtainable in Switzerland.
4. He wrote *Ode to the West Wind.*
5. Cave diving.
6. Motor racing (Paul Newman starred in it).
7. Henry.
8. The ukelele, a Hawaiian name.
9. The lupin.

319

1. Gold coins.
2. In his bath.
3. It is England's highest waterfall.
4. Charles Kingsley.
5. Nottingham, their home city.
6. In *A Day at the Races.*
7. The Archbishops of York and Canterbury respectively. The titles were created by a medieval Pope to stop their rivalry.
8. Charterhouse.
9. Alabaster.

553

1. 217,000 – as of mid-1985.
2. The Labour Party.
3. The Tees.
4. Alexander Solzhenitsyn.
5. Glasgow Celtic.
6. *Mary Poppins.*
7. In Vienna.
8. Richard Strauss.
9. A baboon.

86

1. Who would sail in an umiak?
2. At which battle did the Black Prince 'win his spurs'?
3. Which is the largest state in Mexico?
4. Who wrote the poem *The Dream of Gerontius*?
5. How high is a table-tennis net?
6. Who stars in *High Plains Drifter*?
7. Who had the nickname 'The Colossus of Roads?
8. Which group emerged from Duddleston Manor School?
9. What is the fruit of the blackthorn tree called?

320

1. What, on a menu, is indicated by 'flambé'?
2. Name either of the young kidnappers and murderers of Bobby Franks in 1924?
3. Where did General Wolfe die?
4. In Greek mythology, how many heads had the monster dog Orthos?
5. The Vardon Trophy for the lowest average in the PGA was won in 1970, 1971 and 1972 by which golfer?
6. What is actress Ann-Margret's surname?
7. What nationality was the collaborator Quisling?
8. Who had a hit with the song *Valley of the Dolls*?
9. What is the special characteristic of rodents?

554

1. What is the better-known name of the Parliamentary Commissioner for Administration?
2. When Archbishop Cranmer was burnt at the stake, which portion of his anatomy was found intact in the ashes?
3. 2 November is celebrated in Italy as *what*?
4. What is the decibel level of normal speech?
5. Who is the jockey on Newmarket's famous ghost horse?
6. Who was married to both Frank Sinatra and André Previn?
7. What is Gerald Ford's middle name? (It begins with the letter 'R'.)
8. Who recorded the LP *Camouflage*?
9. To which family of birds does the dabchick belong?

86

1. Probably an Eskimo, as it is an Eskimo boat.
2. Crécy.
3. Chihuahua.
4. Robert Newman.
5. Six inches.
6. Clint Eastwood.
7. Thomas Telford.
8. *Musical Youth.*
9. The sloe-berry.

320

1. That the dish is served flaming.
2. Nathan Leopold. Richard Loeb.
3. In Quebec.
4. Two.
5. Lee Trevino.
6. Olsson.
7. Norwegian.
8. Dionne Warwick.
9. They gnaw.

554

1. The Ombudsman.
2. His heart.
3. 'The Day of the Dead'.
4. 45–55.
5. Fred Archer.
6. Mia Farrow.
7. Rudolph.
8. Rod Stewart.
9. The grebe family.

87

1. Which is reputedly the unluckiest day of the week on which to be born?
2. For how long did Elizabeth I reign?
3. If it is midday in London (GMT), what time is it in Hong Kong?
4. Who was kidnapped in *Kidnapped*?
5. In motor racing, what is the best position at the starting grid called?
6. Better known as an actor, who directed the 1971 film *Kotch*?
7. Which plant was frequently painted by Monet?
8. Who was nicknamed the 'Memphis Flash'?
9. How many vertebrae are there in the human neck?

321

1. Which day of the week is named after the moon?
2. Why did the Saudi censor tear out the diary and political commentary from *The Times* one day in April 1985?
3. French kings used to be crowned at the cathedral of which city?
4. What additional agony was inflicted on the thieves crucified with Jesus?
5. Which is Scotland's most famous athletics stadium?
6. Who, in 1925, played the original 'Phantom of the Opera'?
7. Which numbers flank 20 on a darts board?
8. Which group starred in the film *Rude Boy*?
9. Which part of the eye may be removed and kept in eye banks?

555

1. Which Chinese year coincides with most of 1985?
2. In 1900, how long was the life expectancy of a baby girl?
3. Who is the patron saint of Portugal?
4. Who is the Greek equivalent of the Roman god Jupiter?
5. Which football manager remarked, 'I have just opened the trophy cabinet. Two Japanese prisoners-of-war came out'?
6. Joe Lynch and John Bluthal starred together in which TV series?
7. American Secretary of State, Mr Stevenson – what was his first name?
8. Whose first record was entitled *Rock with the Cavemen*?
9. What is the record number of fleas found on one red squirrel?

87

1. Friday.
2. 45 years.
3. 8.00 pm.
4. David Balfour.
5. Pole position.
6. Jack Lemmon.
7. The water-lily.
8. Elvis Presley.
9. Seven.

321

1. Monday.
2. The fashion page was on the other side, showing bare female arms and legs.
3. Rheims.
4. Their legs were broken.
5. Meadowbank.
6. Lon Chaney.
7. 5 and 1.
8. *Clash.*
9. The cornea.

555

1. The Year of the Bull.
2. 51 years.
3. St George.
4. Zeus.
5. Tommy Docherty, when manager of the downward-sliding Wolves team.
6. *Never Mind the Quality, Feel the Width.*
7. Adlai.
8. Tommy Steele.
9. 13,000 (to the nearest 1,000).

88

1. What does 'nescient' mean?
2. When Napoleon died, where was he buried? (Take care!)
3. From Botswana, in which direction would you go to reach Namibia?
4. What was the first work by Shakespeare to be published?
5. In American football, a team of eleven men may use up to how many substitutes?
6. In film titles, which single word preceded Mountain, Sphinx, Key, Web and Menagerie?
7. Of which large company is Tiny Rowland chairman?
8. Who wrote the *Dance of the Sugar Plum Fairy*?
9. What is a canvas-back?

322

1. To policemen, what does 'CRO' mean?
2. Who was the first European to sail to India?
3. What does 'Long Legs' mean in Nigeria?
4. What was Joe Gargery's trade in *Great Expectations*?
5. The Bologna Trophy is a competition in *what*?
6. What did the sequels to *The Poseidon Adventure* and *The Valley of the Dolls* have in common?
7. The name of which ruler means 'Power of the Trinity'?
8. What nationality was Adolphe Sax, inventor of the Saxophone?
9. Mirabella and Yellow Egg are kinds of what?

556

1. If your speciality is semiotics, what do you study?
2. Before John Paul II, how many Popes were there?
3. Which city has the world's largest school?
4. Who wrote *An Accidental Man* and *The Italian Girl*?
5. What unusual gear did England international footballer Steve Foster wear when playing?
6. Which actor played Churchill in *The Man Who Never Was* and Hitler in *Soft Beds, Hard Battles*?
7. For what sort of artistic work was Arthur Rackham famous?
8. Which instrument does jazzman Miles Davis play?
9. Tocophobia is fear of *what*?

88

1. Ignorant.
2. St Helena. His remains were later brought back to Paris.
3. Due west.
4. The poem *Venus and Adonis*, in 1593.
5. Thirty-two.
6. Glass.
7. Lonrho.
8. Tchaikovsky.
9. A breed of duck.

322

1. Criminal Records Office.
2. Vasco da Gama, in 1497–8.
3. Nepotism – their equivalent of the 'Old Boy Network'.
4. He was a blacksmith.
5. Swimming.
6. Like this book, they began with 'Beyond'.
7. Haile Selassie.
8. He was Belgian.
9. Plum.

556

1. Signs and symbols in linguistics.
2. 263.
3. Calcutta: there are 12,350 pupils at South Point High.
4. Iris Murdoch.
5. A headband.
6. Peter Sellers.
7. Book illustration.
8. The trumpet.
9. Childbirth.

89

1. Which rank comes between Group Captain and Squadron Leader?
2. In 1900, how long was the life expectancy of a baby boy?
3. In 1980, the greatest number of visitors to Britain came from *where*?
4. Who wrote *The Light That Failed*?
5. Which club did Bryan Robson leave to join Manchester United?
6. In the 1976 film *The Class of Miss MacMichael*, who co-starred with Glenda Jackson?
7. What mistake did the Royal Society of Arts make when 'blue plaquing' the former home of the poet Dryden in Gerrard Street, Soho, London?
8. *A Spoonful of Sugar* comes from which musical film?
9. In which dreaded disease does a membrane form across the throat?

323

1. 'Cwt' is short for *what*?
2. In 1949, what became Canada's tenth province?
3. In which valley in Egypt is Tutankhamun's tomb?
4. Which book begins 'It is a truth universally acknowledged, that a single man in possession of a good fortune must be in want of a wife'?
5. How many times was John Francome Champion National Hunt Jockey?
6. Which father and daughter starred in the film *The Chalk Garden*?
7. For what do the letters e. e. stand in e. e. cummings' name?
8. On which part of a guitar do you find the frets?
9. Which was the only British-made tandem rotor helicopter to reach production?

557

1. Tenth wedding anniversaries are represented by which metal?
2. From which reed did the Ancient Egyptians make their books?
3. What did the name Singapore originally mean?
4. Whose sons founded the twelve tribes of Israel?
5. Who had a batting average of 99.94 runs over 52 test matches?
6. Who took over as questionmaster of *Family Fortunes* from Bob Monkhouse?
7. What was Neville Chamberlain's first name?
8. By what name is George Alan O'Dowd better known?
9. Name the first micro-computer that retailed for under £100.

89

1. Wing Commander.
2. 48 years.
3. The USA.
4. Rudyard Kipling.
5. West Bromwich Albion.
6. Oliver Reed.
7. They stuck it on the wrong house!
8. *Mary Poppins*.
9. Diphtheria.

323

1. Hundredweight.
2. Newfoundland.
3. The Valley of the Kings.
4. *Pride and Prejudice*, by Jane Austen.
5. Seven times.
6. John and Hayley Mills.
7. ernest estlin (and he always used lower case letters).
8. On the neck.
9. The Belvedere.

557

1. Tin.
2. Papyrus.
3. Lion City.
4. Jacob's.
5. Don Bradman.
6. Max Bygraves.
7. Arthur.
8. Boy George.
9. The Sinclair ZX80.

90

1. What is a female warlock?
2. Which country was ruled by the House of Braganza until 1910?
3. The people of which nation eat most fish per head?
4. Who is the best-known detective created by Nicholas Freeling?
5. How old was Lester Piggott when he rode his first winner?
6. Who was 007's inept nephew, Jimmy Bond, in the film *Casino Royale*?
7. Which great comic's middle name was Spencer?
8. In which 1985 stage musical did Frank Finlay play Captain Bligh?
9. Laudanum is a tincture of *what*?

324

1. In cookery, what is 'Julienne'?
2. When did Britain introduce equal pay for women in government service?
3. What was the town of Bait Lahm in Israel formerly called?
4. Which famous poet was born in Somersby, Lincolnshire, in 1809?
5. Victor Barna was five times world champion – at *what*?
6. Who made an eight-hour film called *Sleep*, showing a man sleeping?
7. By what name was ambassador Mrs Charles A. Black formerly known?
8. Who composed *Zadok the Priest*?
9. How did Denise-Anne Darval make medical history?

558

1. Which country first used 'catapult' mail to speed up their ship-to-shore postal service?
2. In which king's reign did the Pensioner Parliament assemble?
3. Which country claims more poets per head of the population than any other?
4. Deucalion in Greek myth was the equivalent of which character in the Bible?
5. Who rode his own horses Allibar and Good Prospect in steeplechases?
6. Which film was advertised: 'Five charming sisters on the gayest, merriest manhunt that ever snared a bewildered bachelor!'?
7. Who painted *The Rainbow Landscape*, part of the Wallace Collection?
8. What is a twin-neck Rickenbacker?
9. Where in your body is the cuboid bone?

90

1. A witch.
2. Portugal.
3. The people of Iceland.
4. Piet Van Der Valk, on whom a TV series was based.
5. Twelve years old.
6. Woody Allen.
7. Charlie Chaplin's.
8. *Mutiny!*
9. Opium.

324

1. Vegetables cut into short thin strips.
2. In 1961.
3. Bethlehem.
4. Tennyson.
5. Table-tennis.
6. Andy Warhol.
7. Shirley Temple.
8. Handel.
9. Her heart was the one used in the very first heart transplant.

558

1. France, in 1928.
2. In the reign of Charles II, 1661–9.
3. Hungary.
4. Noah.
5. Prince Charles, in 1981.
6. *Pride and Prejudice*, made 1940.
7. Rubens.
8. An electric guitar.
9. In the foot.

91

1. Of what is linophobia the fear?
2. When did Vesuvius last erupt?
3. On which Channel Island are the Wolf Caves?
4. What were the first words spoken by God to man in the Bible?
5. In 1985, who was the first Swiss ever to take a Wimbledon tennis title?
6. Who was the star of the film *Arthur*?
7. What was Swift Nick Nevison's occupation?
8. To what style music did piano salesman Matt Honk lend his name?
9. By what name is the disease variola better known?

325

1. What kind of eggs come wrapped in sausagemeat?
2. Why, in the mid-eighteenth century, was a cow once hanged?
3. Translate from American into English; 'Turn the faucet on the diapers.'
4. Which daily paper has the largest circulation in Britain?
5. The 'clean and jerk' is a discipline in which event?
6. What certificate had the film *Midnight Cowboy*?
7. Which former editor of *The Times* became Chairman of the Arts Council?
8. Which Peter was first a *Hermit* then a *Trembler*?
9. Linseed oil comes from the seeds of which plant?

559

1. The addition of *what* turns a Martini into a Gibson?
2. Which queen is said to haunt Borthwick Castle in Scotland?
3. Where is the world's largest diamond, *The Star of India*, kept?
4. Which New Testament writer was not Jewish?
5. J.P.R. Williams played for which London Rugby Club?
6. Which dancer stars in the film *Roxie Hart*?
7. Which British painter is a dyed blond?
8. What type of instrument is a virginal?
9. How many different species of the cat family are known to exist?

91

1. Of string.
2. In 1944.
3. On Jersey.
4. 'Be fruitful and multiply'.
5. Heinz Guenthardt (he won the Men's Doubles title).
6. Dudley Moore.
7. He was a highwayman.
8. Honky Tonk.
9. Smallpox.

325

1. Scotch eggs.
2. It was found guilty of witchcraft.
3. 'Turn the tap on the nappies.'
4. The *Sun*.
5. Weightlifting.
6. An X certificate.
7. William Rees Mogg.
8. Peter Noone.
9. Flax.

559

1. An onion.
2. Mary, Queen of Scots.
3. In the Tower of London.
4. St Luke.
5. London Welsh.
6. Ginger Rogers.
7. David Hockney.
8. A keyboard instrument.
9. 37 species.

92

1. What are Thistle, Ninian, Beryl and Piper?
2. At Bomarsund in 1854, what did Charles Lucas win?
3. Which country's defence budget is less than £10 a year, spent on blank ammunition?
4. Who wrote *The Wouldbegoods*?
5. What was the real first name of Everton's great footballer 'Dixie' Dean?
6. Who plays Jessica Fletcher in TV's *Murder, She Wrote*?
7. Who is Jan Lodvik Hoch today?
8. Which rock singer was nicknamed 'Sharon'?
9. Joseph Lister cut the post-operative death rate in his hospital from 43% to 15% by using *what*?

326

1. People in which job in Copenhagen held a 33-year strike, ending in 1961?
2. What was Queen Anne's Fan?
3. How many casino licences are there in London as of July 1985?
4. Who is the patron saint of thieves?
5. What was unique about Wyndham Halswelle's Olympic Gold Medal in 1908 in the 400 metres?
6. In which 1980 film did Bob Hoskins play an East End gang-land boss?
7. What did Kenneth Kaunda do before becoming President of Zambia?
8. In France, what is a Maitrise?
9. What is a zander?

560

1. What is a meshuggener, in Yiddish?
2. Who rode a horse called Black Agnes?
3. Which island's name in its own language is Ellan Vannin?
4. How many written characters does an educated Chinese person know, on average?
5. When Roger Bannister ran the first sub-four-minute mile, who was second?
6. In the 1960s TV serial about 'the Bush Kangaroo', what was the kangaroo called?
7. Which birthday did Shigechiyo Izumi celebrate in 1985?
8. Who were Woglinde, Wellgunde and Flosshilde?
9. In which month does pheasant shooting officially start?

92

1. North Sea oilfields.
2. The first VC, on HMS *Hecla*.
3. Andorra's.
4. E. Nesbit.
5. William.
6. Angela Lansbury.
7. Robert Maxwell, owner of the *Daily Mirror*.
8. Elton John.
9. Carbolic acid, as an antiseptic.

326

1. Barbers' assistants.
2. A rude gesture – thumb to nose, fingers outspread.
3. Twenty.
4. St Nicholas – or St Nick!
5. It was a walk-over – all the other athletes withdrew.
6. *The Long Good Friday*.
7. He was a schoolmaster.
8. A choir school, or cathedral choir.
9. A fish, like a pike.

560

1. A mad or crazy person.
2. Mary, Queen of Scots.
3. The Isle of Man's.
4. Five thousand.
5. Chris Chataway.
6. Skippy.
7. His 120th.
8. The Rhinemaidens in Wagner's opera.
9. In October.

93

1. According to Colonel Sanders, how many herbs and spices are used in preparing Kentucky Fried Chicken?
2. In 1477, King Edward IV outlawed which game?
3. Which Portuguese explorer discovered the Cape of Good Hope?
4. What sort of review did *The Times* give to Darwin's *The Origin of Species*?
5. Where were the 1952 Summer Olympics held?
6. With whom did Peregrine the Penguin, Sally the Seal and Louise the Lamb appear?
7. Which American Indian princess's grave is at Gravesend?
8. In Mozart's *The Magic Flute*, to whom is the magic flute given?
9. What is the incubation period for leprosy?

327

1. Jewish potato pancakes are called *what*?
2. Who was President of the USA at the time of the Wall Street Crash of 1929?
3. What single colour is Libya's flag?
4. How did *The Times* first receive the books of Dickens – with favourable or adverse criticism?
5. Where were the 1968 Winter Olympics held?
6. Who, in *ITMA*, asked, 'Can I do you now, sir?'?
7. Who described wine as 'light held together by water'?
8. Who was 'a merry old soul'?
9. Whey is the watery part of which liquid?

561

1. What are the largest service helicopters in use in Britain?
2. In 1982, which new soft English cheese was marketed?
3. Gulyas soup comes from which country?
4. With whom is Miss Moneypenny in love?
5. On which part of the body is a 'rabbit punch' inflicted?
6. Which actress was nicknamed the *Oomph Girl*?
7. What is the chief piece of equipment needed for playing cribbage?
8. In *The Sound of Music*, how many children were there in the Von Trapp family?
9. In 1985, what reason did a miner give for the presence of eight sticks of dynamite in his shed?

93

1. Eleven.
2. Cricket.
3. Bartholomew Dias.
4. A good review.
5. In Helsinki.
6. Muffin the Mule, in the children's TV series.
7. Pocahontas's.
8. Tamino.
9. It can even be several years.

327

1. Latkes.
2. Herbert Hoover.
3. Green.
4. With adverse criticism.
5. In Grenoble, France.
6. Mrs Mopp.
7. Galileo.
8. Old King Cole.
9. Milk.

561

1. Chinooks.
2. Lymeswold.
3. Hungary.
4. James Bond.
5. On the back of the neck.
6. Ann Sheridan.
7. A standard pack of cards.
8. Seven.
9. Dissolved in water, they would be good for his prize leeks. (Quite true – they are, reputedly, very effective.)

94

1. What is the British name for what Americans call the Fall?
2. Which deceased grand-daughter of Queen Victoria made a trip in April 1985?
3. Of which nation was Ibn Saud the first king?
4. To the nearest 50 years, how old was Noah when the rains came?
5. Which one-time husband of a famous sex symbol was the first to take part in more than 50 World Series games?
6. Who created the TV series *The Sweeney*?
7. Name Prince Henry's elder brother.
8. What did John Shore invent in 1711?
9. What is the main constituent of plaster of Paris?

328

1. What new item came into the UK currency in April 1985?
2. In August 1984, what became the prefix for British vehicle registrations?
3. Which Soviet Republic and American states share a name?
4. How many Forsyte novels did Galsworthy produce?
5. Which pair of British athletes broke the world mile record three times in three days, in 1981?
6. Who narrates *Wildlife on One*?
7. Which French general's name is a byword for discipline?
8. Which instrument was used to play the introduction to *Mrs Dale's Diary*?
9. From what type of rock is marble formed?

562

1. Of what is gamophobia the fear?
2. What age came between the Stone Age and the Iron Age?
3. Elias Ashmole founded *what*?
4. Who wrote the novel *Chocky*?
5. Which electrical device was *not* turned on in April 1985?
6. In which TV series did Jean Marsh play the part of 'Rose'?
7. Who was Jodrell Bank's first director?
8. Who said, in a London *Evening Standard* interview in 1966, 'We're more popular than Jesus now'?
9. How many Tasmanian wolves are there in existence now?

94

1. Autumn.
2. Spain's 'English Queen' – Victoria Eugenia, who died in 1969, but whose remains were flown to Madrid for re-burial.
3. Saudi Arabia.
4. 600 years old.
5. Joe DiMaggio.
6. Ian Kennedy Martin.
7. Prince William.
8. The tuning fork.
9. Gypsum.

328

1. The Welsh £1 coin.
2. The letter B.
3. Georgia.
4. Nine.
5. Steve Ovett and Sebastian Coe.
6. David Attenborough.
7. The name of Général Martinet.
8. The harp.
9. Limestone.

562

1. Marriage.
2. The Bronze Age.
3. The Ashmolean Library at Oxford.
4. John Wyndham.
5. Chelsea FC's electric fence.
6. *Upstairs, Downstairs*.
7. Professor Bernard Lovell.
8. John Lennon.
9. None.

95

1. American police have SWAT teams, meaning *what*?
2. In 19th century London, what job did toshers do?
3. In which country is Latakia, famous for its tobacco?
4. Which game was played with flamingos and hedgehogs in *Alice and Wonderland*?
5. Which sport did Archbishop William Fisher call 'organized loafing'?
6. What did the American quiz *Tic Tac Dough* become in Britain?
7. Which cartoonist sends her characters to Tresoddit, in Cornwall?
8. Which opera by Verdi is based on the play *La Dame aux Camélias*?
9. From which point on a stem do leaves arise?

329

1. When was tea first grown in Ceylon?
2. Which King did Walter Tyrell kill?
3. Which country has the highest mortality rate from snake-bites?
4. Which author said, 'Shooting gives me a good feeling'?
5. Which sport did Mark Twain call 'a good walk spoiled'?
6. In which city was the TV series *Behind Closed Doors* set?
7. In which country is Picasso buried?
8. Which musician did Goethe call 'the human incarnation of the divine force of creation'?
9. In miles per second, how fast must a rocket travel to leave the Earth?

563

1. In Scotland, what are 'champit tatties'?
2. In which unorthodox manner did a division of the French army reach the Battle of the Marne in 1914?
3. In terms of population, what is the world's largest democracy?
4. From which London club did Phileas Fogg set out to go *Around the World in Eighty Days*?
5. Why is Wendy Wimbush associated with Test cricket?
6. Which ex-TV policeman won an Oscar for *Chariots of Fire*?
7. Which US citizen was made an honorary KBE in 1973 for services to broadcasting?
8. Which singer said, 'I don't know anything about music. In my line you don't have to'?
9. Where in the world does the web-toed fishing cat come from?

95

1. Special Weapons And Tactics.
2. They scavenged in the sewers.
3. In Syria.
4. Croquet.
5. Cricket.
6. *Criss Cross Quiz.*
7. Posy Simmonds, in *The Guardian.*
8. *La Traviata.*
9. The node.

329

1. In the 19th century (in 1867, to be precise).
2. William Rufus, in the New Forest.
3. Burma – 15.4 per 100,000.
4. Ernest Hemingway, who shot himself!
5. Golf.
6. Washington, DC.
7. In France, at Aix-en-Provence.
8. Mozart.
9. Seven miles per second.

563

1. Mashed potatoes.
2. In a fleet of 600 taxis.
3. India.
4. The Reform Club.
5. She is, perhaps, the best-known of the regular scorers.
6. Colin Welland, ex-*Z-Cars* actor, who wrote the script.
7. Alistair Cooke.
8. Elvis Presley.
9. From India and Indo-China.

96

1. What is the normal operating temperature of a retail butcher's meat-chiller?
2. Which Egyptian king caused the Great Pyramid of Cheops to be built?
3. Name the main airport of Sydney, Australia.
4. Who was Cain's eldest son?
5. What takes place in Happy Valley, Hong Kong?
6. Who portrayed *Edna, the Inebriate Woman*?
7. What did Jean Nidetch found?
8. According to the *Tremeloes*, what is silence?
9. What closes off the windpipe during the action of swallowing?

330

1. How does an American omelette differ from an English one?
2. When did Big Ben first broadcast on the BBC?
3. Lake Bala is the biggest in which country?
4. How many boys and girls did the Minotaur eat each year?
5. Where did Princess Anne finish in her first flat race?
6. Who say 'Break a leg' as a good luck wish?
7. Who is President of the Girl Guides?
8. During which war was the Turkey-trot a popular dance?
9. Which planet is named after the Roman God who reputedly devoured nearly all his own children?

564

1. What is the main difference between 'British' and 'English' wine?
2. For what do the letters SLA stand – the name of the group who kidnapped Patty Hearst?
3. In which country is Chittagong?
4. Who wrote *The Herries Chronicle*?
5. What was Cassius Clay's middle name?
6. Who was the absent-minded professor in *The Absent-Minded Professor*?
7. In 1930, Ellen Church was the first person to be appointed to which new occupation?
8. In 1964, who had a hit with *Terry*?
9. Cerumen is another name for *what*?

96

1. 1° to 4° Centigrade.
2. King Cheops.
3. Sydney International Airport.
4. Enoch.
5. Horse racing.
6. Patricia Hayes.
7. Weight Watchers.
8. Golden.
9. The epiglottis.

330

1. In spelling. They spell it 'omelet'.
2. In 1923.
3. In Wales.
4. Seven of each.
5. Fourth, on *Against the Grain*.
6. Actors and actresses.
7. Princess Margaret.
8. During World War I.
9. Saturn.

564

1. British wine is made from imported grapes, and English from home-grown.
2. Symbionese Liberation Army.
3. In Bangladesh.
4. Hugh Walpole.
5. Marcellus.
6. Fred MacMurray.
7. Air hostess.
8. Twinkle.
9. Wax in the ears.

97

1. In what does a milliner deal?
2. Which is Cambridge's newest college?
3. What is marketed at Spitalfields in London?
4. Who wrote the play *Betrayal*?
5. Which stroke always begins the swimming medley relay?
6. Which part of his anatomy did Luke Skywalker lose in *The Empire Strikes Back*?
7. In which country was Picasso born?
8. Which group had their first hit with *Speak Like a Child*?
9. In Centigrade, what is the normal body temperature?

331

1. Name the quarter day that falls on 25 March.
2. What was the Labour Party's slogan for 1979?
3. In which city is Aston University?
4. Blue Diamond is a nightclub in which John Le Carré novel?
5. What do you do to clay pigeons?
6. Who was the winner of BBC TV's *Mastermind* in 1985?
7. Who designed the uniforms that the Swiss Guards wear at the Vatican?
8. In 1972 the Council of Europe adopted *what* as its anthem for official occasions?
9. What colour is an emerald?

565

1. A bairn is a Scottish word for *what*?
2. Charles and Henry teamed up in 1906 to make which luxury car?
3. In which range of hills are the Cheddar Caves?
4. Who wrote *Tinker, Tailor, Soldier, Spy*?
5. How many bails sit atop a single cricket wicket?
6. How many finalists are there in BBC TV's *Mastermind*?
7. In 1983, which Labour MP went to the House of Lords with a hereditary peerage?
8. Where was Sir Georg Solti, the naturalized British conductor, born?
9. Which form of power operates the telephone system?

97

1. Hats.
2. Robinson College.
3. Vegetables mainly, and fruit.
4. Harold Pinter.
5. The backstroke.
6. His hand.
7. In Spain.
8. *Style Council.*
9. Just under 37°C.

331

1. Lady Day.
2. 'The Labour Way is a Better Way.'
3. In Birmingham.
4. *Smiley's People.*
5. Shoot them.
6. Ian Meadows.
7. Michelangelo.
8. The choral section from the last movement of Beethoven's Ninth Symphony.
9. Green, normally.

565

1. A young child.
2. The Rolls-Royce.
3. The Mendips.
4. John Le Carré.
5. Two.
6. Four.
7. George Thomas.
8. In Hungary.
9. Electricity.

98

1. What do paparazzi do?
2. Which battle was fought on 13 August, 1704?
3. In which city is the world's largest magistrate's court?
4. Which author said the ideal life was 'good friends, good books and a sleepy conscience'?
5. In which sport could a player 'pick a cherry' or leave a 'picket fence'?
6. Why was the actress Pamela Stephenson turned down by the Magic Circle?
7. Who said, 'Anyone who sees and paints a sky green and pastures blue ought to be sterilized'?
8. What job does Escamillo do in *Carmen*?
9. What is the largest British freshwater fish?

332

1. Which company's base is nicknamed 'Eggcup Towers'?
2. In 1941, how many clothing coupons did you need for a corset?
3. In which state of the USA do most millionaires live?
4. Who wrote about Kimball O'Hara?
5. In which sport is klister used?
6. What is the only British TV quiz show bought and shown by American TV?
7. Of what was Minerva the goddess?
8. Who were Cliff Richard's first backing group?
9. A Shaded Cameo is a kind of *what*?

566

1. On which British island could married women not have their own bank accounts until 1975?
2. Which leader was exiled from Cyprus to the Seychelles in 1956?
3. On which river is Bonn?
4. In mythology, what was the only animal that could kill a basilisk?
5. In which sport could you do a walley?
6. What did Orson Welles call 'the biggest train-set a boy ever had'?
7. Who defeated Jack Jones in the election for Chancellor of London University?
8. Which country won the Eurovision Song Contest in 1975 with *Ding Ding Dong*?
9. What was Britain's first space rocket called?

98

1. They take candid photos, free-lance, of the famous.
2. The battle of Blenheim.
3. In Johannesburg – there are 42 court-rooms.
4. Mark Twain.
5. In ten-pin bowling.
6. Because they refuse to admit women, claiming 'they just can't keep a secret'.
7. Adolf Hitler.
8. He is a bullfighter.
9. The sturgeon, but it is rare.

332

1. TV AM's, which has giant eggcups on its roof.
2. Three, out of sixty-six a year.
3. In California – there were 114,427 in 1985.
4. Rudyard Kipling, in *Kim*.
5. Skiing – it is a wax for skis.
6. *The Krypton Factor*, bought in 1981.
7. Art.
8. *The Drifters*, well before *The Shadows*.
9. Cat.

566

1. On Sark, in the Channel Islands.
2. Archbishop Makarios.
3. On the Rhine.
4. A weasel.
5. In skating – it is a jump.
6. Hollywood.
7. Princess Anne.
8. The Netherlands. It was sung by *Teach-In*.
9. Blue Streak. It was built in 1964.

99

1. How many countries originally formed the Common Market?
2. Which monarch wrote a book about witchcraft called *Daemonologie*?
3. Where do Sards live when they are at home?
4. What are the only weapons with which a werewolf can be killed?
5. What is Linda Fratianne's sport?
6. Which jungle character did Johnny Weissmuller play, after Tarzan?
7. When can a king in chess move more than one square at a turn?
8. *White Boy* was the first single from which group?
9. Of what part of the body is an electroencephalogram taken?

333

1. Who go on a fast during Ramadan?
2. In 1982, the kidnapped US Army Brigadier General James Dozier was rescued. In which country?
3. From which country does the dish *tamale* originate?
4. What was the staple diet of the Israelites in the wilderness?
5. What are the master grades in Judo called?
6. *Boys From the Blackstuff* featured the unemployed of which city?
7. For kidnapping and murdering whose son was Bruno Hauptmann executed in 1932?
8. Which group had a hit with *All Around My Hat*?
9. Where does the tomato plant orginally come from?

567

1. What name is usually given to finely ground tobacco inhaled through the nose?
2. In the Civil War, which battle was fought in the shallow depression of Broad Moor?
3. What is South-West Africa now called?
4. Who wrote the spy novel *A Small Town in Germany*?
5. From which team did Pat Jennnings move to Arsenal?
6. When actors say that they are resting, what do they mean?
7. From which country did the painter Murillo come?
8. According to Del Shannon, how many 'Kinds of Teardrops' are there?
9. Which fuel has octane numbers?

99

1. Six.
2. James I.
3. In Sardinia.
4. A dagger or a bullet fashioned from a silver crucifix.
5. Ice skating.
6. Jungle Jim.
7. When castling.
8. *Culture Club.*
9. The brain.

333

1. Muslims.
2. In Italy.
3. From Mexico.
4. Manna.
5. Dan.
6. Liverpool.
7. Charles Lindbergh's.
8. *Steeleye Span.*
9. South America, although it is now grown worldwide.

567

1. Snuff.
2. The Battle of Naseby.
3. Namibia.
4. John Le Carré.
5. Tottenham Hotspur.
6. They are unemployed at the moment.
7. From Spain.
8. Two.
9. Petrol.

100

1. Which animal is shown on the crest of the Falkland Islands?
2. 'He blew and they were scattered' (in Latin) is the motto on which medal?
3. Which ship canal bypasses the Niagara Falls?
4. Which monster was the offspring of Queen Pasiphaë and a bull?
5. In which city is the Iffley Road running track?
6. To whom was a memorial stone unveiled in Westminster Abbey in 1984?
7. Which large work of art has scenes from Aesop's Fables round its border?
8. Which composer did Rossini say 'has some wonderful moments but awful half hours'?
9. Which flower has a name which means 'nose-twister', because of its strong smell?

334

1. How many hairsbreadths make one inch?
2. Who was the last British king to be crowned in Scotland?
3. Where would you find Dr Johnson's Head and Dr Syntax's Head?
4. What is the most popular name for Christian saints?
5. Which sportsmen dance the Haka?
6. Where, on TV, did Bombadier Beaumont appear?
7. In art, what is 'scumbling'?
8. A Ralph McTell song has sold more sheet music copies than any other in the last forty years. Name it.
9. Which flower has a name which means 'a little sword', because of its leaves?

568

1. What was 'Operation Bishop', carried out by customs officers?
2. When did *The Times* acquire its nickname 'The Thunderer'?
3. Which caves in the Mendips are named after the Saxon word for an animal trap?
4. What did the mild swear word 'Drat!' originally mean?
5. Who won the 1985 Wimbledon Ladies Singles Final?
6. Who played the lead in the films *Dangerous When Wet* and *Million Dollar Mermaid*?
7. In which game might you say, 'J'adoube' to your opponent?
8. Which pop protest singer has been nicknamed 'Barking's Bob Dylan'?
9. In hepatitis, what is inflamed?

100

1. A sheep.
2. The Armada Medal, issued in 1588.
3. The Welland Canal.
4. The Minotaur.
5. In Oxford.
6. To Sir Noël Coward.
7. The Bayeux Tapestry.
8. Wagner.
9. The nasturtium.

334

1. Forty-eight.
2. Charles II, in 1651.
3. On either side of Land's End – they are coastal features.
4. Felix – there are 67, and 64 Johns.
5. New Zealand's rugby players.
6. In the concert party of *It Ain't Half Hot, Mum.*
7. The use of a dry bush to drag paint across a surface.
8. *The Streets of London.*
9. The gladiolus.

568

1. A drugs swoop in which they collected 4.3 tonnes of cannabis – the biggest haul in Western Europe, up until mid-1985.
2. In 1830, under the editorship of Thomas Barnes.
3. Wookey Hole.
4. God rot!
5. Martina Navratilova.
6. Esther Williams.
7. In chess.
8. Billy Bragg.
9. The liver.

101

1. What is Spanish for 'please'?
2. In World War II, what were the German tank divisions called?
3. How many different letters form the Hawaiian alphabet?
4. Which writer has penned a science-fiction book beginning with every letter of the alphabet?
5. What colour flag signifies the end of a motor race?
6. In 1966, which TV play about a homeless young mother made a great impact?
7. Who named the Hawaiian Islands the Sandwich Islands?
8. *The Useless Precaution* was the subtitle of which Rossini opera?
9. In which geological era do we live?

335

1. In England, what is the minimum age at which you may drive a car on public roads?
2. Who founded the US government's Secret Service, in 1861?
3. Which mountain range is called the 'Backbone of Italy'?
4. Who wrote *Atlas Shrugged* and *The Fountainhead*?
5. A local derby match between the Robins and the Pirates at soccer would be held in which city?
6. Which *Times* was first published in 1923?
7. Of whom did Margot Asquith say, 'He could not see a belt without hitting below it'?
8. Who set up Reprise records in the 1960s?
9. As cocks crow, what do turkeys do?

569

1. How are camping sites shown on maps?
2. For how long was William H. Harrison President of the USA?
3. Which European capital is the largest in area?
4. In which city is *The Prime of Miss Jean Brodie* set?
5. Where is the British Show Jumping Derby held?
6. For which company did the TV character Reginald Perrin work?
7. Which American Abstract Impressionist became famous for his 'drip painting'?
8. *Who's Afraid of the Big Bad Wolf?* From which Disney cartoon film does this song originate?
9. Branches of which tree are symbols of peace?

101

1. 'Por favor'.
2. Panzer.
3. Twelve.
4. Andre Norton.
5. A black and white checked flag.
6. *Cathy Come Home.*
7. Captain Cook.
8. *The Barber of Seville.*
9. The Cenozoic.

335

1. Seventeen.
2. Allan Pinkerton. (After founding his own detective agency.)
3. The Apeninnes.
4. Ayn Rand.
5. Bristol (City v Rovers).
6. *Radio Times.*
7. Of Lloyd George.
8. Frank Sinatra.
9. Gobble.

569

1. By pictures of tents.
2. For one month – give or take a day.
3. London.
4. In Edinburgh.
5. At Hickstead.
6. 'Sunshine Desserts.'
7. Jackson Pollock.
8. *The Three Little Pigs.*
9. Branches of the olive tree.

102

1. What type of aircraft were Spitfires and Hurricanes?
2. Which religion's calendar begins in AD622?
3. What does 'Dar es Salaam' mean?
4. A pre-arranged poem was broadcast by the BBC in 1945 so that the French Resistance would know the D-Day invasions were imminent. Which poet wrote it?
5. Which horse won the Fillies Triple Crown in 1985?
6. As what did Doris Day begin her show business career?
7. Whose presence on the battlefield was said to be worth 40,000 men?
8. In the 1940s who was nicknamed 'The Voice'?
9. How many fused bones form the coccyx?

336

1. After how many years' disappearance can a person be legally declared dead?
2. Which war against the Indians was the last fought in America?
3. What is the Italian equivalent of the British 'motorway'?
4. Who wrote *Aurora Leigh*?
5. Where is the HQ of English cricket?
6. Who deals with Top Cat's misdemeanours?
7. Who is Arkady Shevchenko?
8. *Glad All Over* was a No. 1 hit for which group?
9. What is the cowboy term for a motherless calf?

570

1. People of which religion speak Yiddish?
2. Who had herself presented to Julius Caesar in a carpet?
3. What, in the North Sea, are Anne, Corn and Ruth?
4. Which brown bear befriended Mowgli?
5. Which great cricketer also played Rugby for the Barbarians?
6. How many Oscars did *Gigi* win?
7. Who said, 'How can one govern a country that produces over 350 cheeses'?
8. At which New York opera house were *The Who* the first rock group ever to perform?
9. What is hydrogen's atomic number?

102

1. Fighters.
2. The calendar of Islam.
3. 'Gates of Peace'.
4. Verlaine.
5. Oh So Sharp.
6. As a dancer – until she broke her leg.
7. Napoleon Bonaparte's.
8. Frank Sinatra.
9. Four.

336

1. Seven.
2. The Sioux War.
3. Autostrada.
4. Elizabeth Barrett Browning.
5. At Lord's.
6. Officer Dibble.
7. The highest-ranking Soviet diplomat to defect to the West, up to May 1985.
8. *The Dave Clark Five.*
9. Dogie.

570

1. People of the Jewish religion, though fewer and fewer do nowadays.
2. Cleopatra.
3. Oil fields.
4. Baloo.
5. C.B. Fry.
6. Nine.
7. Charles de Gaulle.
8. At the Metropolitan Opera House.
9. One.

103

1. What colour is the starboard light on a ship?
2. Charles Darwin left London in early 1985. How was this possible?
3. Which country owns Bouvet Island in the South Atlantic?
4. 'April is the cruellest month' starts which poem?
5. What is the maximum height of the sole allowed on a high-jumper's shoe?
6. Where do 'points mean prizes' on TV?
7. What do you use to make a 'sanguine' drawing?
8. What unusually composed orchestra played at the Wigmore Hall in July 1985?
9. What is the connection between soda water and sodium?

337

1. What is a group of freemasons called?
2. Rationing of clothes began in 1941 and ended *when*?
3. What is the Hellespont called today?
4. Whose autobiography was called *Hons and Rebels*?
5. In horse racing, what is a 'double carpet'?
6. In which film sequel did Michelle Pfeiffer play the Pink Lady?
7. What do we call paintings known as 'Nature Morte' ('dead nature') in French?
8. Which animals are depicted in Ravel's *L'Enfant et les Sortilèges*?
9. Which metal was called after the German for imp, or goblin?

571

1. Where would you find Fourth Gutter and Palace of Weariness?
2. What did Cunard originally intend to call the liner 'Queen Mary'?
3. Which city has a nightclub area called The Cross?
4. Who called the third volume of his autobiography *An Orderly Man*?
5. Which county cricket club's badge depicts a daffodil?
6. Who plays the visitor from outer space in *Starman*?
7. How is a Divisionist or Pointillist painting done?
8. For which musical instrument does Conlon Nancarrow compose?
9. Which snakes get their name because they produce live young, not eggs?

103

1. Green.
2. *Charles Darwin* is the name of a newly commissioned marine laboratory.
3. Norway.
4. *The Waste Land* by T.S. Eliot.
5. Half an inch, or 13 mm.
6. On *Play your Cards Right.*
7. Red chalk.
8. One of 20 lutes, believed to be the first for 300 years.
9. None at all.

337

1. A lodge.
2. In 1949.
3. The Bosphorus, or Dardanelles.
4. Jessica Mitford's.
5. Odds of 33–1; a 'Carpet' is 3–1.
6. In *Grease II.*
7. Still life paintings.
8. Two Siamese cats.
9. Cobalt. Silver miners thought it a nuisance.

571

1. On your body – they are acupuncture points.
2. *Queen Victoria.*
3. Sydney, Australia.
4. Dirk Bogarde.
5. Glamorgan's.
6. Jeff Bridges.
7. In lots of dots of different colours.
8. The player-piano.
9. Vipers, short for 'vivipera'.

104

1. 'Jack and Jill went up the hill to fetch a pail of water.' What is the basic fallacy here?
2. Which party were the forerunners of the Liberals?
3. What do the Beefeaters guard?
4. In which Dickens novel does Mr Micawber feature?
5. How wide is a field hockey goal?
6. Which film featured the line 'I'm going to make him an offer he can't refuse'?
7. Which Dulles brother was director of CIA?
8. What type of music was Mahalia Jackson renowned for singing?
9. Approximately how many humans are there to each dog in Britain?

338

1. In whose eyes is salt supposedly thrown when the superstitious throw it over the left shoulder?
2. Which two towns formed Budapest, in 1872?
3. Where is the HQ of OPEC?
4. Which doctor wrote *The Keys of the Kingdom*?
5. What are the three disciplines of the Triathlon?
6. 'Are you sitting comfortably?' With which radio programme is this phrase associated?
7. Who immediately preceded Ronald Reagan as President of the USA?
8. *Home on the Range* is the official song of which US state?
9. Which liquid is termed the 'universal solvent'?

572

1. How many pence today would a crown have been worth?
2. Where did the Venerable Bede live?
3. How long is the Pan-American highway?
4. 'All animals are equal, but some animals are more equal than others.' From which book does this come?
5. Which letter of the alphabet might you eat, and which might you drink, to form physical activity?
6. Which British film star said of her autobiography, 'When you look at the things that go on these days, my story reads like Noddy'?
7. What did Jean Merlin reputedly invent in 1760?
8. When was an opera first recorded on record?
9. Name the tubes connecting the nose and ears.

104

1. Wells weren't built at the tops of hills – think of the wasted effort!
2. The Whigs.
3. The Tower of London.
4. In *David Copperfield*.
5. Twelve feet wide.
6. *The Godfather*.
7. Allen Dulles.
8. Gospel music.
9. Ten.

338

1. The devil's.
2. Buda and Pest.
3. In Vienna.
4. Dr A.J. Cronin.
5. Swimming, cycling and running.
6. *Listen With Mother*.
7. Jimmy Carter.
8. Kansas.
9. Water.

572

1. Twenty-five.
2. In Jarrow.
3. 13,000 miles long.
4. *Animal Farm*, by George Orwell.
5. P.T.
6. Diana Dors.
7. Roller skates.
8. In 1903.
9. The eustachian tubes.

105

1. What angle is formed by the clock hands at 3.00?
2. What was Indonesia formerly called?
3. Which is Europe's largest port?
4. In which Dickens novel does the case of Jarndyce v Jarndyce feature?
5. Which Eastern Bloc country led the withdrawal from the 1984 Olympic Games?
6. Which Indian tennis star played in a 'James Bond' film?
7. TV's *Top Crown* features which game?
8. Which famous German composer, born in 1770, died deaf in 1827?
9. The name of which dinosaur means 'Thunder lizard'?

339

1. What is the gastronomic speciality of Whitstable?
2. When was the National Trust founded?
3. What proportion of the world's gold comes from South Africa?
4. Who, in the Bible, was raised from the dead by Jesus?
5. In order to score at squash, what must you have been doing?
6. Robert Redford won an Oscar in 1981 at his first effort as a director. Name the film.
7. Why did Benjamin Disraeli keep the legs of his bed in salt water?
8. Which conductor drowned during a tour of Israel?
9. What is polyvinyl chloride normally called?

573

1. Under which Act can fortune-tellers be apprehended?
2. When was the Bank of England nationalized?
3. Which of London's bridges opens at its centre?
4. What line follows 'Theirs not to reason why'?
5. Famous in another field, who won a Gold Medal for rowing in the 1924 Paris Olympics?
6. Who hosted the BBC programme *Woman's Hour* in 1985?
7. How many heads appear on a standard pack of playing cards?
8. Why did Mexicans originally call cowboys 'Gringos'?
9. By what name is the boon to frying pans polytetrafluoroethylene better known?

105

1. Right-angle, 90°.
2. The Dutch East Indies.
3. Rotterdam.
4. In *Bleak House*.
5. The USSR.
6. Vijay Amritraj.
7. Crown Green Bowling.
8. Beethoven.
9. The brontosaurus.

339

1. Oysters.
2. In 1895.
3. About two-thirds.
4. Lazarus.
5. Serving.
6. *Ordinary People*.
7. So that no evil spirits would influence him while he slept.
8. István Kertesz.
9. PVC.

573

1. The Vagrancy Act of 1824.
2. In 1947.
3. Tower Bridge.
4. 'Theirs but to do and die.'
5. Benjamin Spock.
6. Sue MacGregor.
7. 24. (Two on each picture card.)
8. Because cowboys used to sing to the herds, and the most popular song began 'Green grow the lilacs.'
9. Teflon.

Q

106

1. At the March equinox, how many hours of darkness are there in each 24, all over the world?
2. What iniquitous organization did Nathan Bedford Forrest begin, in 1865?
3. Which was called 'The Dark Continent'?
4. Who wrote *The Adventures of Tom Bombadil*?
5. Which London soccer club wears blue and white hooped shirts?
6. Who played Norman Bates in *Psycho II*?
7. Which fruit did the Reverend Gage first bring to Britain?
8. With what style of music was Bob Marley particularly associated?
9. What colour is lapis lazuli?

340

1. What is the American word for what Britons call a torch?
2. In which year were British gold sovereigns replaced by treasury notes?
3. Which is Europe's busiest airport?
4. From which language does the word 'coffee' originate?
5. Baggataway was the forerunner of which game?
6. In the film *Raiders of the Lost Ark*, what proliferate on the floor of the tomb?
7. Which card game has the same name as an English racecourse?
8. Who played Coco in the musical film *Coco*?
9. How many times the weight of his/her brain is the average human?

574

1. From what does lanolin come?
2. After whom was the liner *Queen Elizabeth* named?
3. In which European city do traffic lights control the water traffic?
4. Which Greek god gives his name to the word 'panic'?
5. How many nets are used in netball?
6. Actress Carole Lombard was killed in a plane crash in 1942. To which actor was she married at the time?
7. Charles Atlas was described as a how-many-pound weakling?
8. In which TV programme were new records voted as 'Hit' or 'Miss' by members of the audience?
9. Name the horizontal bar on which cage birds perch.

106

1. Twelve.
2. The Ku Klux Klan.
3. Africa.
4. J.R.R. Tolkein.
5. Queen's Park Rangers.
6. Anthony Perkins.
7. The greengage.
8. Reggae.
9. Blue.

340

1. A flashlight.
2. In 1914.
3. Heathrow.
4. Turkish.
5. Lacrosse.
6. Snakes.
7. Newmarket.
8. Katharine Hepburn.
9. About forty times.

574

1. Sheep's wool.
2. Queen Elizabeth, the Queen Mother.
3. In Venice.
4. Pan.
5. Two – one hanging from each goal ring.
6. Clark Gable.
7. 97 lb.
8. In *Juke Box Jury*.
9. The perch.

107

1. Apart from the obvious what is a Glasgow Magistrate?
2. The *Resurgam*, which sank on its maiden voyage in 1880, was the first *what*?
3. In Australian slang, a 'crow eater' is a person from *where*?
4. In *Gentleman Jim*, by Raymond Briggs, what was Jim's job?
5. After putting in golf, how long may a player wait to see if a ball balancing on the hole's edge drops in?
6. Which film star was called 'the Golden Girl of Hollywood'?
7. Which politician did his opponents nickname 'The Strangler of Chingford'?
8. Who won an Oscar for his music to the film *Bridge On the River Kwai*?
9. In a cat show, how is a debutante cat different from a maiden?

341

1. In 1985 the US Government set up Radio Marti, to broadcast *where*?
2. Which Antarctic explorer was nicknamed 'The Boss' by his men?
3. Which former home of the Earl of Shrewsbury is now an amusement park?
4. Who was Adam and Eve's firstborn son?
5. Who, in 1984, set up tennis's longest sequence of winning matches, 74 in all?
6. Which film about removal men was written by Jack Rosenthal?
7. From which country do brothers Prince Philip and Prince Laurent come?
8. The play *The Matchmaker* became which musical?
9. In the 1970s, how many pairs of breeding golden eagles were there in England?

575

1. In the British Army, what is a 'wad'?
2. Which Emperor's sarcophagus is in the crypt of Farnborough's Benedictine Abbey?
3. Which country has an equivalent of the SAS called Delta Force?
4. Which heroine in Shakespeare disguised herself as Ganymede?
5. In three-day-eventing, how many penalty points are given for knocking down a show-jumping fence?
6. Who stars in the film *She'll Be Wearing Pink Pyjamas*?
7. Who is known as 'The voice of tennis'?
8. What happened on Tenth Avenue in the ballet by Richard Rodgers?
9. To help which creatures did Devonshire build a £3000 concrete shaft in a disused quarry?

107

1. A herring.
2. Steam-driven submarine.
3. The State of South Australia.
4. First he was a lavatory attendant, then a failed highwayman.
5. Ten seconds – there is a penalty of two strokes if he takes longer.
6. Paulette Goddard.
7. Norman Tebbitt.
8. Malcolm Arnold.
9. A maiden has never won, a debutante has never before been exhibited.

341

1. To Cuba, from Florida.
2. Shackleton.
3. Alton Towers.
4. Cain.
5. Martina Navratilova.
6. *The Chain.*
7. Belgium.
8. *Hello, Dolly*!
9. Only one, in the Lake District.

575

1. It is slang for a sandwich.
2. Napoleon III's.
3. The USA.
4. Rosalind, in *As You Like It.*
5. Ten.
6. Julie Walters.
7. Dan Maskell.
8. Slaughter – it is called '*Slaughter on Tenth Avenue*'.
9. Bats.

108

1. Of what is phobiaphobia the fear?
2. In 1979, two Russians spent how many consecutive days in space?
3. How many states make up the German Federal Republic?
4. Who wrote the novel *The French Lieutenant's Woman*?
5. Which athletic feat by Steve Fonyo, aged 19, raised nearly seven million dollars for charity?
6. Name Katharine Hepburn's sailor doll in the 1981 film *On Golden Pond.*
7. What was Francis Bacon's title?
8. Which tune was played at Peter Sellers's funeral?
9. What is the troposphere?

342

1. Under what age may a child not give evidence in court?
2. What was good news for dogs in 1835?
3. Skyscrapers first appeared in which city?
4. Who, in a *Playboy* magazine interview said, 'I've committed adultery in my heart many times'?
5. Who wear 'silks' to race?
6. In film censorship, for what did the letter 'H' stand?
7. Which Briton climbed Everest at his fourth attempt, aged 50?
8. What is the Irish musical instrument, something like the bagpipes?
9. What is the common name for Nymphaea?

576

1. How many miracles must you have performed to be created a saint?
2. When did France withdraw its troops from NATO?
3. Of where is Valletta the capital?
4. For how many days did Jesus fast in the wilderness?
5. What colour are cricket balls?
6. Who married each other in Canada in 1964 and in Africa in 1975?
7. With which country do you associate Samuel Doe?
8. Who was born at 12 Arnold Grove, Liverpool on 25 February, 1943?
9. Which country developed the first Atom Bomb?

108

1. Fears!
2. 175 days.
3. Ten.
4. John Fowles.
5. He ran across Canada – nearly 5,000 miles – handicapped by having lost a leg at the age of twelve.
6. Elmer.
7. Lord Verulam.
8. *In the Mood.*
9. The lowest layer of the atmosphere.

342

1. There is no lower age limit, provided that the child understands the oath and can be understood.
2. Dog fighting was made illegal.
3. In Chicago.
4. Jimmy Carter.
5. Jockeys.
6. Horror.
7. Chris Bonington.
8. The Uillean pipes, which are not blown into, but squeezed under the arm.
9. Water-lilies.

576

1. Four.
2. In 1966.
3. Malta.
4. Forty.
5. Deep red.
6. Richard Burton and Elizabeth Taylor.
7. Liberia.
8. George Harrison.
9. The USA.

109

1. For what does the 'A' in A-Level stand?
2. What exchange was formed in 1773?
3. How many gondolas are permitted to operate in Venice, by law?
4. Who wrote *What Next in the Law?*, shortly before retiring?
5. In which sport might you perform a telemark?
6. Barbra Streisand and Ryan O'Neal starred in a film, the name of which is a rabbit's catch-phase. Name it.
7. What do the dots on a regular die total?
8. The Pipe and Drums of the Royal Scots Dragoon Guards had a No.1 hit with *what*?
9. What type of lens curves outwards?

343

1. Where would you wear a tiara?
2. In which year in the 1970s were two General Elections held in the UK?
3. What is Santa Clara Valley in California now generally called?
4. Whose body did Mark Antony call 'a bleeding piece of earth'?
5. Which Scottish soccer team plays home matches at Hampden Park?
6. Who hosts TV's *What's My Line*?
7. Which Indian Chief later travelled with Buffalo Bill's Wild West Show?
8. How many symphonies did Tchaikovsky compose?
9. In which organ of the body is the mitral valve?

577

1. What would you probably do with an Eton Mess?
2. What is the city which the Romans called Lutetia now called?
3. Where in London is Speakers' Corner?
4. Who translated *Jabberwocky* for Alice?
5. How many teams are in the Premier Division of the Scottish Soccer League?
6. Paul Hogan features in the series of TV adverts for *what*?
7. What contribution did Linda Sagan, wife of Carl Sagan, make to the spacecraft Pioneer 10 and 11?
8. Which great jazz musician composed the music to the film *Anatomy of a Murder*?
9. In the acronym SCUBA, for what do the letters stand?

109

1. Advanced.
2. The Stock Exchange.
3. 400.
4. Lord Denning.
5. In skiing.
6. *What's Up, Doc*?
7. There are 21 dots, in all.
8. *Amazing Grace.*
9. Convex.

343

1. On your head.
2. In 1974.
3. Silicon Valley.
4. Julius Caesar's.
5. Queen's Park.
6. Eamonn Andrews.
7. Chief Sitting Bull.
8. Six.
9. In the heart.

577

1. Eat it – it is mashed strawberries and cream.
2. Paris.
3. In Hyde Park.
4. Humpty Dumpty.
5. Ten.
6. Foster's lager.
7. She designed the plaques of the nude male and female figures attached to them.
8. Duke Ellington.
9. Self-Contained Underwater Breathing Apparatus.

Q

110

1. In 1985, how much did brewing experts forecast that a pint of beer would cost in AD2000?
2. Which weapon did the Roman gladiators called laquearii use?
3. Where is 'Frisian' spoken?
4. Which heroine in Shakespeare disguised herself as Cesario?
5. Which West Indies cricketer is nicknamed 'Black Diamond'?
6. Who directed the film *Birdy*?
7. What is the title of Judy Chicago's huge work of art which features embroidered place-settings?
8. Which group had their only number one hit with *Blockbuster* in 1973?
9. Which bird builds its own dance-hall?

344

1. Who are the makers of James Bond's cigarettes?
2. Who was founder and first president of the Zoological Society?
3. What do Send, Usk, Werrington and Blantyre have in common?
4. In Shaw's play, what *was* 'John Bull's Other Island'?
5. In which city was the 1982 World Cup Final played?
6. In the classic Bob Newhart sketch, what was the name of the driving instructor?
7. Which former Labour Chief Whip got a life peerage in 1985?
8. Which chart-topping group began at the Rum Runner Club in Birmingham in 1978?
9. What sort of creature is the fish-eating bulldog of Central America?

578

1. Which female, besides the Queen, is on the front of a £10 note?
2. From what illness did George VI die?
3. Where did two Vikings land in 1978?
4. In which play do the central characters call each other Didi and Gogo?
5. Which Briton was trained to win an Olympic gold medal in 1984 by Miklos Nemeth?
6. Which female TV star once asked the questions on *Criss Cross Quiz*?
7. Who stopped believing in Santa Claus when he asked for her autograph?
8. In 1983, who had her first chart record for 28 years with *Where Is My Man*?
9. What is the only cat native to the Old and New Worlds?

110

1. £2.50.
2. A lasso.
3. In Northern Holland.
4. Viola, in *Twelfth Night.*
5. Wayne Daniel.
6. Alan Parker.
7. *The Dinner Party.*
8. *Sweet* – but they had five No. 2 hits.
9. The bower bird of Australia.

244

1. Morlands of Piccadilly.
2. Sir Stamford Raffles – also the colonist of Singapore.
3. They are all detention centres for young offenders.
4. Ireland.
5. In Madrid.
6. Frank Dexter.
7. Bob Mellish.
8. *Duran Duran.*
9. A bat with a dog-like face.

578

1. Britannia.
2. Lung cancer.
3. On the planet Mars.
4. In *Waiting For Godot.*
5. Tessa Sanderson, the javelin champion.
6. Barbara Kelly.
7. Shirley Temple.
8. Eartha Kitt.
9. The lynx.

111

1. What colour is the background to the information signs on British motorways?
2. For what does the 'D' stand in D-Day?
3. The Rhine rises in which country?
4. In which George Eliot book does Maggie Tulliver feature?
5. Which game starts with a face-off?
6. Who said of whom, 'When you've danced with her, you stay danced with'?
7. By what name is Dimitrios Synodinos better known in gambling circles?
8. Who composed the opera *Lohengrin*?
9. Approximately how many million years ago did mammals first appear?

345

1. When telephone dials had letters as well as numbers, which two letters were missing?
2. Which appropriately named people destroyed Rome in AD455?
3. Before Bath was in Avon, where was it?
4. Who wrote, 'Though women are angels, yet wedlock's the devil'?
5. Which Manchester United player was voted 1966 European Footballer of the Year?
6. Which pair of actors starred in the film *The Odd Couple*?
7. Evel Knievel was sentenced to six months in jail for attacking a TV executive with *what*?
8. What is the singer Garfunkel's first name?
9. Chipmunks belong to which family?

579

1. Of which language is Wenyen a variety?
2. Which flag did the Crusaders fly?
3. What is special about the inhabitants of Knighton, a village on the Staffordshire/Shropshire border?
4. Who wrote 'Keep your eyes wide open before marriage and half-shut afterwards'?
5. In which country was cricketer Ted Dexter born?
6. Whose catch-phrase was 'I only asked,' in *The Army Game*?
7. In which century did the painter Tintoretto live?
8. How old was Mozart when he wrote his first symphony?
9. Which was the first re-used spacecraft?

111

1. Blue.
2. Nothing at all – just 'day'.
3. In Switzerland.
4. *The Mill on the Floss.*
5. Ice hockey.
6. Fred Astaire, of Cyd Charisse.
7. Jimmy the Greek.
8. Wagner.
9. 60 million.

345

1. Q and Z.
2. The Vandals.
3. In Somerset.
4. Lord Byron.
5. Bobby Charlton.
6. Jack Lemmon and Walter Matthau.
7. A baseball bat.
8. Arthur, or 'Art'.
9. The squirrel family.

579

1. Chinese.
2. The Cross of St George.
3. They have paid no rates for the last 325 years – thanks to the settlement of a gambling debt of Charles II's.
4. Benjamin Franklin.
5. In Italy.
6. Bernard Bresslaw's.
7. The sixteenth century.
8. Seven.
9. Columbia – the US space shuttle.

112

1. What does 'Post mortem' mean?
2. In which war were jet aircraft first used for fighting?
3. On the shores of which sea is Masada?
4. Who first said, 'Everybody talks about the weather, but nobody does anything about it'?
5. In which athletics event are the greatest heights jumped?
6. Who played Superman in a series of films?
7. According to Mortimer Collins, how old is a man?
8. Who is nicknamed the 'Mother of Country Music'?
9. On which planet, other than earth, did a man-made object first land?

346

1. The Jewish matzo and Indian chapati are both examples of what type of bread?
2. How many Popes have been murdered?
3. From where does the Bank of England obtain its water supply?
4. Who wrote *The Cloister and the Hearth*?
5. Which was the first of the one-day cricket competitions?
6. Who starred in the 1976 film *Dog Day Afternoon*?
7. What New York volunteer crime prevention group did Curtis Sliva begin?
8. Which line precedes 'Oh, what fun it is to ride in a one-horse open sleigh'?
9. Which animal gives its name to a pedestrian crossing?

580

1. How many months have 31 days?
2. Who opened London's Barbican Centre in 1982?
3. ET is the international registration for vehicles from *where*?
4. Into what did Rumpelstiltskin spin straw?
5. In which Olympic jumping event is the take-off board furthest from the landing area?
6. In TV's *Chips*, what is the favoured form of transport?
7. Which world championship takes place each year at the Coxheath Fête?
8. Which great violinist composed works which he claimed were written by Boccherini and Paganini, among others?
9. By what name is Sodium Sesquicarbonate better known in the home?

112

1. After death.
2. World War II.
3. The Dead Sea.
4. Mark Twain.
5. In the pole vault.
6. Christopher Reeves.
7. 'A man is as old as he feels.'
8. Maybelle Carter.
9. On Mars.

346

1. Unleavened.
2. Twenty-six.
3. Its own artesian well.
4. Charles Reade.
5. The Gillette Cup.
6. Al Pacino.
7. The Guardian Angels.
8. 'Jingle bells, jingle bells, jingle all the way.'
9. The zebra or the pelican.

580

1. Seven.
2. Queen Elizabeth II.
3. Egypt.
4. Gold.
5. The triple jump.
6. Motorcycles.
7. The World Custard Pie Throwing Championship.
8. Fritz Kreisler.
9. Bath salts.

113

1. What unlikely National competition is held in Hannibal, Missouri, each year?
2. How much did the USA pay Spain for Florida in 1819?
3. The MiG jet plane is the product of which country?
4. Which of Shakespeare's plays is largely set in Kronberg Castle?
5. Which soccer team's ground is the name of a mainly American game?
6. According to the TV adverts, on what are Cruft's winners invariably fed?
7. Which snooker player used to play professional soccer in Australia?
8. Who composed the song *Over There*, which was popular in World War II?
9. Mercury is mainly discovered within which ore?

347

1. Which part of the tongue registers a 'bitter' taste?
2. In which year was Britain's first proper supermarket opened?
3. Which US state was named after a French king?
4. How was John the Baptist related to Jesus?
5. Who were the first married couple to win Gold Medals in the Olympics?
6. What style bikes were used in the film *ET*?
7. Who painted the *Age of Innocence*?
8. Which was the first American-composed opera performed at La Scala, Milan?
9. To which flower family does the pimpernel belong?

581

1. Approximately what percentage of people have blood group B?
2. What charter did Churchill and Roosevelt sign on HMS Prince of Wales, in 1941?
3. In which US state is the Arlington National Cemetery?
4. Who wrote the Watergate-related autobiography *Blind Ambition*?
5. How many generations of Fraziers did Joe Bugner fight?
6. In which country was actor Stratford Johns born?
7. For what unusual appointment is Mr Frederick Robinson paid £15 per year?
8. Who had a 1961 hit with *My Boomerang Won't Come Back*?
9. What is the 'three fields system'?

113

1. The National Fence-Painting Contest.
2. Five million dollars.
3. The USSR.
4. *Hamlet.*
5. Derby County's Baseball Ground.
6. Pedigree Chum.
7. Eddie Charlton.
8. George M. Cohan.
9. Cinnabar.

347

1. The back.
2. In 1948. (The London Co-op.)
3. Louisiana.
4. He was his cousin.
5. Emil and Dana Zatopek.
6. BMX.
7. Sir Joshua Reynolds.
8. *Porgy and Bess.*
9. The primrose family.

581

1. Nine per cent.
2. The Atlantic Charter.
3. In Virginia.
4. John Dean.
5. Two. Joe first, then his son Marvis.
6. In South Africa.
7. He is the officially appointed Queen's guide to Morecambe Bay.
8. Charlie Drake.
9. A system of crop rotation.

114

1. What name was given to Viking I's landing point on Mars, in 1976?
2. Whom did Jack McCall kill in Deadwood on 2 August 1876?
3. From where in France does Brie cheese come?
4. How many times did the River Styx circle the underworld?
5. *Flying Dutchman* and *Finn* are classes of *what*?
6. Who was the first female to wear men's trousers in public?
7. What craze caused a shortage of plastic piping in the late 1950s, early 1960s?
8. Which Duke Ellington classic was originally called *Dreamy Blues*?
9. Why do flames rise up rather than down?

348

1. Perahera is a festival in which religion?
2. Which German was nicknamed the 'Flying Tailor' in World War II?
3. Where can the Kukukuku tribe be found?
4. What was the eighth plague?
5. Which first-class cricket ground has a tree growing inside the boundary?
6. What was the sequel to the film *Every Which Way But Loose*?
7. In which material is Michelangelo's statue of David sculpted?
8. What are the main differences between Plainsong and Gregorian Chant?
9. Which animals used to guard the temple of Jupiter in Rome?

582

1. For what do the letters 'i.e.' actually stand?
2. Whose life did Flora Macdonald save?
3. In which town were sixty black Africans killed, following a demonstration against 'Pass Laws', in 1960?
4. What was the first name of Webster, of dictionary fame?
5. *Death Valley* is the nickname of the deepest part of which famous US sports stadium?
6. Which Norwegian-born actress's autobiography is entitled *Changing*?
7. How many Britons, prior to Chris Bonington, had climbed Everest?
8. In which country is Bizet's opera *Carmen* set?
9. Which was the first organ to be surgically removed from a person?

114

1. *Bradbury.* (Fêting the sci-fi writer Ray Bradbury.)
2. Wild Bill Hickok.
3. The Brie area, to the east of Paris.
4. Seven times.
5. Yachts.
6. Sarah Bernhardt.
7. The hula-hoop craze.
8. *Mood Indigo.*
9. They are lighter than air.

348

1. In Buddhism.
2. Hermann Göring, because of the variety of different uniforms that he wore.
3. In Papua – New Guinea.
4. A plague of locusts.
5. The St Lawrence ground, in Canterbury.
6. *Every Which Way You Can.*
7. Marble.
8. None – they are the same.
9. Geese.

582

1. Id est.
2. Bonnie Prince Charlie's.
3. In Sharpeville.
4. Noah.
5. Yankee Stadium.
6. Liv Ullman's.
7. Seven.
8. In Spain.
9. The appendix.

115

1. Bluegrass is a style of *what*?
2. Who called himself 'Prince Florizel' when writing to an actress friend?
3. Which Commonwealth city stands on Port Nicholson Bay?
4. Who called his autobiography *Reed All About Me*?
5. What was unique about Primo Carnera's 1933 world title fight against Paulino Uzcudun?
6. In which film did Christopher Lambert play the hero and Ralph Richardson his grandfather?
7. Who used the catchword 'discombobulating'?
8. Who is Annie Mae Bullock?
9. Which small mammal has Pinkus's plates on its skin to compensate for weak eyes?

349

1. Which coin used to be called a bawbee in Scotland?
2. Which Queen was known by the nickname 'Brandy Nan'?
3. Morea is another name for which part of Greece?
4. What was unusual about Ernest Vincent Wright's book *Gadsby*, which contained over 50,000 words?
5. In golf, which club is called a 'Texas wedge'?
6. Which actress is both an expert on pig-farming and a great-niece of Lord Beaverbrook's?
7. Crown Prince Frederick is the heir to which European throne?
8. What was Britain's top-selling single record before *Do They Know It's Christmas*?
9. What actually *is* a cannibal?

583

1. Ragdoll and Korat are kinds of *what*?
2. What did George Washington Goethals begin to build in 1908?
3. In which city does Piccadilly Radio broadcast?
4. To which drug was Sherlock Holmes addicted?
5. What part was played by Michelob in the 1984 Olympic Games?
6. Which famous actor starred in *The Bells*?
7. Crown Prince Felipe is heir to which European throne?
8. Who were Cass, John, Michelle and Denny?
9. How many teeth does a mosquito have?

115

1. Country music.
2. The Prince Regent, later George IV.
3. Wellington, New Zealand.
4. Oliver Reed.
5. It was the only time two Europeans fought for the world heavyweight title.
6. In *Greystoke, The Legend of Tarzan*.
7. Ken Dodd.
8. Tina Turner.
9. The mole.

349

1. The halfpenny.
2. Queen Anne.
3. The Peloponnese.
4. Apart from in the author's name, it contained not one letter 'E'.
5. A putter, when used from off the green.
6. Maria Aitken.
7. The throne of Denmark.
8. *Mull of Kintyre*.
9. One who eats members of its own species.

583

1. Cat.
2. The Panama Canal.
3. In Manchester.
4. Cocaine.
5. It was one of the two official beers.
6. Sir Henry Irving.
7. The throne of Spain.
8. *The Mamas and The Papas*.
9. Forty-seven.

116

1. Who reputedly murdered Sandra Rivett in 1974?
2. How many scenes are there on the Bayeux Tapestry?
3. In Australia, what is a BYO restaurant?
4. Who were Mrs Ford and Mrs Page?
5. The martial arts of tae kwon do and hapkido come from which country?
6. On radio, when Kenneth Williams was Sandy, who was Hugh Paddick?
7. Who painted *Paysage au Soleil Levant*, sold at Sotheby's for £8.15 million in 1985?
8. Who wrote the music for the flop musical *Jeeves*?
9. Which flower has a name which means 'flesh colour'?

350

1. 'Fromologist' was a term coined for collectors of *what*?
2. In which order did the Neolithic, Palaeolithic and Mesolithic ages occur?
3. Why does Germany's highest mountain have a 36-metre concrete tower on its top?
4. Who wrote *The Box of Delights*?
5. What is the cricketing term 'googly' known as in Australia?
6. Which comedian was 'Headmaster of St Michael's'?
7. In which city is there a huge circular painting called the *Panorama Guth*, showing the Australian landscape?
8. Which group's success was greatly helped by Helen Terry?
9. Which fruit's name means 'ugly face' or 'bogey-man' in Spanish?

584

1. Which American protest group is called MADD?
2. What did Lenin do for most of his last year?
3. In which country is mainland Europe's most southerly point, Cape Matapan?
4. Who said, 'A foolish consistency is the hobgoblin of little minds'?
5. A major golf tournament is played over how many holes?
6. In which radio comedy did Pat Hayes play charlady Crystal Jellybottom?
7. Which fashion gimmick did Kathy Hammett invent?
8. Who has had hit records with Phil Everly and with Olivia Newton-John?
9. Which major item in a salad has a name meaning 'milky plant'?

116

1. Lord Lucan.
2. 72.
3. One where you can bring Your Own drink.
4. The Merry Wives of Windsor.
5. Korea.
6. His friend, Julian.
7. Van Gogh.
8. Andrew Lloyd-Webber.
9. The carnation.

350

1. Cheese labels.
2. Palaeolithic, Mesolithic, Neolithic.
3. The Zugspitze is 2964 metres high, so the tower makes it 3000 exactly!
4. John Masefield.
5. A 'bosie', after J.T. Bosanquet.
6. Will Hay.
7. In Alice Springs.
8. *Culture Club*'s.
9. Coconut – the three black marks on its base look like a face.

584

1. Mothers Against Drunken Driving.
2. Collect mushrooms.
3. In Greece.
4. R.W. Emerson.
5. 72 holes.
6. *Ray's A Laugh*.
7. T-shirts with HUGE slogans.
8. Cliff Richard.
9. Lettuce, because of its white 'juice'.

117

1. Which Ford car was a total flop?
2. Name the last remaining King of Spain before it was declared a republic in 1939.
3. Of which major US political party is the ass the symbol?
4. Who wrote *The Playboy of the Western World*?
5. What is Mike Hazelwood's sport?
6. Wile E. Coyote attempts, always unsuccessfully, to capture *whom*?
7. Who is the only US President to have been divorced?
8. Which line precedes 'Four and twenty blackbirds baked in a pie'?
9. Where do you find your occipital artery?

351

1. What does 'a wee' mean, as in 'bide-a-wee'?
2. Which Albanian ruler was known as 'The Lion of Janina'?
3. To which Californian mission do the swallows fly each year, on 19 March?
4. Who described his Antarctic expedition in his book *South*?
5. Who won the 1985 Monaco Grand Prix?
6. What were the words used on the very first gramophone record?
7. Which artist made the canopy over the High Altar in St Peter's, Rome?
8. Which of the orchestral woodwind instruments has the greatest range?
9. What is the male sex hormone?

585

1. Whose day is the second Sunday in May?
2. What was the bombing of London during World War II generally called?
3. Notes of which country are referred to as 'greenbacks'?
4. G.B. Shaw wrote a collection of plays that he termed *Three Plays For Puritans*. Name one.
5. Alain Prost won the 1985 Monaco Grand Prix in which car?
6. Who played Jed Clampett in the TV series *The Beverly Hillbillies*?
7. Of which country is Albert Alexandre Louis Pierre Grimaldi, Marquis de Baux, the Crown Prince?
8. Who had a 1962 hit with *Right Said Fred*?
9. Who made three orbits of the Earth in Friendship 7 in February 1962?

117

1. The Edsel.
2. Alfonso XIII.
3. The Republican Party.
4. J.M. Synge.
5. Water ski-ing.
6. The Road Runner.
7. Ronald Reagan.
8. 'Sing a song of sixpence, a pocket full of rye'.
9. Behind your ear.

351

1. A while.
2. Ali Pasha.
3. Capistrano.
4. Sir Ernest Shackleton.
5. Alain Prost.
6. 'Mary had a little lamb'.
7. Lorenzo Bernini.
8. The clarinet.
9. Testosterone.

585

1. Mother's Day.
2. The Blitz.
3. The USA. (Notes of all denominations are green.)
4. *The Devil's Disciple*; *Caesar and Cleopatra*; *Captain Brassbound's Conversion.*
5. A McLaren-TAG.
6. Buddy Ebsen.
7. Of Monaco.
8. Bernard Cribbins.
9. John Glenn.

118

1. Who produced the *Camargue* car?
2. Who were the *Mayflower*'s passengers on her second journey to America, the Pilgrim Fathers having travelled on her first?
3. From which county did the Tolpuddle Martyrs come?
4. Which magazine uses the mythological winged-horse Pegasus for its logo?
5. How long is the drag-racing 'strip'?
6. Who has presented both *Beat the Clock* and *The Generation Game*?
7. Who, in 1983, brought the World Land Speed Record home to Britain?
8. Who was the first composer to write a concerto for the bassoon?
9. What is a cytologist?

352

1. What is the minimum age at which you may legally purchase fireworks?
2. In which year was the first human heart transplant made?
3. What were *Stoats Nest* and *Bo-Peep Junction*?
4. According to Hyman Kaplan, what is the opposite of 'nightmare'?
5. For what are the two sets of marks awarded to ice-skaters?
6. Name the clown played by James Stewart in *The Greatest Show on Earth*.
7. Kozo Okamoto was released from jail in 1985. What was his crime?
8. Which steel-driving man died trying to beat Captain Tommy's track-laying machine?
9. Which parts of the mandrill monkey are brightly coloured?

586

1. 39.37 inches are the equivalent of which metric measurement?
2. The last battle in 1815 between England and America should never have taken place. Why not?
3. Where was the first British Motor Show held in 1895?
4. According to the nursery rhyme, at what time did Wee Willie Winkie run through the town?
5. How many spectators attended the first soccer Cup Final?
6. Who was the youngest person ever to win an Oscar?
7. Which US President was the fastest Presidential speaker on record?
8. The *High Numbers* became *who*?
9. Which insecticide has been the most influential in controlling malaria?

118

1. Rolls-Royce.
2. Slaves.
3. From Dorset.
4. *Reader's Digest.*
5. A quarter of a mile.
6. Bruce Forsyth.
7. Richard Noble.
8. Vivaldi.
9. A biologist who specializes in the study of cells.

352

1. Sixteen.
2. In 1967.
3. Old stations on the Brighton and South Coast Railway.
4. 'Daymare'.
5. Technical Merit, and Artistic Impression.
6. Button.
7. He was in the Japanese *Red Army* squad responsible for the Lod Airport massacre in 1972.
8. John Henry.
9. Its face and its rump.

586

1. One metre.
2. Because a peace treaty had been signed between the two countries two weeks previously, but no one had told them in New Orleans, where the battle took place.
3. In Tunbridge Wells.
4. Eight o'clock.
5. Approximately 2,000.
6. Shirley Temple, who won one in 1934, at the age of six.
7. John F. Kennedy.
8. *The Who.*
9. DDT.

Q

119

1. What does 'beth' mean, as in Bethlehem?
2. Which is the oldest of the Pyramids?
3. Which country did Prince Sihanouk rule until he was deposed in 1970?
4. Who wrote 'Candy is dandy/But liquor is quicker'?
5. What did Billie Jean King give Bobby Riggs before their famous tennis match?
6. Who made her debut in the 1942 film *In Which We Serve*, when she was eleven weeks old?
7. To what setting does the 'f' stop relate in photography?
8. With what activity do you associate Nat Gonella?
9. Which two mints combine to form peppermint?

353

1. What is the heraldic 'talbot'?
2. Outside which harbour did the *Mary Rose* originally sink?
3. The River Orwell is in which county?
4. Who wrote the science fiction story *Blow Ups Happen*?
5. What sport did Primo Carnera take up after losing his world heavyweight boxing title?
6. In which war was the film *All Quiet on the Western Front* set?
7. Who painted '*The Death of Actaeon*'?
8. Who was Mozart's tutor?
9. Where does an epiphytic plant grow?

587

1. Name the Penlee lifeboat, lost in 1981 with all hands.
2. Which was the only permitted political party in Spain under General Franco?
3. Which English port is nearest to Calais?
4. Who said, 'Let me die with the Philistines'?
5. What does Ed Moses do best?
6. Which Oscar-winning 1930 film was based on a novel by Erich Maria Remarque?
7. What is the jumping cry of parachutists?
8. Who was the first composer to write a concerto for the flute?
9. Heaf tests are used to establish immunity from which disease?

119

1. 'House'.
2. The Pyramid of Zoser, at Saggara.
3. Cambodia.
4. Ogden Nash.
5. A piglet.
6. Juliet Mills.
7. The aperture setting.
8. Music – he was a jazz trumpeter.
9. Spear mint and water mint.

353

1. A hound.
2. Portsmouth.
3. Suffolk.
4. Robert A. Heinlein.
5. Wrestling.
6. World War I.
7. Titian.
8. His father, Leopold Mozart, himself a gifted musician.
9. On another plant.

587

1. The *Solomon Browne*.
2. Falange.
3. Dover.
4. Samson.
5. Hurdle.
6. *All Quiet on the Western Front*.
7. 'Geronimo ...'
8. Vivaldi.
9. Tuberculosis.

120

1. The surface of the Earth is approximately how many times greater than that of the moon?
2. Which large German battleship was sunk on 27 May 1941?
3. After which country is Nova Scotia in Canada named?
4. In Dickens' *Great Expectations*, Miss Havisham stopped her clock at 8.40. Why?
5. Cyclist Eddie Merckx comes from which country?
6. During which war was the film *Bridge on the River Kwai* set?
7. From what does the expression 'above board' come?
8. In the song, what colour ribbons did Johnny promise to buy at the fair?
9. Which drink is flavoured with wormwood?

354

1. What does 'safari' actually mean?
2. Who built Watling Street and the Fosse Way?
3. As seen in so many films, etc., which brand of cigarettes does the massive neon sign in Times Square, New York, advertise?
4. Who wrote, 'He who can, does. He who cannot, teaches'?
5. How do Canadians paddle their canoes?
6. In the *Thunderbirds* TV cartoon series, what colour is Lady Penelope's Rolls-Royce?
7. Whose statue sits in solitary splendour on London's Paddington Station?
8. What is Donovan's surname?
9. What breed is the Dulux dog?

588

1. What is the American name for what the British refer to as 'drawing pins'?
2. From what type of wood was the *Kon-Tiki* raft fashioned?
3. On which continent is the Kalahari desert?
4. Which playwright made his first attempt to ride a bicycle on Beachy Head, and remarked that he wished his audiences laughed as much as the coastguards?
5. Where does racing driver Keke Rosberg come from?
6. Name MGM's lion.
7. Who died in Parkland Hospital, Dallas, on 22 November, 1963?
8. From what type of tree was Tom Dooley hanged?
9. How many ears have bees?

120

1. Six times.
2. The *Bismarck*.
3. Scotland.
4. This was the time at which her wedding had been cancelled.
5. From Belgium.
6. World War II.
7. From cards – the honest players held their cards above the table!
8. Blue.
9. Absinthe, now generally banned.

354

1. Journey.
2. The Romans.
3. Camel.
4. George Bernard Shaw.
5. Kneeling down.
6. Pink.
7. Isambard Kingdom Brunel's.
8. Leitch.
9. It is an Old English sheepdog.

588

1. Thumb-tacks.
2. From balsa wood.
3. Africa.
4. George Bernard Shaw.
5. Finland.
6. Leo.
7. President John F. Kennedy.
8. An oak tree.
9. None.

121

1. How do Americans spell the colour 'grey'?
2. Which Libyan king did Colonel Gaddafi overthrow in 1969?
3. Kosciusko is the highest mountain in which country?
4. Who wrote *An Ideal Husband*?
5. How many players take the field at one time in a Canadian football team?
6. How many curls did Shirley Temple's mother put into her daughter's hair daily?
7. Lord Palmerston was given which nickname, as he reputedly had affairs with three Lady Patrons of the *Almack's Club*?
8. *Iron Maiden* and *Motorhead* are exponents of which type of music?
9. What is Alpha Centauri?

355

1. Whose sword is carried before the monarch at British Coronations?
2. Which monarch ruled England from 1649–60?
3. Where does the Ten Tors walk take place?
4. Who was Methuselah's father?
5. In which single year was cricket included in the Olympics?
6. Of which actor did G.B.Shaw say, 'Simply no brains, all character and temperament'?
7. Margaret Gorman was the first winner of which American contest in 1921?
8. Who had a hit in 1973 with *The Leader of the Gang*?
9. What shape is a volcano?

589

1. Which is Sicily's best known wine?
2. Why were territorial waters originally set at three miles?
3. By what name are we more likely to recognize Sitsang?
4. Who wrote, 'The reason that husbands and wives do not understand each other is because they belong to different sexes'?
5. Which is the longest Olympic track race?
6. Who played Lady Dedlock in BBC TV's *Bleak House*?
7. Elsa Schiaparelli introduced which vivid colour onto the fashion scene in the 1930s?
8. Whose father wore herring boxes in place of shoes?
9. What takes 365 days, 6 hours and 10 minutes?

121

1. Gray.
2. King Idris.
3. In Australia.
4. Oscar Wilde.
5. Twelve players.
6. 56.
7. 'Lord Cupid'.
8. Heavy Metal.
9. A very bright star.

355

1. Edward the Confessor's.
2. None. (Oliver Cromwell had something to do with it.)
3. On Dartmoor.
4. Enoch.
5. In 1900, at the Paris Olympics.
6. Sir Henry Irving.
7. Miss America.
8. Gary Glitter.
9. It is cone-shaped.

589

1. Marsala.
2. This was the maximum firing range of a seashore cannon.
3. Tibet.
4. Dorothy Dix.
5. The 10,000 metres.
6. Diana Rigg.
7. Shocking pink.
8. Clementine's in the song *Oh, My Darling Clementine.*
9. One complete revolution of the Earth around the Sun.

122

1. How many squares are there along each side of *The Times* crossword?
2. Which general addressed his troops in the natural hollow of Cheesefoot Head, near Winchester?
3. Which Berkshire school did Prince Charles attend?
4. Which alphabet has 31 letters?
5. Where can a jockey win the Ritz Club Trophy?
6. Who presented the TV show *Blankety Blank* prior to Les Dawson?
7. What was the actor Samuel Joel Mostel nicknamed, because of his low marks at school?
8. Who was the only Osmond besides Donny to have a solo British number one?
9. What sort of snake do Indian snake charmers usually charm?

356

1. Which garment in English is called after its inventor, but in French is a 'justaucorps'?
2. What happened to US President William Henry Harrison at his inauguration?
3. Which river is the southern boundary between Devon and Cornwall?
4. Which author was born when Halley's Comet came in 1835, and died when it returned in 1910?
5. Which sport uses the terms 'Dundee shuffle' and 'Canadian'?
6. Who is Jimmy Logan's singer sister?
7. During World War II, which country used extra-small stamps called 'bantams' to save paper?
8. Who has said he will never make another album as good as *Highway 61 Revisited*?
9. What sort of creature is a 'Murray grey' in Australia?

590

1. Who kills his wife, his baby and his doctor and has never been executed?
2. What were 'darbies'?
3. Which part of London, once a popular spa, was the home of Keats, Constable and Galsworthy?
4. Who wrote *Ross : Story of a Shared Life*?
5. What is the minimum weight of the baton in a relay race?
6. What was London's first cabaret theatre club called?
7. Robert Graves was an Oxford Professor – of what?
8. Who is the most successful Welsh singer ever in terms of album sales?
9. Which animal appears on the flag of Tanzania?

122

1. Fifteen.
2. Eisenhower, before D-Day.
3. Cheam.
4. The Cyrillic, or Russian alphabet.
5. At Royal Ascot, for riding the most winners.
6. Terry Wogan.
7. 'Zero.'
8. Little Jimmy, with *Long-Haired Lover from Liverpool.*
9. The cobra.

356

1. A leotard.
2. It rained, he caught cold and died of pneumonia shortly afterwards.
3. The Tamar.
4. Mark Twain.
5. Horse racing. They are terms for multiple bets.
6. Annie Ross.
7. South Africa.
8. Bob Dylan.
9. A cow – it is a breed of cattle.

590

1. Mr Punch.
2. Handcuffs, in slang.
3. Hampstead.
4. Norris McWhirter.
5. 50 grams, or $1\frac{3}{4}$ ounces.
6. The Cave of the Golden Calf. It was opened in 1913.
7. Poetry.
8. Tom Jones.
9. The giraffe.

123

1. Where do you place the right palm in a salaam?
2. What was permitted on the roads in Bermuda only from 1946?
3. What is Poland's parliament called?
4. Who wrote *The Woodlanders*?
5. Which colour on an archery target is worth the most points?
6. T.H. White's *The Once and Future King* was the basis for which 1967 film?
7. Which US President lost the sight of one eye as the result of a friendly boxing match?
8. Which country singer has made LPs at two Californian prisons?
9. What percentage of Britain is given over to trees?

357

1. For what do the letters EPNS stand?
2. In which country did the signs of the zodiac originate some 5,000 years ago?
3. The Xingu National Park is in which country?
4. Who described a cynic thus: 'A man who knows the price of everything and the value of nothing'?
5. In which country was soccer's 1982 World Cup held?
6. *Heart of Darkness* by Joseph Conrad was the basis for which 1979 film?
7. Name Fred Astaire's dancing sister.
8. What is the great tenor, Signor Pavarotti's first name?
9. What is a FEFA?

591

1. Which common word both begins and ends with 'und'?
2. Who made a famous ride in the USA on 18 April, 1775?
3. To the nearest hundred, how many islands form the Bahamas?
4. 'Nothing but cabbage with a college education.' What was Mark Twain describing?
5. Where is the Test Match ground Edgbaston?
6. Which classic 1954 film concludes with the line, 'Hello, everybody, this is Mrs Norman Maine'?
7. Who was Max Fleischer's best-known creation?
8. Name Britain's principal opera house.
9. Which nails on the hand grow the slowest?

123

1. On the forehead.
2. The motor car.
3. Seym.
4. Thomas Hardy.
5. Yellow, or gold.
6. *Camelot*.
7. Theodore Roosevelt.
8. Johnny Cash.
9. About 7 per cent.

357

1. Electro-plated nickel silver.
2. In Mesopotamia.
3. In Brazil.
4. Oscar Wilde.
5. In Spain.
6. *Apocalypse Now*.
7. Adele Astaire.
8. Luciano.
9. A Future European Fighter Aircraft.

591

1. Underground.
2. Paul Revere.
3. 700.
4. The cauliflower.
5. In Birmingham.
6. *A Star is Born*.
7. Popeye.
8. Covent Garden.
9. The thumb nail – if right-handed, the left thumb, and vice-versa.

124

1. What name is given to the loading line of a ship?
2. The Treaty of Ghent terminated a war in which year?
3. Where was it announced on the air, 'Vendors of newspapers, chewing-gum etc. are banned from the airport. Gunmen are also banned from the airport'?
4. 'I lift my lamp beside the golden door' is inscribed on which statue?
5. Which game, resembling baseball, uses a larger ball and a smaller pitch?
6. Who played Barbara Hunter in TV's *Crossroads*?
7. Scenes from which city, other than Venice, figure prominently in Canaletto's paintings?
8. In which opera is a silver rose central to the plot?
9. Why do planes fly at high altitudes?

358

1. What is the minimum number of MPs that must take part in a division in the House of Commons?
2. How many silver coins formed the coffin of the Queen of Madagascar, who was buried in 1878?
3. Which international airport is identified by the letters LHR?
4. For how long were the Israelites in the wilderness, in the Bible?
5. How many throwing events are there in a decathlon?
6. Which actor starred in the 1967 film *Two for the Road*?
7. What did William Baffin discover?
8. How many records accompany the Bible and Shakespeare?
9. How do giraffes show affection to each other?

592

1. What is the final stage of passing an Act of Parliament?
2. Over 20 per cent of the population of which country was killed during World War II?
3. King Arthur's tomb is in which town?
4. Who wrote, 'That seems to be the crutch of the matter'?
5. What do the winners of the Indianapolis 500 traditionally drink to celebrate?
6. Which of the Two Ronnies is not incarcerated in Slade Prison?
7. Name the painter brother of William Butler Yeats.
8. Who was the lead singer on the Beatles record *This Boy*?
9. For what does VHF stand?

124

1. The Plimsoll line.
2. 1812.
3. In Beirut, by Beirut Radio – they were obviously cracking down on terrorism.
4. The Statue of Liberty.
5. Softball.
6. Sue Lloyd.
7. London.
8. *Der Rosenkavalier* by Richard Strauss.
9. They use less fuel that way.

358

1. Forty.
2. 30,000.
3. London Heathrow.
4. For forty years.
5. Three. (Shot, discus, and javelin.)
6. Albert Finney.
7. Baffin Island.
8. Eight – on *Desert Island Discs*.
9. By necking – rubbing their necks together.

592

1. The Royal Assent.
2. Poland.
3. In Glastonbury.
4. John Lennon, in *In His Own Write*.
5. Milk.
6. Ronnie Corbett. (The other Ronnie is in prison in the series *Porridge*.)
7. Jack Yeats.
8. Ringo Starr.
9. Very High Frequency.

125

1. What is the missing word – 'Bigamy is having one wife too many. ______, in certain instances, is the same thing'?
2. With which army did the Gurkhas fight in both World Wars?
3. The crew of which ship settled in the Pitcairn Islands?
4. Who wrote, 'A thing of beauty is a joy forever'?
5. At what did Anne Moore excel?
6. Name Barney Rubble's wife.
7. Who were the members of the first Triumvirate?
8. Who bought the Presidential yacht *Potomac*?
9. What is the colour of serum in human blood?

359

1. Which calendar began on 7 October, 3761BC?
2. In 1973, how much did a standard large loaf of bread cost?
3. By what name is Lusitania now known?
4. Whose dying words in Shakespeare's *Romeo and Juliet* were 'A plague o' both your houses'?
5. Four Canon League soccer clubs are called 'Rovers'. Name three.
6. Who played the monster in the original film of *Frankenstein*?
7. Which snooker player carried the Olympic torch in 1956?
8. *I Don't Know How to Love Him* comes from which musical?
9. Although it was not discovered till much later, Percival Lovell predicted the existence of which planet?

593

1. Nostrums are what sort of remedies?
2. Who first navigated the North-West Passage?
3. For what type of displays is Biggin Hill noted?
4. Who wrote, 'Marriage is the alliance of two people, of whom one never remembers birthdays and the other never forgets them'?
5. Who is soccer's Manager of the Year for 1985?
6. Which film is subtitled, *And His Adventures on Earth*?
7. How many men flew the Atlantic before Charles Lindbergh?
8. Which orchestral player normally sits nearest to the conductor?
9. Who showed that mass and energy are equivalent, by the formula $E = mc^2$?

125

1. Monogamy.
2. The British Army.
3. HMS *Bounty.*
4. John Keats.
5. Showjumping.
6. Betty Rubble.
7. Julius Caesar, Pompey and Crassus.
8. Elvis Presley.
9. Yellow.

359

1. The Jewish Calendar.
2. 11p.
3. Portugal.
4. Mercutio's.
5. Blackburn Rovers, Bristol Rovers, Doncaster Rovers and Tranmere Rovers.
6. Boris Karloff.
7. Eddie Charlton.
8. *Jesus Christ, Superstar.*
9. Pluto.

593

1. Patent.
2. Roald Amundsen.
3. Air displays.
4. Ogden Nash.
5. Howard Kendall of Everton.
6. *E.T. The Extra-Terrestrial.*
7. 66. He was the first to do it *solo.*
8. The Leader, or first violin.
9. Einstein.

126

1. Who, in the 17th century said 'Wedlock is a padlock'?
2. Which process was pioneered by Johann Gutenberg?
3. Whose seat is Inverary Castle?
4. Who wrote *The Wreck of the Deutschland*?
5. For which country do the All Blacks play Rugby?
6. Which Peter Sellers film was involved in a High Court case in 1985?
7. Name one of Emmeline Pankhurst's two suffragette daughters.
8. Which first award did Con Conrad's song *The Continental* win?
9. Bombay Duck is, generally, which fish, dried and salted?

360

1. What does 'ibid' mean?
2. What made the Pilgrim Fathers leave England?
3. In which city is Cabot's Tower?
4. Who wrote, 'By all means marry; if you get a good wife, you'll become happy; if you get a bad one you'll become a philosopher'?
5. Name boxer Rahamon Ali's more famous brother.
6. Who hosted *Opportunity Knocks* from 1956–77?
7. From which country did Mata Hari originate?
8. Where does 'a body meet a body'?
9. What do friable substances do easily?

594

1. What time of the day is palindromic?
2. How many of Catherine de Medici's sons became Kings of France?
3. In which British city is the Mayflower Stone?
4. Who wrote, 'Marriage is a ghastly public confession of a strictly private intention'?
5. Buddy and Max were the first names of which boxing brothers?
6. If his T-shirt is to be believed, what is the Hofmeister Bear's name?
7. Who invented the L-Game?
8. Who wrote the six Sun Quartets?
9. How many square metres are there in a hectare?

126

1. John Ray.
2. Printing.
3. The Duke of Argyll's.
4. Gerard Manley Hopkins.
5. For New Zealand.
6. *The Trail of the Pink Panther*.
7. Christabel. Sylvia.
8. The first Oscar for the *Best Film Song of the Year*.
9. Bummalo.

360

1. 'In the same place.'
2. Religious persecution.
3. In Bristol.
4. Socrates.
5. Muhammad Ali.
6. Hughie Green.
7. From Holland.
8. *Comin' Through the Rye*.
9. They crumble.

594

1. Noon.
2. Three.
3. In Plymouth.
4. Ian Hay.
5. The Baer brothers.
6. George.
7. Edward de Bono.
8. Haydn.
9. 10,000.

127

1. Which department store once stood where Regent Street meets Piccadilly Circus?
2. How did Frederick, the Prince of Wales, son of George II, die?
3. Which desert is in Botswana?
4. Which great French novelist once played in goal for Algiers?
5. In which sport did graphics design student Joe Lydon make his name?
6. *Wired* is the story of which American comedian, now dead?
7. For what was Norman Parkinson famous in the 1960s?
8. Which member of a popular duo had a No. 1 hit on his own with *Careless Whisper*?
9. In which science is a rawinsonde used?

361

1. What are the ancient clapper bridges of the West Country made of?
2. US Admiral Rickover was called 'The Father of...' *what*?
3. From which port did both Captain Cook and Francis Chichester sail to go round the world?
4. In the Bible, who followed David as King of Israel?
5. Which British boxer lost world heavyweight title fights to both Muhammad Ali and Floyd Patterson?
6. In which TV series does Pavel Chekov feature?
7. What was Frank Pakenham known as, after he inherited his title?
8. The Herefordshire group *Silence* renamed themselves '*Mott the...*' *what*?
9. Who discovered the four brightest satellites of Jupiter?

595

1. Which airline has Boeing 737s called St Jarlath and St Fachtna?
2. Which US General, nicknamed 'Black Jack', has a missile named after him?
3. Where are remote country areas called 'backblocks'?
4. Who called her autobiography *Voices In My Ear*?
5. What do American golf commentators call a 'snowman'?
6. Who was 'The Man in Black'?
7. Which night-club, founded by Rupert Lycett Green, is named after the casino in *Goldfinger*?
8. *Pink Floyd*'s album *Piper at the gates of Dawn* was named after a chapter in which children's book?
9. Which tree is also called 'golden rain'?

127

1. Swan & Edgar.
2. As a result of a blow from a cricket ball.
3. The Kalahari.
4. Albert Camus.
5. Rugby League.
6. John Belushi.
7. Photography.
8. George Michael of *Wham*.
9. Meteorology, or weather studies.

361

1. Large slabs of stone.
2. The Atomic Submarine.
3. Plymouth.
4. Solomon.
5. Brian London.
6. In *Star Trek*.
7. Lord Longford.
8. *Hoople*.
9. Galileo Galilei.

595

1. Aer Lingus – they are Irish saints.
2. John J. Pershing.
3. In New Zealand.
4. Doris Stokes, the medium.
5. A score of 8 on a hole, because of the figure's shape.
6. Valentine Dyall.
7. Blades.
8. *The Wind in the Willows*.
9. The laburnum.

128

1. In a motor magazine, what does ICE mean?
2. Soviet Marshal Zhukov directed the final assault on *where*?
3. Which capital city stands on a European island called Zealand?
4. How many stations of the Cross are there?
5. In horse racing, what is 'acey deucey'?
6. Who made her first film for 15 years in *The Assam Garden* in 1985?
7. What do you call paintings done on still-wet plaster?
8. Which jazzman leads *The Feetwarmers*?
9. Which creature could you gralloch?

362

1. In Australia, what is a brumby?
2. Which General with the name of a former English county was commander of US forces in Vietnam?
3. What is the capital of Puerto Rico?
4. Which actor called his autobiography *Laughter in the Second Act*?
5. What happened to goalkeeper Bert Trautmann in the 1956 FA Cup Final?
6. Which event in April 1985 gave BBC TV its largest audience ever, after midnight?
7. Who painted *The Cook*, or *Woman Pouring Milk*, in Amsterdam's Rijksmuseum?
8. Who made an album called *Get Your Ya-Yas Out*?
9. If one angle of an isosceles triangle is 110 degrees, what are the other two angles?

596

1. What should you call an undivided double sirloin of beef?
2. What declaration did the Scots Barons send to Pope John XXII in 1320?
3. Which Canadian province is called after a daughter of Queen Victoria?
4. The murder of John Campbell of Glenure in 1752 inspired which novel?
5. In which city is Basin Reserve cricket ground?
6. At County General Hospital, Dr Zorba was the boss of which TV doctor?
7. Which jazz-singer created the words for *Flook*?
8. In which comic opera is Strephon the son of the heroine and the Lord Chancellor?
9. What do you get if you multiply volts by amperes?

128

1. In-Car Entertainment.
2. Berlin, in 1945.
3. Copenhagen.
4. Fourteen.
5. The practice of riding with one short stirrup and one long.
6. Deborah Kerr.
7. Frescos.
8. John Chilton.
9. A deer. It means 'to disembowel'.

362

1. A wild horse.
2. William C. Westmoreland.
3. San Juan.
4. Donald Sinden.
5. He broke his neck, but didn't realize it until afterwards.
6. The final of World Snooker, between Taylor and Davis.
7. Vermeer.
8. *The Rolling Stones*, in 1970.
9. 35 degrees each.

596

1. A baron of beef.
2. The Declaration of Arbroath.
3. Alberta.
4. *Kidnapped*, by Robert Louis Stevenson.
5. In Wellington, New Zealand.
6. Ben Casey.
7. George Melly.
8. *Iolanthe*.
9. Watts.

129

1. When is the Feast of St Stephen?
2. Which edict gave freedom to the Huguenots?
3. Which island has an area of 839,800 square miles?
4. Who wrote, 'It is easier to keep half a dozen lovers guessing than to keep one lover after he has stopped guessing'?
5. What was the mascot of the Los Angeles Olympics?
6. Jack Ryan created the doll Barbie – whose sixth husband was he?
7. Who was accompanied by Sir Joseph Banks on his voyages round the world?
8. Who composed the opera *Russlan and Ludmilla*?
9. How do the cheetah's claws differ from those of the other members of the cat family?

363

1. What were 'Oxford Bags'?
2. Which country was the first to use number plates on cars?
3. Of which country did Queen Margrethe become the first female sovereign for over 500 years?
4. Who wrote, 'Marriage is the only adventure open to the cowardly'?
5. Why is the *America's Cup* so called?
6. Which bird would you pick up if you fancied a chocolate-covered biscuit?
7. What game did William and Isaac Fields invent in 1892?
8. Who wrote both words and music to *Annie Get Your Gun*?
9. What type of creature is a water moccasin?

597

1. How many sides has an obelisk?
2. Who or what was killed by the first bomb dropped on Leningrad in World War II?
3. In which Scottish city was the old prison called *The Tolbooth*?
4. Which ex-*New York Daily News* sportswriter wrote the novel *The Snow Goose*?
5. In which game might you use a cleek?
6. Who plays Bob, the conductor in the film *On The Buses*?
7. Which PM used the phrase, 'You've never had it so good'?
8. What song title did *Frankie and Albert* become?
9. Which is the largest nerve in the human body?

129

1. 26 December.
2. The Edict of Nantes.
3. Greenland.
4. Helen Rowland.
5. Sam, the eagle.
6. Zsa Zsa Gabor's.
7. Captain Cook.
8. Glinka.
9. They cannot be retracted.

363

1. Loose flapping trousers. (Mostly worn in the 1920s.)
2. France.
3. Denmark.
4. Voltaire.
5. Because the first yacht to win the race was called *America*.
6. A Penguin – so say the TV adverts.
7. Ouija.
8. Irving Berlin.
9. A snake – it is another name for a cottonmouth.

597

1. Four.
2. The sole elephant in the zoo.
3. In Edinburgh.
4. Paul Gallico.
5. In golf.
6. Jack Grant.
7. Harold Macmillan.
8. *Frankie and Johnny*.
9. The sciatic nerve.

130

1. Why is the 'drawing room' so called?
2. What did the Dowager Empress Tz'u-Hsi of China order in 1900?
3. From which country do Lancia cars originate?
4. Whose fairy tales were originally reviewed as 'quite unsuitable for children'?
5. Who was the 1985 Football Writers' *Footballer of the Year*?
6. Which film told of Billy Hayes's experiences in a Turkish prison?
7. Which was the first postage stamp bearing Queen Victoria's portrait?
8. Whose dying words were, 'I shall hear in heaven'?
9. What was Dr Charles Towney the first to make in 1960?

364

1. What has been named *Thatcher's Ruin*?
2. When Queen Victoria first ascended the throne, how many pet dogs had she?
3. Before its Federation with Ethiopia, Eritrea was administered by which country?
4. Though turned to stone by Zeus, who continued to cry for her slain children?
5. Whom did England beat in the very first Test Match?
6. Who had his first starring film role in 1933 as the Invisible Man?
7. Thomas Bolsover first used which process, in 1742, in Sheffield?
8. What do hot cross buns cost?
9. How much water is there on the moon?

598

1. What feline device did Percy Shaw invent in 1933?
2. What did the words, 'Not a penny off the pay, not a minute on the day' trigger off?
3. In which county are the Quantocks?
4. Who first wrote, 'It's all Greek to me'?
5. Which national team play their Rugby Union Internationals at Murrayfield?
6. Which actress was nicknamed 'Queen of the Swashbucklers'?
7. Which painter was nicknamed 'le douanier'?
8. Which musical (later a film) is set in Catfish Row?
9. Which star constellation contains Betelgeuse and Rigel?

130

1. The word is a corruption of 'withdrawing room' – to which the ladies retired while the men passed the port.
2. That all foreigners should be killed.
3. Italy.
4. Hans Christian Andersen's
5. Neville Southall.
6. *Midnight Express.*
7. The Penny Black.
8. Beethoven's.
9. A laser.

364

1. A new Somerset cider.
2. Eighty.
3. Great Britain.
4. Niobe.
5. The Australians.
6. Claude Rains.
7. Silver plating.
8. 'One a penny, two a penny . . .'
9. None.

598

1. 'Cat's eyes', for use on the roads.
2. The General Strike of 1926. (They were said by A. J. Coot, Secretary of the Union of Miners.)
3. In Somerset.
4. Shakespeare. (In *Julius Caesar*.)
5. Scotland.
6. Maureen O'Hara.
7. Henri Rousseau, because he was a minor civil servant, before taking up painting.
8. *Porgy and Bess.*
9. Orion.

131

1. Who produce the Scimitar cars?
2. What animal did Canada adopt as an official emblem in 1851?
3. In which country might you alight at a station called Hell?
4. In *War and Peace*, who married Natasha?
5. In competitive gymnastics, how does the men's vault differ from the ladies'?
6. In which film does Jack Lemmon say, 'That's the way it crumbles, cookie-wise'?
7. In what subject did H. G. Wells graduate?
8. Who leads the Sharks in *West Side Story*?
9. Which acid is the basis of vinegar?

365

1. As in 'sword and buckler' what is a buckler?
2. The Old World was all the parts of the world known to Europeans before the discovery of which continent?
3. Which country's national emblem is a rose?
4. What was Abel's occupation?
5. For what other sport is Northampton Town's soccer ground used?
6. What are ridden on the 'Wall of Death'?
7. How many years altogether did the Marquis de Sade spend in prison for sexual offences?
8. What is Hugh Maskela's instrument?
9. Which three animals are associated with the stock market?

599

1. For what would you use a 'half-hunter'?
2. In 1955, Ray Kroc founded which fast food chain?
3. On which estuary does Hull lie?
4. Which ex-US Vice President wrote *The Canfield Decision*?
5. What is the driver's seat in a racing car known as?
6. Mae West and W. C. Fields played together once, in which 1940 film?
7. When Carolyn Farrell was elected as mayor of a town in Iowa, USA, in 1980, what 'first' did she establish?
8. Who was known as Mr Blackpool?
9. Which bird is nicknamed the *Mollymawk*?

131

1. Reliant.
2. The beaver.
3. In Norway.
4. Pierre.
5. The horse is longways on for men and crossways for women.
6. *The Apartment.*
7. Zoology.
8. Bernardo.
9. Acetic.

365

1. A shield.
2. America.
3. England's.
4. He was a shepherd.
5. Cricket. (First-class cricket matches are played there.)
6. Motorbikes.
7. 27 years.
8. The trumpet.
9. Bulls, bears and stags.

599

1. Telling the time – it is a pocket watch.
2. McDonald's.
3. The Humber estuary.
4. Spiro T. Agnew.
5. The cockpit.
6. *My Little Chickadee.*
7. She became the first nun to become mayor of a US town.
8. Reginald Dixon, the organist.
9. The albatross.

Q

132

1. *Bib-Label Lighthearted Lemon-Lime Soda* was its name when this drink first appeared. By what name would we now recognise it?
2. What was 'The King's Time'?
3. Where is Zion National Park?
4. How many volumes were there in the first Encyclopaedia Britannica?
5. Where did the most surprising outbreak of football hooliganism break out on Sunday, 19 May, 1985?
6. With which entertainer do you associate, 'Can you hear me, mother?'?
7. Why is Sungdare Sherpa famous?
8. For every seven white notes on a piano, how many black notes are there?
9. A Dandie Dinmont belongs to which class of dog?

366

1. At what age must a car have its first MOT, in the UK?
2. Who planted the first vineyards in Britain?
3. What cost £46,000 to erect in London's Trafalgar Square?
4. How many of Aeschylus' plays have survived to this day?
5. Which soccer team plays home matches at Roker Park?
6. Which was the first film made in colour to win the *Best Picture* Oscar?
7. In which British paper did the first crossword puzzle appear, in 1924?
8. How did *ABBA* derive their name?
9. A tetrahedron possesses how many faces?

600

1. Which professionals are susceptible to the 'bends'?
2. In which year were 'O' and 'A' Levels first sat?
3. Which profession has produced the most US Presidents?
4. Which dictator wrote the novel *The Cardinal's Mistress*?
5. In which sport is the MacRobertson International Shield awarded?
6. Who starred in *Modern Times*, in 1936?
7. Bill 'Bojangles' Robinson, the dancer, once set a world record for running. How?
8. Both the Beatles and the Rolling Stones featured an Indian instrument on some of their records. Which?
9. What is 8 × 0 × 15?

132

1. 7-UP.
2. A watch in a leather pouch, set by the Post Office in London for the Dublin Post Office and sent by the Irish Mail.
3. In Utah, USA.
4. Three.
5. Outside Peking's *Workers' Stadium* in China.
6. Sandy Powell.
7. He was the first man to climb Mount Everest four times.
8. Five.
9. The terrier class.

366

1. Three years.
2. The Romans.
3. Nelson's Column.
4. Seven.
5. Sunderland.
6. *Gone With The Wind*, made in 1939.
7. The *Sunday Express*.
8. From the initials of the names of the four members.
9. Four.

600

1. Deep sea divers.
2. In 1950.
3. The legal profession.
4. Benito Mussolini.
5. Croquet.
6. Charlie Chaplin.
7. Backwards.
8. The sitar.
9. 0.

133

1. What do the French call a 'cul-de-sac'?
2. Up to 1970 in France, what names were parents allowed to give their children?
3. In which city is the Cathedral of Notre Dame?
4. Which novel by Jacqueline Susann begins, 'The temperature hit ninety degrees the day she arrived'?
5. In which Scottish city is St Johnstone FC based?
6. With whom is the catchphrase 'Hello my darlings' associated?
7. Friedrich Froebel founded what type of school?
8. Which group started the Brother Record recording label?
9. Who first designed a helicopter?

367

1. When is St David's day?
2. How many people died in the worldwide influenza epidemic that followed World War I?
3. Aircraft from Canada are marked with which letter?
4. In 1842, which great American author was appointed as ambassador to Spain?
5. What is known as *Hell's Half-Acre* to golfers?
6. Who starred in the 1926 film *The General*?
7. How many double dominoes are there in a standard set?
8. Which note is four times the length of a crotchet?
9. From what is birds' nest soup made?

601

1. For what do the 3M company's three 'M's stand?
2. Which Chinese revolution occurred in the mid 1960s?
3. Which Scottish city gave its name to one of Hong Kong island's ports?
4. Who wrote *The Descent of Man*?
5. 'c' and 'b' in cricket stand for *what*?
6. The 1951 film *Man of Bronze* was about which American athlete, for many years deprived of his Olympic medal?
7. Which gangster was nicknamed 'Legs'?
8. The *Rolling Stones* had a hit with a Bobby Troup song about which famous highway?
9. Which animal is represented on the Lacoste logo?

133

1. 'Sans-issue'.
2. Only those kept on the list of the Ministry of the Interior.
3. Paris.
4. *Valley of the Dolls.*
5. In Perth.
6. Charlie Drake.
7. Kindergartens.
8. *The Beach Boys.*
9. Leonardo da Vinci.

367

1. 1 March.
2. Over 20 million – more than the number that were killed in the war.
3. The letter C.
4. Washington Irving.
5. The world's largest bunker. (It is in the USA.)
6. Buster Keaton.
7. Seven.
8. A semi-breve.
9. Birds' nests.

601

1. Minnesota Mining and Manufacturing.
2. The Cultural Revolution.
3. Aberdeen.
4. Charles Darwin.
5. Caught and bowled.
6. Jim Thorpe.
7. John Diamond.
8. *Route 66.*
9. The alligator.

134

1. What are Archbishops and Bishops in the House of Lords collectively called?
2. When did the Boston Tea Party take place?
3. For whom was Pennsylvania originally created?
4. 'I must be cruel only to be kind' originates where?
5. Meadowbank Stadium is in which city?
6. Which 'rake' starred in the film *The Boyfriend*?
7. Which Empress laid down many of the Austrian wine laws, several of which are still applicable today?
8. Whose first hit record was *Wuthering Heights*?
9. Name the first space shuttle that orbited the earth.

368

1. Which American President created the dish Chicken à la King?
2. During World War I, for what were 'Q'-ships used?
3. Quezon City was the capital of which country, until 1976?
4. In the Bible, whose wife did David marry?
5. Which two games are played at the All England Club at Wimbledon?
6. Which D.H. Lawrence-based 1969 film starred Glenda Jackson and Oliver Reed?
7. Who was the first General Secretary of the United Nations?
8. Which bell has the lowest note among church bells?
9. Hipparchus the Greek astronomer was the first to use which branch of mathematics?

602

1. What are SERPS?
2. What pension did Charles II give to Colonel Blood for attempting to steal the Crown Jewels?
3. Which ocean separates Europe from the USA?
4. Who described a mugwump as 'A fellow with his mug on one side of the fence and his wump on the other'?
5. In which game might you 'bowl a maiden over'?
6. Who has played Phil Archer on radio for over 30 years?
7. Who designed 'Gorgeous Gussy' Moran's frilly knickers?
8. Which dance was once outlawed in French night clubs?
9. What are measured in angstroms?

134

1. Lords Spiritual.
2. In 1773.
3. Persecuted Quakers.
4. In Shakespeare's *Hamlet*.
5. In Edinburgh.
6. Twiggy.
7. Empress Maria Theresa.
8. Kate Bush's.
9. Columbia.

368

1. Thomas Jefferson.
2. As decoys for German submarines.
3. The Philippines.
4. Uriah's. (Bathsheba.)
5. Tennis and croquet.
6. *Women in Love*.
7. Trygve Lie, of Norway.
8. The tenor.
9. Trigonometry.

602

1. State earnings-related pensions.
2. £300 p.a.
3. The Atlantic.
4. Harold Willis Dodds.
5. In cricket.
6. Norman Painting.
7. Teddy Tinling.
8. The can-can.
9. Wavelengths.

135

1. Who usually represents the Monster Raving Loony Party in by-elections?
2. Which notorious Colonel tried to kidnap the Lord-Lieutenant from Dublin Castle in 1663?
3. What was the country of Jordan called before 1946?
4. Which language did James Joyce learn, just to read some plays?
5. In which sport could you be given a mulligan?
6. What put Hans and Lotte Hass on TV in the 1960s?
7. Which mastermind drafted Macmillan's 'Wind of Change' speech about Africa?
8. Janáček wrote an opera about animals called *The Cunning Little ... what*?
9. A collection of what creatures is called a 'bed'?

369

1. In Scotland, what are fernitickles?
2. Who was the last Prime Minister called Henry?
3. After Paris, what is the largest French-speaking city?
4. Whose first book was *Call For The Dead* in 1961?
5. The first Test cricket ground in England was the Oval. What was the second?
6. Which *East Enders* scriptwriter has the same name as a 1921 book of poems by W.B. Yeats?
7. Which famous British playwright was fined at the age of 19 for refusing to be conscripted into the Army?
8. From which country do the instrumental group *Tangerine Dream* come?
9. What is a collection of parrots called? It suggests there are only two of them.

603

1. What is the name given to the first day of Holy Week?
2. What was the occupation of Elbridge Gerry?
3. Which Irish county was once called King's County?
4. In which book by Len Deighton did Harry Palmer appear?
5. What happens after 85 overs in a Test match in cricket?
6. In which film did Lotte Lenya play the villainous Rosa Klebb?
7. Which Duke is the hereditary Grand Falconer of England?
8. Which duo have spent almost as many weeks in the album charts as the Beatles?
9. A collection of what is called a rabble?

135

1. Screaming Lord Sutch.
2. Thomas Blood, who later had a go at the Crown Jewels.
3. Transjordan.
4. Norwegian, to read Ibsen.
5. Golf – it is a free shot in a friendly game.
6. They were famous for underwater filming.
7. Sir David Hunt.
8. *Vixen.*
9. Oysters.

369

1. Freckles.
2. Herbert Henry Asquith.
3. Montreal.
4. John Le Carré's.
5. Old Trafford, Manchester.
6. Michael Robartes.
7. Harold Pinter.
8. West Germany.
9. A company.

603

1. Palm Sunday.
2. He was a politician. (He is remembered in the word 'gerrymandering'.)
3. Offaly.
4. None of them – the hero had no name, but was called Harry Palmer in the films.
5. A new ball can be used.
6. *From Russia With Love.*
7. The Duke of St Albans.
8. Simon and Garfunkel.
9. Rats.

136

1. Maria Montessori introduced modern methods to which profession?
2. What was the sign for gladiators' lives to be spared?
3. Where is the NASA Space Centre?
4. Who wrote, 'It is love that is sacred. Marriage and love have nothing in common. We marry only once but we may love twenty times. Marriage is law and love is instinct'?
5. Who were the first winners of soccer's Rous Cup, in 1985?
6. Who wrote the play *The Cocktail Party*?
7. Which poet was sailing his boat *Ariel* when he drowned, in 1822?
8. By what name is Beethoven's sixth symphony known?
9. The binary number system uses which two numbers?

370

1. For what do the letters IDD stand, in relation to telephones?
2. The military coup in Portugal in 1974 was termed *what*?
3. In America, what is the ground floor of a building called?
4. From which illness did Dostoevsky's *The Idiot* suffer?
5. Since the end of World War I, which is the only soccer team never to have left the English First Division?
6. What is the Flintstones' pet dinosaur called?
7. Sir Edmund Hillary and Sir Vivian Fuchs first crossed which continent overland?
8. Who had a hit with the *Ying Tong Song*?
9. Hyracotherium was an early form of which modern animal?

604

1. How many stars are visible to the naked eye?
2. In which year was Idi Amin of Uganda deposed?
3. What language do Austrians speak?
4. Who wrote, 'The music at a marriage procession always reminds me of the music of soldiers marching to battle'?
5. What compete in the Fastnet race?
6. Who is Virginia McKenna's husband?
7. What great painter and inventor did King François I employ?
8. Who wrote the march *Crown Imperial* for the coronation of George VI?
9. Which breed of dog hunts hares?

136

1. Teaching.
2. Thumbs-up
3. In Houston, Texas.
4. Guy de Maupassant.
5. Scotland.
6. T.S. Eliot.
7. Percy Bysshe Shelley.
8. The Pastoral.
9. 0 and 1.

370

1. International Direct Dialling.
2. The Revolution of Flowers.
3. The first floor.
4. Epilepsy.
5. Arsenal.
6. Dino.
7. Antarctica.
8. The Goons.
9. The horse.

604

1. 5776
2. In 1979.
3. German.
4. Heinrich Heine.
5. Yachts.
6. Bill Travers.
7. Leonardo da Vinci.
8. William Walton.
9. The beagle or greyhound.

137

1. What is a 'burqa'?
2. Where was Joan of Arc burned at the stake?
3. In which street does the Prime Minister live?
4. How did Samuel Pepys conclude his daily diary?
5. Racing which vehicles has Renato Molinari been World Champion?
6. Who was the sixth Dr Who?
7. Cedric Gibbons, the designer of the Oscar statuette, won it himself how many times?
8. Who starred as the cornet player 'Red' Nichols in the 1959 film *The Five Pennies*?
9. What does the average person's skin weigh?

371

1. Which country is eaten for Christmas dinner?
2. How old was Henry V when he fought at the Battle of Shrewsbury in 1403?
3. In which English county is Boston?
4. To which head of the CIA did Ian Fleming dedicate *The Spy Who Loved Me*?
5. How many runs are awarded to the batting side if a fielder stops the ball with his hat or cap?
6. What was Sarah Bernhardt's eccentric bed?
7. Of what does 70% of house dust usually consist?
8. How many mourners accompanied Mozart to his pauper's grave?
9. What is the common name of NaCl?

605

1. What do Italians call 'hors d'oeuvre'?
2. How was Queen Victoria related to Wilhelm II of Germany?
3. From where do the drinks ouzo and retsina originate?
4. Which three place names was Eliza Doolittle taught to pronounce correctly?
5. Which baseball fielding position is behind home plate?
6. Who played Hawk in the film *Hawk the Slayer*?
7. By what repeated name was Bingo previously called?
8. *Is There Something I Should Know* was which group's first No. 1 hit?
9. Which form of cancer was named after the pathologist who isolated it in 1832?

137

1. An overall body garment for women, with slits for the eyes.
2. At Rouen.
3. Downing Street.
4. 'And so to bed.'
5. Power boats.
6. Colin Baker.
7. Eleven times.
8. Danny Kaye.
9. About six pounds.

371

1. Turkey.
2. Fifteen.
3. Lincolnshire.
4. Allen Dulles.
5. Five. (Well, it's not quite cricket!)
6. A coffin.
7. Flakes of human skin.
8. One.
9. Salt.

605

1. Antipasti.
2. She was his grandmother.
3. Greece.
4. Hertford, Hereford and Hampshire.
5. Catcher.
6. John Terry.
7. Housey Housey.
8. *Duran Duran*'s.
9. Hodgkin's Disease.

138

1. Which anniversary of Alcoholics Anonymous was celebrated in 1985?
2. Which PM did Dimitri Tsafendas murder in 1966?
3. Where is the famous Blue Grotto?
4. Who wrote the poem *The Rape of the Lock*?
5. What makes the puissance event in show jumping spectacular?
6. They now call it *Ponderosa* on US TV, but in Britain we still see the programmes under the original name. What is it?
7. Yoshimasa Waha was the first man to do *what*?
8. Which great song composer wrote Dwight D. Eisenhower's campaign song, *I Like Ike*?
9. Which crab does not have its own homegrown shell?

372

1. On which wedding anniversary does one give lace?
2. In which year did British Summer Time begin?
3. Which country has 'Bullet' trains?
4. Who was the doubter among the apostles?
5. What is Jahangir Khan's game?
6. In 1971, which actor won an Oscar for playing two people in one film – *Cat Ballou*?
7. Approximately how many letters does Marjorie Proops receive per annum?
8. Paul McCartney originally gave the name *Scrambled Eggs* to which Beatles hit?
9. How thick is the Earth's atmosphere?

606

1. What does 'Fitz' mean, in 'Fitzherbert' and the like?
2. Name either of the American Presidents who died on 4 July, 1826.
3. Which famous fictional detective lives in St Mary Mead?
4. Which constellation in the sky is named after the giant hunter of Greek mythology?
5. Who said that the reason he was chosen to advertise after-shave was that 'no one can call me poofy'?
6. Which West End play was first staged on 25 November, 1952?
7. Who flew around the world in *Winnie May*?
8. Which animal, in the song, is connected with 'Doh'?
9. Emperor, Rockhopper and Jackass are all types of *what*?

138

1. Its fiftieth.
2. Dr Verwoerd of South Africa.
3. In Capri.
4. Alexander Pope.
5. The height of the fences.
6. *Bonanza.*
7. Ski down the Matterhorn.
8. Irving Berlin.
9. The hermit crab.

372

1. The thirteenth.
2. In 1925.
3. Japan.
4. Thomas.
5. Squash.
6. Lee Marvin.
7. 30,000.
8. *Yesterday.*
9. About 37½ miles.

606

1. 'Son of'.
2. John Adams. Thomas Jefferson.
3. Miss Jane Marple.
4. Orion.
5. Henry Cooper.
6. *The Mousetrap.*
7. Wiley Post.
8. 'A deer, a female deer.'
9. Penguin.

139

1. Which Nobel Prize does Norway award?
2. Against whom did Admiral Duncan fight the Battle of Camperdown in 1797?
3. Which city was Sutona in the Domesday Book, and still has an area called Sutton?
4. In Ian Fleming's book, at which game does Goldfinger cheat by using a radio?
5. What are Acorn and Mother Goose?
6. Which film star has been nicknamed 'the Hockey Stick'?
7. Who was 'Rawhide' during his election campaign?
8. What did Peter Goldmark invent after listening to classical music at a party?
9. What is the heaviest flying bird of prey?

373

1. How many letters were *not* used as suffixes on car registration plates?
2. Whose chief assistant was Wynkyn de Worde?
3. Which city's symbol is the winged lion of St Mark?
4. Which poet helped write a mystery story called *The Death of the King's Canary*?
5. In athletics, races over more than what distance begin from a curved starting-line?
6. Who wrote the play *The Little Foxes*?
7. Which famous comedian came third in a competition to find the person who most looked like him?
8. In Japanese music, what is a wagon?
9. What is the most malleable metal?

607

1. How many sixpences were there in a guinea?
2. The Petty Bag Office was part of what?
3. Which African capital city has a name which means 'elephant's trunk' in Arabic?
4. In which Shakespeare play does a statue apparently come to life?
5. Kenya has won the Rahim Jivraj Cup most often – in which sport?
6. *Three's Company* was the US title for which British TV comedy about flat-sharing?
7. William, Patrick, Jon, Tom, Peter and Colin have all been *who*?
8. To which pop group did Lol Creme and Kevin Godley formerly belong?
9. Approximately how fast can a racehorse race?

139

1. The Peace Prize.
2. The Dutch.
3. Plymouth.
4. Canasta.
5. Two races of the fillies' Triple Crown in the USA.
6. Julie Andrews.
7. Ronald Reagan – his Secret Service code name.
8. The long-playing record.
9. The condor.

373

1. Five – I, O, Q, U and Z.
2. The printer William Caxton's.
3. Venice's.
4. Dylan Thomas.
5. Over 800 metres.
6. Lillian Hellman.
7. Charlie Chaplin.
8. A six-foot zither with silk strings.
9. Gold.

607

1. 42.
2. The Court of Chancery, until it was abolished in 1889.
3. Khartoum.
4. In *The Winter's Tale*.
5. In hockey.
6. *Man About The House*.
7. *Doctor Who*.
8. *10 c.c.*
9. About 35 m.p.h.

140

1. Locomotive 4472 is better known by what name?
2. Tamerlane assumed what name in the fourteenth century?
3. In which English county is the world's narrowest street, called *Squeeze-Belly Alley*?
4. In *Tarka the Otter*, what type of creature is Old Nog?
5. In which town are the international-standard Derby Swimming Baths?
6. With whom was the phrase 'Before your very eyes' associated?
7. Who founded London's first birth-control clinic, in 1921?
8. As what was Karl Bohm famous?
9. How much milk does an average cow produce in an average year?

374

1. For how long is the normal British passport valid?
2. Who first claimed Australia for Britain in 1770?
3. Which country did Mark Twain describe as 'Mother of history, grandmother of legend, and great-grandmother of tradition'?
4. Which American magazine once printed a nine-page face-to-face interview with the Devil?
5. Which two colours can official table-tennis balls be?
6. What is the concluding line of the *Merry Melodies* cartoon series?
7. Who succeeded William Burns as chief of the FBI?
8. Who composed the symphony known as *The Clock*?
9. Which rays produce a sun tan?

608

1. On which date does the new car registration year begin in the UK?
2. The Romans built forts at towns whose names end with *what*?
3. Logan International Airport serves which American city?
4. Of whom did Shakespeare write, 'Age cannot wither her, nor custom stale her infinite variety'?
5. In which country does Benfica play home matches?
6. In which TV series does Fozzie Bear feature?
7. Poet John Snow was perhaps better known for which activity?
8. *Pipes of Peace* was whose first solo No. 1 hit?
9. What is a young zebra called?

140

1. The *Flying Scotsman*.
2. Great Khan.
3. In Cornwall.
4. A heron.
5. In Blackpool
6. Arthur Askey.
7. Marie Stopes.
8. A conductor.
9. 1,000 gallons.

374

1. Ten years.
2. Captain James Cook.
3. India.
4. *Life*.
5. White or yellow.
6. 'That's all, folks!'
7. J. Edgar Hoover.
8. Haydn.
9. Ultraviolet rays.

608

1. 1 August.
2. -caster, -cester, or -chester.
3. Boston, Massachussets.
4. Cleopatra.
5. Portugal.
6. *The Muppets*.
7. Cricket.
8. Paul McCartney's.
9. A colt.

141

1. With whose sword was Sir Francis Chichester knighted?
2. Who formed the Royal Ballet Company in France?
3. How much did the US pay Spain for the Philippines in 1898?
4. In which of Shakespeare's plays is the gathering of the plant samphire referred to as a 'dreadful trade'?
5. Which British athlete became World Superstar Champion?
6. Who played the part of swimmer Annette Kellerman in the film *Million-Dollar Mermaid*?
7. Who painted *Cypresses with a Star*?
8. Who was Derek, of *Derek and the Dominoes* fame?
9. For what were Shetland ponies mainly used in the nineteenth century?

375

1. Which washing machine used to be advertised by a large frog, complete with voice-over by Alan Bennett?
2. Of which country was Patrice MacMahon President in the late 19th century?
3. Which English county possesses the greatest amount of coastline?
4. Who wrote the play *The Lady's not for Burning*?
5. In archery, how many arrows are used in a York round?
6. The National Theatre was involved in an obscenity trial in 1985, because of which play?
7. Who commanded the British at the Battle of Bunker Hill?
8. What was the theme song for the Harry James big band?
9. What is the more colloquial name for *Monstera deliciosa*?

609

1. For what is 'Mrs' an abbreviation?
2. Throughout all history, which was the biggest Empire?
3. Who succeeded Warren Hastings as Governor-General of India?
4. In which country are classical plays called 'Noh' plays?
5. Why are the Brierly Turk, the Darley Arabian and the Godolphin Arabian famous?
6. By what name was Rosine Bernard better known?
7. Whose last words were, 'How were the circus receipts today at Madison Square Garden?'?
8. *Age of Consent* was which group's first LP?
9. Name Britain's premier flower show.

A

141

1. Sir Francis Drake's.
2. Louis XIV, the Sun King, himself a ballet dancer.
3. $20 million.
4. In *King Lear*.
5. Brian Hooper.
6. Esther Williams.
7. Van Gogh.
8. Eric Clapton.
9. Hauling coal – they were pit ponies.

375

1. Servis – which went into liquidation.
2. France.
3. Cornwall.
4. Christopher Fry.
5. 144.
6. *The Romans in Britain*.
7. General Thomas Gage.
8. *Ciribiribin*.
9. The Swiss cheese plant.

609

1. Mistress.
2. The British Empire.
3. Lord Cornwallis.
4. In Japan.
5. They are the three stallions from which all thoroughbred racehorses are descended.
6. Sarah Bernhardt.
7. P.T.Barnum's.
8. *Bronski Beat*'s.
9. The Chelsea Flower Show.

142

1. Of what is Blue Vinney a type?
2. With which PM did George Tierney fight a duel on Putney Heath in 1798?
3. Famed in song, where is Mandalay?
4. In which Shakespeare play do Publius Cicero and Popilus Lena feature?
5. Which great cricketer also played soccer for England in 1901?
6. Which racing driver took part in the film *Caravan to Vaccares*?
7. Which Queen's face appears on playing cards?
8. In which year did the Woodstock Festival take place?
9. What is the maximum measurement for earthquakes on the Richter scale?

376

1. How is the weight of a ship ascertained?
2. In 1924, Eastbourne commuters complained about dirty carriages. What was the reply of Southern Region's General Manager, Sir Robert Walker?
3. In which country are the Ox Mountains?
4. How many times does the word 'Christian' appear in the Bible?
5. Why did Gillette give up their cricket sponsorship?
6. The hype line to which film was 'They're Young – They're in Love – and They Kill People'?
7. In 1973, which Royal couple moved into Gatcombe Park?
8. Which actress and singer had a great success with her LP *Stoney End*?
9. What is the chemical symbol for ice?

610

1. What sort of exam is a 'viva voce'?
2. When were Westerners first permitted to enter Nepal?
3. Which country's civil aviation marking letter is 'G'?
4. Which Indian Princess did Peter Pan rescue from Captain Hook?
5. In which year was the FA Centenary Cup Final?
6. Which porn film ran for ten years at the Pussycat Theatre in Los Angeles?
7. Which British physicist discovered the nucleus of the atom?
8. Which brothers wrote *I Got Rhythm*?
9. By what initials is Deoxyribonucleic acid better known?

142

1. Of cheese.
2. William Pitt the Younger.
3. In Burma.
4. *Julius Caesar.*
5. C.B.Fry.
6. Graham Hill.
7. That of Elizabeth of York, wife of Henry VII.
8. In 1969.
9. Twelve.

376

1. By the volume of water it displaces.
2. 'It was entirely due to the filthy habits of passengers.'
3. In Ireland.
4. Three.
5. Because they felt that the public now associated them more with cricket than with razors.
6. *Bonnie and Clyde.*
7. Princess Anne and Captain Mark Phillips.
8. Barbra Streisand.
9. H_2O, the same as for water.

610

1. An oral exam.
2. In 1950.
3. Britain's.
4. Princess Tiger Lily.
5. In 1972.
6. *Deep Throat.*
7. Ernest Rutherford.
8. George and Ira Gershwin.
9. DNA.

143

1. Who might call a soldier a 'pongo'?
2. Where in Britain did the Ordovices live?
3. Which Great Lake is in Utah?
4. Which famous playwright once edited *Woman's World* magazine?
5. What is natation?
6. Who played the lead in BBC TV's cop thriller *Target* in 1977?
7. Which Duke is the Earl of Ulster's father?
8. Which LP was top of the album charts for every week in 1959?
9. Which part of a man's body can swell to ten times its normal size when he's excited?

377

1. 'Timbrology' was an early name for *what*?
2. How did Amy Robsart die in 1560?
3. Which record is held by Loch Morar?
4. Which heroine fell in love with Count Vronsky?
5. 'Turnverein' was an old name for a club in which sport?
6. Who was the Dickensian-sounding colleague of Tracey Ullman and Lenny Henry on TV?
7. Which art historian was always called 'K' by his friends?
8. What German name do we use for the instrument called 'jeu de timbres' in French?
9. Which instrument can separate two liquids by spinning them at high speed?

611

1. Who made a record called *Derek & Clive*, sold with a paper bag to be sick into?
2. What did the Rochdale Pioneers start?
3. In which country is the geyser after which all other such springs are named?
4. Who wrote the play staged by the National Theatre in 1982 with a real boat floating on stage?
5. Who is the youngest player ever to win the Men's Singles title at Wimbledon?
6. Who was 'the Man you love to Hate'?
7. Which Yorkshire author was called 'Jolly Jack' because he grumbled so much?
8. What is the shortest No. 1 record?
9. What could you measure on a modified Mercalli Scale?

143

1. A sailor.
2. In North Wales.
3. Great Salt Lake.
4. Oscar Wilde, in 1884.
5. Swimming.
6. Patrick Mower.
7. The Duke of Gloucester.
8. The *South Pacific* soundtrack.
9. The pupil of the eye.

377

1. Stamp-collecting, or philately.
2. Of a broken neck. She *apparently* fell downstairs.
3. It is the deepest lake in Britain.
4. Anna Karenina.
5. Athletics.
6. David Copperfield, in *Three of a Kind*.
7. Kenneth Clark, later Lord Clark.
8. Glockenspiel.
9. A centrifuge.

611

1. Peter Cook and Dudley Moore.
2. The Co-operative Movement.
3. In Iceland.
4. Alan Ayckbourn. (*Way Upstream* was the play.)
5. Boris Becker, aged 17 years, 7 months, 7 days.
6. Erich von Stroheim, the 'heavy' actor.
7. J.B. Priestley.
8. *It's Not Unusual*, by Tom Jones.
9. An earthquake.

144

1. In criminal slang, what is a 'peter'?
2. What were Henry VIII's invasions of Scotland in 1544 and 1545 called?
3. Which country has the world's largest National Park?
4. Which famous butler's first name was Reginald?
5. Which football club's home ground has the same name as a battle of 1066?
6. Who was 'the Virginian' on TV?
7. Who was thrown out 'with nothing but a fine-tooth comb'?
8. Who formed The *E-Street Band* as his backing group?
9. What does a Spaniard call a solano, and an Australian a willy-willy?

378

1. Where is the Royal Tournament held in Britain?
2. Who benefited from the Speenhamland System?
3. The world's largest car ferry sails from Travemunde to *where*?
4. In Dickens, whose mother was Agnes Fleming?
5. Colonel Jose Aresti of Spain devised the scoring rules for which spectacular sport?
6. John Pilger's documentary *Year Zero* was about which country?
7. 'Protect Your Planet' is a slogan of which group?
8. Which 1967 LP did critics in 1977 vote the best rock album of all time?
9. What sort of creature do Australians call a 'paddy melon'?

612

1. What is a 'sleepout' in Australia?
2. What was a Nilometer used to measure?
3. The longest known canoe journey, nearly 9,000 miles, started at New Orleans, and finished *where*?
4. What does 'The Game Chicken' teach Toots to do in *Dombey and Son*?
5. Which sport did E. C. Goode revolutionise with a rubber mat from a chemist's shop counter?
6. Which TV doctor was assisted by Dr Steven Kiley?
7. Comedian Frankie Howerd won the first Post Office competition for doing *what*?
8. Which musical note is 'double-croche' in French?
9. What does a petrologist study?

144

1. A safe.
2. The Rough Wooing – he was annoyed about the failure of marriage plans for his son.
3. Canada. (Wood Buffalo N.P., in Alberta.)
4. Jeeves's.
5. Chelsea. (Stamford Bridge.)
6. James Drury, in the 1960s.
7. Bill Bailey, in the song.
8. Bruce Springsteen.
9. A wind.

378

1. At Earls Court.
2. Poor people and low earners.
3. Helsinki, across the Baltic.
4. She was Oliver Twist's mother.
5. Aerobatics.
6. Cambodia.
7. Friends of the Earth.
8. *Sergeant Pepper's Lonely Hearts Club Band.*
9. A small wallaby.

612

1. An extension built on to a house.
2. The height of the Nile.
3. Alaska.
4. Box.
5. Table tennis – he stuck the pimpled rubber to his bat.
6. Marcus Welby, MD.
7. Sticking stamps on envelopes.
8. The semi-quaver, or 'double-hook'.
9. Rocks.

Q

145

1. Which legendary ship is doomed to sail for ever?
2. What was the official language of the Roman Catholic church until 1964?
3. The Devil's Cataract is part of which falls?
4. Which of Ian Fleming's books first appeared in the USA under the title *Too Hot to Handle*?
5. Who succeeded Bob Paisley as Manager of Liverpool FC?
6. Which was the Beatles' second film?
7. Who created *The Gambols*?
8. Who had a big hit with *Lily the Pink*?
9. If you styled yourself a caliologist, what would you do?

379

1. What is the Antonov 124's claim to fame?
2. What were the British troops called by the Americans in their war against them?
3. What, in May 1985, were 'privatised' at King's Cross Station?
4. Who was the first woman to win a Nobel Prize for Literature?
5. Name the new cup awarded for the first time in 1985 to the victors of an annual England/Scotland soccer match.
6. In which US town was the film *American Graffiti* set?
7. Comedian Red Skelton became famous for painting *what*?
8. Which comedy pair recorded *Goodbye-ee* in 1965?
9. Which two fruits combine to form the loganberry?

613

1. What did the unlikely trio of Francis Bacon, Bjorn Borg and Aaron Copland have in common in 1985?
2. Which of the Seven Wonders of the Ancient World was at Ephesus?
3. What is the capital of Jersey?
4. Who wrote the poem *Fern Hill*?
5. Who retired as Manager of Liverpool FC on 29 May 1985?
6. Who starred in the film *Z*?
7. How many points are scored at cribbage for making '15'?
8. Name Freddie Mercury's first solo single.
9. Which of the five senses normally dims first?

145

1. *The Flying Dutchman.*
2. Latin.
3. The Victoria Falls.
4. *Casino Royale.*
5. Joe Fagan.
6. *Help!*
7. Barry Appleby.
8. *Scaffold.*
9. Study birds' nests.

379

1. It is the world's largest aircraft. (It has a 272-foot wingspan and can carry 150 tons 5,000 miles)
2. 'Redcoats' – also 'Lobsters'.
3. The lavatories.
4. Pearl S. Buck, in 1938.
5. The Rous Cup.
6. In Modesto.
7. Clowns.
8. Peter Cook and Dudley Moore.
9. The blackberry and the raspberry.

613

1. Their entries had been omitted from *Who's Who*! 'The computer must have hiccupped', said the publishers.
2. The Temple of Diana.
3. St Helier.
4. Dylan Thomas.
5. Joe Fagan.
6. Yves Montand.
7. Two.
8. *Love Kills*
9. Smell.

146

1. What is the function of a ship's scuppers?
2. Why was being a midwife a particularly hazardous occupation in the sixteenth century?
3. Which is the oldest university in the USA?
4. In which country is Orwell's *1984* set?
5. Kyu and Dan are grades in which sport?
6. What colour are the lenses in 3-D glasses?
7. In which city was Eva Perón reburied in 1971?
8. Who leads the 'Jets' in *West Side Story*?
9. Do not ask arachnophobics this question ... In English country areas, approximately how many spiders inhabit each acre?

380

1. In built-up areas in Britain, between which hours must drivers not toot?
2. How did J.K. Stanley improve the bicycle, in 1885?
3. What do the Pedaung women of Burma use to stretch their necks?
4. Prince Vlad, 'The Impaler', was the real-life model for whom?
5. 'The Aces' is the nickname of which speedway team?
6. Name the car that is the star of *The Love Bug*.
7. What was Jaqueline Cochrane's claim to women's aviation fame?
8. A US state took as its state song the title song from a Broadway musical – later a film. Which state, and which song?
9. Which bird gives its name to a pedestrian crossing?

614

1. What is the shape of traffic signs on which instructions are given?
2. What gave rise to the superstition that it is unlucky to walk under ladders?
3. What is the sacred river of the Hindu religion?
4. Who wrote *The Blessed Damozel*?
5. In which activity might you perform a camel spin?
6. 'Come with me to the Casbah' was said by Charles Boyer to whom, in the 1938 film *Algiers*?
7. What colour gloves does a snooker referee wear?
8. Who wrote the song *Days of Wine and Roses*?
9. Which hormone controls the level of glucose in the blood?

146

1. They drain away excess water.
2. Because if a baby died, the midwife was accused of being a witch.
3. Harvard.
4. Oceania.
5. Judo.
6. Red and green.
7. In Madrid.
8. Tony.
9. Approximately 50,000.

380

1. Between 11.30 p.m. and 7.00 a.m.
2. He made one with wheels of equal size.
3. Brass rings.
4. Count Dracula.
5. Belle Vue, Manchester.
6. Herbie.
7. She was the first female to fly faster than the speed of sound.
8. Oklahoma, and *Oklahoma*.
9. The pelican.

614

1. Circular.
2. Before gallows were invented, people were executed by hanging them from the top rungs of ladders.
3. The Ganges.
4. Dante Gabriel Rossetti.
5. Ice-skating.
6. No-one! This famous line was never uttered in the film.
7. White.
8. Henry Mancini.
9. Insulin.

147

1. The Borobudur is the largest in the world. What is it?
2. As what did Romans use catacombs?
3. What is the first name of the majority of the men on Corfu?
4. Who was reading *The Imitation of Christ* by Thomas à Kempis when he died?
5. How many people does the largest Olympic bobsleigh hold?
6. Who preceded Trevor Nunn as the Artistic Director of the Royal Shakespeare Company?
7. Who was the famous father of the film director Jean Renoir?
8. *On The Street Where You Live* comes from which musical?
9. What is the name for a pigeon's young?

381

1. What is the vessel called that holds the baptismal water?
2. When did the first ship sail through the Panama Canal?
3. What is the time difference between Perth, Scotland, and Perth, Australia?
4. Which poem begins, 'He did not wear his scarlet coat'?
5. Which Wimbledon winner once won an Olympic Silver Medal for Archery?
6. Windsor Davies and Don Estelle are both in which TV comedy series?
7. Who won the 1983 Embassy World Indoor Bowls Crown?
8. Who composed the banned song *Give Ireland Back to the Irish*?
9. Which is the lightest metallic element?

615

1. What is the international language of air traffic control?
2. What implements did the early Japanese dentists use to extract teeth?
3. Which river, 68 miles in length, is wholly within Wales?
4. Why was an Adam's apple so called?
5. How many times has Sebastian Coe won the Olympic 1500 m race?
6. Which country saw the FA Cup Final 'live' for the first time in 1985 on TV?
7. Which number is at the 3 o'clock position on a darts board?
8. How old was Dolly Parton when she made her first record, *Puppy Love*?
9. Who designed the fighter-bomber, the Mosquito?

147

1. A pagoda.
2. As burial places.
3. Spiro.
4. Pope John Paul I.
5. Four.
6. Peter Hall.
7. Pierre August Renoir, the painter.
8. *My Fair Lady*.
9. Squab.

381

1. The font.
2. In 1913.
3. Eight hours.
4. *The Ballad of Reading Gaol* by Oscar Wilde.
5. Charlotte Dodd.
6. *It Ain't Half Hot, Mum*.
7. Bob Sutherland.
8. Paul McCartney.
9. Lithium.

615

1. English.
2. Their fingers.
3. The River Towy.
4. According to legend, a piece of that fateful apple stuck in Adam's throat.
5. Twice.
6. China.
7. Six.
8. Thirteen.
9. Sir Geoffrey de Havilland.

148

1. What do the letters NATO stand for?
2. In 1941, what did it cost to broadcast the very first TV commercial in the USA?
3. 'Big Muddy' is the nickname of which US river?
4. For what were King Arthur's knights searching?
5. Name the twin brothers who took the Gold and Silver Medals in the Men's Slalom at the 1984 Winter Olympics?
6. Who died in *The Blue Lamp* and was reincarnated in Dock Green?
7. What were (are?) Mods' favoured form of conveyance?
8. Complete the Elton John title, *Don't Shoot Me* ...
9. During which months should you not eat oysters?

382

1. Name three of the five official languages of the United Nations.
2. Who was the first English king to obtain a divorce?
3. 'Ecosse' is French for which country?
4. According to Greek legend, who solved the riddle of the Sphinx?
5. Tessa Sanderson won a Gold Medal in which event at the 1984 Olympics?
6. The state of Iowa, USA, shares its nickname with which M*A*S*H character?
7. For what is Eddie Kidd famous?
8. Who wrote the music for *I Only Have Eyes for You*?
9. Approximately how many pints of blood pass through the kidneys each minute?

616

1. On which day was Solomon Grundy buried?
2. Name the first primates to return from space unharmed. (28 May 1959.)
3. The word 'tawdry' is derived from the name of which fair, near Ely?
4. Huldrefolk feature in which country's folklore?
5. Who won the Silver Medal for the men's 800 metres in the 1984 Olympics?
6. Who was the first man to appear on the cover of *Playboy* magazine?
7. Which great architect once wrote, 'A house is a machine for living in'?
8. The Kirov ballet is based in which city?
9. Apart from the obvious, what is a 'Scorched Carpet'?

148

1. North Atlantic Treaty Organisation.
2. Nine dollars.
3. The Missouri.
4. The Holy Grail.
5. Phil and Steve Mahre.
6. PC George Dixon (Jack Warner).
7. Motor scooters.
8. *I'm Only the Piano Player.*
9. Those with 'R's in their names.

382

1. English, French, Spanish, Russian and Chinese.
2. Henry VIII.
3. Scotland.
4. Oedipus.
5. Javelin.
6. Hawkeye.
7. Motorcycle stunting.
8. Harry Warren.
9. Two and a half pints.

616

1. On Sunday.
2. Abel and Baker – two chimpanzees.
3. St Audrey.
4. Norway's.
5. Sebastian Coe.
6. Peter Sellers.
7. Le Corbusier.
8. In Leningrad.
9. A moth.

149

1. What is the common name for hypermetropia?
2. The 10,000 lb atomic bomb dropped on Hiroshima was given which diminutive nickname?
3. From which country do Citroën cars originate?
4. Which bawdy French writer was a monk?
5. Who was the first woman to win three track Gold Medals at one Olympics?
6. 'We Never Close' was the boast of which London theatre?
7. Who painted *Guernica*?
8. Which bell has the highest note among church bells?
9. What type of creature is a cottonmouth?

383

1. In heraldry, what are 'attires'?
2. The Great Exhibition of 1851 collected a profit of £150,000, a not-inconsiderable amount in those days. How was it spent?
3. Mahammad Ajeeb is which British city's first black mayor?
4. Who wrote, 'Marriage always demands the greatest understanding of the art of insincerity possible between two human beings'?
5. How many players are there in a handball team?
6. Which film company's logo is called the *Proud Lady*?
7. Which great cartoonist is nicknamed 'Sparky'?
8. Who was band leader Herb Miller's more famous older brother?
9. What does a nucivorous animal eat?

617

1. What unlikely national competition is held in Raleigh, Mississippi, each year?
2. The prototype of which undersea vessel was originally built in 1624?
3. Manchuria is a province of which country?
4. Who tells the stories in the *Arabian Nights*?
5. Who has won the most Olympic athletics medals?
6. Whose products are 'bootiful' in TV adverts?
7. Olivia Newton-John's grandfather Max Born won a Nobel Prize for *what*?
8. Which group had a big hit with *Whiskey in the Jar*?
9. What is added to rubber to vulcanize it?

149

1. Long-sightedness.
2. 'Little Boy'.
3. France.
4. Rabelais.
5. Wilma Rudolph, in 1960.
6. The Windmill.
7. Pablo Picasso.
8. The treble.
9. A snake.

383

1. Stag's antlers.
2. In founding the South Kensington Museum.
3. Bradford's.
4. Vicki Baum.
5. Eleven.
6. Columbia Pictures.
7. Charles Schultz.
8. Glenn Miller.
9. Nuts.

617

1. The National Tobacco-Spitting Contest.
2. The submarine.
3. China.
4. Scheherazade.
5. Paavo Nurmi. (9 Gold, 3 Silver.)
6. Bernard Matthews's.
7. Physics.
8. *Thin Lizzie*.
9. Sulphur.

150

1. Approximately what percentage of Britain's food is home-produced?
2. Up to the reign of Henry VIII (and some way into his too), a person could be hanged for eating meat on one day of the week. Which day?
3. In which country is Galilee?
4. In which imaginary country is *The Lion, the Witch and the Wardrobe* set?
5. Who won soccer's 1985 European Cup-Winners' Cup Final?
6. Who plays The Master in TV's *The Master*?
7. What type of person is 'mattoid'?
8. How many reeds are used to play a clarinet?
9. How many degrees do the interior angles of a triangle add up to?

384

1. What is the nickname given to a vicar's neckwear?
2. Who came to power in Malta in 1974?
3. Which are Russia's two most heavily populated cities?
4. What kind of creature was Richard Adam's *Shardik*?
5. What is on the front of England Test Cricketers' sweaters?
6. Name the only film in which Lionel, Ethel and John Barrymore appeared together.
7. With which No. 1 public enemy did Herbert Youngblood break out of prison in 1934?
8. Which band leader had a name in common with that of a former Prime Minister?
9. To the nearest 1,000, how many types of reptiles are there?

618

1. Who is the Bishop of Rome?
2. To whom did Lady Astor once say, 'If you were my husband, I'd flavour your coffee with poison'?
3. How many time zones are there in South America?
4. Whom do Janeites revere?
5. What name is given to the back person in a tug-of-war team?
6. Who said, 'Give him the money, Barney'?
7. How many pieces are there in a tangram puzzle?
8. Whom did Mark Chapman kill in New York?
9. What is the collective name for herons?

150

1. About 55 per cent.
2. Friday.
3. In Israel.
4. In Narnia.
5. Everton.
6. Lee Van Cleef.
7. A combination of genius and fool.
8. One.
9. 180°.

384

1. A dog-collar.
2. Dom Mintoff.
3. Moscow and Leningrad.
4. A bear.
5. Three lions. (Couchant, or lying down.)
6. *Rasputin and the Empress.*
7. John Dillinger.
8. Ted Heath.
9. 6,000.

618

1. The Pope.
2. Winston Churchill.
3. Three.
4. Jane Austen.
5. The anchorman.
6. Wilfred Pickles.
7. Seven.
8. John Lennon.
9. A siege.

151

1. What was very noticeably on strike from July to October 1979?
1. Which king won the Battle of the Spurs?
3. How many towers does New York's World Trade Center have?
4. Which poet invented the nine-line stanza named after him?
5. Which Australian has twice been the defeated finalist in the World Snooker Championship?
6. What do Americans call weekly or fortnightly repertory in the theatre?
7. What vocal feat did Errol Bird manage to do for $10\frac{1}{4}$ hours in 1979?
8. From which country does the dance called 'Cueca' come?
9. Who, or what, is the siamang of Sumatra?

385

1. Who promised, 'From 6.45 a.m. to Lights Out at 9.30 p.m. life will be conducted at a brisk tempo'?
2. What was the nickname of Richard de Clare that suggests a weapon – or a drink?
3. In which town did a rich wool merchant found Blundell's school, in 1604?
4. Who wrote a story in which a sculptor makes a doll model of Captain Alexander Hepburn?
5. What was Dick Pope Jnr the first person to do bare-foot?
6. The first episode of which TV comedy about three pious men was called *The Tower of London*?
7. Why was Helen Morgan sacked as Miss World in 1974?
8. What sort of music did Ira D. Sankey compose?
9. How many yards, on average, does a giant tortoise move in one minute?

619

1. Iron horse is CB slang for what vehicle?
2. In Anglo-Saxon times, who had a wergild six times greater than a ceorl?
3. Where is Australia's Lake Surprise?
4. Which 83-year-old comedian called his autobiography *The Third Time Around*?
5. Which professional sport did hurdler Renaldo Nehemiah take up after athletics?
6. Whose middle name is Paradine?
7. Which prize did Mairead Corrigan and Betty Williams win in 1976?
8. In music, what is SPAM?
9. If you use a vigesimal system, in what scale do you count?

151

1. The ITV network.
2. Henry VIII, in 1513, against France.
3. Two.
4. Spenser, for *The Faerie Queene*.
5. Eddie Charlton.
6. Stock theatre.
7. Yodel.
8. Chile.
9. A gibbon – a member of the ape family.

385

1. William Whitelaw, promising a 'short sharp shock' to young offenders.
2. Richard 'Strongbow'.
3. In Tiverton, Devon.
4. D.H. Lawrence – *The Captain's Doll.*
5. Water-ski. (In 1947.)
6. *The Goodies*, in 1970.
7. Because she was an unmarried mother.
8. Religious music – hymns.
9. About five yards.

619

1. A motorcycle.
2. A thane, or thegn.
3. In the Tanami Desert.
4. George Burns.
5. American Football.
6. David Frost's.
7. The Nobel Peace Prize.
8. The Society for the Publication of American Music.
9. Units of twenty.

152

1. Who said, 'Modern society greets gold as its Holy Grail'?
2. What did Charles Townshend do in 1767 that the Americans hated?
3. Laval, Verdun, Hull and Sherbrooke are among the main cities of which province?
4. Which novelist married Zelda?
5. Which great tennis player (5 ft $4\frac{1}{2}$ inches tall) said, 'If you're small, you better be a winner'?
6. Which comedian played Grandpa Smallweed in *Bleak House* on TV?
7. Which French writer's funeral did 50,000 people attend in April 1980?
8. What is the English title of Franz Lehar's opera *Die Lustige Witwe*?
9. Which great early medical man came from Kos, the Greek island?

386

1. In 1943, what food was listed on the Strand Palace Hotel menu as 'Ballotine de jambon Valentinoise'?
2. The Crown Jewels James II took when he fled were given back by his descendants – to which king?
3. What do the Dutch call Surinam?
4. What was Grace Metalious's only best-selling novel?
5. The Sunbrite World Pairs Championship is held in what sport?
6. Why were a John Wayne Western on BBC 1 and snooker on BBC 2 interrupted on May 5th, 1980?
7. Whom did former Playmate of the Year Patti Macguire marry?
8. Which modern invention did Menotti use for the title of an opera in 1974?
9. Which gas did William Ramsay isolate in 1895?

620

1. In 1943, what food was listed on the Strand Palace Hotel menu as 'Assiette Froide'?
2. How many barrels of powder did Guy Fawkes and his friends put in Parliament's cellars?
3. What name did Podgorica take, in honour of Yugoslavia's leader?
4. Which novelist's name, rearranged, makes 'Our best novelist, senor'?
5. Which country played its first cricket Test match in 1932?
6. Which character does Derek Fowlds play in *Yes, Minister*?
7. Which pioneer of birth control reckoned she'd be canonized within 200 years?
8. From which country does the war trumpet called a puukaaea come?
9. In which science did James Jeans become famous?

152

1. Karl Marx, in 1867.
2. As Chancellor, he put a tax on tea.
3. Quebec, in Canada.
4. F. Scott Fitzgerald.
5. Billie-Jean King.
6. Charlie Drake.
7. That of Jean-Paul Sartre.
8. *The Merry Widow.*
9. Hippocrates. (He inspired the Hippocratic Oath.)

386

1. Hot Spam. (It was during the period of food rationing.)
2. To George IV, in 1807 – 119 years later!
3. Suriname.
4. *Peyton Place.*
5. Speedway racing.
6. To show the SAS storming the Iranian Embassy in London.
7. Jimmy Connors.
8. *The Telephone.*
9. Helium, not previously known on earth.

620

1. Cold Spam. (It was during the period of food rationing.)
2. About 30.
3. Titograd.
4. The name of Robert Louis Stevenson.
5. India.
6. Bernard Wooley, the Minister's Private Secretary.
7. Dr Marie Stopes.
8. From New Zealand.
9. Astronomy.

153

1. According to the saying, spring is here when you can cover how many daisies with your foot?
2. In 1808, Maria Paradis was the first woman to scale which mountain?
3. Ford Dearborn, USA, is now which city?
4. Gollum features in which book?
5. Which is the world's most famous bobsleigh run?
6. What was Lorraine Chase's reply to the question, 'Were you truly wafted here from Paradise?'?
7. Whom does Marcie call 'Sir' in *Peanuts*?
8. On what did Yankee Doodle ride into town?
9. Which star constellation contains Betelgeuse and Rigel?

387

1. What is the Irish Parliament's equivalent of the letters M.P.?
2. Who, aged 21, was the youngest General in the American Civil War?
3. The Dogger Bank is in which sea?
4. Who wrote *Midnight's Children*?
5. Who was the captain of India's World Cup-winning cricket team in 1983?
6. Whose cry was 'Wakey, Wakey'?
7. What was US President Herbert C. Hoover's middle name?
8. Whose third symphony was known as *The Polish*?
9. On the Beaufort scale, what number represents 'calm air'?

621

1. Which tap in a dwelling *must* connect directly to the water mains?
2. Which party did William Gladstone represent?
3. On which river is Eel Pie Island?
4. 'Once more into the breach, dear friends, once more' comes from which play?
5. From which country does jockey Steve Cauthen come?
6. What part does Michael Jackson play in the film *The Wiz*?
7. In the USA, which President's birthday is a national holiday?
8. Which singing sisters were named Maxene, LaVerne and Patty?
9. Which is considered to be the most destructive insect?

153

1. Five.
2. Mont Blanc.
3. Chicago.
4. *The Hobbit* by J.R.R. Tolkien.
5. The Cresta Run.
6. 'Nah, Luton Airport.'
7. Peppermint Patty.
8. A pony.
9. Orion.

387

1. TD.
2. General George Custer.
3. The North Sea.
4. Salman Rushdie.
5. Kapil Dev.
6. Billy Cotton's.
7. Clark.
8. Tchaikovsky's.
9. 0.

621

1. The cold water tap in the kitchen.
2. The Liberal Party.
3. The Thames.
4. Shakespeare's *Henry V*.
5. The USA.
6. The scarecrow.
7. George Washington's.
8. The Andrews Sisters.
9. The locust.

154

1. Who reputedly clocked up £19,000 in parking fees, in 1985?
2. What was the focal point of the Paris Exhibition of 1889?
3. Originally, what was Brisbane, in Australia?
4. Which line follows, 'What is this life, if, full of care,'?
5. In which Olympic event did Dana Zatopek win a Gold Medal?
6. Which film, whose title relates to playing cards, did Marlon Brando both star in and direct?
7. After which Surveyor General of India was a mountain named?
8. In which year was BBC TV's *The Old Grey Whistle Test* first broadcast?
9. What is the common name for *Hamamelis*?

388

1. At what time during daylight is your shadow shortest?
2. How tall was Olduvai Man, whose bones were discovered in 1959?
3. Where is the British Army's ordnance depot?
4. Who wrote the novel *The Bridges of Toko-Ri*, based on events in the Korean War?
5. Which team was the first to win all UEFA trophies?
6. Which 'Professional' played in *The Cuckoo Waltz*?
7. Salisbury Cathedral was built in which style?
8. *I, Me, Mine* was the last song that they recorded together, in early 1970. Who?
9. What is the common name for asteroidea?

622

1. With what is Amnesty International mainly concerned?
2. Which of the Seven Wonders of the Ancient World was at Halicarnassus in Turkey?
3. Which is the largest of the Scandinavian countries?
4. Who wrote *Cold Comfort Farm*?
5. Which horse races form the English Triple Crown?
6. Which child actress's autobiography is entitled *My Young Life*?
7. Who created Pig-Pen, Schroeder and Rerun?
8. How many people dance a 'pas de deux'?
9. What was the code name for the first atomic bomb, exploded in New Mexico in 1945?

154

1. President Banda of Malawi. He left his Boeing 747 parked at Heathrow for his private stay in Britain, *after* his official visit.
2. The Eiffel Tower.
3. A penal colony.
4. 'We have no time to stand and stare.'
5. The Women's Javelin event.
6. *One-Eyed Jacks*.
7. Sir George Everest.
8. In 1972.
9. Wych-hazel, or witch-hazel.

388

1. At midday.
2. About four feet tall.
3. At Bicester.
4. James Michener.
5. Juventus FC.
6. Lewis Collins.
7. English Gothic.
8. The Beatles.
9. Starfish.

622

1. The conditions of political prisoners.
2. The Mausoleum of King Mausolus.
3. Sweden.
4. Stella Gibbons.
5. The Derby, the St Leger and the 2,000 Guineas.
6. Shirley Temple's.
7. Charles M. Schultz – in *Peanuts*.
8. Two.
9. *Day of Trinity*.

155

1. Which organization's motto is 'Courtesy and Care'?
2. Which flag day did Douglas Haig organise?
3. Varna (Bulgaria), Brasov (Romania) and Donetski (USSR) were all once called what?
4. What word, that now means chaos or tumult, did Milton create for the capital of Hell?
5. Who lost three Wimbledon finals in the same year, in 1977?
6. What TV series told the story of Dr Richard Kimble, a pediatrician?
7. Which art-loving millionaire bought Sutton Place in Surrey in the 1950s?
8. The player of which instrument do rock musicians call 'professor'?
9. How is the structure of a fish's heart different from a mammal's?

389

1. Which newspaper used the slogan 'Are You Getting It Every Day?'?
2. Housteads is the best-preserved fort *where*?
3. Which county did Henry VIII call 'the most beastly slice in England'?
4. Which author created characters named Car Darch, Joshua Jopp and Levi Lickpan?
5. What was Cuban athlete Alberto Juantorena's original sport?
6. *Bwana Devil*, the first 3-D film, promised you *what* in your lap?
7. Who painted *Le Jardin du Poète*, sold for $6 million in 1980?
8. Which country won the Eurovision Song Contest in 1979 with *Hallelujah*?
9. Which colourless fluid carries blood corpuscles round the body?

623

1. During World War II, why did the BBC say there would be no women newsreaders?
2. Which king was called 'the Black Boy' when young?
3. Which city got its name because Snot and his tribe once lived there?
4. Who wrote a novel about medieval Florence called *Romola*?
5. Which Australian was four times the defeated Wimbledon Men's Singles finalist?
6. Angela Lansbury plays Jessica Fletcher in which TV series?
7. Who painted *Where do we come from? What are we? Where are we going?*?
8. Which rock singer picked his name because a spirit called herself that at a séance?
9. What is measured in QO2 units?

155

1. The Automobile Association's.
2. Poppy Day, when he was President of the British Legion.
3. Stalin.
4. Pandemonium.
5. Betty Stove.
6. *The Fugitive.*
7. J. Paul Getty.
8. The piano.
9. It has only two chambers, not four.

389

1. The *Sun.*
2. On Hadrian's Wall.
3. Lincolnshire.
4. Thomas Hardy.
5. Basketball.
6. A lion.
7. Van Gogh.
8. Israel, sung by *Milk and Honey.*
9. Plasma.

623

1. 'They might have to read bad news.'
2. Charles II.
3. Nottingham.
4. George Eliot.
5. Ken Rosewall.
6. *Murder, She Wrote.*
7. Gauguin.
8. Alice Cooper.
9. How much oxygen is breathed.

156

1. According to folklore, who is the only person that can capture a unicorn?
2. Which comet is featured on the Bayeux Tapestry?
3. Only one US state does not model its laws on the British system. Which?
4. Who wrote *Thérèse Raquin*?
5. What is the name of the French tennis tournament?
6. Where, in the South of France, is the famous film festival held?
7. Who invented the swing-wing plane?
8. Which London orchestra made the soundtrack for *Star Wars*?
9. What colour are the hottest stars?

390

1. When children reach two, what proportion of their adult height are they?
2. In 1614, Countess Bathory was executed for what alleged crime?
3. The Temple of Athene in Athens is better known by what name?
4. The fabled monster known as the Chimera had a lion's head, dragon's tail, and the body of which animal?
5. Where is the Sheffield Shield a major cricketing trophy?
6. Who plays Tarzan in the film *Tarzan and the Huntress*?
7. Why should US Presidents avoid being elected in a year ending with a zero?
8. Which pair had a hit with *I Got You Babe*?
9. What type of apes inhabit the Rock of Gibraltar?

624

1. How long is one term of office for a US senator?
2. Between which two cities were the Punic Wars fought?
3. Which American state has the fewest inhabitants?
4. Which family features in John Steinbeck's novel *The Grapes of Wrath*?
5. What is the name given to the projectile in curling?
6. Of whom was the remark made, 'Now there's a broad with a future behind her'?
7. Who created Flash Gordon?
8. Who wrote the song *Beautiful Dreamer*?
9. Of what fruit is Norfolk Giant a variety?

156

1. A virgin.
2. Halley's Comet.
3. Louisiana.
4. Emile Zola.
5. Roland Garros, held in Paris.
6. At Cannes.
7. Barnes Wallis.
8. The London Symphony Orchestra.
9. Blue.

390

1. Half. (This is just the average.)
2. Being a vampire.
3. The Parthenon.
4. A goat.
5. In Australia.
6. Johnny Weissmuller.
7. Because, since 1840, everyone who has done so has died in office.
8. Sonny and Cher.
9. Barbary apes.

624

1. Six years.
2. Carthage and Rome.
3. Alaska.
4. The Joads.
5. The stone.
6. Marilyn Monroe.
7. Alex Raymond.
8. Stephen Foster.
9. The raspberry.

157

1. Which food in Britain gets its name from the Portuguese word for quince jam?
2. What did the Weasel, Buster and Checker do in 1963, with some help?
3. Westbury Down is the highest point of *what*?
4. The ghosts of Peter Quint and Miss Jessel the governess appear in which story?
5. In cricket, Middlesex won the last *what* in 1980?
6. What was the radio programme called that became TV's *Candid Camera*?
7. Which doctor used to buy oysters for his cat, Hodge?
8. Which singer was married to Kris Kristofferson from 1973 to 1980?
9. The pylorus is the exit from what?

391

1. Where will you see the motto 'E Pluribus Unum', or 'one out of many'?
2. Which great man was nicknamed 'Copper Nose', 'Ruby Nose' and 'The Brewer'?
3. Which river is called Abbai or Al-Bahr locally?
4. In Shakespeare, Bardolph is remarkable for what?
5. Whose figure appears on the weathercock at Lord's?
6. Where was the film *Ryan's Daughter* set?
7. Why did Nancy Reagan say a woman is like a teabag?
8. Who is the first person mentioned in the Beatles song *Ob-la-di, ob-la-da*?
9. What do growers do if they vernalize a plant?

625

1. What is the American equivalent of our Post Code?
2. In 1492, Pope Innocent VIII, who was in a coma, was given a blood transfusion from three young men. What happened?
3. In Wyoming, what is an Indian paintbrush?
4. Who said, 'Bah, humbug!' when wished a Merry Christmas?
5. What is the heaviest of the three swords used in fencing?
6. Which British film star once wore a mink bikini in a gondola in Venice?
7. Which guide-book did Raymond Postgate begin in 1951?
8. In which Puccini opera does Minnie own a pub called The Polka?
9. What does rock look like if it is called 'saccharoidal', in geology?

157

1. Marmalade.
3. They became the Great Train Robbers.
3. Salisbury Plain.
4. *The Turn of the Screw*, by Henry James.
5. Gillette Cup. (Its name changed subsequently.)
6. *Candid Microphone* – of course!
7. Dr Samuel Johnson.
8. Rita Coolidge.
9. The stomach. It is the muscle round the opening to the duodenum.

391

1. On all USA coins and banknotes.
2. Oliver Cromwell.
3. The Nile.
4. His large red nose.
5. That of Old Father Time.
6. In Ireland.
7. 'You can't tell how strong she is until you put her in hot water.'
8. 'Desmond has a barrow in the market place.'
9. They chill it to encourage flowering.

625

1. The Zip Code.
2. He died, and so did the three young men.
3. The name of the State Flower.
4. Scrooge.
5. The épée – it can weigh up to 770 grams.
6. Diana Dors, in 1955.
7. *The Good Food Guide.*
8. *The Girl of the Golden West.*
9. Sugar.

158

1. What is a STOLPORT?
2. When did the first mid-air collision between two passenger aircraft happen?
3. On which street is the New York Stock Exchange?
4. What did the word 'lady' originally mean?
5. How did the Jockey Club upset the firm of Durex?
6. When Hattie McDaniel won an Oscar for Best Supporting Actress in *Gone With the Wind*, what 'first' did she achieve?
7. Which dancer was nicknamed 'The Mayor of Harlem'?
8. *Keeps Rainin' All the Time* is the subtitle for which song?
9. What is the more usual name for the pelargonium?

392

1. When is Twelfth Night?
2. Which company made the first jet airliner, Comet 1?
3. Wearing what colour does a bride traditionally marry, in China?
4. Which poem by Rupert Brooke begins, 'If I should die, think only this of me'?
5. Which New Zealander reached the Wimbledon Men's Singles final in 1983?
6. Which Hitchcock film was shot in Bodega Bay, California?
7. To which Public Enemy No. 1 is there a memorial in Nashville, Tennessee?
8. Who had her first major hit in 1964 with *Anyone Who Had a Heart*?
9. How often do *The Floralies of Ghent* take place?

626

1. By what name is the homely Marullus Lacrymans better known?
2. How did the knight of old issue a personal challenge?
3. At which University did Britain's first Professor of Parapsychology take up his post?
4. Which poem begins, 'I sprang to the stirrup, and Joris, and he'?
5. Peter Shilton and Ray Wilkins both won their 70th England soccer caps in the same match. Against which team?
6. By what name was Tula Ellice Finklea better known?
7. Why was William Taynton famous?
8. Which US President used *High Hopes* as his campaign song?
9. On the roads, which are the commonest electric powered vehicles?

158

1. A Short Take Off and Landing Airport.
2. In 1956.
3. Wall Street.
4. Loaf-kneader.
5. By saying that *Durex* wasn't a suitable name for a horse, and refusing to allow it to be registered.
6. She was the first black person to win an Oscar for acting.
7. Bill 'Bojangles' Robinson.
8. *Stormy Weather*.
9. Geranium.

392

1. 6 January.
2. De Havilland.
3. Red.
4. *The Soldier*.
5. Chris Lewis.
6. *The Birds*.
7. John Dillinger.
8. Cilla Black.
9. Every five years – it is Europe's most spectacular flower show.

626

1. Dry rot.
2. By throwing down a glove.
3. At Edinburgh University.
4. *How They Brought the Good News From Ghent to Aix*, by Browning.
5. Scotland.
6. Cyd Charisse.
7. He was the first person to be televised. (By Baird.)
8. John F. Kennedy.
9. Milk floats.

Q

159

1. What are the four dimensions?
2. Who was America's first Republican President?
3. What does Finland call England?
4. Who wrote the poem *A Song for St Cecilia's Day*?
5. What was table-tennis originally called?
6. 'Mother of Mercy, is this the end of Rico?' is the concluding line to which Edward G. Robinson film?
7. Where is Lord Nelson buried?
8. Which governor of Louisiana composed the song, *You Are My Sunshine* in 1940, as his campaign song?
9. How many chambers has the human heart?

393

1. How many gross are in a great gross?
2. Approximately how old is the wheel?
3. Between which two countries were the Opium Wars of 1839–42 fought?
4. How often, according to legend, does the town Brigadoon appear?
5. In 1979, which Briton was voted World Male Athlete of the Year?
6. *Planet of the Apes* was based on which Pierre Boulle book?
7. Which gangster was killed by federal agents in front of the Biograph Theatre, Chicago?
8. How old was Leopold Stokowski when he first conducted an orchestra?
9. What is the collective term for rhinoceroses?

627

1. For how many years are passports for children valid?
2. Prior to Henry VIII, how were monarchs addressed?
3. Of which US state is Indianapolis the capital?
4. Who sprang from the head of Jove, fully grown?
5. Give the surname of brothers Ian and Greg, who have both captained Australia at cricket.
6. The 1955 film *Rebel Without a Cause* was based on which book?
7. Which are the only two types of chess piece able to make the first move?
8. 'A, You're Adorable.' What is 'B'?
9. What does 'kangaroo' mean in aborigine?

159

1. Length, width, depth and time.
2. Abraham Lincoln.
3. Englanti.
4. John Dryden.
5. *Not* Ping-pong, but Gossamer. (*Gossima* was the trade name.)
6. *Little Caesar.*
7. In St Paul's Cathedral. (*Not* under his column!)
8. Jimmie Davis.
9. Four.

393

1. Twelve.
2. 5,000 years.
3. Britain and China.
4. Once every 100 years, for one day only.
5. Sebastian Coe.
6. *Monkey Planet.*
7. John Dillinger.
8. Twelve.
9. A crash.

627

1. Five years.
2. 'Your Highness' or 'Your Grace'.
3. Indiana.
4. Minerva. (Athena, in Greek myth.)
5. Chappell.
6. *Children of the Dark* by Irving Shulman.
7. Pawns and knights.
8. 'So beautiful.'
9. 'I do not know.' (That's the answer!)

160

1. For what does ER stand?
2. In 1916, where did the Easter Rising take place?
3. In which country is the source of the River Tigris?
4. Who said, 'If in doubt, tell the truth'?
5. When black Nubas engage in their traditional bouts of wrestling, what curious thing do they first do to their bodies?
6. Who starred as the two airline pilots in the 1945 film *The Way to the Stars*?
7. What type of clothing did John B. Stetson produce?
8. Who made the LP *An Innocent Man*?
9. For what do the letters UHF stand?

394

1. What emblem does the Jaguar car sport?
2. The practice of kissing what part of the Pope's anatomy was abolished in 1773?
3. Which of the Three Musketeers shared a name with a Greek mountain?
4. Why did Zeus have Prometheus chained to a rock?
5. Who won soccer's Canon League in the 1984–85 season?
6. When was Raquel Welch born?
7. Who coined the phrase for FBI agents – 'G-Men'?
8. Which composer was born in Bonn in 1777?
9. Which is the lightest of the elements?

628

1. What are 'Angels on horseback', as a snack?
2. At Trafalgar, who was Nelson's No. 2?
3. Which is Europe's oldest university?
4. In which language have the words 'alcohol' and 'sugar' their origin?
5. Which two teams share Elland Road?
6. For what do the letters 'FF' stand, on videos and cassette recorders?
7. What nationality was Jacques Brel, the singer?
8. Who succeeded Arthur Fiedler as conductor of the 'Boston Pops' orchestra?
9. Which food substance is formed in plants by the influence of light on chlorophyll?

160

1. Elizabeth Regina.
2. In Dublin.
3. In Turkey.
4. Mark Twain.
5. They paint them white.
6. Michael Redgrave and John Mills.
7. Hats.
8. Billy Joel.
9. Ultra High Frequency.

394

1. A jaguar.
2. His toe.
3. Athos.
4. Because he gave fire to the human race.
5. Everton.
6. In 1942.
7. George 'Machine Gun' Kelly.
8. Beethoven.
9. Hydrogen.

628

1. Prunes or oysters wrapped in bacon.
2. Admiral Collingwood.
3. The University of Salerno, in Italy.
4. Arabic.
5. Leeds United (Soccer) and Hunslet (Rugby).
6. Fast forward.
7. Belgian.
8. John Williams.
9. Starch.

161

1. Broadly, what is a curriculum vitae?
2. Elected in 1867, who was Canada's first PM?
3. What is the actual meaning of 'Himalayas'?
4. Who wrote the *Cautionary Verses*?
5. What did Bobby Riggs give Billie-Jean King before their much fêted tennis match?
6. Who played James Bond in the film *Live and Let Die*?
7. Who said, 'I have always thought that every woman should marry, and no man'?
8. What nationality was pianist Julius Katchen?
9. Where in the human body is the 'Circle of Willis'?

395

1. Why did Amazon women reputedly cut off their right breasts?
2. How many of the Tolpuddle Martyrs were named James?
3. Which sea separates Italy and Yugoslavia?
4. Which French author fought over 1,000 duels?
5. In 1985, which soccer team won a major cup, yet were relegated to Division 2?
6. Which zany group made the film *The Life of Brian*?
7. Who said, 'Marriage means exchanging the hurly-burly of the chaise longue for the deep peace of the double bed'?
8. Whose first major hit was *Mandy*?
9. Which bird is also known as the windhover?

629

1. What do three short blasts on a ship's siren mean?
2. Who headed the Gestapo in World War II and is still a wanted war criminal?
3. Cars from which country carry the international registration letter A?
4. Better known as a novelist, who wrote the play *The Potting Shed*?
5. Which is the longest Olympic swimming distance?
6. Who directed *Day for Night*?
7. Which great artist designed the United Nations building in New York?
8. The song cycle *On Wenlock Edge* was composed by whom?
9. Which animals jump highest?

161

1. A summary of qualifications and experience – most usually requested when applying for a job.
2. John A. MacDonald.
3. 'Abode of snow.'
4. Hilaire Belloc.
5. An inflatable 'Sugar Daddy'.
6. Roger Moore.
7. Benjamin Disraeli.
8. American.
9. At the base of the brain.

395

1. So they would not get in the way of their bowstrings.
2. Three.
3. The Adriatic.
4. Cyrano de Bergerac.
5. Norwich City, who won the Milk Cup.
6. The Monty Python team.
7. Mrs Patrick Campbell.
8. Barry Manilow's.
9. The kestrel.

629

1. 'Full speed ahead.'
2. Heinrich Müller.
3. Austria.
4. Graham Greene.
5. 1,500 metres.
6. François Truffaut.
7. Le Corbusier.
8. Ralph Vaughan Williams.
9. Antelopes.

162

1. What is the nickname of the plane designed to be the US President's aerial command post if nuclear war breaks out?
2. In medieval times, how tall was the average man?
3. Of what is 350 Fifth Avenue, New York, the official address?
4. Who wrote *Kes*?
5. Competitors are electrically wired to determine the validity of hits in which sport?
6. Who repeatedly stole Judy's sausages?
7. Who painted the Rokeby Venus?
8. Of which group was Martha Reeves the lead singer?
9. What is the minimum number of degrees in a reflex angle?

396

1. What colour is the paper which sets out government policy to be discussed?
2. Which English king lost his head?
3. Where are the Frigid Zones? (Remember, this section is Geography.)
4. Invariably, how old is Little Orphan Annie?
5. How many faults are incurred by a rider who falls off, in show jumping?
6. At how many frames per second does cinema film move?
7. Which Briton won the Nobel Prize for Literature in 1958?
8. In the song *Fly Me to the Moon*, which two planets are mentioned?
9. Which part of the body is the palate?

630

1. Which government department has responsibility for immigration?
2. Who was set adrift by his mutinous crew in 1789?
3. Which is the nearest city to Spaghetti Junction?
4. Who first wrote of 'Cloud Cuckoo Land'?
5. Who were the first winners of cricket's Gillette Cup?
6. In the film *Star Wars*, what was Hans Solo's space vehicle called?
7. Excluding the reds, what is the total value of the other colours in snooker?
8. Of which group was Phil Spector married to the lead singer?
9. What is the collective term for oxen?

162

1. The 'Doomsday Plane'.
2. 5′6″ tall.
3. The Empire State Building.
4. Barry Hines.
5. Fencing.
6. The crocodile. (In Punch and Judy.)
7. Velasquez.
8. *The Vandellas.*
9. 181°.

396

1. Green.
2. Charles I – who was beheaded.
3. The areas between the Polar circles and the Poles.
4. Eleven.
5. Eight.
6. 24 frames per second.
7. Bertrand Russell.
8. Jupiter and Mars.
9. The roof of the mouth.

630

1. The Home Office.
2. Captain William Bligh.
3. Birmingham.
4. Aristophanes.
5. Sussex.
6. *Millenium Falcon.*
7. Twenty-seven.
8. *The Ronettes.*
9. A yoke.

163

1. What did the US motor trade call 'Borax'?
2. For what were the Skylon and Dome of Discovery built?
3. What is the largest island belonging to Denmark?
4. In which city was the Encyclopaedia Britannica first printed?
5. Up to September 1983, which cricketing country had never won a Test match?
6. In *The Caine Mutiny*, with what does Captain Queeg continually fiddle?
7. Which make of car, gold-plated and with zebra-skin seats, did Lady Docker once own?
8. Which pop singer, born Michael Barrett, changed his name officially to Clark Kent?
9. What term is used for two spacecraft joining together in space?

397

1. Which museum is in Cambridge Heath Road, Bethnal Green?
2. Near where was the battle of Pinkie fought in 1547?
3. In which country is the Blue Mountains National Park?
4. Which author lived at Ayot St Lawrence?
5. In which make of car did James Hunt begin his Grand Prix career?
6. Which TV humorist inherited the title Lord Glenavy?
7. Which actress (married to Stringer Davies) was related to Tony Benn?
8. In what subject does rock singer Chuck Berry have a college diploma?
9. How old must a cat be to enter a cat show Senior class?

631

1. What product of great value is produced by a special mill at Laverstoke in Hampshire?
2. Who first made a fortune from literature in England?
3. Which country calls itself 'Druk-yul', or 'Druk Gyalkhap', meaning 'Realm of the Dragon'?
4. Joseph Smiggers was a perpetual Vice-President of which club?
5. Essex cricketer David Acfield twice competed for Britain in the Olympics – in which sport?
6. Which former office-boy in an ad agency produced *Chariots of Fire*?
7. What colour socks does Peter O'Toole always wear for luck?
8. What connection was there between the deaths of Keith Moon and Mama Cass Elliott?
9. Brontophobia is fear of *what*?

163

1. Chrome trim that was just decorative.
2. The 1951 Festival of Britain.
3. Greenland.
4. In Edinburgh, in 1768.
5. Sri Lanka – but they had played only eight.
6. Two large ball-bearings.
7. A Daimler.
8. Shakin' Stevens, *not* Superman!
9. Docking.

397

1. The Museum of Childhood.
2. Edinburgh. (The English won.)
3. In Australia.
4. George Bernard Shaw.
5. A Hesketh.
6. Patrick Campbell.
7. Margaret Rutherford.
8. Hairdressing.
9. Two years.

631

1. Paper for British banknotes.
2. Alexander Pope, for translating Homer. (£8,000 was a lot in the early 18th century!)
3. Bhutan, which means 'end of the land'.
4. The Pickwick Club, in *The Pickwick Papers*.
5. Fencing. (In 1968 and 1972.)
6. David Puttnam.
7. Green.
8. They died in the same apartment.
9. Thunder.

164

1. What does a dolmen look like?
2. There were two at Heliopolis, Egypt. One went to New York's Central Park, the other to London's Embankment. What are they?
3. In which country could you stay in a parador?
4. Which poet did Oscar Wilde call 'an English saint in side whiskers'?
5. Which greyhound racing track did the BBC buy for £30 million?
6. In *Hi-de-Hi* what colour coat does Peggy long to wear?
7. What does an oenophile like?
8. For which hit musical was *Shut Up And Dance* an early planned title?
9. Golden Queen, Sigmabush and The Amateur are all kinds of *what*?

398

1. About whom did Kruschev say, 'He was bursting with an impatient desire to rule the world'?
2. Who did Lord Wavell say was 'always expecting rabbits to come out of empty hats'?
3. In which gulf is Anticosti Island?
4. Which poet had a face 'like a wedding cake left out in the rain'?
5. What nickname is given to the Northumberland Plate, run at Newcastle?
6. Which famous satirical TV programme had its last showing late on December 28th, 1963?
7. Which sport did actor Tom Selleck formerly play?
8. Which pop singer from Coventry was once a singing monk at medieval banquets?
9. How is a camel's blood different from that of all other mammals?

632

1. Which American actress said, 'I'm as pure as the driven slush'?
2. What did the Nazis plan to do in Operation Bernhard?
3. The Canal de Yucatan is between Mexico and which island?
4. Which novelist, who died in 1931, had 'Enoch' as his first name?
5. In which sport could you 'hang five'?
6. In which army film did Hywel Bennett and Wayne Sleep appear, with David Bowie as an extra?
7. Which 1890s artist did Oscar Wilde call 'a monstrous orchid'?
8. Which instrument does pop singer Phil Collins play?
9. The age of *what* can be estimated by Galvayne's Groove?

164

1. It is a large stone, with a hole in the centre. (In the West Country it is called a tolmen.)
2. The obelisks known as Cleopatra's Needles.
3. Spain – it is a state-owned hotel.
4. Matthew Arnold.
5. White City, for their new radio HQ.
6. Yellow.
7. Wine.
8. *West Side Story*.
9. Tomato.

398

1. Mao Tse-Tung.
2. Winston Churchill.
3. The Gulf of St Lawrence, Quebec.
4. W.H.Auden.
5. The Pitmen's Derby.
6. *That Was The Week That Was*.
7. Basketball, at UCLA.
8. Paul King.
9. It has oval red blood cells – all other mammals have round blood cells.

632

1. Tallulah Bankhead.
2. Produce masses of forged British bank-notes.
3. Cuba.
4. Arnold Bennett.
5. In surfing. (It means one's toes hang over the edge of the board.)
6. *The Virgin Soldiers*.
7. Aubrey Beardsley.
8. The drums. (He started when he was five.)
9. A horse. (It is found on a tooth.)

165

1. From what forerunner of paper does paper take its name?
2. Britain began using postage stamps in 1840. How long did it take America to follow suit?
3. In which year was snow first known to fall in the Sahara Desert?
4. To what sort of urn did Keats write an ode?
5. What medal did Fatima Whitbread win in the 1984 Olympics?
6. In which country was Yul Brynner born?
7. Which referee made history by sending a player off in the 1985 FA Cup Final?
8. Where was 'The Cotton Club' situated?
9. What is the plural of grouse?

399

1. What is the other name for an auctioneer's hammer?
2. During World War II what petrol substitute was used by many vehicles?
3. In which country does the River Po flow?
4. Who, in 1900, wrote *The Interpretation of Dreams*?
5. In which year was wind surfing first included in the Olympic games?
6. Who played the liner's Captain in the 1974 film *Juggernaut*?
7. 'Roy G. Biv' is a mnemonic for *what*?
8. Ignaz Joseph Pleyel was a very successful piano manufacturer. But which great composer's pupil was he?
9. What do sessile flowers lack?

633

1. Who operates the Red Star delivery service?
2. Who was murdered by Nathuran Godse, in 1948?
3. From which country do Skoda cars come?
4. Who said, 'Nothing that is worth knowing can be taught'?
5. What vehicle did Allan Abbott race to a world record?
6. *Change Lobsters and Dance* is the title of which Austrian actress's autobiography?
7. What was Molière doing when he died?
8. By how much does a dot after a musical note increase its length?
9. What is the collective term for bears?

165

1. Papyrus.
2. Seven years.
3. In 1979.
4. Grecian.
5. A Bronze, for the Women's Javelin event.
6. In Japan.
7. Peter Willis.
8. In Harlem, New York – it was a night club famed for its jazz.
9. Grouse.

399

1. A gavel.
2. Methane gas.
3. Italy.
4. Sigmund Freud.
5. In 1984.
6. Omar Sharif.
7. The colours of the spectrum, in order.
8. Haydn's.
9. Stalks.

633

1. British Rail.
2. Mahatma Gandhi.
3. Czechoslovakia.
4. Oscar Wilde.
5. The bicycle.
6. Lilli Palmer's.
7. Acting in one of his own plays.
8. Half the length again of the original.
9. A sleuth.

166

1. What colour is 'bianco' wine?
2. In 1976, where did two Vikings land?
3. In which town may be found the oldest Christian church still in use?
4. Name the house in *Gone With The Wind.*
5. How many Gold Medals did Russia's Yelena Shushunova win at the 1985 European Women's Gymnastic Championships?
6. In *Brideshead Revisited*, who is Lord Sebastian Flyte's father?
7. On which game is Hugh Kelsey a prolific writer?
8. In which Gilbert and Sullivan operetta are Dick Deadeye and Ralph Rackstraw characters?
9. Why do folk avoid face-to-face confrontations with people with halitosis?

400

1. Which part of the vegetable mange-tout is eaten?
2. Who was the last English king to be killed in battle?
3. McCarren Airport serves which American city?
4. Where is Graham Greene's novel *The Comedians* set?
5. Who, in 1963, was voted 'Young Cricketer of the Year'?
6. In which film were these the final words, 'Louis, I think this is the beginning of a beautiful friendship'?
7. Which US President had once been a professional male model?
8. *Bright Mohawk Valley* was the original title of which song, more often played as an instrumental?
9. For what does the acronym BASIC stand, in computer jargon?

634

1. What is the word for both a sharp pull and an American?
2. Who immediately preceded Abraham Lincoln as US President?
3. Which New York avenue is nicknamed the 'Great White Way'?
4. What does Robert Burns describe as a 'Wee, sleekit, cow'rin, tim'rous beastie'?
5. What is the longest foot race in the Olympics?
6. In the films, what was Tarzan's chimpanzee called?
7. Which congressman for California had won the Olympic decathlon?
8. Which country singer's autobiography is named after her greatest-selling hit, *Stand by your Man*?
9. Where, in your house, would you find sodium chloride?

166

1. White.
2. On Mars.
3. In Bethlehem.
4. Tara.
5. Four.
6. The Marquis of Marchmain.
7. Bridge.
8. *HMS Pinafore.*
9. Because they have bad breath.

400

1. All of it.
2. Richard III.
3. Las Vegas.
4. In Haiti.
5. Geoffrey Boycott.
6. *Casablanca.*
7. Gerald Ford.
8. *Red River Valley.*
9. Beginner's All purpose Symbolic Instruction Code.

634

1. Yank.
2. James Buchanan.
3. Broadway.
4. A mouse.
5. The 50 km Road Walk.
6. Chita.
7. Bob Mathias (1952).
8. Tammy Wynette's.
9. In your salt cellar.

167

1. By what name is the Shinkansen better known?
2. Pope Gregory the Great first declared which city to be the centre of the Christian Church?
3. What is Sinology?
4. Who wrote, 'Marriage is like life in this – that it is a field of battle and not a bed of roses'?
5. Which soccer team plays home matches at Turf Moor?
6. *The Virgin Soldiers* was made into a film. But who wrote the book?
7. In which form of art did Donatello specialise?
8. Who wrote both words and music to *Call Me Madam*?
9. Who discovered the element sodium?

401

1. Which constellation is symbolized by twins?
2. In what ratio did the French cavalry outnumber the victorious English at the Battle of Agincourt?
3. If you were a Selenite, where would you live?
4. Who succeeded Wordsworth as Poet Laureate?
5. What colour belts do beginners wear, in Judo?
6. Name the Flintstones' daughter.
7. Who first said, 'There never was a good war or a bad peace'?
8. From what material are marimbas made?
9. What is Iceland's national symbol?

635

1. From which one type of grapes is the wine Asti Spumante made?
2. Who asked the oracle at Ammon whether the murderers of his father (Philip II) had all been punished?
3. Which old hunting cry became the name of part of London's West End?
4. Who were Cain and Abel's parents?
5. How high is a badminton net at its centre?
6. Which professional wrestler played Thunderlips in the film *Rocky III*?
7. What is the title of the head of the Campbell clan?
8. Who was the conductor of the Black and White Minstrels?
9. To which order of birds do budgies belong?

167

1. The 'bullet' train. (Of Japan.)
2. Rome.
3. The knowledge of things connected with China and the Chinese.
4. R.L. Stevenson.
5. Burnley.
6. Leslie Thomas.
7. Sculpture.
8. Irving Berlin.
9. Sir Humphrey Davy.

401

1. Gemini.
2. 5 to 1.
3. On the moon.
4. Alfred, Lord Tennyson.
5. White.
6. Pebbles.
7. Benjamin Franklin.
8. Wood.
9. A falcon.

635

1. The Muscat grape.
2. Alexander the Great.
3. So-ho! (Soho.)
4. Adam and Eve.
5. Five feet.
6. Hulk Hogan.
7. The Duke of Argyll.
8. George Mitchell.
9. The parrots.

168

1. How many masts does a ketch have?
2. Which king was said to have been 'crowned' with his mother's bracelet at nine months?
3. What is the city of Caerdydd called in English?
4. Which poet, who died in 1915, had the middle name 'Chawner'?
5. What do Americans call 'natural English'?
6. On 1930s radio, what did lodgers, rabbits, commercial travellers and honeymoon couples have in common?
7. What are you doing if you employ Naismith's formula to find out how long it will take?
8. *Sing a Rude Song* was a musical about which music-hall star?
9. What is the only nut native to the USA?

402

1. Kernmantel is one of the two types of *what*?
2. Which King barred his wife from Westminster Abbey during his coronation?
3. What is the biggest department store in Moscow's Red Square?
4. Which great poet did Charles Lamb call 'an archangel a little damaged'?
5. 'Navy ride' and 'snap down' are terms from which sport?
6. Which film star's first names were Roscoe Conkling?
7. What is a spelunker's hobby?
8. To which group does Joe Leeway now belong, after being their roadie?
9. What sort of animal was Grimbert in the old stories about Reynard the Fox?

636

1. What is the equivalent of a cowboy in Australia?
2. Which English king's wife, Berengaria, never came to England?
3. America's gold is stored at Fort Knox, but where is its silver stored?
4. Which singer called his autobiography *Yes I Can*?
5. For which football team did Muhren, Thijssen, Wark and Mariner all once play?
6. In which TV series did Dirk Benedict play Lt. Starbuck?
7. Which artist said, 'Bullfighters are the priests of a Spanish god who sacrifices himself'?
8. What sort of music sounds like what Cinderella heard at midnight?
9. Why are American 'quarter horses' so called?

168

1. Two.
2. Henry VI.
3. Cardiff.
4. Rupert Brooke.
5. A spin or twist put on a ball, as in billiards.
6. They were all banned as subjects for jokes.
7. Planning a cross-country hike.
8. Marie Lloyd.
9. The pecan.

402

1. Climbing rope. (The other is cable-laid.)
2. George IV.
3. GUM.
4. Samuel Taylor Coleridge.
5. Wrestling.
6. 'Fatty' Arbuckle's. (1887–1933.)
7. Exploring caves. (It is the American word.)
8. *The Thompson Twins.*
9. A badger.

636

1. A stockman.
2. Richard I's.
3. At West Point.
4. Sammy Davis Jr.
5. Ipswich Town.
6. *Battlestar Galactica.*
7. Salvador Dali.
8. Ragtime! Sorry about that ...
9. They are very fast over a quarter of a mile.

169

1. On what shape traffic signs are warnings displayed?
2. Who, in 1901, became MP for Oldham?
3. For what do the letters PC stand, on an Ordnance Survey map?
4. In which book are the Houyhnhnms introduced?
5. Who opened the 1936 Olympic Games?
6. In which 1957 film did Nancy and Ronald Reagan both appear?
7. Sir Sidney Nolan painted which outlaw many times?
8. In the song *Lullaby of Broadway* which two restaurants are mentioned?
9. What is probably the most dangerous point in a space trip?

403

1. At the September equinox, how many hours of daylight are there in the 24, all over the world?
2. During World War II Mussolini banned all comic strips bar one. Which?
3. Apart from shaking hands, what is the other traditional way of greeting one another in Tibet?
4. The poem *Metroland* was written by which Poet Laureate?
5. For which county did Bob Willis play cricket?
6. In *Jaws*, how is the shark finally killed?
7. Who painted *Tahitian Women Bathing*?
8. From where does calypso music originate?
9. How many hours' sleep per 24 does an antelope need?

637

1. Approximately how many individual journeys are made on the London Underground annually?
2. What killed some 300,000 people in Calcutta, in October 1737?
3. From what are the majority of buildings in Aberdeen constructed?
4. Name Paddington Bear's antique-shop-owner friend.
5. How many different strokes are usually used in a medley swimming race?
6. Who played Kid Shelleen in the film *Cat Ballou*?
7. Which racing driver became World Superstars Champion in 1981?
8. Name two of Verdi's three operas called after Shakespearian characters.
9. Which mineral has the human body in the greatest abundance?

169

1. Triangular.
2. Winston Churchill.
3. Public convenience.
4. *Gulliver's Travels*.
5. Adolf Hitler.
6. *Hellcats of the Navy*.
7. Ned Kelly.
8. Angelo's and Maxi's.
9. Re-entry to the earth's atmosphere.

403

1. Twelve.
2. Mickey Mouse.
3. By bumping foreheads.
4. Sir John Betjeman.
5. Warwickshire.
6. It is blown up with dynamite.
7. Paul Gauguin.
8. The West Indies.
9. One.

637

1. 500 million.
2. An earthquake.
3. Granite.
4. Mr Gruber.
5. Four.
6. Lee Marvin.
7. Jody Scheckter.
8. *Falstaff, Otello* and *Macbeth*.
9. Calcium.

170

1. The National Economic Development Council. How is it commonly known?
2. What is the Sealed Knot Society?
3. After which race of people is the Caribbean named?
4. Which TV quizmaster wrote a detective story called *Landscape with Dead Dons*?
5. What is an Ace to a golfer?
6. What are known as 'Horse Operas'?
7. What award was finally made to Alfred Dreyfus?
8. At what age was Buddy Holly killed?
9. What is the common name for Vanessa Atalanta?

404

1. Who went to tell the King that the sky was falling down?
2. Who was the first US President to wear long trousers?
3. In which country is *La Stampa* a national newspaper?
4. Whose was the first recorded burial?
5. Where were soccer's World Cup Finals held in 1982?
6. What does Stringfellow Hawke pilot?
7. A painting done in shades of a single colour is called *what*?
8. In which film was the song *White Christmas* first heard?
9. Which animal did G. K. Chesterton describe in a poem as 'the devil's walking parody'?

638

1. From where is the public permitted to watch in the House of Commons?
2. What were Britain's enemies in World War II collectively called?
3. Which Scottish castle was the scene of Duncan's murder?
4. Which magician befriended Carrot?
5. Who scored Southampton's goal in the 1976 FA Cup Final?
6. Which was the world's first teletext service?
7. Homepride's chief flour-grader will always be associated with whose voice?
8. Which father and daughter had a 1967 hit with *Something Stupid*?
9. According to Ophelia in *Hamlet*, for what is rosemary?

170

1. Neddy.
2. An historical society which, for example, re-enacted the Battle of Sedgemoor in July 1985.
3. The Caribs.
4. Robert Robinson.
5. A hole-in-one.
6. Wild West films.
7. The Legion of Honour.
8. Twenty-two.
9. The Red Admiral, a butterfly.

404

1. Chicken Licken.
2. Thomas Jefferson.
3. In Italy.
4. That of Sarah, Abraham's wife.
5. In Spain.
6. *Airwolf.*
7. A monochrome.
8. *Holiday Inn.*
9. The donkey.

638

1. The Strangers' Gallery.
2. The Axis.
3. Glamis Castle.
4. Catweazle.
5. Bobby Stokes. (A correction of Quiz 56, Q.5 in *The Ultimate Trivia Quiz Game Book*. Thanks to all those who wrote in pointing this out.)
6. ITV's *Oracle.*
7. John Le Mesurier's.
8. Frank and Nancy Sinatra.
9. Remembrance.

171

1. Eponymous words are derived from *what*?
2. Who had the codename Colonel Warden Thugheart in World War II?
3. In which county is the privately-run Bluebell Line?
4. From which Oscar Wilde work do these words come, 'Twenty years of romance make a woman look like a ruin, but twenty years of marriage make her something like a public building'?
5. Which country did Emile Zatopek represent with distinction?
6. What was Christine Jorgensen's original name?
7. Which pirate captained the ship *Adventure Galley*?
8. Which city's walls fell due to the blast of trumpets?
9. Which animal has most often been named Chanticleer?

405

1. Of whom did Winston Churchill say, 'A modest little man with much to be modest about'?
2. St Bruno of Cologne founded which religious order in 1084?
3. In the mouth of which bay do the Aran Islands lie?
4. Where does the phrase 'All hell broke loose' originate?
5. Which country has competed in all the modern Olympic games?
6. What colour are E.T.'s eyes?
7. Which Mafia leader was killed in a New York barbershop in 1957?
8. Which patriotic American song did Katherine Lee Bates write?
9. Barnes Wailis's 'bouncing bomb' was codenamed *what*?

639

1. Who said, 'The only thing I really mind about going to prison is the thought of Lord Longford coming to visit me'?
2. Which war began at Fort Sumter?
3. Which French Ministry is known as *le quai d'Orsay*?
4. Who wrote of Spain in *A Rose in Winter*?
5. Which is the final event of the heptathlon?
6. On which TV programme did the Beatles make their first major TV appearance in 1963?
7. What did Samuel Crompton invent?
8. The name of King Gama's daughter is the name of which Gilbert and Sullivan operetta?
9. Which is the largest variety of penguin?

171

1. The names of people.
2. Winston Churchill.
3. In Sussex.
4. *A Woman of No Importance.*
5. Czechoslovakia.
6. George Jorgensen.
7. Captain Kidd.
8. Jericho's.
9. The cock.

405

1. Clement Attlee.
2. The Carthusian Order.
3. Galway Bay.
4. In Milton's *Paradise Lost.*
5. Great Britain.
6. Blue.
7. Albert Anastasia.
8. *America the Beautiful.*
9. *Upkeep.*

639

1. Richard Ingrams, editor of *Private Eye.*
2. The American Civil War.
3. The Foreign Ministry.
4. Laurie Lee.
5. The 800 metres.
6. *Thank Your Lucky Stars.*
7. The spinning mule.
8. *Princess Ida.*
9. The emperor penguin.

172

1. A Geisha girl makes up her face in what colour?
2. The ship *The Eye of the Wind* set out in 1978 to follow the same round-the-world course as that of which navigator?
3. Name either of Kent's cathedral cities.
4. Who wrote the book of fairy tales called *A House of Pomegranates*?
5. Charles Bannerman was the very first cricketer to score *what*, in 1877?
6. Who directed the film *La Strada*?
7. Which dancer said, 'I just put my feet in the air and move them around'?
8. From what are the instruments in a steel band normally formed?
9. What colour is the live wire in a modern three-pin plug?

406

1. According to Ian Fleming, how many times can you live?
2. Who married Isabella of Castile in 1469?
3. According to the song, over which cliffs will there be bluebirds?
4. Conan Doyle's Wiggins led which gang of urchins?
5. Which European Championships were held at Crystal Palace on 22 June 1985?
6. Which TV series was based on Paul Scott's *The Raj Quartet*?
7. How are Mother Theresa and the inventor of dynamite connected?
8. Who had a 1958 hit with *Who's Sorry Now*?
9. Ascorbic acid is another name for which vitamin?

640

1. Why is 'Edwards' a good name for a one-fingered typist?
2. In which year did the minimum school-leaving age rise to 16 in Britain?
3. Which sea has no outlet?
4. In Greek mythology, what did Charybdis form?
5. Where is cricket's Shell Shield contested?
6. Into *what* was the stolen bullion fashioned in the film *The Lavender Hill Mob*?
7. Who, when asked how he kept so fit at 70, replied 'Gin and cigarettes'?
8. Where is the Fenice opera house?
9. What type of dog is a bitzer?

172

1. White.
2. Sir Francis Drake.
3. Canterbury and Rochester.
4. Oscar Wilde.
5. The very first run of the very first Test match – for Australia.
6. Fellini.
7. Fred Astaire.
8. Oil drums.
9. Brown.

406

1. Twice. (*You Only Live Twice.*)
2. Ferdinand.
3. Dover.
4. The Baker Street Irregulars.
5. The Octopush Championships. (Underwater hockey.)
6. *The Jewel in the Crown.*
7. Mother Theresa won the Nobel Peace Prize – the awards being instigated by Alfred Nobel, the inventor of dynamite.
8. Connie Francis.
9. Vitamin C.

640

1. All the letters of his name are in a block on the standard keyboard.
2. In 1973.
3. The Dead Sea.
4. A whirlpool.
5. In the West Indies.
6. Toy Eiffel Towers.
7. Denis Thatcher.
8. In Venice.
9. A mongrel.

173

1. What is the bookmakers' signalling system called?
2. Who caused Offa's Dyke to be built in the eighth century?
3. Who, in 1977, said, 'Iran is an island of stability in one of the more troubled areas of the world'?
4. Who said, 'You go first and I'll precede you'?
5. Which horse won the 1985 Epsom Derby?
6. Name Alf Garnett's daughter, played by Una Stubbs in the TV series *Till Death Us Do Part*.
7. Abraham Zapruder filmed the assassination of which US President?
8. What did she wear with her hulahula skirt?
9. The positive electrode is the anode. What is the negative one called?

407

1. Who is the head of Bristow's firm, in Frank Dickens' cartoon strip?
2. Over which ancient country did Hammurabi rule?
3. With which country's cuisine is nan bread chiefly associated?
4. Who wrote *Wilhelm Meister*?
5. What happened to the Oxford crews in the Boat Races of 1925 and 1951?
6. Who was the Oscar-winning star of the film *Hamlet*?
7. Whose father said, 'They'll never do it. It is only given to God and angels to fly'?
8. Why did two major theatre circuits ban P.J. Proby's act as obscene, in 1965?
9. What do ailurophiles love?

641

1. Romark the Hypnotist collided with *what* shortly after setting off to drive blindfold through the centre of Ilford?
2. As what was Gil Eanes famed in the fifteenth century?
3. Thebaw was the last king of which country?
4. What is Gatsby's first name?
5. Who is known as 'The Doc' in soccer?
6. For what was Vesta Tilley best known?
7. How is Prince William related to Prince Edward?
8. What type of choral work is Handel's *Messiah*?
9. 'No mere machine can replace a reliable and honest clerk.' About what was this said?

A

173

1. Tic-tac.
2. King Offa.
3. President Jimmy Carter.
4. Mrs Malaprop – in Sheridan's *The Rivals.*
5. *Slip Anchor.*
6. Rita.
7. John F. Kennedy.
8. Red feathers, according to the song.
9. The cathode.

407

1. Sir Reginald Chester Perry.
2. Babylonia.
3. India's.
4. Goethe.
5. They sank.
6. Laurence Olivier.
7. Bishop Wright, father of Orville and Wilbur.
8. Because his trousers kept splitting.
9. Cats.

641

1. A police van.
2. As an explorer and navigator.
3. Burma.
4. Jay.
5. Tommy Docherty.
6. Male impersonations.
7. He is his nephew.
8. It is an oratorio.
9. The typewriter.

174

1. What was unusual about the three saints Willibald, Wallburga and Winebald?
2. Where did Napier take an 1868 expedition to rescue Britons held hostage by Theodore, the ruler?
3. What is built on Jenkins Hill in Washington, D.C.?
4. In the James Bond books, who is Bond's Scots housekeeper at his London flat?
5. Which sport is played at Wankhede Stadium?
6. Who starred in a flop musical *The Three Musketeers*, then became a prince in *Dynasty*?
7. Which Sioux Indian chief's real name was Tashunca-Uitco?
8. Under what name did Don Van Vliet form the *Magic Band* in 1964?
9. What are zoonoses?

408

1. Bedford Fillbasket, Peer Gynt and Thor are all *what*?
2. The explorer Jacques Cartier and his men were cured of *what* by brewing up the leaves of the white pine?
3. Which country produces the most coal?
4. According to Conan Doyle, what was detective Holmes's first name?
5. In which game do you hear the terms 'blots', 'bearing off', and 'tables'?
6. Which film had six sections, starting with 'The Set-Up' and 'The Hook'?
7. What nickname was given to President Rutherford Hayes's wife because she wouldn't serve alcohol in the White House?
8. Which singer was nicknamed 'Queen of Disco'?
9. In 1885, Gunnar Gavelin rode from Stockholm to Moscow in 27 days – on *what*?

642

1. What sort of Australian food is a floater?
2. Which dancing religion did Wovoka create for the Paiute Indians in the 1880s?
3. Which great explorer's middle name was Janszoon?
4. What is odd about the tiger Sabor in the Tarzan books?
5. From which country does the football team Valkeakosken Haka come?
6. Which Friendly Ghost gets a bad time from Fatso, Lusso and Lazo?
7. What did the Royal Victoria Coffee House eventually become?
8. For which product did Barry Manilow sing the jingle 'You Deserve A Break Today'?
9. Who discovered that coal-tar naphtha and rubber could make cloth waterproof?

174

1. They were two brothers and a sister, who lived in the 8th century.
2. Abyssinia. (Napier was successful.)
3. The Capitol.
4. May
5. Cricket, in Bombay.
6. Michael Praed.
7. Crazy Horse, who fought at Little Big Horn.
8. Captain Beefheart.
9. Animal diseases caught by man.

408

1. Types of Brussels sprouts.
2. Scurvy – it was rich in vitamin C.
3. Russia.
4. William – William Sherlock Scott Holmes.
5. In backgammon.
6. *The Sting*, made in 1973.
7. 'Lemonade Lucy'.
8. Donna Summer.
9. On the back of a large pet pig.

642

1. Meat pie in soup.
2. The Ghost Dance religion.
3. Abel Tasman, discoverer of New Zealand.
4. There are no tigers in Africa.
5. Finland. (They have played in the European Cup.)
6. Caspar.
7. London's Old Vic theatre.
8. McDonalds hamburgers.
9. Charles Macintosh, hence the name of the raincoat.

175

1. To date, the majority of Popes have been of what nationality?
2. What colour was the Red Baron's plane in World War I?
3. BMW cars come from which country?
4. The author of *Marriage and Morals* gained a Nobel Prize in 1950. Who was it?
5. Which soccer team is nicknamed the 'Hatters'?
6. What are the highest theatre and concert seats jocularly known as?
7. Who summoned a British Cabinet delegation at 6.00 a.m. one day, then smiled and said, 'This is my day of silence, but please go on talking'?
8. What was Barbra Streisand's contribution to the film *The Eyes of Laura Mars*?
9. Why is seaweed a good thing to eat?

409

1. What is the name for the study of the efficiency of people working?
2. Of which order of architecture is the Parthenon in Athens?
3. What is the approximate population of Brazil?
4. Who is 'The Fat Owl of the Remove'?
5. To whom did National Coach Tom McNab once say, 'You're a bum runner and you'll never make a decathlete'?
6. Where was the first Royal Variety Show staged in 1930?
7. Who was *Time* magazine's 'Man of the Year' in 1942?
8. The song *Alice Blue Gown* comes from which operetta?
9. 'Eye of newt, and toe of frog, wool of bat and tongue of dog.' Sounds appetising! Who cooked this concoction?

643

1. Where on the body are cummerbunds worn?
2. Who passed more than 300 death sentences at the 'Bloody Assizes'?
3. The TV character Robert Ironside acts as a crime consultant in which city?
4. How long did Alex Haley take to write *Roots*?
5. Australia's cricket team came to Britain in 1985, but which other (unlikely) national side visited and played matches at club level?
6. Who played Sugar Cane in the film *Some Like it Hot*?
7. Who said, 'The finest eloquence is that which gets things done'?
8. Which great partnership first met in The Royal Gallery of Illustration in London?
9. What is the snowline?

175

1. Italian.
2. Red.
3. Germany.
4. Bertrand Russell.
5. Luton Town.
6. 'The Gods'.
7. Gandhi.
8. She sang the title song.
9. It has a very high iodine content.

409

1. Ergonomics.
2. Doric.
3. 125 million.
4. Billy Bunter.
5. Daley Thompson.
6. At the London Palladium.
7. Joseph Stalin.
8. *Irene.*
9. The Three Witches in *Macbeth.*

643

1. Round the tum.
2. Lord Chief Justice George Jeffreys.
3. San Francisco.
4. 11 years.
5. Italy.
6. Marilyn Monroe.
7. David Lloyd George.
8. Gilbert and Sullivan.
9. The level above which snow never completely melts.

176

1. Who publishes *The War Cry*?
2. Which country used the first aeroplane in war?
3. Where would you find Queen's Island?
4. Which school did Jennings, Darbishire and Co. attend?
5. The Iroquois Cup is awarded in which game?
6. Which Peter Bogdanovitch film is based on the life of Rocky Dennis?
7. Which cowboy actor owns the California Angels baseball team, five radio stations and a hotel in Palm Springs?
8. The Vuillaume family were famed for making *what*?
9. Otitis affects which organs of the body?

410

1. Apart from his fiddlers, for what else did Old King Cole call?
2. Why were trade signs, rather than names, once hung outside shops?
3. The Iguassu Falls are in which country?
4. Name the high priest's servant whose ear Peter cut off.
5. Why did bowling change from 9 to 10 pins in the USA?
6. In the USA, for what is a Clio awarded annually?
7. To whom did her agent say, 'You'd better learn secretarial work, or else get married'?
8. What is gathered in May on a cold and frosty morning?
9. Approximately how many earth years does Neptune take to orbit the sun?

644

1. Charlotte Beyser Bartholdi was the model for which statue?
2. What happened to letter post in 1968 in the UK?
3. Tea ceremonies play important roles in which country?
4. Who wrote, 'Marriage has many pains, but celibacy has no pleasures'?
5. The old Indian game of Poona is now called what, in its modern form?
6. The 1983 film *The Boys in Blue* featured which comedian duo?
7. Who goes first in *Go*?
8. Which singer starred in the *Matt Helm* series of films?
9. What, and how old, is a teg?

176

1. The Salvation Army.
2. Italy, in their Turkish war of 1911.
3. In Belfast.
4. Linbury Court Preparatory School.
5. Lacrosse.
6. *Mask.*
7. Gene Autry.
8. Violins.
9. The ears.

410

1. His pipe and his bowl.
2. Because few folk could read.
3. In Argentina.
4. Malchus.
5. To outwit the old law which forbade the playing of 9 pins.
6. The best TV commercial.
7. Marilyn Monroe.
8. Nuts.
9. 165 years.

644

1. The Statue of Liberty.
2. Class distinction – it was divided into first and second class.
3. In Japan.
4. Samuel Johnson.
5. Badminton.
6. Tommy Cannon and Bobby Ball.
7. Black.
8. Dean Martin.
9. A sheep – aged two years.

177

1. What are the first ten amendments to the US Constitution called?
2. What took place in 1897 at Bonanza Creek, Alaska?
3. What service did the Reverend John Flynn begin in Australia?
4. *Summoned by Bells* is which Poet Laureate's autobiography, in verse?
5. Why did BBC commentator Tommy Woodroffe eat his hat, in 1938?
6. What is the main British actors' newspaper called?
7. Why did Gainsborough paint his *Blue Boy*?
8. Sir Frederick Ashton's ballet *Rhapsody* is danced to what music?
9. Experiments with which vegetable helped Mendel formulate the basic laws of heredity?

411

1. Of what is clinophobia the fear?
2. Who first used hand grenades?
3. In which county is the Naze?
4. Name the Cyclops who imprisoned Odysseus.
5. Which river runs under The Oval cricket ground?
6. Which colour do actors consider to be unlucky on stage?
7. Which Dorothy L. Sayers novel features cards and card games as chapter headings?
8. Which music hall artist made the song *Boiled Beef and Carrots* popular?
9. What colour bones has the garfish?

645

1. 'We shall fight on the beaches, we shall fight on the landing-grounds, we shall fight in the ____ and in the streets.' What is missing?
2. When did Britain come off the Gold Standard?
3. Where is the Quirinal Palace?
4. Who was the world's first baby?
5. Who did Richard Raskind become in 1977?
6. Which appropriately named play is set in a women's Turkish bath?
7. Where is the Walker Art Gallery?
8. Which great soprano is Catalan?
9. Of what are the cells of honeycombs made?

177

1. The Bill of Rights.
2. The Klondike gold rush.
3. The Flying Doctor Service.
4. John Betjeman.
5. Commentating on the 1938 FA Cup Final he said, 'If there's a goal now, I'll eat my hat.' There was, and he was a man of his word.
6. The *Stage*.
7. To prove to art critics that blue needn't be a cold, dull colour.
8. *Rhapsody on a Theme of Paganini*, by Rachmaninov.
9. Peas.

411

1. Going to bed.
2. The Mongols, under Khubla Khan.
3. Essex.
4. Polyphemus.
5. The Effra.
6. Green.
7. *Unpleasantness at the Belladonna Club.*
8. Harry Champion.
9. Bright green.

645

1. 'Fields'.
2. In 1931.
3. In Rome.
4. Cain.
5. Renee Richards – and was barred from entering both the US Tennis Open and Women's events.
6. *Steaming.*
7. In Liverpool.
8. Monserrat Caballé.
9. Beeswax.

178

1. Founded in 1702, what was London's first daily newspaper?
2. In which year was the first baby born on Antarctica?
3. Honolulu is on which of the Hawaiian islands?
4. To what was the 'listener' on his way when buttonholed by the Ancient Mariner?
5. With which sport and which country would you associate the *City Slick Sidewinders*?
6. Who was the husband of Lucille Ball in the TV series *I Love Lucy*?
7. How did the painter Turner study a storm at sea?
8. Which singer wrote the cookbook *Cooking for You Alone*?
9. Red iron oxide is more commonly called *what*?

412

1. What does the culinary term 'farci' mean?
2. Approximately how many Volkswagen *Beetles* were manufactured?
3. Of which country is Maseru the capital?
4. Name the popular pre-flight free magazine distributed at Heathrow and Gatwick Airports.
5. Which ex-West Ham player became commissioner of the North American Soccer League?
6. Which Scots comedian is the brother of singer Annie Ross?
7. Barbara Hulanicki and husband Stephen FitzSimon began *what*?
8. Which song was banned while the Queen toured Canada in 1960?
9. In which constellation are the Seven Sisters?

646

1. What kind of criminal was known as a 'leather-lifter' in the USA?
2. The *Cutty Sark* was what kind of ship?
3. What is the (human) population of Australia?
4. Who wrote the play *The Quare Fellow*?
5. Which member of the English aristocracy won an Olympic Gold Medal for the 400 metres hurdles?
6. Who played Pope Julius II in the 1965 film *The Agony and the Ecstasy*?
7. Name Atari's first video game.
8. Whose first symphony is named *Winter Daydreams*?
9. Are hermaphrodites male or female?

178

1. The *Daily Courant.*
2. In 1978.
3. Oahu.
4. A wedding.
5. Baseball. They play in England.
6. Desi Arnaz. (And in real life, too.)
7. By having himself strapped to a ship's mast.
8. Johnny Mathis.
9. Rust.

412

1. 'Stuffed'.
2. Fifteen million.
3. Lesotho.
4. *Airport.*
5. Phil Woosnam.
6. Jimmy Logan.
7. The shop 'Biba'.
8. *The Battle of New Orleans.*
9. The Pleiades.

646

1. A pick-pocket.
2. A tea clipper.
3. About fifteen million.
4. Brendan Behan.
5. Lord Burghley, in 1928.
6. Rex Harrison.
7. *Pong.*
8. Tchaikovsky's.
9. Both.

179

1. Which rather special date is said to be Superman's birthday?
2. Which English king was ransomed for 150,000 marks in 1194?
3. In which city is the Gefion Fountain, which shows the goddess ploughing with her four sons, who had been turned into oxen?
4. In the church year, what is 28 December?
5. What name is used for the sport of riding a three-ski tricycle over water?
6. Which TV cops used the call-sign 'Zebra 3' from a red-and-white Ford Torino?
7. Which flower is Mary Quant's logo?
8. Which Beatles song begins 'Flew in from Miami Beach BOAC'?
9. Which scientific 'year' ended in 1958 after 18 months?

413

1. Where did Dr Edward Gibson spend Christmas, 1973?
2. When Gerald Ford became President, who was his (unelected) Vice President?
3. Where can you see the Peter and Paul Fortress and the battleship Aurora?
4. Which mystery writer also wrote *The Man Born To Be King*, a life of Jesus?
5. What is the diameter of the centre circle in soccer?
6. In which film did an invisible dragon called Elliot appear, or rather, *not* appear?
7. What was 'Professor Longhair', or Ron Byrd, good at?
8. Jazzmen Theodor Navarro and Thomas Waller both used the same nickname – *what*?
9. In 1969, after Apollo VII journeyed round the moon, how late was it when it got back?

647

1. What very useful food item did Italo Marcioni invent in 1903?
2. Who was the last British monarch to have his statue erected during his lifetime?
3. In which capital city does the Old Town, called 'Gamla Stan', stand on four islands?
4. Who is the most famous fictional student of Wittenberg University?
5. What did the Irish rugby player, D.B. Walkington, wear except when making a tackle?
6. Why did child film star Jackie 'Butch' Jenkins give up acting in the 1940s?
7. Which famous couple got divorced in 1809?
8. Who, just before take-off, said 'Where the hell are the parachutes?'?
9. The USSR's ship *Lenin* was the first atomic-powered *what*?

179

1. 29 February.
2. Richard I.
3. In Copenhagen.
4. The feast of the Holy Innocents in remembrance of the babies put to death by order of King Herod.
5. Aquabobbing – invented in Switzerland in 1967.
6. Starsky and Hutch.
7. The daisy.
8. *Back in the USSR.*
9. International Geophysical Year.

413

1. Orbiting the Earth in Skylab.
2. Nelson Rockefeller.
3. In Leningrad.
4. Dorothy L. Sayers.
5. Twenty yards.
6. *Pete's Dragon.* (1977.)
7. Rock 'n' roll piano playing, in its early days.
8. 'Fats.'
9. Eleven seconds.

647

1. The icecream cone.
2. Edward VII – it stands in Tooting Broadway.
3. In Stockholm.
4. Hamlet.
5. A monocle.
6. Because he developed a stutter.
7. Napoleon and Josephine. 'Not tonight, Josephine!'
8. Bandleader Glenn Miller, whose plane disappeared in 1944.
9. Ice-breaker.

180

1. Who or what do Francophiles admire?
2. The Liberty Bell was ringing for the funeral of Chief Justice John Marshall when *what* happened?
3. In which country is Salonika?
4. Which of Shakespeare's plays ends with the words 'Go bid the soldiers shoot'?
5. Peter O'Sullevan normally commentates on which sport?
6. What began early in the day on 17 January 1983?
7. For what was Humphrey Repton famous?
8. For what would you train at White Lodge?
9. What is the main source of atomic energy?

414

1. What is known as the 'Flying Hamburger'?
2. Which king of England's two German mistresses were known as 'Elephant and Castle'?
3. Over which islands did Queen Liliuokalani rule?
4. In which Dickens novel does this line feature, 'Be very careful o' widders all your life, 'specially if they've kept a public house'?
5. What colour flag tells racing drivers that the race has started?
6. Who co-starred with Laurence Harvey in the film *Room at the Top*?
7. Who designed the Cenotaph in Whitehall?
8. Who had a 1959 hit with *Living Doll*?
9. Why do people in Madley in Herefordshire observe the skies?

648

1. Who are known as 'The Bill'?
2. Who were paid for the first time in 1911?
3. In which country is Kabul?
4. Who is Cedric Errol better known as?
5. In which activity might you adopt the 'crucifix' position?
6. Television stars Vivien, Rick, Nigel and Mike – who are they?
7. Which French painter, born in Limoges in 1841, began his career painting on porcelain?
8. Decca's Dick Rowe said this in 1962 about a group, 'We don't like the sound – guitar groups are on the way out.' Which group?
9. How do the tails of monkeys and apes differ?

180

1. France and the French – not Franco!
2. Its historic crack appeared.
3. In Greece.
4. *Hamlet.*
5. Horse-racing.
6. Breakfast TV.
7. Landscape gardening.
8. Ballet dancing.
9. Uranium.

414

1. A German high-speed train.
2. George I's.
3. The Hawaiian Islands.
4. *Pickwick Papers.*
5. Green.
6. Simone Signoret.
7. Sir Edward Lutyens.
8. Cliff Richard.
9. A British satellite tracking station is established there.

648

1. The police.
2. MPs.
3. In Afghanistan.
4. Little Lord Fauntleroy.
5. In gymnastics, on the rings.
6. The Young Ones.
7. Renoir.
8. The Beatles.
9. Apes don't have tails.

181

1. Who helps Yogi Bear out of his troubles with the Ranger?
2. To prevent invasions during which wars were Martello towers originally erected in Britain?
3. Which is the world's most northerly capital city?
4. 'We are absolutely certain of the authenticity of this biography.' The publishers said this about which proven fraud?
5. What is the mascot for the 1986 Commonwealth Games?
6. Which actor wrote the play *The Man in the Glass Booth*?
7. Which snooker player received an MBE in 1985?
8. In which country is a koto most usually played?
9. Which is the next largest quadruped to the elephant?

415

1. Which PM introduced Premium Bonds?
2. Joanna the Mad reigned in which country in the early 16th century?
3. Which famous collection is housed in Manchester Square, London?
4. In Greek mythology, how many eyes had the giant Argus?
5. What is the minimum permitted weight for a professional heavyweight boxer?
6. Who plays Sam Whiskey in the 1969 film *Sam Whiskey*?
7. 'God's in his heaven, all's right with the world.' Who wrote it?
8. The *Swan Chorus* is in which Wagner opera?
9. Mariner IX orbited which planet in 1971?

649

1. Who summons the Commons to the Lords to hear the Queen's speech?
2. A 'Penny Bazaar' in 1887 started which great chain of stores?
3. The first six Presidents of the USA came from two states. Name either state.
4. What trade did Joseph teach Jesus?
5. How long is a volleyball court?
6. Film producer Irving Thalberg said, 'Forget it. No Civil War picture ever made a nickel', on being offered a film in 1938. Which?
7. What are potsherds, objects dealt with by archaeologists?
8. What is the official folk dance of the USA?
9. Friesian cattle are named after which province in Holland?

181

1. Boo Boo.
2. The Napoleonic Wars.
3. Reykjavik, the capital of Iceland.
4. Clifford Irving's biography of Howard Hughes.
5. Mac – the Scottie dog.
6. Robert Shaw.
7. Ray Reardon.
8. In Japan.
9. The hippopotamus.

415

1. Harold Macmillan.
2. In Spain.
3. The Wallace Collection.
4. One hundred.
5. 12 st. 7 lb.
6. Burt Reynolds.
7. Robert Browning.
8. *Lohengrin*.
9. Mars.

649

1. Black Rod.
2. Marks and Spencer.
3. Virginia and Massachusetts.
4. Carpentry.
5. Sixty feet.
6. *Gone With the Wind*.
7. Fragments of broken pot.
8. The Square Dance.
9. Friesland.

Q

182

1. What is the traditional way of signing a Valentine card?
2. Who was known as 'Stupor Mundi'?
3. The 39th parallel separates Canada from the USA; but what does the 38th parallel separate?
4. In which hospital is Richard Gordon's *Doctor in the House* set?
5. Who won the 1985 FA Cup Final?
6. In which 1969 film remake did Peter O'Toole and Petula Clark star?
7. Who painted *View of the Stour*?
8. Who composed the music for the ice-dancers Karen Barber and Nicky Slater's *Dragon Dance*?
9. What animal is the symbol of Millwall FC?

416

1. London cabby George King applied to join the United Nations as a delegate from *where*?
2. Simon de Montfort led the Barons' revolt against which king?
3. Which is the oldest city on the South American continent?
4. Who first translated Homer's *Odyssey* and *Iliad* into English?
5. 'Excuse me, Mr Umpire, but have I taken this batsman's wicket?' What is the usual way of asking this question?
6. Who replaced Pamela Sue Martin as Fallon, in *Dynasty*?
7. From what did Marie Curie die?
8. Christopher Robin went down with *whom*?
9. In a hunt, what is the 'brush'?

650

1. Where, on a dress, might you find a mutton-leg?
2. How many countries, in 1950, signed The European Convention of Human Rights?
3. Where is Valencia Island?
4. Who wrote, 'There's no form of prayer in the liturgy against bad husbands'?
5. Between which two points is the Fastnet yacht race sailed?
6. In *The Dukes of Hazzard*, how are Bo and Luke Duke related?
7. Publisher George Palmer Putnam was married to which aviator?
8. *B. Bumble and the* ______. Name the pop group.
9. Name Kattomeat's paw-scooping cat, as seen in their ads.

182

1. No signature – keep 'em guessing.
2. Frederick II, Holy Roman Emperor (1212–50).
3. North Korea from South Korea.
4. St Swithin's Hospital.
5. Manchester United.
6. *Goodbye, Mr Chips.*
7. John Constable.
8. Mike Batt.
9. The lion.

416

1. Venus. (He was rejected.)
2. Henry III, in 1261.
3. Lima, in Peru.
4. Alexander Pope.
5. 'Howzat?'
6. Emma Samms.
7. Leukaemia, caused by radiation.
8. Alice.
9. The fox's tail.

650

1. The top of the sleeve, which is extensively puffed at the shoulder and upper arm and tapers to fit closely to the forearm.
2. Fifteen.
3. Off the south-west coast of Ireland.
4. George Farquhar.
5. Cowes and the Fastnet Rock.
6. They are cousins.
7. Amelia Earhart.
8. *Stingers.*
9. Arthur.

183

1. Which motor manufacturers make the Dyane?
2. Who commanded the Prussian troops at the Battle of Waterloo?
3. What do Americans call what we call 'chips' – the edible kind?
4. In Greek mythology, who is both sister and wife to Zeus?
5. Over what distance is The Oaks run?
6. June Havoc, the Broadway and Hollywood star, had an equally famous sister. Who?
7. What explanation did Chris Lloyd give for Carol Thatcher's co-authorship of *Lloyd on Lloyd*?
8. Who wrote *Maple Leaf Rag*?
9. The mastiff and the greyhound were crossed to produce which breed?

417

1. The largest ships tend to carry *what*?
2. John Young sneaked what food on to his spacecraft in 1965?
3. On 12 June 1985, a Boeing 727 was blown up at Beirut Airport. To which country did it belong?
4. Tobias Smollett wrote *The Adventures of Peregrine* ______. What word is missing?
5. Which games take place at Braemar, annually?
6. Nicolai Poliakoff – under what name was he universally loved?
7. During World War II, in correspondence with Churchill, whose code reference was 'Naval Person'?
8. From which Puccini opera does the aria *Nessun' dorma* come?
9. A bristlecone pine tree in California has what distinction?

651

1. What does l.c. mean to a printer?
2. Over which country was King Peter II reigning when it was declared a republic in 1945?
3. St Thomas, St Croix and St John are the three largest islands in which group?
4. Who created Long John Silver?
5. In which year was the Davis Cup first contested?
6. On which actor's face is Captain Marvel's based?
7. Which Queen said, 'So that's what hay looks like'?
8. *The Blue Danube* is written in which dance tempo?
9. Which poet had a Newfoundland dog called Boatswain?

183

1. Citroën.
2. General von Bülow.
3. French fries.
4. Hera.
5. 1½ miles.
6. Gypsy Rose Lee.
7. 'No one else asked.'
8. Scott Joplin.
9. The Great Dane.

417

1. Oil – they are oil tankers.
2. A corned beef sandwich.
3. Jordan.
4. *Pickle.*
5. The Highland Games.
6. Coco the clown.
7. Franklin D. Roosevelt's.
8. *Turandot.*
9. That of being the oldest known living thing in the world.

651

1. Lower case, i.e. not capital letters.
2. Yugoslavia.
3. The Virgin Islands.
4. Robert Louis Stevenson.
5. In 1900.
6. Fred MacMurray's.
7. Queen Mary, wife of George V.
8. In waltz time.
9. Lord Byron.

184

1. When does the Russian Orthodox Church celebrate Christmas?
2. How were affairs of honour formerly settled?
3. Which royal residence was built on the site of a former leper colony?
4. Who wrote *A Connecticut Yankee in King Arthur's Court*?
5. Forty all – what is the call in tennis?
6. Who said, 'The play was a great success but the audience was a failure'?
7. Who drove a coach and four across Morecambe Bay in May 1985 – the first such crossing for 130 years?
8. Who was the male lead in *The Birth of the Blues* (1941)?
9. By what name is the cotton worm otherwise known, especially in the USA?

418

1. When we have a drought in the UK, how do we usually solve the problem?
2. During which war did the term 'Fifth Column' originate?
3. What do we call what Hungarians call the 'Duna'?
4. For what is the Booker McConnell Prize awarded annually?
5. Which job in sport did Bob Jenkins lose in 1985?
6. Who starred in 143 Robin Hood adventures on TV in the fifties and sixties and died in June 1985?
7. How many times did Sir Isaac Newton marry?
8. Which telephone number was the title of a Glenn Miller favourite?
9. What is the favourite food of the death watch beetle?

652

1. Which was the first British retail store group to allow customers to withdraw cash with their in-house charge cards?
2. Prior to 1851, where was Marble Arch?
3. What is 'un poisson d'avril' in France?
4. Pease-blossom; Cobweb; Moth. Which is the missing fairy?
5. In which yacht race did 13 competitors die in 1979?
6. Who was Popeye's girlfriend?
7. The great architect Charles Jeanneret was better known by what name?
8. Who sang with *The Luvvers*?
9. During its lifespan, what takes the following forms; parr, smolt, grilse?

184

1. 7 January.
2. By fighting duels.
3. St James's Palace.
4. Mark Twain. (Samuel Clemens.)
5. Deuce.
6. Oscar Wilde.
7. Prince Philip, Duke of Edinburgh.
8. Bing Crosby.
9. The boll weevil.

418

1. By appointing a Minister of Drought – it always rains the next day!
2. The Spanish Civil War. (1936–1939.)
3. The River Danube.
4. The best novel of the year.
5. Head of Umpires at Wimbledon – for giving a press interview.
6. Richard Greene.
7. He never did.
8. *Pennsylvania 6500.*
9. Wood.

652

1. Debenhams – from September 1985.
2. In front of Buckingham Palace.
3. An April Fool.
4. Mustard-seed. (In Shakespeare's *A Midsummer Night's Dream.*)
5. The Fastnet Yacht Race.
6. Olive Oyl.
7. Le Corbusier.
8. Lulu.
9. A salmon.

Q

185

1. Where is the Golden Temple, the holy place of Sikhism?
2. In 1780, which was the first US state to abolish slavery?
3. What does Australia actually mean?
4. What was Thackeray's middle name?
5. Which Yorkshire soccer club, in Division 1 in 1970, was in Division 4 by 1979?
6. *Penmarric* was turned into a TV serial, but who wrote the book?
7. Who designed Princess Elizabeth's wedding dress, in 1947?
8. What raises the strings of a violin and sends their vibrations to the body of the instrument?
9. Who invented enamel?

419

1. What would you burn in a thurible?
2. Name one of the three main battles of the English Civil War.
3. What is the official language of Kenya?
4. Lew Wallace wrote *Ben Hur*. What rank did he hold during the American Civil War?
5. How far is it between consecutive baseball bases?
6. Frances de la Tour played which character in *Rising Damp*?
7. Who said, 'Men are generally more careful of the breeding of their horses and dogs than of their children'?
8. Which pair wrote *Jesus Christ, Superstar?*
9. The pimpernel belongs to which family of plants?

653

1. Which religion was founded by Guru Baber Nanak?
2. What was Richard Parker's claim to fame in 1797?
3. How many tides a day has Southampton?
4. From where does the line, 'All hope abandon, ye who enter here' come?
5. Name two of the three US horse races that comprise their Triple Crown.
6. What type of hat does Donald Duck favour?
7. What was designer Chanel's first name?
8. Who composed *Keep the Home Fires Burning*?
9. What is a female hedgehog called?

185

1. At Amritsar.
2. Massachusetts.
3. 'Southern Land'.
4. Makepeace.
5. Huddersfield Town.
6. Susan Howatch.
7. Norman Hartnell.
8. The bridge.
9. Bernard Palissy.

419

1. Incense.
2. Edgehill, Marston Moor and Naseby.
3. Swahili.
4. That of General.
5. Thirty yards.
6. Miss Jones.
7. William Penn.
8. Tim Rice and Andrew Lloyd Webber.
9. The Primrose family.

653

1. Sikhism.
2. He led the Nore Mutiny.
3. Four.
4. Dante's *Inferno*.
5. The Kentucky Derby, the Preakness and the Belmont Stakes.
6. A sailor's hat.
7. Coco was the name she favoured, but also accept her real name, Gabrielle.
8. Ivor Novello.
9. A sow.

186

1. In which prison was Dr Crippen hanged?
2. Which famous ship did Captain Langsdorff sink off Uruguay in 1939?
3. Which difficult-to-visit country calls itself 'Land of the Eagles'?
4. Sir John Oldcastle was said to be the model for which Shakespeare character?
5. Which sport did the Irish canon Rev. William Grey introduce to Japan?
6. Which Hollywood producer said he made 'beautiful films for beautiful people'?
7. What did Jean François Marie Arouet decide to call himself?
8. Which song was inspired by the sea battle of Quiberon in 1759?
9. Every summer Moscow suffers from a plague of 'pookh'. What is it?

420

1. Who wouldn't pay homage to a hat in Altdorf market place?
2. What did the 'Sons of Liberty' do in 1773, disguised as Red Indians?
3. Which city did the Arno river flood in 1966?
4. About which book did some say 'John, print it' in 1678?
5. For which country did cricketer Viv Richards play soccer in the World Cup?
6. Which film star said, 'I started out to be a sex fiend, but I couldn't pass the physical'?
7. Chinese Empress Tzu Hai, who died in 1908, once insisted her royal train could be driven only by whom?
8. What did Mozart forget to write for *Don Giovanni*?
9. What did Dr Simpson first use in an operation on 12 November 1847?

654

1. Which English company owns the George V Hotel in Paris?
2. What killed Prince Albert in 1861?
3. Where is the miniature city of Madwodam, near its country's Parliament?
4. In Hardy, Dumpling, Fancy, Tidy and Loud preferred to be milked by which dairymaid?
5. What did Pagan Swallow win in 1985, in his last race?
6. Which film star was America's most decorated soldier of World War II?
7. Who painted *The Water Seller of Seville*, now in the Wellington Museum?
8. In the Barbra Streisand song, who are 'the luckiest people in the world'?
9. Apart from being a bargain, what is a 'snip' when referring to a horse?

186

1. In Pentonville, in 1910.
2. His own, the *Graf Spee*.
3. Albania.
4. Falstaff.
5. Hockey, early this century.
6. Louis B. Mayer, of MGM.
7. Voltaire.
8. *Hearts of Oak*.
9. A shower of the fine fluffy seeds of female poplar trees – it gets *everywhere*!

420

1. William Tell.
2. They dumped tea overboard in the incident known as 'the Boston Tea Party'.
3. Florence.
4. *The Pilgrim's Progress*, according to Bunyan.
5. Antigua.
6. Robert Mitchum.
7. Eunuchs, but her advisers persuaded her otherwise.
8. The overture. He wrote it on the day of the first performance.
9. Chloroform.

654

1. Trust House Forte.
2. Typhoid, a result of bad drains.
3. The Hague, in Holland.
4. Tess, of *Tess of the D'Urbervilles*.
5. The Greyhound Derby.
6. Audie Murphy.
7. Velazquez.
8. 'People who need people.'
9. A small white mark on the forehead, or elsewhere on the body.

Q

187

1. When an MP wishes the public galleries to be cleared, what does he say to the Speaker?
2. During the 18th century, what form of tax was introduced to raise money for road improvements?
3. For what is the Isle of Harris famed?
4. Who wrote *Trilby*?
5. Why are Sheffield Wednesday called 'Wednesday'?
6. In which town was the film *Santa Fé Trail* premièred?
7. Which ball starts in the middle of the table at snooker?
8. Holly Johnson is a member of which group?
9. Where on their bodies do bees carry the pollen they collect?

421

1. Which drink has 'The real thing' as its advertising slogan?
2. Which is the oldest surviving trading company in the world, dating from 1670?
3. Approximately how many Indonesian islands are inhabited?
4. Who wrote *Lolly Willowes*, the first book ever to be offered to the Book-of-the-Month Club?
5. The Wanderers were the first team to win which cup?
6. Who starred in the TV programme *The Blood Donor*?
7. Why was Dr Samuel Mudd's name mud?
8. Who was the original stage *Evita*?
9. Which gas, in solid form, is called 'dry ice'?

655

1. What is the Spanish equivalent of the English name John?
2. 'Hobby horses' were an early form of what vehicle?
3. How many tons of barley are grown in the UK each year for brewing?
4. Who wrote *The Cask of Amontillado*?
5. In the 1982 Soccer World Cup Finals, which was the only country to score against England?
6. How did Martha Graham become famous?
7. Hampton Court was originally the residence of which cardinal?
8. Who composed the *James Bond* film theme?
9. How many eyes have most types of spider?

187

1. 'Mr Speaker, I spy strangers.'
2. Tolls.
3. Tweed.
4. George du Maurier.
5. Because the team was founded by butchers who played on their half-day off – Wednesday.
6. In Santa Fé.
7. Blue.
8. *Frankie Goes To Hollywood.*
9. On their hind legs.

421

1. Coca Cola. (Coke.)
2. The Hudson Bay Company.
3. 3,000.
4. Sylvia Townsend Warner.
5. The FA Cup.
6. Tony Hancock.
7. Because he set the broken leg of John Wilkes Booth, the assassin of Abraham Lincoln.
8. Elaine Paige.
9. Carbon dioxide.

655

1. Juan.
2. The bicycle.
3. About two million.
4. Edgar Allan Poe.
5. France.
6. She was a renowned dancer and choreographer.
7. Cardinal Wolsey.
8. John Barry.
9. Eight.

188

1. What is the base of bourbon whiskey?
2. Which king of England was nicknamed 'Lackland'?
3. Of which country is Ruritania now part?
4. Which bird did not return to Noah's Ark?
5. Who was the first person to play over 100 singles matches at Wimbledon?
6. TV's *Two's Company*: Elaine Stritch was one. And the other?
7. Sir John Suckling is reputedly the inventor of which popular card game?
8. Which German-born composer was naturalised in Britain in 1727?
9. What colour is a blue tit's breast?

422

1. Which motor manufacturer makes the 'Esprit'?
2. To which king was Muckle John court jester?
3. Which is Thailand's longest river?
4. At which pub did Chaucer's Pilgrims meet before leaving for Canterbury?
5. *Diomed* was the very first winner of which classic race?
6. Which actress, star of *Butterflies* among others, has been voted 'Funniest Woman on TV'?
7. Who was discovered in Australia, when he was mistaken for Lord Lucan?
8. When mares eat oats and does eat oats, what do little lambs eat?
9. Why was the massive Shire horse originally bred?

656

1. 'Finders keepers, losers ______'?
2. For what was Lady Hamilton incarcerated?
3. In which French city is the most perfume made?
4. Slave Josiah Henson's life story was the basis for the central character in which book?
5. Which member of the Royal Family fell off the horse *Good Prospect*?
6. Who does Compo fancy in *Last of the Summer Wine*?
7. What was Joseph Conrad's initial problem as a writer of English novels?
8. Who 'laughed to see such sport' before the dish ran away?
9. About how long does it take a red blood corpuscle to make a complete circuit of the body?

188

1. Corn.
2. King John.
3. None – it existed only by courtesy of novelist Anthony Hope.
4. The dove.
5. Billie-Jean King.
6. Donald Sinden.
7. Cribbage.
8. George Frideric Handel.
9. Yellow.

422

1. Lotus.
2. Charles I.
3. The Mekong River.
4. The Tabard.
5. The Epsom Derby.
6. Wendy Craig.
7. John Stonehouse.
8. Ivy.
9. To carry men in heavy armour.

656

1. Weepers.
2. Debt.
3. Grasse.
4. *Uncle Tom's Cabin.*
5. Prince Charles.
6. Nora Batty.
7. He arrived in England as an adult, with no knowledge of English!
8. The little dog.
9. About one minute.

189

1. How many brothers did Prince Philip, Duke of Edinburgh, have?
2. Lady Astor, the first woman to take her seat in the Commons, was MP for which city?
3. The islands of Murano, Burano and Torcello are part of which city?
4. About which war was *The Red Badge of Courage* written?
5. In Portuguese bullfights, the bull is not killed – so what do the 'forcados' do?
6. In which city was Station KDSA the first to transmit radio programmes?
7. Which elderly artist worked lying down by sticking coloured paper on his canvas?
8. What was Franz Liszt's *real* first name?
9. Which inventor said his machine stopped women doing the only thing that kept them quiet?

423

1. Why did the great jockey Fred Archer commit suicide in 1886?
2. In 1914, Miss M. Allen and Miss E. Harburn became England's first women *what*?
3. Which capital city has a twice-weekly Feira da Lado, or Thieves' Market?
4. Which fictional spy-hunter was called 'The Head Eunuch' by his first boss?
5. Which country won their first and only Olympic gold medal when Josy Bartel won the 1500 metres in 1952?
6. In which TV cop series were Lopaka and Steele the two detectives?
7. Who kept a lion in his garden in St John's Wood as a model for his sculptures?
8. Which music video became, in 1984, the first to sell more than 100,000 in Britain?
9. From which country did the physicist and chemist Ernest Rutherford come?

657

1. What did Ras Tafari Makonnen become, in 1930?
2. Why was Kaiser Leopold I repeatedly put into a freshly-killed pig when a baby?
3. What is the only Eastern European country to have diplomatic relations with Israel?
4. Who created Marguérite Gauthier?
5. Which motor-racing circuit was at Weybridge?
6. Byron Barr was the real name of an actor who won an Oscar for *They Shoot Horses Don't They?* What was his professional name?
7. The Hall of Fame for *who* is at Owensboro, Kentucky?
8. Which musical contained *Ma Belle Marguérite* and *This Is My Lovely Day*?
9. If a person suffers from retropulsion, they have a tendency to do *what*?

189

1. None – he had four sisters.
2. Plymouth, the Sutton division.
3. Venice.
4. The American Civil War. (Stephen Crane wrote it.)
5. They wrestle with the bull, as a team.
6. In Pittsburgh, in 1920.
7. Henri Matisse.
8. Ferencz.
9. Isaac Singer. He thought hand-sewing kept women quiet!

423

1. Because he couldn't keep his weight down.
2. Policewomen, in Grantham, Lincs.
3. Lisbon.
4. George Smiley, created by John Le Carré.
5. Luxembourg.
6. *Hawaiian Eye.*
7. Landseer, when doing the Trafalgar Square lions.
8. The video showing the making of *Thriller.*
9. New Zealand.

657

1. Haile Selassie, Emperor of Ethiopia.
2. He was a premature baby – they thought it would help him gain strength.
3. Romania.
4. Alexandre Dumas, fils.
5. Brooklands.
6. Gig Young.
7. Cowboys.
8. *Bless the Bride* (1947).
9. Walk backwards.

190

1. In which month does the Trooping the Colour ceremony take place?
2. Why did J.H. Thomas resign from the House of Commons in 1936?
3. Which mythical animal is seen on the Welsh flag?
4. Where did the pig keep the ring for which the Owl and the Pussycat paid him one shilling?
5. What was Fred Spofforth's Test Match 'first'?
6. Which was TV's famous rag and bone merchant series?
7. Which chess piece can never be captured?
8. Which musical instrument was sold at Sotheby's for £286,000 in April 1985?
9. Which incense comes from the resin of the Boswellia tree?

424

1. Who wrote, 'Life does not cease to be funny when people die any more than it ceases to be serious when people laugh'?
2. Which battle marked the end of the American War of Independence?
3. Which is the smallest of the Great Lakes of North America?
4. Name Miss Jane Marple's writer nephew.
5. Which twins played cricket for the successful Surrey side of the 1950s?
6. In which play does Woody Allen ask Humphrey Bogart for advice?
7. Whose diaries often contained the words 'And so to bed'?
8. Which song begins 'Maxwelton's braes are bonnie'?
9. What is the collective word for a group of turtles?

658

1. Who is believed to have been buried in The Turin Shroud?
2. How many Princesses of Wales preceded Princess Diana?
3. What is the commonest three-letter ending to surnames in Sweden?
4. Whose last play, written when he was 93, was *Buoyant Billions*?
5. Marine Ball is a shallow-water version of which sport?
6. *Charlie and the Chocolate Factory* was made into a film in 1971. Who wrote the book?
7. In which game is one player always dummy?
8. What type of instruments are chordophones?
9. What is a female elephant called?

190

1. In June, on a Saturday – they say it rains less in June!
2. Because of suspected Budget leaks.
3. A dragon.
4. At the end of his nose.
5. He scored the first-ever Test Match hat-trick – in 1879.
6. *Steptoe and Son.*
7. The king.
8. A Stradivarius violin.
9. Frankincense.

424

1. George Bernard Shaw.
2. The battle of Yorktown.
3. Lake Ontario.
4. Raymond West.
5. Alec and Eric Bedser.
6. Woody Allen's *Play It Again Sam.*
7. Samuel Pepys's.
8. *Annie Laurie.*
9. A bale.

658

1. Jesus Christ.
2. Eight.
3. 'son'.
4. George Bernard Shaw's.
5. Water polo.
6. Roald Dahl.
7. Bridge.
8. Stringed instruments.
9. A cow.

191

1. Who created the *Let's Parler Franglais* series?
2. To arrest whom did Chief Supt. Jack Slipper go to Brazil in 1974?
3. What did Mrs Joan Charleston inherit in 1985?
4. What was Jesus' first miracle?
5. Who won his first Grand Prix tennis title in 1985 – the Stella Artois singles at Queens Club, London – aged just 17?
6. What nationality was the detective Mr Moto?
7. In the USA, which teacher was the subject of a famous trial, for teaching Darwin's theory of evolution?
8. Which heavy metal group takes most of its name from a dirigible?
9. By what name is the vegetable *pisum sativum* better known?

425

1. For what do hedonists live?
2. What was the Act of Supremacy, declared by Henry VIII?
3. What came between Byzantium and Istanbul?
4. How many of the twelve apostles are saints?
5. In which sport might a Hereford Round feature?
6. Who plays Michael Corleone in the film *The Godfather*?
7. Who said, 'History is littered with wars that no-one believed would happen'?
8. In what activity do members of the Grand Order of Guisers indulge?
9. Why do visitors to Fidel Castro's home have scent splashed on them?

659

1. 'Something old, something new . . .' What else?
2. In the USA, who were Gold Star mothers?
3. Which was the first European country to introduce a compulsory AIDS test for blood donors?
4. In Norse mythology, who caused Balder's death?
5. In 1985, what unusual decision was taken by the Wimbledon seeding committee?
6. Who was 'Private Benjamin' in 1980?
7. Where would you most usually see the works of Barry Fantoni?
8. Ron Wood and Rod Stewart were once together in which group?
9. In which discipline did the Greek scholar Euclid specialize?

191

1. Miles Kington.
2. The Great Train Robber, Ronnie Biggs.
3. An entire Tudor village.
4. Changing water into wine.
5. Boris Becker of Germany.
6. Japanese.
7. John Scopes.
8. *Led Zeppelin*.
9. The pea.

425

1. Pleasure.
2. That the King of England was head of the Church of England.
3. Constantinople. (The same city has had three names.)
4. Ten.
5. Archery.
6. Al Pacino.
7. Enoch Powell.
8. Traditional folk dancing.
9. Because his new 'minder' – a huge python – is trained to kill anyone without the scent on them.

659

1. 'Something borrowed, something blue.'
2. Those whose sons were killed in World War I.
3. France.
4. The giant Loki.
5. They created joint top seeds in the Ladies' Singles.
6. Goldie Hawn.
7. In *The Times Diary*. (He is a cartoonist.)
8. *The Faces*.
9. Mathematics.

192

1. Who or what is 'Gloire de Dijon'?
2. Who thought of the idea of the Great Exhibition of 1851?
3. Which US city is nicknamed the 'Mile High City'?
4. *Lloyd on Lloyd* is a tennis book written by Chris and John Lloyd. But who is the third co-author?
5. Who was the first player ever sent off in an FA Cup Final?
6. Who played Arthur Fallowfield in *Beyond Our Ken*?
7. For what was the late Sir Donald Coleman Bailey famous?
8. Who used *When the Blue of the Night Meets the Gold of the Day* as his theme song?
9. What is the collective name for a group of leopards?

426

1. Pure marble is what colour?
2. In which year did a nuclear-powered submarine first sail under the North Pole?
3. How deep is Loch Ness?
4. Which newspaper was run by 'directors, managers, pensioners, students, MPs and a sprinkling of the peerage, headed by a couple of Duchesses'?
5. Which sport was first practised in 1958?
6. What was Chief Inspector Clouseau's first name?
7. Alexei Leonov was the first to do *what*, in space?
8. With whose clown did the *Everley Brothers* have a No. 1 hit?
9. What tree was named after Scotsman David Douglas?

660

1. What, in the field of public transport, is meant by OPO?
2. Where was the murderer Dr Crippen heading for when he was caught?
3. Where do Angelinos live?
4. Who wrote, 'All is gas and gaiters'?
5. How many members of Manchester United's 1985 cup final team had not yet represented their respective countries?
6. The film *The Bridges at Toko-Ri* was set during which war?
7. Jimmu Tenno was the first emperor of which country?
8. In Roger Miller's 1965 hit *King of the Road* for how much were rooms to let?
9. Which is the missing common blood group – AB, B, O?

192

1. It is a yellow hybrid tea rose.
2. Albert, the Prince Consort.
3. Denver, Colorado.
4. Carol Thatcher.
5. Kevin Moran, of Manchester United, in 1985.
6. Kenneth Williams.
7. Inventing the Bailey bridge, used by Allied troops in the second half of World War II.
8. Bing Crosby.
9. A leap.

426

1. White.
2. In 1958.
3. 750 feet. (Plenty of room for Nessie.)
4. *The Times*, during the General Strike of 1926.
5. Hang-gliding.
6. Jacques.
7. Walk.
8. *Cathy's*.
9. The Douglas fir.

660

1. One Person Operation of trains and buses.
2. Canada.
3. In Los Angeles.
4. Charles Dickens.
5. None.
6. The Korean War.
7. Japan.
8. 50 cents.
9. Group A.

193

1. What did Rickenbacker make in the 1930s that was nicknamed 'frying pan'?
2. Who belonged to the 'Cockyoli Birds', then led 'the Hooligans' when he joined the Tory party?
3. What is the capital of Bosnia-Hercegovina, part of Yugoslavia?
4. Who created Colonel Charles Russell, fictional Head of the British Security Service?
5. On what sort of surface do the Dutch play a form of bowls called Klootschien?
6. Who linked Perry Mason and Chief Ironside?
7. Which Norwegian artist painted *Summer Landscape* which became, in 1978, the most valuable object ever sold at auction in Sweden?
8. Which great musical opened at Lincoln's Inn Fields on 29 January 1728?
9. What do you look at to see if someone has trichoglossia?

427

1. 'Yellow pages' in a telephone directory are what colour in Australia?
2. Which Prime Minister did Aneurin Bevan call 'the juvenile lead'?
3. In which country are the Swabian Mountains?
4. From which country did detective writer Ngaio Marsh come?
5. For which sport would you use a variometer?
6. Which famous actor was once presumed lost and dead when exploring the Amazon river?
7. A pair of *what* did Lorenzo Ghiberti spend 23 years making, then take 27 years on the next pair?
8. What sort of rock music did the Coventry group, the *Specials AKA* create?
9. How do you look if you have chlorosis, a severe form of anaemia, or iron deficiency?

661

1. What did Charles Nessler invent, after watching wig-makers in South Molton Street in 1905?
2. Which Irish P.M. and President was born in New York in 1882?
3. What is 'Gebel Tariq', named after a Moorish chief called Tariq, called today?
4. Who wrote *Verses on the Death of Dr Swift*, about the author of *Gulliver's Travels*?
5. What is the diameter of the hole, in golf?
6. For their work in which film were both Gladys Cooper and Stanley Holloway nominated for Oscars?
7. In Italian art, what is a 'mandorla', or 'almond'?
8. What sort of instrument is a Ludwig 'Speed King'?
9. If you had a pain in your gluteus maximus, where would you feel it?

193

1. An electric guitar.
2. Winston Churchill.
3. Sarajevo.
4. William Haggard.
5. Along roads. Really, it is a sort of long-distance throwing.
6. Raymond Burr, the actor who played both roles on TV.
7. Edvard Munch.
8. *The Beggar's Opera.*
9. The tongue – it is a hairy or coated tongue.

427

1. Pink.
2. Anthony Eden.
3. In West Germany.
4. New Zealand.
5. Gliding.
6. Albert Finney
7. Doors for the Baptistry in Florence.
8. Two-Tone music.
9. Green in coloup!

661

1. Permanent waving for hair.
2. Eamon de Valera.
3. Gibraltar.
4. Jonathan Swifthimself.
5. 4½ inches.
6. *My Fair Lady.* (Neither won.)
7. A sort of halo, round the whole body.
8. A bass drum with foot-pedals.
9. In the bottom, or buttock.

194

1. In a restaurant, what are kormas and vindaloos?
2. Who was mainly instrumental in forming a model industrial community in Scotland early in the 19th century?
3. What do folk traditionally fly in Korea at New Year?
4. Who wrote, 'Consistency is the last refuge of the unimaginative'?
5. For which country did Kazimierz Deyna play soccer?
6. Who first presented BBC TV's *Grandstand*?
7. Who is the Head of State for Canada?
8. A Kabuki is *what*?
9. Which organs of the body would be affected by nephritis?

428

1. What does 'ersatz' mean?
2. Which Primate of All Ireland was executed in 1681?
3. Where are the Ribbon Falls?
4. Who wrote limericks and *A Book of Nonsense*?
5. How many Olympic heavyweight boxing Gold Medals did Teophilio Stevenson win?
6. Which best-selling novel, written by a Supreme Court judge of the USA, was made into a film in 1959?
7. Sir Isaac Newton left school early to take up which career?
8. Wagner wrote the opera *Götterdämmerung*. What does this mean?
9. Titan is the largest moon of which planet?

662

1. What is Greek for the letter 'E'?
2. Who was the last US President to have been a General in the army?
3. What is LASER 558?
4. Who wrote *Brideshead Revisited*?
5. Who won the 1936 Olympic Decathlon, then became yet another Olympian to play Tarzan in films?
6. How old was Cary Grant when his daughter Jennifer was born?
7. How did James Chalmers improve postage stamps?
8. What does the musical term 'ritardando' mean?
9 For what do insects use their spiracles?

194

1. Types of curry.
2. Robert Owen.
3. Kites.
4. Oscar Wilde.
5. Poland.
6. David Coleman.
7. Queen Elizabeth II.
8. A Japanese musical play.
9. The kidneys.

428

1. Substitute.
2. Oliver Plunkett.
3. In California, USA.
4. Edward Lear.
5. Three.
6. *Anatomy of a Murder*.
7. Farming.
8. Twilight of the Gods.
9. Saturn.

662

1. Epsilon.
2. Dwight D. Eisenhower.
3. A ship-based radio station, 14 miles off the east coast of England.
4. Evelyn Waugh.
5. Glenn Morris.
6. 62.
7. He made them adhesive.
8. Slow down.
9. To breathe through – they are pores in their sides.

Q

195

1. Who went to sea in a sieve?
2. In 1914, which country had the largest air force?
3. The Ashburton Treaty determined the boundaries between which two countries?
4. Who created the character of Starveling the Tailor?
5. For what is 'canter' short?
6. Who played Kharis in the 1942 film *The Mummy's Tomb*?
7. Who created the 'New Look' in 1947?
8. What did Queen Elizabeth I ban in churches?
9. Which is the oldest extant breed of horse?

429

1. Of what is etymology the study?
2. Who was the first English Prince of Wales?
3. Where is Montego Bay?
4. Who wrote *The Leatherstocking Tales*?
5. Who is Old Jem, at Lord's Cricket Ground?
6. Which was the first film based on Bram Stoker's *Dracula*?
7. Who broke pilot Wiley Post's round-the-world speed record?
8. The scale played in semitones is called *what*?
9. What is about half the sulphuric acid produced used for?

663

1. Ambrosia and nectar were food and drink to whom?
2. What was Sir Thomas Sopwith's best-known World War I aviation creation?
3. Where in Canada does London stand on the River Thames?
4. On what did Marley's ghostly face first appear to Scrooge in Dickens' *A Christmas Carol*?
5. On what is spaceball played?
6. What is Ensign Chekov's function in *Star Trek*?
7. Who, according to Disraeli, was 'inebriated with the exuberance of his own verbosity'?
8. Who founded Les Ballets Russes, in France?
9. What sort of animal is Sooty's glove-puppet friend Sweep?

195

1. The Jumblies, in Edward Lear's poem.
2. France.
3. Canada and the USA.
4. William Shakespeare.
5. Canterbury Gallop.
6. Lon Chaney Jr.
7. Christian Dior.
8. Hymn singing.
9. The Arab.

429

1. The derivation of words.
2. Edward II.
3. In Jamaica.
4. James Fenimore Cooper.
5. The scarecrow.
6. *Nosferatu*.
7. Howard Hughes.
8. Chromatic.
9. The manufacture of artificial fertilizers.

663

1. The Greek gods.
2. The biplanes called Sopwith Camels.
3. In Ontario.
4. A doorknocker.
5. On trampolines.
6. He is a navigator.
7. William Gladstone.
8. Diaghilev.
9. A dog.

Q

196

1. When the Eddystone lighthouse was dismantled in 1882, where was it rebuilt?
2. What title did Pope Leo X give Henry VIII in 1521?
3. In which English town is Harvard House, built by the grandfather of the US college's founder?
4. Who called himself 'The Great Beast' and 'The Wickedest Man Alive'?
5. Before the wooden golf tee was invented, what did players put the ball on?
6. For their work in which 1966 film were all four stars nominated for Oscars, though only the two women won?
7. The sculpting stone called Purbeck marble is actually *what*?
8. Carl Perkins had only one British hit, with a song he wrote. Namely?
9. What sort of creature is Venezuela's 'Horseman', or 'Cattle Tyrant'?

430

1. In which country do they massage cows with gin to produce tender beef ?
2. What did the Marines capture, then defend, in 1704?
3. What is on top of each of the Kremlin's five tallest towers?
4. In which country in 1904 did the only known first edition of Shakespeare's *Titus Andronicus* turn up?
5. Why was the victory of Pebbles in the 1985 Eclipse Stakes remarkable?
6. Who was *The Man in the White Suit* in the 1951 film?
7. Which game are the Pilgrim Fathers known to have played on the *Mayflower*?
8. Why was the song *Refrains* by Lys Assia remarkable?
9. What does Teschen disease affect?

664

1. In what field of activity did A.S. Neill make his name at Summerhill?
2. What tradition was begun in Hyde Park by the bread riots of 1855?
3. Which motorway connects Bristol and London?
4. About which poet did W.B. Yeats say, 'He is the handsomest man in England, and he wears the most beautiful shirts'?
5. What 'first' did Viv Anderson accomplish in 1978?
6. Who took his role in *The Winds of War* because 'it promised a year of free lunches'?
7. Which painter's middle name was Harmensz?
8. Which 15-year-old rock singer was launched as 'Little Miss Dynamite'?
9. Which island was the home of the Blue Vanga, the Scaly Ground Roller and the Dodo?

196

1. At Plymouth Hoe.
2. 'Fidei Defensor', or 'Defender of the Faith'.
3. In Stratford-on-Avon.
4. Aleister Crowley, dabbler in black magic.
5. Little piles of sand.
6. *Who's Afraid Of Virginia Woolf?*
7. A hard limestone.
8. *Blue Suede Shoes.*
9. A bird – a flycatcher which sits on the backs of cattle.

430

1. Japan.
2. Gibraltar.
3. A large red star.
4. In Sweden, at Malmö.
5. She was the first filly to win in 100 years.
6. Alec Guinness.
7. Darts.
8. It was the first winner of the Eurovision Song Contest, in 1956, for Switzerland.
9. Pigs.

664

1. Education – he founded his own school.
2. The tradition of people speaking at Speakers' Corner.
3. The M4.
4. Rupert Brooke.
5. He became the first black footballer to play for England.
6. Robert Mitchum.
7. Rembrandt's.
8. Brenda Lee, in 1960.
9. Madagascar.

Q

197

1. Who owns Snoopy?
2. The Act of Settlement barred those of which religion from becoming British sovereigns?
3. The Camargue is an area in which country?
4. Who wrote *The Trumpet Major*?
5. In 1954, who was the first BBC Sports Personality of the Year?
6. What does Road Runner say?
7. Name one of the three painters who founded the Pre-Raphaelite Brotherhood.
8. Bob Marley and *who*?
9. What is a John Dory?

431

1. Wippell's – who or what are they?
2. During World War I, who was the Kaiser of Germany?
3. Which country has the highest proportion of elderly people in the world?
4. Who wrote, 'Never trust a husband too far, nor a bachelor too near'?
5. Who organises the World Haggis Hurling Championship?
6. Who spied for the Allies, and was Adolf Hitler's favourite actress?
7. In 1876, which sureshot did Frank Butler marry?
8. The John Gabel Entertainer was the first *what*?
9. What is the temperature on the surface of the sun?

665

1. Members of which religion don't have haircuts or shave?
2. Which club, founded in 1950, innovated credit cards?
3. Which country has the highest literacy rate in Africa?
4. Who wrote *The Third Policeman* and *At Swim-Two-Birds*?
5. For which country did Ferenc Puskas play soccer?
6. Who was the Oscar-winning star of the film, *Song of Bernadette*?
7. What is reputedly the most popular participant pastime in the USA?
8. What is the better-known title of Mozart's opera *The Rake Punished*?
9. What is the name commonly used for the magnetic storms which occur on the surface of the sun?

197

1. Charlie Brown, in the comic strip *Peanuts*.
2. Roman Catholics.
3. France.
4. Thomas Hardy.
5. Christopher Chataway.
6. 'Beep Beep.'
7. Sir John Millais, William Holman Hunt and Dante Gabriel Rossetti.
8. *The Wailers*.
9. A fish.

431

1. Ecclesiastical tailors.
2. Wilhelm II.
3. Austria.
4. Helen Rowland.
5. The World Haggis Hurling Association. (Who else?)
6. Greta Garbo.
7. Annie Oakley.
8. Juke box.
9. 6,000° Centigrade.

665

1. Sikhism.
2. Diners Club.
3. Algeria.
4. Brian O'Nolan, under his pen-name Flann O'Brien.
5. Hungary.
6. Jennifer Jones.
7. Fishing.
8. *Don Giovanni*.
9. Sunspots.

198

1. The word 'platonic' is derived from whose name?
2. Which army did Napoleon defeat at the Battle of Jena?
3. Wilton, where the carpets come from, is in which county?
4. Which book begins 'Call me Ishmael'?
5. C.B. Fry, the cricketer, was once invited to be King of *where*?
6. How many children has Mia Farrow?
7. Which painter wrote the book *Noa Noa*, about Tahiti?
8. Which country's national anthem is called *Breth Flamurit te per bashkuar*?
9. What type of bird is a jabiru?

432

1. Which name is common to the constellation Crux and a variety of Poker?
2. On the 11th hour of the 11th day of the 11th month in 1918, what ended?
3. Treasure Island sits in which US bay?
4. 'Deuteronomy' means *what*?
5. England first played in Soccer's World Cup when?
6. Which burglar have John Barrymore, Ronald Coleman and David Niven all played in films?
7. Who was Aristotle's mentor?
8. Which of Schubert's symphonies was 'The Unfinished'?
9. Who was the recipient of the first Nobel Prize for Physics?

666

1. What is the time in Paris when it is midnight (GMT) in London?
2. From which British king did America fight for independence?
3. Which is England's most northerly county?
4. With which relative did Heidi go to live in the mountains, in the book *Heidi*?
5. Which soccer league club are 'Alexandra'?
6. Whose first starring role was in the 1923 film *Where the North Begins*?
7. *Seascape: Folkestone* was sold in 1984 for a record £7,300,000. Who painted it?
8. Of *where* are Gilbert and Sullivan's pirates?
9. Who developed the 'steady-state theory' relating to the origins of the universe?

198

1. Plato's.
2. The Prussian Army.
3. Wiltshire.
4. *Moby Dick* by Herman Melville.
5. Albania. (He declined.)
6. Three natural, and four adopted.
7. Paul Gauguin.
8. Albania's. (And a pat on the back for the brave questioner attempting this tongue-twister.)
9. A South American stork.

432

1. Southern Cross.
2. World War I.
3. San Francisco Bay.
4. 'The second law.'
5. In 1950.
6. Raffles.
7. Plato.
8. The Eighth, not his last, but his penultimate.
9. Wilhelm Röntgen. (He developed X-rays.)

666

1. 1.00 a.m.
2. George III.
3. Northumberland.
4. Her grandfather.
5. Crewe.
6. Rin Tin Tin's.
7. J.M.W. Turner.
8. Penzance.
9. Sir Fred Hoyle.

199

1. How many years after the event is the tercentenary celebrated?
3. Wat Tyler and his followers came to London from which county?
3. Which is Africa's second largest country?
4. Who wrote the collection of novels called *A Dance to the Music of Time*?
5. At which game do Oxford and Cambridge compete for the Bowring Bowl?
6. Who played Miss Marple in the 1962 film *Murder, She Said*?
7. Who expelled more than 80,000 Asians from Uganda?
8. Who is the 'Frankie' in Sister Sledge's song?
9. How many toes has an ostrich on each foot?

433

1. Who is the most-quoted Chinese philosopher?
2. Which king's illegitimate son was James Scott, Duke of Monmouth?
3. Where is the Bay of Pigs?
4. In Dickens' *Our Mutual Friend*, how does Melvin Twemlow describe the House of Commons?
5. What is the maximum following wind permitted for sprint records to be recognised in athletics?
6. Who wrote the play *Death of a Salesman*?
7. Who introduced transcendental thinking?
8. From where did Burlington Bertie come, in the song?
9. What does an analgesic kill?

667

1. Who is Bristow's boss?
2. In 1973, how much was a gallon of petrol?
3. Chittagong is in which country?
4. Name the famous novelist daughter of Sir Leslie Stephen, editor of the *Dictionary of National Biography*.
5. Which sports commentator waffled, 'The obvious successor to Brearley at the moment isn't obvious'?
6. The ads for which lager exhort you to 'Follow the Bear'?
7. Who is Lord of the Isles?
8. Which king had a hit with *Ramblin' Rose*?
9. Which British scientist was called the 'Father of Modern Physics'?

199

1. 300 years.
2. Kent.
3. Algeria.
4. Anthony Powell.
5. Rugby Union.
6. Margaret Rutherford.
7. Idi Amin.
8. Frank Sinatra.
9. Two.

433

1. Confucius.
2. Charles II's.
3. In Cuba.
4. 'The best club in London.'
5. Two metres per second.
6. Arthur Miller.
7. Immanuel Kant.
8. Bow.
9. Pain.

667

1. Mr Fudge – in the cartoon strip by Frank Dickens.
2. 55 pence.
3. Bangladesh.
4. Virginia Woolf.
5. Trevor Bailey.
6. Hofmeister.
7. Prince Charles.
8. Nat 'King' Cole.
9. Sir Joseph Thomson.

200

1. One of whose many names is 'Old Harry'?
2. In what language was the Magna Carta written?
3. In which country are there the most motorbikes per capita?
4. Who was the 'Beloved Disciple'?
5. Name either of the unconnected activities at which Sheila Young has been World Champion.
6. Michael Aldridge is the newest member of which popular TV series?
7. W.W.Mitchell was chiefly instrumental in setting down the rules of which game?
8. What kind of song is a Noël?
9. At what speed must you travel to escape the Earth's velocity?

434

1. What type of food are you likely to eat in a trattoria?
2. How did Edward VII determine that his weekend guests had eaten well?
3. Why does the Duchy of Cornwall (the Prince of Wales' estate) seem to be misnamed?
4. In mythology, Stheno and Euryale were *what*?
5. Which cricketer was nicknamed 'The Don'?
6. In which 1980 mercenary adventure film did Christopher Walkden star?
7. Which colour is said to be the most restful to the eye?
8. How were Richard and Johann Strauss related?
9. Who said, 'The great ocean of truth lay all undiscovered before me'?

668

1. It was said that some unemployed people chose to stay at the seaside and collect their benefits, so having a free holiday. What was this 'scandal' nicknamed?
2. Who said, 'I have nothing to offer but blood, toil, tears and sweat'?
3. On which continent did Speedway racing have its origins?
4. On which day was man created?
5. What takes place in a 'salle d'armes'?
6. Moses Lamarr, who died in August 1985, was the voice of which Disney cartoon character?
7. In which county is Constable's painting *The Haywain* set?
8. For what was Balanchine famed?
9. How often does a moose shed its antlers?

200

1. The devil's.
2. Latin.
3. In Bermuda.
4. John.
5. Cycling (sprint) and speed skating.
6. *Last of the Summer Wine.*
7. Bowls.
8. A Christmas carol.
9. 25,000 m.p.h., or 7 miles per second.

434

1. Italian.
2. He weighed them – both on arrival and departure – and was affronted if they hadn't put on pounds!
3. Less than one fifth of its acreage lies in Cornwall.
4. Gorgons.
5. Sir Donald Bradman.
6. *The Dogs of War.*
7. Green.
8. They weren't.
9. Isaac Newton.

668

1. The 'Costa del Dole.'
2. Winston Churchill.
3. Australia.
4. The sixth.
5. Fencing.
6. Pluto.
7. In Suffolk.
8. Ballet – he was the most famous ballet master and choreographer of the New York Ballet School.
9. Annually.

201

1. Who said, 'Why should I question the monkey when I can question the organ grinder?'?
2. Which US President's father was an Ambassador to Britain in 1939?
3. Which mountain do Tibetans call 'Mother of the Snows'?
4. From which mountain did Moses first see Canaan?
5. Until 1980 there were nine ways of getting out in cricket. Now there are ten – what was the addition?
6. What did Frank Lloyd Wright call 'Chewing gum for the eyes'?
7. Who painted *Christ at Emmaus*?
8. Which group did Roy Wood form after leaving *The Move*?
9. Against which crime should tortoise owners be vigilant?

435

1. Which nation invented fireworks?
2. What did the letters ARP stand for during World War II?
3. Where, in Britain, are wild reindeer found?
4. Name the blowpipe-toting Andaman Islander in Conan Doyle's *The Sign of Four*.
5. Which Bill, an ex-Rugby star, received an OBE in the 1985 New Year Honours List?
6. What is *Star Wars*' Luke Skywalker's home planet called?
7. Who was the immediate successor to the fashion designer, Christian Dior?
8. The musical term 'molto allegro' means *what*?
9. What is a dikdik?

669

1. 'Red sky at night is the ______'s delight' What is missing?
2. In which year did China lease Hong Kong to Britain?
3. What is the meaning of a red rectangle on an Ordnance Survey map?
4. Who was the wife of Menelaus?
5. Steve O'Shaughnessy is an unusual name for a cricketer. What was his claim to fame?
6. What were the puppets Pinky and Perky?
7. Camrose trials are held to select national teams for which game?
8. Who pulled pussy out of the well?
9. Who conducted a dangerous experiment, flying a kite in a storm, which established that lightning was a form of electricity?

201

1. Aneurin Bevan.
2. John F. Kennedy's father – Joseph Kennedy.
3. Mount Everest.
4. Mount Pisgah.
5. 'Timed out' – a new batsman must step on to the field within two minutes of a wicket falling.
6. Television.
7. Rembrandt.
8. *Wizzard.*
9. 'Tortoise-rustling' for, since the ban on imports, tortoises can fetch between £50 and £150 (1985.)

435

1. The Chinese.
2. Air-Raid Precautions.
3. In the Cairngorm Mountains.
4. Tonga.
5. Beaumont.
6. Tatooine.
7. Yves Saint Laurent.
8. 'Very quickly.'
9. A small antelope.

669

1. 'Shepherd.'
2. In 1841.
3. It indicates a main railway station.
4. Helen of Troy.
5. He equalled the record for the fastest first-class century, held by P.G.H. Fender, in 1983.
6. Pigs.
7. Bridge.
8. Little Tommy Stout, in the nursery rhyme.
9. Benjamin Franklin.

202

1. 'The Voice of Britain' is the subtitle of which national daily?
2. During which war did 'Popski's Private Army' function?
3. With which country's cuisine are biryani dishes chiefly associated?
4. Who was the first leader of the Israelites?
5. For which county did W.G. Grace play cricket?
6. What did the fictional character Mary Poppins use for transport?
7. How did the painter Paul Klee describe drawing?
8. Which conductor of the BBC Concert Orchestra for some 20 years received an MBE in 1985?
9. Which is the smallest species of partridge?

436

1. Who married the Owl and the Pussycat?
2. To whom was Louis XVI of France married?
3. How large is the Hungarian Navy?
4. In which language was the Gutenberg Bible printed?
5. Why was Dora Ratjen's 1936 Olympic High Jump Gold Medal repossessed?
6. Who played the Countess in the 1967 film *The Countess from Hong Kong*?
7. Form a mill – remove one of your opponent's playing pieces. What is the game?
8. What was Pan's instrument?
9. Which breed of dog is most used for police work in Britain?

670

1. Which motor manufacturers make the Civic?
2. Which sauce is named after the Battle of Mahón?
3. Which horse measures some 360 feet across?
4. Alfred Jingle features in which Dickens novel?
5. How many hits to the body win an épée fencing bout?
6. How was the actor John Drew related to John, Lionel and Ethel Barrymore?
7. Who said, 'A producer shouldn't get ulcers, he should give them'?
8. Marguerite Porter, one of the Royal Ballet's principal dancers, retired in her prime in June 1985. Whom did she blame?
9. What colour is a citrine?

202

1. The *Daily Express.*
2. World War II.
3. India's.
4. Moses.
5. Gloucestershire.
6. Her umbrella.
7. 'Taking a line for a walk.'
8. Sidney Torch.
9. The quail.

436

1. 'The turkey who lives on the hill.'
2. Marie Antoinette.
3. Hungary is land-locked and has no navy.
4. In Latin.
5. Because 'she' was a man.
6. Sophia Loren.
7. Nine Men's Morris.
8. The pipes.
9. The German Shepherd, or Alsatian.

670

1. Honda.
2. Mayonnaise.
3. The White Horse at Uffington, Berkshire.
4. *Pickwick Papers.*
5. Three.
6. He was their uncle.
7. Sam Goldwyn.
8. The critics.
9. Yellow. (It is a gemstone.)

203

1. What is the lifespan of the average US dollar bill?
2. Who did pilot Roy Brown shoot down on 21 April, 1918?
3. Which rock in the Central Desert of Australia is famed for its colour changes?
4. According to Edward Lear, who lived on the Coast of Coromandel in the woods?
5. The Hon. Lionel Tennyson captained England at what game?
6. Who is associated with a tickling stick?
7. Sheikh Mujibur Rahman was the first President of *where*?
8. To which common musical instrument is a samisen most similar?
9. Which sex chromosome from the father means 'it's a girl'?

437

1. Which religious group did John Nelson Darby found?
2. Who kept a daily account of the Great Plague and Great Fire of London?
3. Beside Paraguay, which is the only land-locked country in the Americas?
4. Who described poverty as 'The greatest of evils and the worst of crimes'?
5. Which boxing match was termed 'The Rumble in the Jungle'?
6. In *The Wizard of Oz*, in which land did Dorothy first touch down?
7. Who painted *The Lunch on the Grass* which caused quite a stir when first exhibited?
8. Who had a hit with *The Locomotion*?
9. Whatever was Quetzalcoatlus Northropi?

671

1. What was remarkable about Balaam's ass?
2. E. Oxford, 1842; J. Francis, 1842; J. Bean, 1842; W. Hamilton, 1849; R. MacLean, 1882. All attempted and failed at the same enterprise, which can never be achieved now. What was it?
3. In which county is Savernake Forest?
4. In which novel is Britain named *Airstrip One*?
5. What starts a tennis rally?
6. Who starred with Sean Connery in *Dr No*, the first Bond film?
7. What age was Albert Einstein before he was able to speak?
8. Who wrote *Hark, the Herald Angels Sing*?
9. Which bird runs fastest?

203

1. $1\frac{1}{4}$ years, on average.
2. The 'Red Baron'.
3. Ayers Rock.
4. The Yonghy-Bonghy-Bo.
5. Cricket.
6. Ken Dodd.
7. Bangladesh.
8. A guitar.
9. An X chromosome.

437

1. The Plymouth Brethren.
2. Samuel Pepys.
3. Bolivia.
4. George Bernard Shaw.
5. Muhammad Ali *v.* George Foreman, held in Zaire in 1974.
6. Munchkin Land.
7. Edouard Manet.
8. Little Eva.
9. It is believed to be the largest flying creature the world has seen – it had a wingspan of 36 feet.

671

1. It could talk.
2. They all tried to assassinate Queen Victoria.
3. In Wiltshire.
4. In *Nineteen Eighty-Four*, by George Orwell.
5. The service.
6. Ursula Andress.
7. Four.
8. Charles Wesley.
9. The ostrich.

204

1. How many people were killed in the St Valentine's Day massacre?
2. Which territory did Romania acquire in 1920?
3. Which country is ruled by the House of Orange?
4. Who constructed the labyrinth for Minos, in Greek mythology?
5. Apart from his stick, with what else may a hockey player stop the ball?
6. Which book by Enid Bagnold was made into a film?
7. A picture worth over £2,000,000 was stolen from the Dulwich Picture Gallery for the third time. Who painted it?
8. Known as a virtuoso on the violin, Paganini was also a master of another instrument. Which?
9. Which explosive was invented by Ascanio Solaro?

438

1. From what does London's Fleet Street derive its name?
2. Which company made the jet fighter ME 262?
3. The wine 'Lacryma Christi' comes solely from the slopes of which mountain?
4. Who wrote, 'Oh what a tangled web we weave, when first we practise to deceive'?
5. Axel Paulsen gave his name to a jump in which activity?
6. Whom did Ryan O'Neal portray in the film *A Bridge Too Far*?
7. Which US President was a Quaker?
8. Who had a hit in 1970 with *Abraham, Martin and John?*
9. Which cords are protected by the Adam's apple?

672

1. What is the time in Tokyo when it is 5.00 p.m. (GMT) in London?
2. When were the Dead Sea Scrolls discovered?
3. What is America's equivalent to Britain's Sandhurst?
4. Who wrote *Inside the Third Reich*?
5. Where did baseball have its origins?
6. Who played Michelangelo in the 1965 film *The Agony and the Ecstasy*?
7. During the Boer War, which future South African PM captured future British P.M Winston Churchhill?
8. *The Useless Precaution* was the subtitle of which Rossini opera?
9. Which bird is a kleptomaniac?

204

1. Seven.
2. Transylvania.
3. Holland.
4. Daedalus.
5. His hand.
6. *National Velvet.*
7. Rembrandt.
8. Guitar.
9. Nitro-glycerine.

438

1. The River Fleet – now covered over.
2. Messerschmitt.
3. Mount Vesuvius.
4. Sir Walter Scott.
5. Ice skating.
6. General James Gavin.
7. Herbert Hoover.
8. Marvin Gaye.
9. The vocal cords.

672

1. Midnight.
2. In 1947.
3. West Point.
4. Albert Speer, Hitler's architect.
5. In 18th-century England – there is even a reference to baseball in Jane Austen!
6. Charlton Heston.
7. Louis Botha.
8. *The Barber of Seville.*
9. The magpie.

Q

205

1. Which British cheese is often termed the 'King of Cheeses'?
2. Which is the world's longest mountain range?
3. To become President of the USA, for how many years must you have lived there?
4. In which country is Pearl Buck's *The Good Earth* set?
5. Willie Banks broke an athletics world record in 1985, which had stood since 1968. Which?
6. What is the NFT?
7. Billy Breen, after 30 years, sought fame and changed his name to *what*?
8. What does the 'frog' do on a violin bow?
9. What is the colloquial name for 'cutis anserina'?

439

1. If you owned a Tompion, what could you tell by it?
2. 'Death will come on swift wings to those that disturb the sleep of the Pharaohs.' This curse seemed to come true for many of those associated with the opening of which tomb?
3. Who was Abilene's famous marshal?
4. *Tenderness* was the original title of which D.H. Lawrence novel?
5. Who rode the 1985 Epsom Derby winner to a seven-length victory?
6. Who wrote *Pennies from Heaven* for television?
7. For what did 92-year-old Alfred Bestell receive his MBE in 1985?
8. Who was the Oscar-winning star of the musical film *Cabaret*?
9. Which planet, just visible to the naked eye, is four times greater in diameter than the earth?

673

1. Who always receives and understands messages by radio?
2. Who succeeded Henry VIII?
3. Where would you find the Nursery End?
4. Who wrote the poem beginning 'The best laid schemes o' mice an' men/Gang aft agley'?
5. In which sport might you use a shime-waza?
6. In the radio series *The Archers*, who keeps the village shop?
7. Who did Alf Lomas replace as Leader of the European Parliament's Labour group?
8. From which work does Handel's famous *Largo* come?
9. Which cat is called the 'Hidden Paw' by T.S. Eliot?

205

1. Stilton.
2. The Andes, in South America.
3. Fourteen years, at least.
4. In China.
5. The record for the triple jump – the new record is 58 feet, $11\frac{1}{2}$ inches.
6. The National Film Theatre.
7. Larry Grayson.
8. It tightens (and loosens) the hairs.
9. Goose pimples.

439

1. The time – it is a type of clock.
2. Tutankhamun's.
3. Wild Bill Hickok.
4. *Lady Chatterley's Lover*.
5. Steve Cauthen.
6. Dennis Potter.
7. His *Rupert Bear* strip.
8. Liza Minelli.
9. Uranus.

673

1. Roger.
2. His son, Edward VI, aged 10.
3. At Lord's Cricket Ground.
4. Robert Burns.
5. In Judo – it is a throttling technique.
6. Martha Woodford, played by Molly Harris.
7. Barbara Castle.
8. His opera *Xerxes*.
9. Macavity, the mystery cat.

206

1. Where is 'Glitter Gulch'?
2. The king of which country became, in 1902, the first monarch to pass a driving test?
3. Which is the world's most northerly capital of an independent nation?
4. Who wrote *The Bafut Beagles* and *The Drunken Forest*?
5. Which sports 'spin-off' was invented by John Jervis Barnard in 1922?
6. Who was *The Man From Atlantis*?
7. Which game has a name which means 'the sparrows'?
8. Mark Knopfler is guitarist with which group?
9. What has varieties called Hungarian, Lucombe, Red and Pin?

440

1. What unusual form of payment did 'Madam' Cynthia Payne receive from her customers in Streatham?
2. What did French revolutionaries replace, in 1793, with 'festivals of the fruits of the earth'?
3. The Jagiellonian University is the oldest in which country?
4. Who wrote, 'Cover her face; mine eyes dazzle; she died young'?
5. From which country does the football team Lokomotiv Plovdiv come?
6. Which TV personality with her own show once played Dick Whittington in a panto at Bognor Regis?
7. Who once said his plays were about 'the weasel under the cocktail cabinet'?
8. Levi Stubbs Jr was the lead singer of which vocal quartet?
9. Which bird lays an egg weighing about a quarter of the adult bird's weight?

674

1. In Austria, you might eat Guglhupf – what is it?
2. Who was surprised to be met at Father Point, in Canada, by Inspector Dew in 1910?
3. The 'Catalan Talgo' train runs from Barcelona to *where*?
4. Upon whom is the character of Paul Morel in *Sons and Lovers* based?
5. Heber's Calendar and Pond's Sporting Kalendar contained early rules for what?
6. In which film did Julie Christie play Lara?
7. Serigraphy is another name for what process?
8. On a piece of music, 'D.C.' means *what*?
9. What does a maggot become?

206

1. It is a nickname for Las Vegas.
2. Italy.
3. Reykjavik, Iceland.
4. Gerald Durrell.
5. The Football Pools.
6. Patrick Duffy.
7. Mah-jong.
8. *Dire Straits.*
9. The oak tree.

440

1. Luncheon vouchers.
2. Saints' days.
3. Poland. (It is at Cracow.)
4. John Webster, in *The Duchess of Malfi.*
5. From Bulgaria.
6. Esther Rantzen.
7. Harold Pinter.
8. *The Four Tops.*
9. The kiwi.

674

1. Sponge cake.
2. Dr Crippen.
3. Geneva. (It takes 9½ hours.)
4. D.H.Lawrence, the author of the book.
5. Horse racing.
6. *Doctor Zhivago.*
7. Silk-screen printing.
8. Da capo, or 'go back to the beginning'.
9. A fly.

207

1. Which popular soft drink was created by Caleb B. Brabham?
2. Which stone did Edward I steal?
3. In which city is the Guggenheim Museum?
4. Which of Isaac's children was hirsute?
5. How many throwing events are there in the Decathlon?
6. Mia Farrow's father, John Farrow, won an Oscar for his script of which film?
7. Which king in a pack of cards is always in profile?
8. Minnie the *what* was the theme song of Cab Calloway's band?
9. About what did the ubiquitous 'they' say, 'Very clever, but it will never replace the horse'?

441

1. What is a Pyrrhic victory?
2. What goaded Parliament into passing the Clean River Act in 1870?
3. Prior to Nairobi, what was the capital of Kenya?
4. 'There's a divinity that shapes our ends.' From where does this line come?
5. Who said, 'When the FA get into their stride, they make the Mafia look like kindergarten material'?
6. Whose catchphrase is 'Shut that door'?
7. Which puzzle was first introduced in 1832?
8. Which people first wrote down music?
9. What is an abalone?

675

1. The Germans called them 'Panzerschiffe.' What did we call them?
2. How much older was Queen Elizabeth I than Mary, Queen of Scots?
3. In 1979, the ship *Ashdod* was the first Israeli ship to sail through *where*?
4. Who wrote *The First Men on the Moon*?
5. Now better known in another field, who was leading in the 1956 Grand National on *Devon Loch* when he fell?
6. Which was Alfred Hitchcock's first film as sole director?
7. 'Good Grief' is which cartoon character's favourite expression?
8. Who had a No. 1 hit with *What Do You Want?*
9. What was the very first TV set called?

207

1. Pepsi-Cola.
2. The stone of Scone.
3. In New York.
4. Esau.
5. Three. (The shotputt, the discus and the javelin.)
6. *Around the World in 80 Days.*
7. The King of Diamonds.
8. *Minnie the Moocher.*
9. The motor car.

441

1. One in which the cost of winning is more than the gain.
2. The Thames smelled so vilely that sitting in the Houses of Parliament was virtually impossible, due to their close proximity to it.
3. Mombasa.
4. Shakespeare's *Hamlet.*
5. Brian Clough.
6. Larry Grayson's.
7. The jigsaw puzzle.
8. The Greeks.
9. A type of shell fish.

675

1. Pocket battleships.
2. About nine years.
3. The Suez Canal.
4. H.G. Wells.
5. Dick Francis.
6. *The Pleasure Garden.*
7. Charlie Brown's.
8. Adam Faith.
9. A 'televisor'.

208

1. Who said, when interviewed in 1969, 'No woman in my time will be Prime Minister'?
2. Who was Rosie the Riveter?
3. In which country are Lakes Titicaca and Poopo?
4. What was Robinson Crusoe's first clue that his island was inhabited?
5. Which 1965 cycling world champion died during the 1967 Tour de France?
6. Who wrote the *Poldark* books, which were turned into a TV serial?
7. Which President did Judge Sarah Hughes swear in at short notice?
8. Which unripe vegetables inspired Booker T. and the MGs?
9. In which year did Sir Richard Woolley, Astronomer Royal, say 'Space travel is utter bilge'?

442

1. Which prison was demolished to make way for the Old Bailey?
2. Which writer, in 1374, was appointed Controller of Customs and Subsidy of Works, Skins and Hides?
3. What distinction has the Condor railway station in Bolivia?
4. 'Many's the long night I've dreamed of cheese – toasted mostly.' Which *Treasure Island* character said this?
5. Which racecourse crosses the Melling Road?
6. Which actress wrote the play *Diamond Lil*?
7. Who loved Ethel le Neve?
8. What does a belly-man do?
9. Of what is chalk composed?

676

1. What is the minimum age at which you can stand for Parliament in the UK?
2. After which unsuccessful trip was Sir Walter Raleigh executed?
3. Renault cars hail from which country?
4. In Dorothy L. Sayers's *Gaudy Night*, who finally accepts Lord Peter Wimsey's proposal of marriage?
5. On which racecourse is the Cesarewitch run?
6. Rupert Davies is known for playing which fictional detective?
7. Which painter once stated, 'A painter who has the feel of breasts and buttocks is saved'?
8. What type of dancers were Antonio and Rosario?
9. The false plane tree is more commonly called *what*?

208

1. Margaret Thatcher.
2. It was the name given to female factory workers in America during World War II.
3. In Bolivia.
4. He found a human footprint in the sand.
5. Tommy Simpson, of Britain.
6. Winston Graham.
7. Lyndon Johnson.
8. 'Green Onions.'
9. 1956. And in 1957 . . .

442

1. Newgate.
2. Geoffrey Chaucer.
3. It is the highest in the world.
4. Ben Gunn.
5. Aintree.
6. Mae West.
7. Dr Crippen.
8. He makes the soundboards of pianos.
9. The skeletons of minute animals.

676

1. Twenty-one.
2. His search for El Dorado.
3. France.
4. Harriet Vane.
5. Newmarket.
6. Inspector Maigret.
7. Renoir.
8. Flamenco.
9. The sycamore.

209

1. What is pumice stone made of?
2. Why was the American comic strip *Bringing Up Father* nicknamed the *Wall Street Comic Strip* in 1948?
3. Which is the USA's southernmost city?
4. Who wrote, 'We are all in the gutter, but some of us are looking at the stars'?
5. In which sport might you perform a 'Lutz' or 'Choctaw'?
6. What is actor George C. Scott's middle name?
7. Who first said 'Little things affect little minds'?
8. Which unlikely pair recorded *Peace on Earth* together?
9. How many times its own length can an average frog jump?

443

1. What do *remueurs* do in the champagne-making process?
2. Who inaugurated the 5-year plan in Russia in 1928?
3. On which river is the Hoover Dam?
4. According to legend, how many heads had Hydra?
5. In 1985, who won the 100th Scottish Cup Final?
6. Who was the chairman of the 1985 Brain of Britain radio quiz show?
7. What do you tiddle with your squidger and hope to pot?
8. According to Johnny Preston's 1959 hit, with whom is *Running Bear* in love?
9. Which cereal crop is grown in the greatest quantity in the UK?

677

1. What is the present name for Sing Sing prison?
2. Name the 'lost city' that supposedly once existed in the Atlantic Ocean.
3. Which European capital begins and ends with 'O'?
4. Lennie and George are the central characters of which John Steinbeck novel?
5. What age horses run in the US Kentucky Derby?
6. Suzanne Sommers made her début in which 1973 film, with the words 'I love you'?
7. Who wrote his autobiography in cell 7 at Landsberg Prison?
8. In which Mozart opera is there a character called Leporello?
9. Which animal can live at the highest altitude?

209

1. Hardened volcanic lava.
2. Because it incorporated a coded message for stock market investors 'in the know'.
3. Honolulu.
4. Oscar Wilde, in *Lady Windermere's Fan.*
5. In ice-skating.
6. Campbell.
7. Benjamin Disraeli.
8. Bing Crosby and David Bowie.
9. About twelve times.

443

1. They shake the bottles.
2. Stalin.
3. The Colorado River.
4. Nine.
5. Glasgow Celtic.
6. Robert Robinson.
7. The wink – in tiddleywinks.
8. Little White Dove.
9. Barley.

677

1. Ossining.
2. Atlantis.
3. Oslo.
4. *Of Mice and Men.*
5. Three-year-olds.
6. *American Graffiti.*
7. Adolf Hitler.
8. In *Don Giovanni.*
9. The yak.

210

1. Why were unmarried women termed spinsters?
2. Which Archbishop of Canterbury divorced Henry VIII from Catherine of Aragon?
3. Where is Kodiak Island?
4. Who wrote, 'In the spring a young man's fancy lightly turns to thoughts of love'?
5. Which county plays cricket at Edgbaston?
6. Who produced, directed, wrote and starred in the film *Citizen Kane*?
7. Marie Dupuis, a maid of the household, often posed for which painter?
8. Which Gilbert and Sullivan operetta is subtitled *Castle Adamant*?
9. Which plant is sometimes called 'Elephant's-ears'?

444

1. Who slept in Baby Bear's bed?
2. Who was the most famous rider of the horse Aethelnoth?
3. Speke Airport serves which city?
4. Name Moses' elder brother?
5. Which soccer star beat the jockey Bob Champion in a 100-yard charity camel race in 1982?
6. On the first night of the Royal Shakespeare Company's production of *Othello*, what happened to John Gielgud's beard?
7. Which statesman married Yvonne Vendroux in 1921?
8. How many notes are there in the pentatonic scale?
9. What is the collective word for a group of mules?

678

1. A polygraph was the first form of *what*?
2. Of which country was Eric Bloodaxe king?
3. What do the French call Brittany?
4. To which poet was Sylvia Plath married?
5. How often does Giant Haystacks, the wrestler, have to buy new beds?
6. Which singer stars in the film *Don't Look Back*?
7. Name the two Churchills who both died on 24 January.
8. What was Winifred Atwell's instrument?
9. Where do mosquitoes lay their eggs?

210

1. Because they were supposedly occupied in spinning their wedding clothes.
2. Thomas Cranmer.
3. In the Gulf of Alaska.
4. Alfred, Lord Tennyson.
5. Warwickshire.
6. Orson Welles.
7. Renoir.
8. *Princess Ida*
9. The begonia.

444

1. Goldilocks.
2. Lady Godiva.
3. Liverpool.
4. Aaron.
5. Jimmy Greaves.
6. It fell apart. (The press had fun with this at the time.)
7. Charles de Gaulle.
8. Five.
9. A barren.

678

1. Lie detector.
2. Of Norway.
3. Bretagne.
4. To Ted Hughes, now the Poet Laureate.
5. About every three months.
6. Bob Dylan.
7. Lord Randolph, in 1985, and Sir Winston, in 1965.
8. The piano.
9. In water.

211

1. The ascetics who lived on top of pillars were called what?
2. Which religion came into being in 1469?
3. In which country are the Adirondack Mountains?
4. 'The boy stood on the burning deck' during which battle?
5. In which country is the game pelota particularly popular?
6. Which actor married, among many others, Miss Birmingham and Miss Muscle Beach?
7. What was the surname of the brothers John and William who made the first breakfast cereal?
8. Which common instrument does the Greek bazukia most closely resemble?
9. From what is solar energy derived?

445

1. For which New York paper did Karl Marx once write?
2. Who was director of music at St Mark's Cathedral in Venice from 1613 until his death in 1643?
3. What are China's two capitals?
4. Who wrote, 'Marriage is popular because it combines the maximum of temptation with the maximum of opportunity'?
5. Which member of the Royal Family was the BBC Sports Personality for 1971?
6. What, in the TV series about Frank, is the name of Frank Spencer's wife?
7. Which Israeli PM was born David Green?
8. Which colour bottom was popular in the 1920s – as a dance?
9. At what age does a dog first need a licence?

679

1. Who first taught that the one permanent thing is change?
2. When was the Great Wall of China built?
3. Which American President's ancestors occupied Sulgrave Hall, Northants?
4. Who wrote, 'Call no man unhappy until he is married'?
5. Who said, 'I am the only woman who does not have a sweat problem'?
6. Who played Joy Adamson in the film *Born Free*?
7. Jungle Alexandras and Jock Scots are used in which activity?
8. What was the surname of brothers Tommy and Jimmy, of big band fame?
9. Apart from the obvious – like washing – what else persuades lice to leave the human body?

211

1. Stylites – after Simon Stylites.
2. Sikhism.
3. In the USA.
4. The Battle of the Nile. (1798.)
5. In Spain.
6. Mickey Rooney.
7. Kellogg.
8. The guitar.
9. The sun.

445

1. The *New York Tribune.*
2. Claudio Monteverdi.
3. Taipei and Beijing. (Peking.)
4. George Bernard Shaw.
5. Princess Anne.
6. Betty.
7. David Ben-Gurion.
8. Black. (The Blackbottom.)
9. Six months.

679

1. Heraclitus.
2. In 246 BC.
3. George Washington's.
4. Socrates.
5. Martina Navratilova.
6. Virginia McKenna.
7. Fishing – they are types of fly.
8. Dorsey.
9. The body temperature rising – as happens when one is ill.

212

1. At what time did Cinderella's coach turn back into a pumpkin?
2. Which king was the first to go to see an FA Cup Final?
3. Which country has the highest road accident rate in Europe?
4. Which play introduced Lady Bracknell?
5. When did the skater Robin Cousins trip over, at the 1980 Winter Olympics?
6. Which actress's autobiography was entitled *My Double Life*?
7. To whom is Esther Rantzen married?
8. Who was termed 'Queen of the Music Halls'?
9. Which animals' evidence can be admissible in US courts of law?

446

1. What shape is a baguette diamond?
2. When the *Mayflower* sailed to America, how many men were on board?
3. Which French city is famed for mustard?
4. The Rostovs and Bolkonskys feature in which novel?
5. At the inception of colour TV in Britain, which was the first major sporting event covered by the BBC?
6. Which actor was incarcerated in Reading Gaol for six months from Christmas 1984, for cocaine smuggling?
7. In religious art, what does the anchor symbolise?
8. In June 1985, which singer was a hijack hostage?
9. To which family of trees does the cedar belong?

680

1. Which child is 'loving and giving'?
2. Where would you find a vambrace, a gorget and a sabaton together?
3. Where is Trafalgar, after which the battle was named?
4. Who wrote the poem *The Lady of the Lake*?
5. Where is the Bislett Stadium, where so many world athletics records have been set?
6. Who was called 'The Voice of the BBC'?
7. Which Pope died on 29 September 1978?
8. To which ballet dancer was Roberto Arias married?
9. What, in fact, was the Piltdown Man – subject of the great hoax?

212

1. At midnight.
2. George V.
3. Greece.
4. *The Importance of Being Earnest.*
5. On the steps of the podium as he went up to receive his gold medal.
6. Sarah Bernhardt's
7. Desmond Wilcox.
8. Marie Lloyd.
9. That of a bloodhound.

446

1. Rectangular.
2. Seventy-four.
3. Dijon.
4. *War and Peace* by Leo Tolstoy.
5. The Wimbledon Tennis Championships.
6. Stacy Keach.
7. Hope.
8. Demis Roussos.
9. The pines.

680

1. Friday's child.
2. On a suit of armour.
3. In Spain.
4. Sir Walter Scott.
5. In Oslo.
6. Richard Dimbleby.
7. Pope John Paul I.
8. Margot Fonteyn.
9. An orang-utan.

Q

213

1. What is béchamel, in cookery?
2. Marshal Soult, Duke of Dalmatia, was whose Chief of Staff at Waterloo?
3. Where is Stonecutter's Island?
4. Which book is a prelude to *The Lord of the Rings*?
5. The Australian cricketer Billy Murdoch scored what 'first' in 1884?
6. In which 1967 film does Sandy Dennis star as a teacher at the Calvin Coolidge High School?
7. Who said, 'Language is the dress of thought'?
8. Who wrote, 'There's No Business Like Show Business'?
9. Which creature has been the symbol of medicine for centuries?

447

1. What percentage of adults in the UK sleep in the nude?
2. What was the World War I slang for 'no more' or 'finished'?
3. What is the population of Bangladesh?
4. Which Shakespearian character said, 'I am constant as the Northern star'?
5. Which American comedian said, 'I've seen cricket and I know it isn't true'?
6. Sacheen Littlefeather accepted whose Oscar award for Best Actor?
7. Who is the cartoonist behind The Gambols strip?
8. Approximately how many hours would it take to play all of Joseph Haydn's works?
9. Which live creatures did doctors of old keep in their medical bags?

681

1. Whose ghost is said to haunt Kensington Palace?
2. Who passed the law forbidding the killing of game in Royal Forests?
3. Which is the world's oldest continent?
4. Who wrote the short story *The Canterville Ghost*?
5. To which swimmer is swimmer Roland Matthes married?
6. Who starred in the film, *What A Crazy World*?
7. Name Queen Victoria's first Prime Minister.
8. Who was the top recording artist in the world in 1964, according to the US magazine *Billboard*?
9. Who won *Time* magazine's Man of the Year award for 1982?

213

1. A white sauce.
2. Napoleon's.
3. In Hong Kong.
4. *The Hobbit.*
5. The first double-century in a Test Match.
6. *Up the Down Staircase.*
7. Dr Samuel Johnson.
8. Irving Berlin.
9. The snake.

447

1. About 20 per cent.
2. 'Napoo'.
3. 92 million.
4. Julius Caesar.
5. Danny Kaye.
6. Marlon Brando's – for his part in *The Godfather.*
7. Barry Appleby.
8. More than 300 hours.
9. Leeches.

681

1. George II's.
2. William the Conqueror.
3. Australia.
4. Oscar Wilde.
5. To Kornelia Ender.
6. Joe Brown.
7. Lord Melbourne.
8. Cliff Richard.
9. Not a man at all, but The Computer. (Which is why it is in this section.)

214

1. Jean Dunant, who founded the Red Cross, was the first to win which prize?
2. What title did Leo Tolstoy have?
3. Which islands are the world's top salt producers?
4. Which Somerset Maugham novel features the painter Paul Gauguin?
5. With which sport is Colonel Abner Doubleday associated?
6. Who played the pirate leader Captain Geoffrey Thorpe in the 1940 film *The Sea Hawk*?
7. Which Venetian painted *The Paradise*?
8. Which Gounod opera was based on a story by Goethe?
9. Which continent is home to the wombat?

448

1. What does the *Daily Express*'s 'masthead' logo depict?
2. Argentina's free health service was founded in 1870. When was it abolished?
3. Which country produces the most rice?
4. Who wrote the thriller *The Five Red Herrings*?
5. Who, while commentating on a Test Match, said, 'The bowler's Holding, the batsman's Willey'?
6. The autobiography of which actor, writer and director is entitled *Dear Me*?
7. For what was Palladio famed?
8. Which station broadcasts records on 208 m?
9. Why was the metal indium so named?

682

1. 'Some are born great, some achieve greatness, and some have greatness thrust upon them.' From where does this famous phrase originate?
2. Which revolution began on 7 November 1917?
3. Mount Ararat is in which country?
4. With which book did Salman Rushdie win the Booker Prize in 1981?
5. FIM is the administering body of which sport?
6. Name Michael Crawford's best-known portrayal.
7. Who was the last British Governor of Kenya?
8. What was Russ Conway's instrument?
9. The degree Ch.B. is a degree in *what*?

214

1. The Nobel Peace Prize.
2. He was Count Leo Tolstoy.
3. The Bahamas.
4. *The Moon and Sixpence.*
5. Baseball. (In 1839 he was credited with both the name and laying down the rule. Later research suggests that he didn't invent the name.)
6. Errol Flynn.
7. Tintoretto.
8. *Faust.*
9. Australia.

448

1. A crusader.
2. In 1977.
3. China.
4. Dorothy L. Sayers.
5. Brian Johnston.
6. Peter Ustinov.
7. Architecture.
8. Radio Luxembourg.
9. Because of its indigo colour.

682

1. Shakespeare's *Twelfth Night.*
2. The Russian Revolution.
3. Turkey.
4. *Midnight's Children.*
5. Motorcycling.
6. Frank Spencer.
7. Malcolm Macdonald.
8. The piano.
9. In surgery. It means Bachelor of Surgery.

215

1. Mrs Elizabeth Robinson was the first woman to address which assembly?
2. Approximately how many humans inhabited England at the time of the Domesday Book?
3. What was Manchester's Airport called before 1955?
4. Who wrote the poem *On the Grasshopper and the Cricket*?
5. Who was the first Englishman to achieve a batting average of 100 in a first-class cricket season?
6. Name Alfred Hitchcock's first 'talkie'?
7. About whom did Kitty Muggeridge say, 'He rose without trace'?
8. How many maids were a-milking?
9. Which metal is commonly used as a shield against radiation?

449

1. From what did Samson derive his strength?
2. In which year did the St Valentine's day massacre take place?
3. Which country has the shortest railway?
4. Who used the name Robert Markham when he wrote *Colonel Sun* – featuring James Bond?
5. 'Shoeless' Joe Jackson played which game?
6. Who directed the films *Saboteur* and *The Lady Vanishes*?
7. In which city is the great Prado art gallery?
8. 'Pizzicato' to 'arco'. What does the music tell you to do?
9. Where is Britain's largest horse fair held annually?

683

1. What was the first letter transmitted in Morse Code by transatlantic wireless signal?
2. During which decade were the Liberals last in power?
3. What is the language of the Bahamas?
4. According to the Bible, what were God's first words?
5. From which country did runner Emile Puttemans hail?
6. For what did Carol Reed win his Oscar with the film *Oliver*?
7. Which domino contains the fewest pips?
8. Which comedian had a hit with *Love is Like a Violin*?
9. Experiments with two cans and some kitchen scales led to which form of transport?

215

1. The House of Commons.
2. About two million.
3. Ringway Airport. (It is now Manchester International.)
4. John Keats.
5. Geoffrey Boycott.
6. *Blackmail.*
7. David Frost.
8. Eight.
9. Lead.

449

1. His hair.
2. In 1929.
3. Afghanistan. (Less than half a mile in total.)
4. Kingsley Amis.
5. Baseball.
6. Alfred Hitchcock.
7. In Madrid.
8. Change from plucking to bowing.
9. At Appleby.

683

1. 'S'.
2. The 1920s.
3. English.
4. 'Let there be light.'
5. From Belgium.
6. His work as director.
7. The double blank.
8. Ken Dodd.
9. The Hovercraft.

216

1. What letter on a ship's flag signifies 'Yes'?
2. Which country has been ruled by the Al Khalifah family since 1783?
3. 'Breaking the ice' is a well-known phrase, but from where is it reputed to come?
4. Name all three Brontë sisters.
5. Who scored the winning goal in the 1985 FA Cup Final?
6. How many autobiographies has Shirley MacLaine written?
7. Who painted *The Little Girl In White*?
8. Who wrote the choral work *Carmina Burana*?
9. Where do turtles head when they hatch?

450

1. Which Queen has a London mainline station named after her?
2. Who was the first Chancellor of the German Federal Republic?
3. In which country was the Portuguese dictator Caetano overthrown in 1974?
4. Who wrote, 'Marriage is a sort of friendship recognised by the police'?
5. Who was the BBC Sports Personality of the years 1967 and 1970?
6. Name the clown which is used in promoting the McDonald's hamburger chain.
7. Who drives a car with the number plate 1 PRO?
8. Whom did Sir Thomas Beecham refer to as 'that Milanese purveyor of spaghetti'?
9. Jaundice turns the skin what colour?

684

1. What is Greek for the letter 'S'?
2. In 1914, the wife of a French Minister shot the editor of which French national newspaper?
3. Which country has the highest birthrate in Europe?
4. What does the Feast of the Passover commemorate?
5. Hookers and props play which game?
6. Who was the Oscar-winning star of the film *Gaslight*?
7. How old was Lucrezia Borgia when she first married?
8. Who made his orchestra rehearse playing 'For he's a jolly good fellow' when he was about to be knighted?
9. Which member of the carp family is most commonly kept as a pet?

216

1. The letter C.
2. Bahrain.
3. At each stop of the Irish Mail the porters changed the foot-warmers, and passengers got into conversation.
4. Charlotte, Emily and Anne.
5. Norman Whiteside.
6. Two.
7. James Whistler.
8. Carl Orff.
9. For the sea.

450

1. Queen Victoria.
2. Konrad Adenauer.
3. In Angola.
4. Robert Louis Stevenson.
5. Henry Cooper.
6. Ronald.
7. Ray Reardon.
8. Toscanini.
9. Yellow.

684

1. Sigma.
2. *Le Figaro.*
3. Albania – where parenthood is encouraged.
4. The deliverance of the Jews from Egypt.
5. Rugby.
6. Ingrid Bergman.
7. Twelve.
8. Sir Malcolm Sargent.
9. The goldfish.

217

1. Who sailed the vessel *Tigris* – a boat made of papyrus?
2. Who said, 'A Conservative government is an organised hypocrisy'?
3. Of the ten radio stations in Bhutan, what do eight solely transmit?
4. Who wrote the book *The Wizard of Oz*?
5. Dressed as whom did Bobby Riggs arrive for his tennis match *v.* Billie-Jean King?
6. Who played Miss Jane Marple in the 1964 film *Murder Ahoy*?
7. When did President Brezhnev, of the Soviet Union, die?
8. Which American composed the music for the ballets *Billy the Kid* and *Rodeo*?
9. How many legs has a scorpion?

451

1. Which novel featured an invention known as the 'Feelies'?
2. When Queen Victoria made her first rail journey in 1842, she travelled to Slough from which London station?
3. In which city is the Anne Frank Museum?
4. What pen name did the US Supreme Court judge use to write his best-seller, *Anatomy of a Murder*?
5. What name was given to England's 1932–33 tour of Australia?
6. Which actor was the star of the film *Death Wish*?
7. Of which royal personage is Frances Roach the mother?
8. *Manru* was the only opera written by which composer-pianist?
9. The coypu is the largest *what* in Britain?

685

1. On average, for how long does an ordinary light bulb last?
2. Who was the leader of the Tolpuddle Martyrs?
3. In which county is the Forest of Dean?
4. Who has the second longest entry in the *Oxford Dictionary of Quotations*?
5. For which country did Ranjitsinjhi play Test cricket?
6. In which film does a beautiful horse lose its head?
7. Who painted *The Four Freedoms*, a frequently reproduced painting?
8. Which suffragette composed *March of the Women*?
9. Who was the first Englishman to become a Matador de Toros?

217

1. Thor Heyerdahl.
2. Benjamin Disraeli.
3. Flood warnings.
4. L. Frank Baum.
5. King Henry VIII.
6. Margaret Rutherford.
7. In November 1982.
8. Aaron Copland.
9. Eight.

451

1. *Brave New World*, by Aldous Huxley.
2. Paddington.
3. In Amsterdam.
4. Robert Traver.
5. The 'Bodyline' series.
6. Charles Bronson.
7. The Princess of Wales.
8. Paderewski.
9. Rodent.

685

1. 750 hours.
2. George Loveless.
3. In Gloucestershire.
4. Alfred, Lord Tennyson.
5. England.
6. *The Godfather*.
7. Norman Rockwell.
8. Dame Ethel Smyth.
9. Henry Higgins.

218

1. In America's Annual National Rattlesnake Sacking Contest, how many rattlesnakes must be bagged?
2. In which city did the Peterloo massacre of 1819 occur?
3. Andorra has the highest minimum voting age in the world. What is it?
4. Who wrote, 'As to marriage or celibacy, let a man take which course he will, he will be sure to repent'?
5. Which British racing driver won four Grand Prix races in 1963?
6. In which film did Charlie Chaplin portray a clown?
7. Martha Graham is renowned for *what*?
8. What was John Lennon doing when he was shot?
9. What is a Rhodesian Ridgeback?

452

1. How old was William Gladstone when he became PM for the fourth time?
2. Who took the Red Army on The Long March?
3. Which country has the highest sand dunes in the world?
4. Who wrote of Natty Bumpo in a number of novels?
5. To what did Marvin Hagler change his name by deed poll in 1982?
6. Who, on TV, said, 'Oooh, you are awful, but I like you' and accompanied this with a clout from a handbag?
7. What is Barbie the doll's boyfriend's name?
8. What form of music was Jacopo Peri believed to be the first to have composed?
9. Who is Charley in John Steinbeck's novel *Travels With Charley*?

686

1. Why may you not take the mickey out of President Canaan Banana of Zimbabwe because of his name?
2. Whose ear did Spanish pirates sever, in 1739?
3. On which mountain is Kibo Peak?
4. Who wrote the book *Sex Scandals*, published in 1985?
5. How much did Stan Bowles reputedly bet that his then club, QPR, would win the 1975–76 Football League Championship?
6. What was the name of the comedy, revived by the RSC in 1976, which starred Alan Howard and Norman Rodway?
7. What was the ransom demanded for Eugene Paul Getty in 1973?
8. To what did the group *Tyrannosaurus Rex* change its name?
9. Lady's Slipper is a variety of which flower?

218

1. Ten.
2. In Manchester.
3. Twenty-five.
4. Socrates.
5. Jim Clark.
6. *Limelight.*
7. Choreography, mainly.
8. Autographing his LP *Double Fantasy* – for his killer!
9. A breed of dog.

452

1. Eighty-four.
2. Mao Tse-tung.
3. Algeria.
4. James Fenimore Cooper.
5. Marvellous Marvin Hagler.
6. Dick Emery.
7. Ken.
8. Opera.
9. His dog, a poodle.

686

1. Because he passed a law in 1983 making it a crime if you do.
2. Robert Jenkins, which act led to 'The War of Jenkins' Ear'.
3. Mount Kilimanjaro.
4. Christine Keeler.
5. £6,000 – and they didn't!
6. *Wild Oats.*
7. Three million dollars.
8. *T. Rex.*
9. The orchid.

219

1. Which city is the base of the secret society called the 'Camorra'?
2. In 1819, King John VI of Portugal had a special throne made to help him do *what*?
3. The Duke of Wellington once lived in Merrion Square – in which city?
4. Who wrote *The Leopard Hunts In Darkness*?
5. What was unusual about the way Len Hutton got out at the Oval in 1951, playing South Africa?
6. In *From Here To Eternity*, why did the Montgomery Clift character refuse to box?
7. Artists who painted 'Singeries' showed which animals pretending to be human?
8. In the opera *Moses and Aaron* the second act ends with a dance before which idol?
9. Food canning was invented about 1830. How long was it before can-openers were invented?

453

1. In which country were safety matches invented in 1852?
2. How many dollars could you get for a pound during the US Civil War?
3. On which island are Fort St Elmo and the castle of St Angelo?
4. Which author threatened to charge the BBC double if they used his first name, which he thought 'too English'?
5. In which sport did Tony Pawson and Bobby Smithers become world champions in 1984?
6. In which US state was the MGM musical *Seven Brides For Seven Brothers* set?
7. What accident killed the Dutch artist Carel Fabritius in 1654?
8. Who composed the 'Drumroll' or 'Paukenwirbel' Symphony in 1795?
9. What was the name of the Wright Brothers' first practical biplane, in 1905?

687

1. Early this century, what did Americans buy called 'twofers'?
2. By what Arabic name meaning 'lord' do we know Rodrigo Diaz de Vivar?
3. Which city has adjacent museums containing the *Fram* and the *Kon-Tiki*?
4. Which Poet Laureate was the son of a Danish sculptor, and wrote *Love's Last Shift*?
5. By the laws of the game, what may a footballer not wear?
6. In the 1946 film *The Seventh Veil*, what was Ann Todd's job?
7. Which comedian became chairman of the Ramblers' Association in 1985?
8. Who was inspired by Thomas Hardy's work to write *Egdon Heath* in 1927?
9. In which hospital was Alexander Fleming researching when he found penicillin in 1928?

219

1. Naples.
2. Hear better – it had speaking tubes built in.
3. In Dublin.
4. Wilbur Smith.
5. He was given out for obstructing the field.
6. He had once blinded a man in the ring.
7. Monkeys.
8. The Golden Calf.
9. Over 50 years. They were first known in 1885. Until then, they used chisels!

453

1. In Sweden.
2. Twelve.
3. On Malta.
4. George Bernard Shaw.
5. Angling.
6. Oregon.
7. The gunpowder magazine next door to his studio blew up.
8. Haydn. (No. 103 in E flat major.)
9. Flyer III.

687

1. Cigars, at two for 25 cents.
2. El Cid.
3. Oslo.
4. Colley Cibber.
5. Anything dangerous to another player.
6. She was a concert pianist.
7. Mike Harding.
8. Gustav Holst.
9. St Mary's, Paddington.

220

1. Psephology is the study of *what*?
2. Which two languages are on the Rosetta Stone?
3. In which country is Cook Mountain?
4. Name the Brontë *brother*.
5. Who were the beaten finalists both in the 1974 and 1978 World Cup?
6. Holmfirth is the setting for which popular BBC TV series?
7. Which judge, who held court in a saloon, was nicknamed 'The Law West of the Pecos'?
8. How many reeds has a bassoon?
9. In what do whales congregate?

454

1. How many people form a nonet?
2. Which was the largest concentration camp formed by the Nazis in World War II?
3. Which wall is about 1,500 miles in length?
4. Who wrote *Salar the Salmon*?
5. What was M.P. Betts's goal-scoring first?
6. Which actress stars in the 1979 film *Bloodline*?
7. Which American, just before being hanged as a spy by the British, said, 'I only regret that I have but one life to lose for my country'?
8. From which country does the dijeridu come?
9. Which British scientist discovered the electron?

688

1. What is cupidity?
2. Whose nickname was 'Tumbledown Dick'?
3. Mount Godwin Austen is more regularly called what?
4. Who wrote *A Town Like Alice*?
5. Who said to Joe Bugner, 'Stay pretty. Whatever happens, stay pretty'?
6. In the *Rocky* films, what is Rocky's surname?
7. Bryan Organ's portrait of whom was put on show at the National Portrait Gallery, just before her marriage?
8. Which Gilbert and Sullivan opera is subtitled *The Merryman and his Maid*?
9. How many lives has a cat?

A

220

1. Election results.
2. Egyptian and Greek.
3. In New Zealand.
4. Branwell.
5. Holland.
6. *Last of the Summer Wine.*
7. Judge Roy Bean.
8. Two.
9. Schools.

454

1. Nine.
2. Auschwitz.
3. The Great Wall of China.
4. Henry Williamson.
5. He scored the very first goal in the very first FA Cup Final.
6. Audrey Hepburn.
7. Nathan Hale.
8. Australia.
9. Sir Joseph Thomson.

688

1. Greed for gain.
2. Richard Cromwell, son of Oliver.
3. K 2.
4. Nevil Shute.
5. Muhammad Ali.
6. Balboa.
7. Lady Diana Spencer.
8. *The Yeoman of the Guard.*
9. One.

221

1. What said 'Oranges and Lemons'?
2. What pulled the first trains?
3. What are the two official languages of Canada?
4. Of what figure of speech are 'hrrmph', 'maiow' and 'pow' all examples?
5. Where is the HQ of Lancashire County Cricket?
6. The TV series *Who Pays the Ferryman?* was set on which island?
7. Who said 'An editor is a man who separates the wheat from the chaff, and then prints the chaff'?
8. Whom did Sir Thomas Beecham try to keep out of his orchestras?
9. Of what is the barber's red and white striped pole the symbol?

455

1. What is the English equivalent of the Greek letter 'lambda'?
2. Who murdered George, Duke of Buckingham, in 1627?
3. What does one traditionally throw into Rome's Trevi fountain?
4. Whose drawings first appeared in the book *Is Sex Necessary?*?
5. To whom did Muhammad Ali say, 'You're the Chump and I'm the Champ'?
6. Whose very first company was called the 'Laugh-O-Gram Corp'?
7. Which Nobel Prize winner has appeared in the pages of *Wisden Cricketers' Almanac*?
8. Who was the first black entertainer to win an Emmy?
9. Which is the largest manufacturer of aircraft in the world?

689

1. What number is represented by the Roman numeral M?
2. Which European country was last at war in 1814?
3. How many litres of spirits a year does the average Soviet citizen drink?
4. What is the first line of Walter de la Mare's poem *Silver*?
5. In adverts for which toothpaste did Billie Jean-King take part?
6. In which city is the Royal Exchange theatre?
7. St Thomas Aquinas was a member of which order of friars?
8. Which Elvis Presley film was based on the novel *A Stone For Danny Fisher*?
9. Which sex chromosome from the father means 'it's a boy'?

221

1. The bells of St Clement's.
2. Horses.
3. English and French.
4. Onomatopoeia.
5. At Old Trafford.
6. Crete.
7. Adlai Stevenson.
8. Women.
9. A bleeding, bandaged arm, as barbers originally doubled as surgeons.

455

1. The letter L.
2. John Felton.
3. Coins.
4. James Thurber's.
5. Sonny Liston.
6. Walt Disney's.
7. Samuel Beckett.
8. Harry Belafonte.
9. Boeing.

689

1. 1,000.
2. Sweden.
3. Eight.
4. 'Slowly, silently, now the moon'
5. Colgate.
6. In Manchester.
7. The Dominicans.
8. *King Creole*.
9. The Y chromosome.

Q

222

1. What is the Greek for the letter 'K'?
2. Who once abolished St Valentine's day in England?
3. Which London street is nicknamed 'The Street of Ink'?
4. How wide was the hat worn by the Quangle Wangle in Edward Lear's poem?
5. What curious maritime sporting achievement did Frédéric Beauchêne accomplish in 1979?
6. Who played John Cleese's wife in *Fawlty Towers*?
7. By what name is 'Lexico' universally known today?
8. Who composed the opera *Norma*?
9. What is guano?

456

1. Initials are all the rage nowadays, but why is ASH opposed to FOREST?
2. Which famous liner was launched in 1967?
3. How do Americans pronounce the letter 'Z'?
4. For how long was Robinson Crusoe marooned?
5. Which are the only two countries to have won the Americas Cup?
6. Who said, 'A man in the house is worth two in the street'?
7. Breakfast Time's first weather forecaster was who, wooed from Thames TV?
8. Name the theme song from the TV series *Minder*.
9. By what name is daltonism commonly known?

690

1. Who is called, among many other things, 'Old Poker'?
2. Which uncle of Queen Victoria's was Belgium's first king?
3. In which Irish county is Tralee?
4. How many chapters does the book of *Obadiah* contain in the Bible?
5. At what minimum age are horses raced?
6. Well known for playing everyone's mum, who played Mrs Hutchison in TV's *The Liver Birds*?
7. Which part of his anatomy did Marty Feldman insure?
8. In which city is the record company *Tamla Motown* based?
9. Name the bear that disappeared while filming a TV commerical for toilet rolls.

222

1. Kappa.
2. Oliver Cromwell – quite a spoilsport!
3. Fleet Street.
4. 102 feet wide.
5. He wind-surfed round Cape Horn.
6. Prunella Scales.
7. *Scrabble.*
8. Bellini.
9. Sea bird droppings.

456

1. ASH is an anti-smoking lobby, FOREST a pro-smoking lobby.
2. *QE2.*
3. 'Zee.'
4. Over 28 years.
5. America and Australia.
6. Mae West.
7. Francis Wilson.
8. *I Could Be So Good For You.*
9. Colour-blindness.

690

1. The devil.
2. Leopold I.
3. Kerry.
4. Just one.
5. Two years.
6. Mollie Sugden.
7. His eyes.
8. In Detroit, USA. (Mo-town, short for motor-town, is the nickname of Detroit.)
9. Hercules.

223

1. How long does an ostrich egg take to cook?
2. What was the cause of the American Civil War?
3. Which is the smallest of the four oceans?
4. Approximately how many different words did Shakespeare use in his plays?
5. Which player stands on the mound in the middle of the diamond in baseball?
6. What happens at the start of every *Quincy* TV programme?
7. What was First Lady 'Lady Bird' Johnson's real first name?
8. Why is the song that Christine Jorgensen features in her night club act *I Enjoy Being a Girl* particularly apt?
9. Which is the world's shortest snake?

457

1. In what has the surname 'Coward' its origin?
2. It was called Trans-Western Airlines when Howard Hughes owned it. What is it now called?
3. In which country does the largest variety of flowers grow?
4. How did the Basilisk kill its enemies?
5. How many points are awarded to the winner of a Grand Prix motor racing event?
6. *Z Cars* was set in which town?
7. How is Skipper related to Barbie – the doll?
8. Who had a No. 1 hit with *Cars*?
9. Gas consumption is measured in what units?

691

1. Relating to museums, for what is 'V. and A.' an abbreviation?
2. Aventine, Palatine and Viminal are three of which seven?
3. 'Pays de Galles' is French for which country?
4. What made Tristan and Isolde fall in love?
5. The Hospitals Cup is competed for in which game?
6. The advent of which technique made it unnecessary for a film to be made with a different cast for each country?
7. Who sailed *Robertson's Golly* across the Atlantic in 1976?
8. For how long was Tchaikovsky married?
9. Why is it anti-social to allow a lion to eat you?

223

1. About 40 minutes.
2. The question of slavery.
3. The Indian Ocean.
4. 25,000.
5. The pitcher.
6. All the officers present pass out when Quincy uncovers a body.
7. Claudia.
8. She underwent a sex change operation.
9. The thread snake.

457

1. The job of cow-herd.
2. Trans-World Airlines, or TWA for short.
3. In South Africa.
4. Just by looking at them.
5. Nine.
6. Seaport.
7. She is her younger sister.
8. Gary Numan.
9. Therms.

691

1. Victoria and Albert.
2. The seven hills on which Rome was built.
3. Wales.
4. The magic potion that they both drank.
5. Rugby Union.
6. Dubbing.
7. Claire Francis.
8. One month.
9. Because once it has tasted human flesh it becomes a man- and woman-eater for life.

224

1. What does 'ad hoc' mean?
2. Name the first British steamship to cross the Atlantic.
3. Name two of the four English counties which, prior to 1974, began with the letter C.
4. Who was Salome's mother?
5. Who managed Nottingham Forest to victory twice in the European Cup?
6. The film *Champions* featured which activity?
7. Who described one of Turner's paintings as 'A tortoise-shell cat having a fit in a platter of tomatoes'?
8. What type of solo dancing developed on street corners in the 1980s?
9. Which bird's bill is said to hold more than its belly?

458

1. Who said, 'Please be informed that there is a Santa Claus'?
2. Which inquisition started in 1478?
3. How much did the USA pay Spain for the Virgin Islands in 1917?
4. Who was the Roman goddess who equated with the Greek Hera?
5. What is Brian Hooper's athetics event?
6. Whose vital statistics are 70–30–32?
7. Many people have more than one claim to fame, but who both produced *Gone With The Wind* and founded Pan Am?
8. What is fake about snake-charmers playing music?
9. Against what disease would a Sabin vaccine be given?

692

1. Where would you wear a sombrero?
2. What was the Allied Forces password during the D-Day landings?
3. Name Canada's longest river.
4. Which book begins 'Mr Salteena was an elderly man of 42 . . .'?
5. Who died on Coniston Water in 1967?
6. Who plays Stan Butler in the film *On The Buses*?
7. Who is called the 'Father of Modern Chemistry'?
8. *Ol' Man River* was written about which river?
9. 92 is the atomic number for which element?

224

1. 'For a specific purpose.'
2. *Great Western*.
3. Cornwall, Cambridgeshire, Cumberland and Cheshire.
4. Herodias.
5. Brian Clough.
6. Steeplechasing.
7. Mark Twain.
8. Break dancing.
9. The pelican's.

458

1. Jim Lovell, the first astronaut to go behind the dark side of the moon.
2. The Spanish Inquisition.
3. $25 million.
4. Juno.
5. The pole vault.
6. Miss Piggy's.
7. Cornelius Vanderbilt Whitney.
8. Snakes are deaf.
9. Poliomyelitis.

692

1. On your head.
2. 'Mickey Mouse.'
3. The MacKenzie.
4. Daisy Ashford's *The Young Visiters*.
5. Sir Donald Campbell.
6. Reg Varney.
7. Anton Lavoisier.
8. The Mississippi.
9. Uranium.

225

1. The Hadrosaurs (now extinct) are often called 'duck-billed' *what*?
2. When the English Civil War began, in which city did Charles I raise his standard?
3. Which US city was called 'Porkopolis' because of its meat-packing industry?
4. Lydia Languish is the heroine of which Sheridan work?
5. What is the unique characteristic of Rotterdam Golf Club's course?
6. In which US city did the action of *The Sting* take place?
7. Which great artist was a shepherd boy when Cimabue saw him draw a lamb on a slate?
8. How many holes does a French flageolet have?
9. What is the common name for the wild rose or eglantine?

459

1. Which make of car has a model called Mulsanne Turbo?
2. The Domesday Book was rebound in how many volumes for its 900th anniversary?
3. Which city is farthest south, Madrid, Naples, Lisbon or Ankara?
4. By what name do we know Perrault's story *Cendrillon?*
5. Which professional sport did England full-back Alastair Hignell take up after quitting rugby?
6. What is the only Oscar-winning film whose title begins with 'U'?
7. Which fashion designer is the daughter of ballroom dancing champions from Kent?
8. Which great American invented a 'harmonica', a set of tuned glass bowls?
9. How many times per minute does a whale's heart beat?

693

1. In South Africa, what is called 'mealies'?
2. Which country's republican revolutionaries were called 'charcoal burners'?
3. Where do the 'gendarmeria pontificia' work?
4. What was Mr Root's profession, according to *The Henry Root Letters*?
5. What did the Earl of Winchelsea rename the White Conduit Cricket Club?
6. In which TV comedy series did Maureen Lipman run a magazine advice column?
7. Which word for a hooded cloak is also used for a game?
8. Who wrote operas called *Hugh the Drover* and *Sir John In Love*?
9. Removal of which sugar makes fruit soften when boiled?

225

1. Dinosaurs.
2. In Nottingham.
3. Cincinnati.
4. *The Rivals*.
5. It is 8 metres below sea level, the lowest in the world.
6. In Chicago.
7. Giotto.
8. Six: four in front, and two behind.
9. The sweet-briar.

459

1. Bentley.
2. Five. (It used to be two.)
3. Lisbon.
4. *Cinderella*.
5. Cricket, for Gloucestershire.
6. *Underworld*, made in 1928.
7. Zandra Rhodes.
8. Benjamin Franklin.
9. Between nine and ten.

693

1. Maize.
2. Italy's – the Carbonari.
3. In the Vatican – they are the police.
4. A fishmonger.
5. The Marylebone Cricket Club, in 1787.
6. *Agony*.
7. Domino.
8. Ralph Vaughan Williams.
9. Pectin.

226

1. Who commit patricide?
2. Who said, in 1933, 'I am insulted by the persistent assertion that I want war. Am I a fool? War! It would settle nothing'?
3. England consists of approximately how many square miles?
4. Whose name did God change to Israel?
5. Which successful jockey comes from Kentucky and rides in Britain?
6. Aged 79, who won an Oscar playing in the film *The Sunshine Boys*?
7. On which poet's tombstone in Rome is inscribed, 'Here lies one whose name was writ in water'?
8. In which country did modern ballet begin in the 17th century?
9. Sooty, the glove puppet – what animal is he?

460

1. Whose egg is 'good in parts'?
2. Which war was named after the Israeli participants' holy day?
3. Of which country was Antioch the ancient capital?
4. Who saw the first rainbow, according to the Bible?
5. What was Bobby Moore accused of stealing in 1970, when in Bogotá for the World Cup?
6. Who, of *Terry and June* fame, received an OBE in 1985?
7. Who resigned as P.M. of Canada in 1984, after sixteen years in the post?
8. From which film does the song *Secret Love* come?
9. Where would you be if you sat on a howdah?

694

1. When is Lammas day?
2. In 1906 HMS *Dreadnought* was launched from which dock yard?
3. In the village of Staphorst in Holland, what is the prerequisite for a girl marrying?
4. Sleeping Beauty's father ordered all *what* to be burned?
5. Why was Severiano Ballesteros disqualified from the US Open in 1980?
6. In which of Tom Stoppard's plays did Michael Hordern and Diana Rigg co-star?
7. What is a shard, to an archaeologist?
8. Who wrote both words and music to *King's Rhapsody*?
9. Which is the main element in the human body?

226

1. Children who kill their fathers.
2. Adolf Hitler.
3. 50,000. (50,333, to be precise.)
4. Jacob's.
5. Steve Cauthen.
6. George Burns.
7. That of John Keats.
8. In France.
9. A bear.

460

1. The curate's egg.
2. The Yom Kippur War.
3. Syria.
4. Noah, and his family.
5. An emerald bracelet, though it was obvious that he could not have done so.
6. June Whitfield.
7. Pierre Trudeau.
8. *Calamity Jane*.
9. On top of an elephant.

694

1. 1 August.
2. Portsmouth.
3. She *must* be pregnant!
4. Spinning wheels.
5. He arrived at the first tee ten minutes late.
6. In *Jumpers*.
7. A piece of pottery. (And to non-archaeologists, too.)
8. Ivor Novello.
9. Oxygen.

Q

227

1. Which PM cut the working week to three days?
2. What name is given to the battle won by Nelson in Aboukir Bay?
3. From which country do Fiat cars come?
4. Who wrote the Mr Moto series of novels?
5. Who described golf as 'An ineffectual attempt to direct an uncontrollable sphere into an inaccessible hole with instruments ill-adapted for the purpose'?
6. Which Shakespeare play do actors refer to as 'the Scottish play'?
7. Who leads the new Tory group, Conservative Centre Forward?
8. Which opera house's roof is designed to look like the sails of a yacht?
9. Acrux is the brightest star in which constellation?

461

1. 'Man, an ingenious assembly of portable plumbing.' Who said it?
2. The temple of Diana was constructed from which material?
3. Harare is the capital of which country?
4. Which fictional detective lived at 14 Farraway Street?
5. Which East German won both the athletics sprint races at the 1972 Olympics?
6. Who led the group that killed the actress Sharon Tate and others in 1969?
7. Who were the first to play dominoes?
8. Which rock musical features Frank N. Furter, Riff-Raff, Brad and Janet?
9. How many legs have arachnids?

695

1. Which *Peanuts* character loves the little red-headed girl?
2. What service, started in Britain in July 1635, helped people keep in touch?
3. Which country contains at least half the population of South America?
4. Who wrote, 'Though the mills of God grind slowly, yet they grind exceeding small'?
5. How many days before a championship would Bjorn Borg stop shaving?
6. In Alfred Hitchcock's film *The Lady Vanishes*, what was suspicious about the nun on the train?
7. Who said, 'All I know is that I am not a Marxist'?
8. How many No. 1 hits had the Beatles?
9. Who raised the lioness Elsa from a cub?

227

1. Edward Heath (but only temporarily).
2. The Battle of the Nile.
3. Italy.
4. John Phillips Marquand.
5. Winston Churchill.
6. *Macbeth.*
7. Francis Pym.
8. That of the opera house in Sydney, Australia.
9. The Southern Cross.

461

1. Christopher Morley.
2. Marble.
3. Zimbabwe.
4. Hercule Poirot.
5. Renate Stecher – the women's 100 metre and 200 metre Gold Medallist.
6. Charles Manson.
7. French monks.
8. *The Rocky Horror Show.*
9. Eight. (They are spiders.)

695

1. Charlie Brown.
2. The Royal Mail.
3. Brazil.
4. Longfellow, in *Retribution*, translating the work of Friedrich von Logan.
5. Four.
6. She was wearing high heels.
7. Karl Marx.
8. Seventeen (in Britain).
9. George and Joy Adamson.

288

1. Peter the Great of Russia claimed they were 'a useless embarrassment' and levied a tax on them. What were they?
2. How were Prince Albert and Queen Victoria related, apart from being married?
3. Which London bridge comes between Southwark Bridge and Tower Bridge?
4. Who is father of the Jewish race?
5. What is Bernhardt Langer's game?
6. Who played Christ in the film *Johnny Got His Gun*?
7. Elsie and ______ Waters. Which sister of the comedy duo is missing?
8. Which composer did Clara Wieck marry?
9. How long do hen eggs take to hatch?

462

1. Which canal has the same name as a type of hat?
2. Who used to use a claymore?
3. What was a 'London Particular' – fortunately now a thing of the past?
4. Who drank poison to save Peter Pan?
5. Which cricketer was nicknamed 'Fiery Fred'?
6. Name Gotham City's Police Chief in TV's *Batman*?
7. Which is the lowest-ranked suit at bridge?
8. What did Amati make?
9. Where is the Achilles tendon on the body?

696

1. What are floors on ships called?
2. Who led the Arabs into Damascus, in 1918?
3. In which US state is New Orleans?
4. Who appropriately wrote *Last Flight*?
5. What is a shiai?
6. Where do the Munchkins live, according to *The Wizard of Oz*?
7. How did Prince William of Gloucester die, in 1972?
8. On which instrument is Kyung Wha Chung a virtuoso?
9. The 'green revolution' is *what*?

228

1. Beards.
2. They were cousins.
3. London Bridge.
4. Abraham.
5. Golf.
6. Donald Sutherland.
7. Doris
8. Robert Schumann.
9. Three weeks.

462

1. The Panama.
2. Scottish Highlanders – it was a two-edged sword.
3. A dense fog, or smog.
4. Tinkerbell.
5. Fred Trueman.
6. Chief O'Hara.
7. Clubs.
8. Violins, mostly.
9. In the heel.

696

1. Decks.
2. T.E. Lawrence, Lawrence of Arabia.
3. In Louisiana.
4. Amelia Earhart.
5. A judo contest.
6. In Munchkin Land.
7. In an air crash.
8. The violin.
9. The development of high-yield crops.

229

1. By law, at what age must children begin their education in the UK?
2. During World War II, which group had a great reputation as night fighters with knives?
3. What is the Aletsch?
4. Who was said to have given Abraham the Black Stone, which is in the Great Mosque at Mecca?
5. Which county plays cricket matches at Headingley?
6. Whom does Worzel Gummidge love?
7. For what is Eric Hosking famous?
8. What is a calliope?
9. What is the best natural fertiliser?

463

1. For what occupation would you train at Norlands?
2. For what public spectacle did crowds come to Tyburn?
3. Which part of London is termed the 'Square Mile'?
4. Who married Miriam Larkins?
5. Who won the first of her Wimbledon singles titles in 1978?
6. Who played the Chinese detective, Mr Wong, in five films?
7. Aged 60, Leonardo da Vinci began painting with his left hand. Why?
8. What, in the song, is itsy-bitsy, teeny-weeny'?
9. How is it that mongooses which attack cobras are unaffected by the snakes' venom?

697

1. Who created Badjelly and Dulboot?
2. How were Kings Richard I and John related?
3. What is the height of the letters in the Hollywood sign, just outside Hollywood?
4. *The White Peacock* was whose first novel?
5. Riposte and parry are terms used in which sport?
6. Bernard Cribbins is the voice of which bird?
7. The children of which ex-MP turned journalist are named Pericles and Petronella?
8. Who put Pussy in the well?
9. Where on the body are bicuspids found?

229

1. At five.
2. The Gurkhas.
3. The largest glacier in Europe. (It is in Switzerland.)
4. The Archangel Gabriel.
5. Yorkshire.
6. Aunt Sally.
7. Bird photography.
8. A steam organ.
9. Guano, or bird droppings.

463

1. You would train to become a nanny.
2. Public hangings.
3. The City.
4. Mr Polly. (H. G. Wells.)
5. Martina Navratilova.
6. Boris Karloff.
7. Because his right arm became paralysed.
8. 'Yellow polka-dot bikini.'
9. They move so fast that they are rarely bitten!

697

1. Spike Milligan, in his books for children.
2. They were brothers.
3. 50 feet tall.
4. D. H. Lawrence's.
5. Fencing.
6. Busby, in the British Telecom ads.
7. Woodrow Wyatt.
8. Little Tommy Green.
9. In the mouth – they are teeth.

230

1. Who, when told that the reason he lost the Labour leadership to Harold Wilson because he was so rude to people when he was drunk, replied, 'What makes them think I'm rude to them just because I'm drunk?'?
2. What was the forerunner of the plate?
3. Which country did the League of Nations expel in 1939 for attacking Finland?
4. Who wrote the novels *One Fat Englishman* and *Jake's Thing*?
5. In which sport would you use a shinai?
6. In which 1967 film did Simon and Garfunkel's *Sounds of Silence* feature?
7. Who painted the picture *Rain, Steam and Speed*?
8. Whose waltz should last just a minute?
9. What is a baroque pearl?

464

1. At what age are you considered to be responsible for fastening your own car seat belt?
2. Who became the Mayor of London during the reign of Richard II?
3. What provides 99 per cent of Brunei's income?
4. Who writes crime stories featuring Mr Ripley?
5. Dig, set, spike. What is the game?
6. In which 1960 film do Frank Sinatra and friends rob a number of Las Vegas casinos?
7. What do we call the game the Arabs call Shatranj?
8. In which US city is pianist Liberace's museum sited?
9. Which breed of dog has a black tongue?

698

1. What can a traveller get free, if in limited quantities, at the gate of Winchester's Hospital of St Cross?
2. Which two Custers died at the Little Big Horn?
3. In which ocean is Madagascar?
4. Where did Gulliver find himself tied to the ground?
5. In which sport is a telemark a turn?
6. The Ruby Slipper Award is made to what kind of actors?
7. Who painted *Nude Descending a Staircase*?
8. Andreas Ludwig Priwin is better known by what name?
9. Who was the pupil told at the age of 10, 'Albert, you will never amount to much'?

230

1. The late Lord George-Brown.
2. A slice of stale bread.
3. Russia.
4. Kingsley Amis.
5. In kendo – it's a practice weapon.
6. *The Graduate.*
7. J.M.W. Turner.
8. Chopin's.
9. One of irregular shape.

464

1. Fourteen.
2. Dick Whittington.
3. Oil and gas.
4. Patricia Highsmith.
5. Volleyball.
6. *Oceans 11.*
7. Chess.
8. In Las Vegas.
9. The Chow-Chow.

698

1. Bread and beer. (It is known as 'Wayfarers' Dole.')
2. George and Tom.
3. In the Indian Ocean.
4. In Lilliput.
5. In skiing.
6. Child actors.
7. Marcel Duchamps.
8. André Previn.
9. Albert Einstein.

231

1. On which aircraft carrier did Prince Andrew serve during the Falklands conflict?
2. Who was nicknamed 'Old Noll'?
3. What lies between St James's Palace and Lancaster House in London?
4. Which Welsh poet died in New York in 1953?
5. Who rode *Alleged* to victory in both the 1977 and 1978 Prix de l'Arc de Triomphe?
6. Who are BBC TV's *Dear Ladies*?
7. Henry McCarty was better known by what name?
8. Who sang for *Money, Money, Money*?
9. With whose welfare is the Blue Cross concerned?

465

1. Which crisps do the ads claim are 'Britain's noisiest'?
2. The *Lusitania* belonged to which shipping line?
3. In which country is the ngultrum the unit of currency?
4. Who wrote the clerihew, 'Geography is about maps/But biography is about chaps'?
5. Heide Schuller was the first woman to take which oath in 1972?
6. Which British director leads an international troupe of actors, based in Paris?
7. A portrait of King Philip IV of Spain was destroyed in an arson attack in Zurich in 1985. Who was the painter?
8. Who had a hit with the *Sounds of Silence*?
9. From which animal does coney fur come?

699

1. On which day did Solomon Grundy marry?
2. Who was the great son of Philip of Macedonia?
3. Where would you spend kyats and pyas?
4. Name the labrador in Sheila Burnford's book *The Incredible Journey*.
5. Who was the first amateur athlete to promote a product in TV ads?
6. Stephanie Turner played which rank police officer in *Juliet Bravo*?
7. How many cases of typhoid did 'Typhoid Mary' cause in New York?
8. Which piano manufacturers used to describe their product as 'The Instrument of the Immortals'?
9. Which bird's cry sounds like 'A little bit of bread and no cheese'?

231

1. HMS *Hermes*.
2. Oliver Cromwell.
3. Clarence House.
4. Dylan Thomas.
5. Lester Piggott.
6. Dr Evadne Hinge and Dame Hilda Bracket.
7. Billy the Kid – or William Bonney, his other alias.
8. Abba.
9. Animals. (But people in the USA.)

465

1. Golden Wonder.
2. Cunard.
3. Bhutan.
4. Edmund Clerihew Bentley. (Their originator.)
5. The Olympic Oath.
6. Peter Brook.
7. Rubens.
8. Simon and Garfunkel.
9. The rabbit.

699

1. Wednesday.
2. Alexander the Great,
3. In Burma.
4. Luath.
5. Sebastian Coe.
6. Inspector.
7. About 1,300.
8. Steinway.
9. The yellowhammer's.

232

1. Which political party did Sir Robert Walpole lead?
2. Cyrano de Bergerac loved whom?
3. Great Inagua and Cat Island belong to which group of islands?
4. Who was the father of Shem, Ham and Japheth?
5. For which country did Raman Subba Row play Test cricket?
6. Which actress had to get fat fast for her part in the film *Steaming*?
7. In 1980, which non-underpants-wearing snooker player's trousers split during a televised match?
8. Who wrote both words and music to *The Dancing Years*?
9. Which US state has the mayflower for its state flower?

466

1. Who ran through the town in his nightgown?
2. In World War II which battle saw the first defeat of the strong Japanese Navy?
3. Fort York in Canada is now named *what*?
4. Who created Professor Branestawm?
5. What is the more colloquial name for the dressage exercise 'piaffer'?
6. Who, from *Dad's Army*, wrote the play *Ghost Train*?
7. Which greetings cards company did Joyce C. Hall found, back in 1913?
8. Which composer sat for his portrait by the painter Renoir?
9. The raising of 33,000 lb one foot high in one minute is termed one unit of *what*?

700

1. John Smith, DDS. What is his professsion?
2. When the *Mayflower* sailed to America, how many women were on board?
3. What do Germans call what we call motorways?
4. From which play do these lines come, 'What's in a name? That which we call a rose by any other name would smell as sweet'?
5. In 1985, who won the French Open women's tennis singles title for a record sixth time?
6. In which film did Groucho Marx play Rufus T. Firefly?
7. To which city would you go to see Salvador Dali's painting of the crucifixion?
8. Where did the hula hula dance originate?
9. Who wove messages in her web to save Wilbur the Pig?

232

1. The Whigs.
2. Roxanne.
3. The Bahamas.
4. Noah.
5. England.
6. Felicity Dean.
7. Bill Werbeniuk's.
8. Ivor Novello.
9. Massachusetts. (Appropriately.)

466

1. Wee Willie Winkie.
2. The Battle of Midway.
3. Toronto.
4. Norman Hunter.
5. Spanish-walk.
6. Arnold Ridley.
7. Hallmark Cards.
8. Wagner.
9. Horsepower.

700

1. He is a dentist.
2. Twenty-eight.
3. Autobahns.
4. Shakespeare's *Romeo and Juliet.*
5. Chris Evert-Lloyd.
6. *Duck Soup.*
7. To Glasgow.
8. In Hawaii.
9. Charlotte the spider, in the children's book *Charlotte's Web*, by E.B. White.

233

1. Whose mistress was reputedly the model for Britannia?
2. In World War I, what were 'Little Willies'?
3. What is 'Salop' short for?
4. Name the maid of the fictional detective, Miss Jane Marple?
5. The first batsman to score centuries in both innings of a Test Match was an Australian. Who?
6. The Screen Actors' Guild Annual Award was first presented in 1965. Who was its first recipient?
7. Which painter did ballet dancer Olga Koklova marry in 1918?
8. Für *who*, by Beethoven?
9. To which bird family does the mocking bird belong?

467

1. Which motor manufacturers make the Dino?
2. Which train was robbed in the Great Train Robbery of 1963?
3. Approximately how long is the Suez Canal?
4. Of which country is Shakespeare's Cymbeline king?
5. In 1899, Albert Trott, batting for MCC against the Australians at Lord's, achieved a unique feat. What was it?
6. Who said, of Louis B. Mayer's funeral, 'The reason so many people showed up at his funeral was because they wanted to make sure he was dead'?
7. Who wrote *Here Lies Eric Ambler*?
8. Who 'sang for his supper'?
9. Which disease killed thousands of elm trees in the 1970s in Britain?

701

1. Where would you wear a Tam o'Shanter, should you want to?
2. Who was the only US President to be impeached?
3. 'Montezuma's Revenge' is said to affect visitors to Mexico. What is its other nickname?
4. Which 'set' or 'series' of novels did Balzac write?
5. Which was the first soccer club to issue computer identity cards?
6. Which humorist played Mr Micawber in the 1935 film *David Copperfield*?
7. Who painted *The Virgin with a Parrot*?
8. John Denver named which of his songs after Jacques Cousteau's research ship?
9. What does 'vermicelli' literally mean?

233

1. Charles II's.
2. Tanks.
3. Shropshire.
4. Gwen.
5. Warren Bardsley.
6. Bob Hope.
7. Pablo Picasso.
8. Elise.
9. The thrush family.

467

1. Ferrari.
2. The Aberdeen Express.
3. 104 miles.
4. Of Britain.
5. He hit a six which cleared the pavilion.
6. Samuel Goldwyn.
7. Eric Ambler – it is his autobiography.
8. Little Tommy Tucker.
9. Dutch elm disease.

701

1. On your head.
2. Andrew Johnson. (Not Richard Nixon.)
3. The 'Aztec Two-Step'. (It means stomach trouble.)
4. *The Human Comedy.*
5. Chelsea FC.
6. W.C.Fields.
7. Rubens.
8. *Calypso*
9. 'Little worms.'

234

1. The East London Christian Mission became *what*, in 1878?
2. The first European Parliamentary elections in Britain were held in which year?
3. Egyptians are reputedly the descendants of which of Noah's sons?
4. Who has the longest entry in the *Oxford Dictionary of Quotations*?
5. In 1980, Giant Haystacks broke his ribcage whilst wrestling in Kuwait. What was his next problem?
6. The Antoinette Perry Award is presented for Broadway successes. What is the common name?
7. Who composes the comic strip *BC*?
8. The dancer Robert Helpmann hailed from where?
9. To which bird family does the nightingale belong?

468

1. What are cowboys' leggings called?
2. Which US President died during his fourth term of office?
3. On which river does Gateshead stand?
4. Who drank from a bottle labelled 'Drink Me'?
5. Dave Whelan broke a leg in an FA Cup Final. To what rule change did this lead?
6. For what does BAFTA stand?
7. Who said, 'A good marriage would be between a blind wife and a deaf husband'?
8. 'Your tiny hand is frozen.' In which opera does this well-known aria occur?
9. Who gave President Kennedy his dog Pushinka?

702

1. At the age of 12, which future US President said, 'Mother, I want to be an old-fashioned lawyer who can't be bought by crooks'?
2. Which letters were termed the 'Willy-Nicky Correspondence'?
3. Chatsworth, the stately home, is in which county?
4. Who died from wearing a shirt steeped in a centaur's blood?
5. 100–1 outsider *Foinavon* was an unlikely winner of the 1967 Grand National. What helped him win?
6. Alan Bates and Oliver Reed wrestled naked in which film?
7. Who said to whom, 'You're on my bloody feet, Fred'?
8. What does 'ff', commonly written on sheet music, mean?
9. What is the unit of weight in the metric system?

234

1. The Salvation Army.
2. In 1979.
3. Ham.
4. William Shakespeare.
5. He was too big for the ambulance called to take him to hospital.
6. The Tony Award.
7. Johnny Hart.
8. Australia.
9. The thrush family.

468

1. Chaps.
2. Franklin D. Roosevelt.
3. The Tyne.
4. Alice. (In *Alice in Wonderland*.)
5. The permitting of substitutes.
6. British Academy of Film and Television Arts.
7. Michel de Montaigne.
8. In *La Bohème* by Puccini.
9. Premier Nikita Krushchev.

702

1. Richard M. Nixon.
2. Those between the Tsar and the Kaiser in the early part of the 20th century.
3. Derbyshire.
4. Hercules.
5. The rest of the surviving runners fell at the 23rd fence.
6. *Women in Love*.
7. Norman Tebbit to Fred Bishop, busy rescuing him after the Brighton bombing.
8. 'Very loud' (fortissimo).
9. The gram, or gramme.

A CHOICE OF PENGUINS

The Time Out London Guide
The Time Out Paris Guide
The Time Out New York Guide

Compiled by *Time Out* magazine – with twenty years' experience of providing information about events and entertainment – these guides are different: witty, humorous and thoroughly readable. Jam-packed with information, the Time Out guides will show you a good time in the *real* London, Paris or New York.

Raw #2 Edited by Art Spiegelman and Françoise Mouly

Raw returns with an all-new collection of avant-garde American, European and Japanese commix – and a new chapter of *Maus*. '*Raw* ... indicates how far comics have come from their early, invincible innocence' – *Newsweek*

I: The Philosophy and Psychology of Personal Identity Jonathan Glover

From cases of split brains and multiple personalities to the importance of memory and recognition by others, the author of *Causing Death* and *Saving Lives* tackles the vital and vexed questions of personal identity. 'Fascinating' – Anthony Storr

War and Peace Leo Tolstoy

This massive chronicle portrays Russian life during and after the Napoleonic War. Few would dispute its claim to be regarded as the greatest novel in any language.

The Penguin Guide to Ancient Egypt W. J. Murnane

This unique and authoritative guide describes the ancient sites and monuments of Egypt, and places them within the context of their time and within the realities of the present day.

Plants from the Past David Stuart and James Sutherland

As soon as it is planted, even the most modern garden can be full of history, whether overflowing with flowers domesticated by the early civilizations of Mesopotamia or with plants collected in the Himalayas for Victorian millionaires.

A CHOICE OF PENGUINS

Miss Manners' Guide to Rearing Perfect Children Judith Martin

Whether she is discussing playground etiquette or teenage parties, how to cope with toddlers' birthdays or a fiancé abruptly introduced to unsuspecting parents, the author brings to child-rearing the same high-minded hilarity, the same firm insistence on proper behaviour, that made her *Guide to Excruciatingly Good Behaviour* such a huge bestseller.

The End of the Affair Graham Greene

The frank, intense account of a love affair and its mystical aftermath. 'For me one of the most true and moving works of my time, in anybody's language' – William Faulkner

The Life of Samuel Johnson James Boswell

Hailed by Macaulay as the best biography ever written and by Carlyle as a book 'beyond any other product of the eighteenth century', this work today continues to enjoy its status as a classic of the language.

March Violets Philip Kerr

Berlin, 1936, was full of March Violets, late converts to National Socialism. For Bernie Gunther business was booming, especially in the missing-persons field. So when Hermann Six hired him to find the murderers of his daughter and son-in-law, Gunther was glad for the variety...

The Penguin French Newsreader Ian MacDonald

Using self-test exercises based on original French newspaper articles, this convenient language aid will help improve your understanding of contemporary colloquial French.

My Life as a Man Philip Roth

'Roth's best novel ... no writer alive can sustain a full-length novel at as high a decibel level as Philip Roth' – *Newsweek*. 'Philip Roth is one of the country's finest, most forceful, intelligent and serious contemporary writers' – *The New York Times*

A CHOICE OF PENGUINS

The Time Out Film Guide Edited by Tom Milne

The definitive critical guide to more than 9,000 films. World cinema – from the first talking pictures to the latest releases – assessed by two decades of *Time Out* magazine's reviewers. 'In my opinion the best and most comprehensive' – Barry Norman

Modern Ireland 1600–1972 R. F. Foster

'Late twentieth-century history at its very best, as readable and as important a book in its own field as James M. McPherson's *Battle Cry of Freedom*' – Andrew M. Greeley in *The New York Times Book Review*

The Literature of the United States Marcus Cunliffe

A general introduction to the main themes and figures of the American literary scene, from colonial times to the present day. 'A very good book indeed' – D. W. Brogan in the *Guardian*

The Posters of Glasnost and Perestroika Victor Litvinov

Following the success of the *The Soviet Political Poster*, this stunning large-format full-colour book brings together 144 of the posters generated by Gorbachev's first four extraordinary years as Soviet leader.

Clinging to the Wreckage John Mortimer

The unforgettable, bestselling autobiography of the creator of Rumpole. 'Exceptionally touching and funny' – *The Times*

Selected Stories Nadine Gordimer

'A magnificent collection worthy of all homage' – Graham Greene. 'Nadine Gordimer's work is endowed with an emotional genius so palpable one experiences it like a finger pressing steadily upon the pulse' – *Village Voice*